scorch

a novel

a.d. nauman

Contents

Contents

LIST OF ILLUSTRATIONS

PROLOGUE

By the end of the nineteenth century, the Seven Seas had just about dried up as wellsprings of adventure, mystery, and romance. In the course of a few dozen previous centuries, those waters had enlivened history with dazzling yarns of exploration and discovery, glamour and glory, storm and shipwreck, danger and disaster, destruction and death. That storybook era was now virtually closed and, for all working purposes, the Seven Seas had been finally conquered. Men of the breed of Columbus and Da Gama, Drake and Cook, Ericsson and Frobisher were now obsolete, because, within the coastal confines of the waters, your nautical explorer had simply run out of space.

Unless, of course, some unlikely success should one day follow the pathetic efforts of those dreamy characters who persisted in assaulting the Eighth Sea, the limitless ocean of the air. It was by no means an imaginary sea, as the birds were daily demonstrating. And it held fabulous possibilities with which the Seven Seas could not compete, for its shoreline was the whole world and its shipping could establish ports of call anywhere on earth—if someone could devise shipping that could use it.

However, as the twentieth century came in, prospects were painfully remote; the scattered experiments that had been going on for years with gasbags and incredibly fragile gliders seemed to promise nothing more helpful than a few yards of dithering flight before the customary crash. With rare exceptions, the world of practical men was heartily unimpressed, for it was reasonably obvious that thin air could never usefully support anything resembling the traffic that had taken centuries to develop on the waters.

As it turned out, even the wildest dreams of the most ardent pioneers proved to be tame and shy; the Air Age, from primitive infancy to complex maturity, was established before the new century was half over. So swift was the conquest of the air that the strange possibility arose for one individual to take part in the main parade of events and to tell its story as a personal adventure.

However, among those who took to the air in the early stages of the fight and stayed there to see it through, there were not many who survived to tell the story; for if the conquest of the air was swift, it was not easy—Nature had never designed man to go up into the air, and she had a vast repertoire of dirty tricks for knocking him out of it, so that the casualties of that struggle were notoriously high.

Somehow I managed, with improbable good luck, to survive practically every kind of flying for half a century on both sides of the Atlantic, starting before the First World War at the controls of a primitive "box-kite," a marvel of its time, and winding up at the controls of a four-jet transport, at which nobody marvels any more. My survival was all the more surprising because, especially during the long years when progress was mostly by trial and error, I became a sort of rolling stone of aviation, working in many fields as a professional specialist in investigating the unknown and the untried, testing new types of airplanes and equipment and exploring new possibilities of putting them to work. It was a form of employment that offered an instructive and exciting life, but not a long one; yet it seems to have been long enough to suit the purposes I had vaguely in mind when I started.

This story, then, is an effort to picture the evolution of aviation as it took shape within the workaday life of one pilot who saw most of it.

THE EIGHTH SEA

CHAPTER I

"Previous Experience Unnecessary"

There was a time, now fast receding into a hazy past, when the arts and practices of piloting airplanes were generally regarded as a daring and romantic occupation but not as a commendable profession for young men with sane aspirations toward a reasonably prosperous future. The haphazard business of early aviation—if you could call it a business— was unencumbered by any sound knowledge or experience, so that any hopeful aspirant was free to try his hand at the game; the result was that the flying community was liable to attract a strange variety of unlikely recruits.

As a recruit I was as unlikely as anyone, and I have often wondered just what it was that impelled me to elbow my way, against formidable odds, into a business of which I knew practically nothing and for which I seemed to possess singularly outstanding disqualifications.

In early 1913 I had never seen an airplane closer than a couple of miles away, and I had never met anyone even remotely connected with flying. I used to read with mild interest the quaint accounts of flying events that occasionally appeared in the newspapers, but if I thought much about aviation at all I usually classified it with such antics as swimming the Channel or climbing the Alps—perfectly useless amusements but probably a lot of fun for those who liked that sort of thing. Yet somehow, before the end of the year, I had burned behind me such boats as I had, and had scraped a small and uncertain toe hold in a struggling aviation concern that was not at all sure it had any use for me.

Perhaps my job had something to do with it. Family financial circumstances had cut short my apparently promising scholastic program in England and had landed me on a bookkeeper's stool in a bank in Paris, with a salary of 150 francs ($30) a month and some slight family influence that ensured for me carefully mapped prospects for slow but regular promotion in the worthy profession of banking. It was a job of high respectability, solid security—and deadly dullness. Possibly in some dim corner of my skull I reflected unconsciously that, if I didn't care to face a lifetime in banking, the precarious business of aviation was about as far from it as I could hope to get. Anyway, I began to have daydreams of being an aviator—very vague dreams indeed, because I had not the least notion of what aviators were supposed to be useful for or what I, as an aviator, was ever likely to accomplish. However, this faint ambition was a strictly abstract sentiment, with no sort of plan behind it, and I kept the idea to myself as a slightly disreputable secret.

Lightning struck one Sunday afternoon in the songworthy Paris springtime. Walking along the bank of the river Seine near Saint-Cloud I saw, moored to some trees, something that turned out to be an Henri Farman biplane on floats. It was my first close view of an airplane. Guarding it was a mechanic who seemed glad to relieve his boredom by answering my numerous curious questions. The conversation warmed up to the point where he allowed me to climb onto a float and up into the pilot's seat. He let me work the controls and explained their action. At that moment a reasonable imitation of a celestial vision flashed before me: my future belonged in the pilot's seat, and I had better do something about it.

From that day on, my mind worked overtime wondering how to tackle the impossible. I could see no way to approach even the fringes of aviation. I knew nobody in the business, nor anybody who knew anybody. My capital was nil; my salary barely housed and fed me. I was a poor sort of mechanic, and my small stock of mathematics and physics would be hard to sell in a newborn industry suffering from chronic indigence. In 1913 that struggling business would have no room for a youth of eighteen with no money and no other assets beyond a vague enthusiasm. I had some prosperous relatives, but it was they who had put me into my banking job, and I knew too well what they would do if I asked them to help me out of a safe job and into a trade that offered little physical and no financial future.

After weeks of befuddled scheming, I worked out a desperate mail campaign. From various publications I found in the YMCA, I made out a list and wrote to everyone I could discover who seemed to own an airplane. My feeble pitch was to suggest some airplane improvement, adding with appalling optimism that I would like a chance to work on the idea. This was not quite as absurd as it might seem today; the primitive state of the art left it wide open to new suggestions even from amateurs, and occasionally some crazy idea made headway.

I will pass over the dreary discouragement of most of those who bothered to reply. But from Claude Grahame-White, already famous in England and America, I received a shred of hope. His company was completing England's biggest airplane, a five-seat biplane intended to attain all of fifty-five miles an hour—and it happened that, in my letter, I had recklessly suggested that one day there would be huge planes capable of carrying more than twenty passengers at as much as a hundred miles an hour. A ludicrous idea, no doubt—but G-W didn't think so.

It seemed to him, he wrote, that my untutored enthusiasm might turn into something useful if I had some training, and he offered to let me join his company as an engineering apprentice; I would not be paid anything, but he would waive the usual apprenticeship fees. This was really a very generous offer, for in those days it was customary to pay substantial fees for several years to learn a skilled trade. But still I was up against a brick wall. If I could last out financially for a year, I was sure I could learn enough to be worth some pay—but where was I to get the money to last out with?

Then I remembered that nebulous affair of the bank bonus. These Continental banks paid a staff bonus based on the annual profits of the branch; it could range from nothing much to a large percentage of a year's salary, and it came in one welcome lump. Cautiously I pumped the chief accountant on the subject. Confidentially he told me that the profits of the branch were running high; my bonus might even reach a thousand francs, but, of course, it would not be payable yet for about six months. On such an amount I could take a very slim chance, but in six months Grahame-White would probably have changed his mind or forgotten me.

Without much hope, I secured an interview with the bank manager, told him my whole unlikely story, and asked diffidently if there was any chance that my bonus could be advanced. No doubt I bent the facts a little, intimating that my invitation from the famous Grahame-White was a pressing one and that what I needed was merely starting funds. Mr. Polejaieff must have lunched very well that day, for he listened to my hesitant request with a benign and fatherly air, discoursed glowingly on the marvels of flight, arranged an advance on my bonus, and wished me luck.

A couple of weeks later I walked into Grahame-White's small office at Hendon Aerodrome, about eight miles north of London. I was pretty good at dreaming in those days, but I could not possibly have dreamed at that moment that I was starting on the first lap of a fifty-year course.

I recognized Claude immediately from his numerous published photographs. He was thirty-four years old, tall, dark, and handsome in the approved adventurer tradition, with a loud voice and a breezy manner— the popular ideal of the "intrepid birdman." For a moment he was evidently struggling politely to remember who on earth I was. I reminded him. Years later he admitted to me that, at that moment, he had a vague hope that I had come to the wrong office; I was tall, thin, with round shoulders and eyeglasses, and I know I looked far more like the bank clerk I had just been than the ornament of aviation that I hoped to become. However, he recovered rapidly, switched on his renowned dazzling smile, and after a few words of cordial welcome, passed me over to his manager, Richard Gates, in the next office.

Gates, himself an occasional pilot of modest abilities, was a square-built, hard-shelled old army man, tough enough for the uphill job of keeping an aviation company solvent in those days. He greeted me with a heavy scowl; he promptly made it clear that he didn't approve of a non-paying apprentice and that he regarded me as one of G-W's more regrettable acts of charity. For several tortured minutes I could see myself being thrown back into the cold, dull world of banks and commerce. However, said Gates finally, seeing that he seemed to be stuck with me he would give me a chance; as an apprentice I would be expected to learn, by working on the job, airplane design and construction, metal- and woodworking, and the handling of airplanes in the field—but if I didn't work hard and learn fast I wouldn't be around long.

Later on, I realized that Gates was merely giving me the hard, swift kick that I needed to propel me from dreams into action. Thereafter he never missed a chance to give me gruff signs of encouragement, and having found out about my flimsy finances, he arranged to pay me a small but helpful wage long before I would have had the nerve to ask for it.

Gates sent me along to report to the workshops foreman, Jimmy Rickard, an acid little man in blue overalls who told me to show up in the metalworking shop at six-thirty the next morning. For a few seconds, as I left the shop, I felt a sense of letdown; the clatter of the tools, the rattle of the machines, the grime of the benches—these had been no part of my glittering dream of riding the skies. But as I walked toward the main gates, I saw two planes taking off from the field. My spirits started to rise again—soon I would be living among those wondrous planes. By some preposterous miracle I had actually been admitted into the strange new world of aviation. I had no idea what sort of future I was heading for, but I was happy—in some vague fashion I seemed to be on my way.

CHAPTER II

THE STATE OF THE ART—1913

Perhaps I should draw a starting line for my story by sketching the shape of aviation at the time it admitted me to its thin ranks; some of this is generally familiar, some possibly not.

The best-remembered date in aviation history is December 17, 1903, the day on which the Wright brothers are credited (not without furious opposition in some captious quarters) with making the first powered flights; for historical purposes it is justly celebrated as the day of aviation's birth. But that event passed unheralded, and several years went by while the world heard nothing to convince it that any useful progress was being made with flying machines; so for practical purposes that famous date has little more than statistical significance. It was not, in fact, until about 1910 that aviation really took off on its non-stop flight to glory.

My suggestion of the year 1910 in that respect may be sufficiently unorthodox to call for some explanation, and I might start by drawing attention to a dramatic statistic: between 1903 and the end of 1909 only one man, a passenger, was killed in an airplane crash; in 1910 alone more than thirty men died in flying accidents. So the course of events between 1903 and 1910 is probably worth a review.

It is still hard to realize that reports of the Wrights' initial achievements were firmly ignored or even derided by the press and public of the day. However, at least some of this neglect must be attributed to the reticence of the Wrights themselves, for those two painstaking geniuses well understood that many problems were yet to be faced, and public disregard enabled them to work along in welcome obscurity for another year or more improving their device, learning how to handle it, and studiously developing the control patents that proceeded from their careful experiments.

By 1905 they felt that they had evolved a useful invention: a navigable ship of the air. They wanted to put it on the market so that others could make practical use of it, but there their interest evidently ended. They were not adventurers with an inclination to spend time and money exploring the skies; they were hard-working artisans with an ingenious product to sell. But there was no rush of customers; the cautious brothers undertook no publicity program that might have convinced the world of the genuinely scientific progress they had made, and for a few more years most of their efforts were devoted to private attempts to sell what they had. Meanwhile various inventors in other countries had gone into the business of wobbling off the ground in their own versions of flying machines, many of which differed radically from the Wrights' device.

It was not until 1908 that Wilbur Wright, flying in France, astonished the small world of flying enthusiasts with demonstrations of the very superior progress the brothers had made during those quiet years as compared with that of their competitors. These exhibitions helped them to make some money with the sales of a number of planes. More importantly, however, they were also able to show that their competitors could make little progress unless they used a system of controls that infringed the Wrights' patents, so that eventually those patents proved to be their major asset. From then on, the Wrights sat back on their monument as the pioneers of controllable flight and pretty well passed out of the picture of progress. Other inventors doggedly carried on.

By 1909 the Wrights and the increasing number of other experimenters had left the world in no doubt that flying machines could be made that would really fly. But nobody had yet demonstrated that these flimsy contraptions could do anything useful when they did fly. A skeptical world assigned them their place as fascinating toys for inventors, cranks, daredevils, and showmen.

And then, in July of 1909, Louis Blériot flew across the English Channel.

The startling importance of that flight is little appreciated even today. By itself it wasn't really much of a flight: something less than thirty miles in calm air—with a crash at the end of it. And Blériot wasn't trying to prove anything; he was simply after a nice prize offered by a London newspaper. But it was the first flight in which a flying machine did something more than just fly. For it demolished Britain's historic insularity. Britannia ruled the waves. Britain was Mistress of the Seven Seas, behind whose ramparts she had been proudly invulnerable for centuries. Now Blériot's little bit of a flight gave her public notice that, on the Eighth Sea, she was wide open to attack—and so it was to prove in two world wars.

In the faraway America of the Wrights, Blériot's flight had probably little more than sporting significance. But in the war-conscious countries of Europe, and particularly in France, the effect was more profound; the flight created a subtly deep impression, among thoughtful men of action, that somehow there must be a serious future for the airplane. It attracted to aviation a class of people who were not especially interested in how flying machines were made; they knew only that they wanted to fly.

Thus it was that, by the significant year of 1910, an entirely new breed of men had begun everywhere to take to the air. They were different in outlook from the careful and cautious inventor-aviators of earlier years, whose minds ran mainly to the mechanisms of their products. The newcomers were men of action and adventure, people who wanted to explore the newly opened ocean of the air, to fly faster, higher and farther, to carry bigger loads to more places; they were ready to take all kinds of risks to find out what new things airplanes could be made to do. The inventors and designers now followed where these men led, and a rash of new designs, sane and silly, broke out to meet their needs. The airplane was no longer a quaint gadget; it was an instrument of impetuous action. The battle for the air had started, and the heavy casualties of 1910 made it clear that the fight was going to be tough.

From 1910 onward American progress in aviation surprisingly dropped far behind. The American influence brought to Europe so impressively by Wilbur Wright in 1908 had rapidly disappeared; with the virtual retirement of the Wrights, the only outstanding American name in the field of practical design was that of Glenn Curtiss. On the other hand, the principal countries of Europe steadily built up aircraft industries, which though still small and financially feeble, were widely exploring the technical field under a score of names that would become famous in the world war that was slowly creeping near.

In 1913, technology had only just started to accelerate, and there had been few basic design developments since 1910. Most of the same models of airplanes—those that were any good—were still in general use, some of them cleaned up a bit or showing minor improvements. A number of new designs of merit had appeared, and many more with no merit at all. Design was chiefly a matter of art and intuition, with occasional traces of science mixed in here and there. Experience was too meager for any particular design pattern to predominate; it was strictly a matter of the designer's personal taste as to whether the propeller or elevators went in front or behind, or whether he preferred monoplanes, biplanes, triplanes, or some other fancy arrangement. Freak designs were always cropping up from geniuses in quest of a short cut to fame; earlier freaks kept disappearing, to be replaced by newer freaks. Performance estimates were pure guesswork or bragging, and new types quite commonly failed to get off the ground.

Airplanes had now been flown off the water, first somewhat sketchily by Henri Fabre in France, and later in practical fashion by Glenn Curtiss in America. This was a notable piece of progress, although it gave the cynics a chance to observe that airplanes could now sink as well as crash.

Airplanes of French design dominated the market in most countries. The simple and docile Blériot monoplane had probably the widest general sales; the fast but tricky Morane-Saulnier monoplane appealed to pilots of more daring inclinations, while the big Farmans and similar biplanes were preferred by those who liked a lot of wing area for very slow landings. There were numerous other designs, of small to medium popularity. A few English designs, almost all with French engines, were beginning to earn respect. There were several good German designs, which, because of their heavy-looking automobile-type engines, seemed Teutonically clumsy compared with the more graceful French planes, and they were limited mostly to German use.

Between 1910 and 1913 several types of better and lighter engines had come into general use, most of them French. But engine reliability continued to hover not far above the zero point. This did not disturb us unduly; we wanted light engines and we presumed that it would be too much to expect reliability and lightness at the same time. The British, for no obvious reason, continued to lag dismally in the field of engine design, a neglect for which they were to be severely punished in the coming war.

The art of piloting was still in a completely primitive state and, except in the case of a few experts, the main objectives were to stay right way up, avoid stalling, and land without crashing. However, the experts killed themselves with just as much abandon as the novices, simply because they took more chances.

Government control over aviation activities would have seemed a ghastly idea if it had occurred to anybody. But apart from certain design and inspection controls for planes sold to the military, there would be no official regulation until 1919 in Europe and 1927 in the U.S.A. Supervision was exercised over sporting contests, records, and races by national Aero Clubs affiliated with the Fédération Aéronautique Internationale (FAI); these clubs were usually old-established affairs that had originally been balloon clubs and automatically became aviation clubs when airplanes came into existence. The Aero Clubs issued pilots' certificates to those who passed their simple flight tests; a pilot had no need for such a certificate if he cared to fly without one, but it was a valued hallmark of elementary competence to anyone who wanted to call himself a pilot.

In 1913, therefore, aviation was still in its primitive "flying-machine" stage. Airplanes could fly, but that was about all; they were a long way yet from being capable of any really useful service. Another year was to pass before a great war would compel the world to adopt aviation as a serious business.

CHAPTER III

NEVER A DULL MOMENT

After my terse interview with the workshops foreman, I went to look for lodgings in the sprawling rows of little suburban houses in the neighborhood. Most of these catered to the numerous permanent and transient population of Hendon airfield, with accommodations ranging from cheap and simple diggings for mechanics and artisans to slightly more pretentious rooms for well-off students or visitors. There was no local hotel, and the nearest pub was a couple of miles up the Edgware Road—a long way to go when hardly anyone owned a car. It was a tight little community, where nobody was interested in anything but flying and everyone knew everyone else.

For twelve shillings and sixpence (about $3) a week I found lodgings with Mrs. Curtis not far from the aerodrome gates, four beds to a bedroom, and plain but generous feeding. Two of my roommates were Frank Goodden and Freddy Dunn, both of whom were destined to become well-known pilots and to lose their lives in test flying.

Early next morning, with no fancy preliminaries, I was put to work to start my training as helper to John Slack in the metalworking shop, a cold and drafty barn of a place where the only way to get warm on a winter's morning was to find something to take to the welding shop and spend as long as possible getting it welded. Later in the day the chief engineer, John North, gave me a general talk on what my program as an apprentice was going to be. I think North was greatly impressed with the wide extent of my ignorance, and nothing on earth seemed less likely than the fact that a few years later I would be the test pilot for several of North's most successful designs.

Apprentices—there were about a dozen of us—had a fairly regular schedule of training. We were rotated through the various fabrication, repair, and engine-overhaul shops, in which we spent more or less time according to the state of business in the factory. Most evenings there were courses or lectures on theoretical subjects by the chief engineer or his principal assistants, or perhaps by some visiting expert. Our major aim was to qualify for the design and engineering office, where we would learn drafting and get a chance to work on whatever new design project was on hand. However, our schedule was far from rigid, because we were encouraged to pick up all the practical experience we could among the exceptionally varied flying-field activities that were a feature of life at Hendon.

The days of specialists were not yet dreamed of, and an apprentice was expected to learn as much as possible about as many things as possible. The textbooks of aviation were not yet written; the flying business was groping, by motley processes of trial and error, toward the discoveries upon which the textbooks would later be founded. The only way we could learn anything was by doing it—or trying to. Knowledge that is commonplace today came to us bit by bit, day by day, sometimes as a novelty, sometimes as a surprise, and often as a shock or a tragedy. Airplanes were designed and put together mostly by inspiration, and we tested the results the only way we knew how: by putting the planes into the air—if they would fly.

So it was important to us to supplement our formal factory training with all the field experience we could find. A Grahame-White apprentice was well situated to collect that sort of experience, because the company had to reach for income in all directions in order to stay in business. The airplane market was too scanty for any outfit to survive on airplane sales alone, unless it happened to be an offshoot of some other, supporting business. The Wrights, for example, had bravely financed their historic experiments from the proceeds of their little bicycle business, and Blériot had a flourishing trade in automobile accessories.

The Grahame-White Company, with G-W's flair for showmanship and Gates's business acumen, had organized itself to do something of everything connected with flying, and it probably approached nearer to prosperity than any other independent concern in the business. First of all, it owned Hendon Aerodrome, a flying field of about three hundred acres close to London, which almost automatically became the center of British flying. Probably more aviation was concentrated at Hendon at that time than anywhere else in the world, except perhaps for a couple of French flying fields.

Along one side of the field were rows of barnlike hangars, which were rented out as bases for a strange assortment of flying schools, as workshops for sundry constructors and inventors, or as storage for the innumerable visiting airplanes. G-W's own small factory built trainer boxkites, Morane-Saulnier Model G monoplanes under license from France, and several models of mixed success that its own design office produced. The company ran its own flying school. It went after racing and contest prizes, even employing its own racing pilot, an incredibly taciturn American named Walter Brock, who won all the big cross-country races of 1914 (and with whom I corresponded regularly until his death in Chicago in 1964).

Then, of course, there were the frequent and famous Hendon Air Shows, which drew a steady flow of coinage into the G-W coffers— I shall have more to say about these. A profitable restaurant was set up, resented only by the staff of the G-W design office, because it obstructed their view of the flying. There were few, if any, aviation activities that the apprentice could not find at Hendon.

The factory workshops probably did far more work on repairs than on new construction, for crashes were always with us, and structural casualties came in from all directions. Spare parts were rare. We hardly ever had drawings to work to, practically everything was a handmade job, and we learned to perform strange miracles of improvisation and ingenuity to get some wreck back into the air. These shops also handled our endless hopeful experiments, and in one famous case we improvised a very successful airplane, the G-W "Lizzie," from the wreckage of three different types.

So spare time for apprentices was unknown and unwanted. Day and night, fair weather and foul, seven days a week, there was always something to do as long as we could stay awake. Invariably there was someone around the field who wanted a hand with an engine overhaul, a wreck recovery, an experimental job, or something of the sort. For visiting pilots we did everything from servicing their machines to finding them local lodgings. I don't remember that anyone ever expected to get paid for this indiscriminate assistance; spare money was scarce around Hendon, but now and then we might scrounge a lunch or a dinner in the restaurant from some grateful pilot or operator.

However, if a visiting pilot brought in a new or unfamiliar type of airplane and wanted our help, it was an affair of honor for us to extract the promise of a ride in his plane, in which, perhaps, he would let us try the controls. By such minor blackmail I promoted rides in planes of a wide variety of designs, some of which were wonders in their day but have long since been forgotten.

The Hendon Flying Shows started from modest efforts of the company to collect a little gate money from the curious, and they rapidly became a national institution. Weather permitting, every Saturday and Sunday, and sometimes Wednesday, we put on a show consisting of races around the pylons, stunt flying such as it then was, and passenger joy rides. The shows were another outlet for apprentice activity: we sold tickets, started propellers, filled tanks, timed racers, checked turns at the pylons, and explained to a puzzled public such technical mysteries as how a pilot got back to earth if his engine stopped. These shows drew all kinds of people and became important social, technical, and sporting gatherings. So when a constructor or a pilot, from any country, wanted to show off his plane or himself, he usually turned up sooner or later at a Hendon show. We came to know just about everybody connected with international aviation. We handled a vast variety of airplane types, and we picked up all sorts of ideas from listening to the various sales talks of designers, the opinions of mechanics, and the yarns of pilots.

Pylon racing would, many years in the future, be practically regulated out of business, because too many fatal accidents occurred when high-speed planes became bunched on turns. But at a time when sixty-five miles an hour was a creditable full-throttle speed, an air race over a circuit of two or three miles, with five pylons, produced the general atmosphere of a Roman chariot race. The public got to know the different planes and pilots, bookies set up stands in the enclosures, and regular race-track rituals were observed.

Passenger joy rides provided only nominal revenue, for the perils of flight were always well advertised and customers were few. Sometimes a good crash at one meeting would increase the crowd of thrill seekers at the next one, but joy ride income slumped accordingly.

Before World War I, "stunt flying" was limited to looping (which the French pilot Adolphe Pégoud had popularized in September 1913) and steep banking. These were quite enough to amaze the spectators of that day; such antics as intentional spins and rolls would not be known for another two or three years.

Crashes were, of course, a normal feature of flying in that era, and it was the general public understanding that anyone who went up into the air and got down without a crash was either very clever or very lucky. Anything could cause a crash in days when engines were skittish, stability was a questionable curiosity, controls were erratic, structures were delicate, and piloting consisted largely in staggering along close to the stalling point. We knew nothing about stalling except that it was full of mystic perils and was to be avoided at all costs. We tried, of course, to learn whatever we could from any crash, and the Aero Clubs had accident-investigating committees; but most crashes remained unexplained, simply because flying held too many mysteries for us to know where to start looking for causes. We just assumed that airplanes naturally crashed every so often.

My first experience of a fatal crash was that of George Lee Temple, early in 1914. I was flying in a Blériot, at about fifteen hundred feet, as passenger with Walter Brock, and we casually watched Temple, who was flying his own single-seat Blériot a little to our right. He went into a dive, and then continued right on over until he struck the ground very precisely upside down. Brock landed close to the wreck and we ran over to it. I lifted up the tail, and the gruesome object that dangled down from the safety belt showed us that Temple was beyond our services. Everybody had theories about the cause of the crash, but nobody produced any usable evidence. Some thought Temple must have fainted and fallen forward onto his controls; others guessed he was trying to copy Pégoud's early attempts at an "outside" loop and had misjudged his altitude.

At the inquest on Temple, the coroner's jury did its best to contribute to the future safety of flight. A juryman asked a witness whether, if the plane had been fitted with a landing gear on top as well as underneath, it would have landed all right. The surprised witness could only stammer that, well—er—yes, as a matter of fact it probably would have. Whereupon the jury brought in a verdict of "accidental death," adding a recommendation that in future all airplanes should be fitted with landing gears both above and below.

Richard Gates was to meet his death several months later in finding out something that ought to have been perfectly obvious to us, but wasn't until the accident happened. Night flying shows in fine weather had been getting popular at Hendon; Frank Goodden had been giving impressive demonstrations by looping with small lights around the wings of his Caudron biplane. Landings were made by the light of kerosene-soaked flares in cans, which were intended to provide perspective rather than illumination—so the pilot landed into the pattern of the lights. Gates thought we should have a permanent floodlight installation, so he procured a small searchlight and decided to try it out himself one night. Gates took off and flew around for a while, and then we saw his boxkite appear out of the darkness heading toward the searchlight, apparently for a landing. We watched the forward elevator drop as the plane went into its glide, and until too late it didn't occur to us, or evidently to Gates either, that he was now close enough to the light to be blinded by it. The boxkite went straight on into the ground. We worked a long time removing what was left of a man who had been one of the few sound businessmen in aviation.

However, if we air people couldn't explain our crashes, that didn't deter the newspapers from doing so. One day, after a pilot had been killed through causes unknown to us, an inquisitive reporter discovered that the pilot had been suffering from a bad head cold. He made a brilliant deduction: everyone knew how delicate a job it was to balance an airplane in flight, so the chances were that the pilot had sneezed and thereby lost control. And was it not possible that many other mysterious air accidents had been caused by sneezing? The paper took the idea so seriously that it produced an editorial about it, and for a brief while the sneeze loomed as a major hazard of aviation.

Another great press discovery was "the deadly sideslip." Airplanes were so often seen to fall on the nose after what looked like a sideslip at low altitude. It wasn't until years later that we knew that this "sideslip" was simply the beginning of a spin that had started too close to the ground to look like a spin. Today we call it an "incipient spin," and it still ranks high as a cause of crashes to pilots who manage to stall close to the ground. However, the press told us just how to handle this menace: never bank at low altitudes—always keep your turns flat and you will be quite safe.

Students' crashes were in a class by themselves. We became used to watching students emerge unhurt or slightly bent from wrecks that would have killed any experienced pilot. I have seen students, confused, flustered, or lost in sheer hopelessness, perform feats that no skilled pilot could carry out on purpose. I have seen watchers on the ground clutching each other in nervous agony while some student, blissfully unconscious of danger, offered Death a wide-open opportunity, which Death sportingly declined to accept. I don't remember any student fatalities in the Grahame-White school while I was there, in spite of some spectacular wrecks. We had a fair amount of bloodshed as well as a number of broken bones—including the case of a student who landed a boxkite in the top of a big tree, tried to climb down, and broke a leg falling out of the tree.

CHAPTER IV

PASSPORT TO FLIGHT

My initial infatuation with life among the wondrous airplanes was a form of happy insanity, which kept me more than content for two or three months. But when logical thinking showed signs of returning, it seemed obvious that I would never make much progress with airplanes unless I could fly them, a consideration that brought me up against my next insuperable problem. For Gates had long before made it clear that my apprenticeship did not include learning to fly; if I wanted to do that I would have to pay the regular flying school fee. This was £75 ($375), a lot of money in those days and an utterly prohibitive sum by my financial standards.

However, having already accomplished the impossible once, by getting as far as Hendon, I thought I might as well take a crack at the next impossibility.

Before World War I there existed nothing remotely resembling the "flight training" of later years. The schools did not pretend to be able to teach much in days when there were still few accepted techniques, even among experienced pilots. All they offered the student was the chance to get his FAI pilot's certificate, which we called a "ticket" or "brevet." The tests for this document consisted of a few flights in calm air in which you flew several "figure eights," wide enough to require only slight banking, and made a few power-off landings. There was, as I said before, no such thing as an official pilot's license, and when the student passed these FAI tests the school's responsibility ended. He was supposed to have "learned to fly," and anything he learned after that was whatever he could pick up for himself in whatever flying he could latch onto; he then developed his own style and techniques to suit his own tastes and aptitudes.

At that time, before war came along to change the whole picture, only a small percentage of students had much prospect of carrying on with the expensive pastime of flying, once they had taken their tickets. Many of them lost interest after the novelty had worn off and were content to have a pilot's brevet to exhibit to admiring friends. Some of them were wealthy young men who could afford to buy an airplane; but crashes were frequent and costly, insurance was out of the question, and often their first crash was their last flight—one way or another. But there were a few flying jobs to be found, especially if the pilot was a reasonably good mechanic, for aviation activities were slowly expanding. With my usual gratuitous optimism I was confident that I could get a flying job if I could get my ticket. If . . .

One day I found myself in the office with Grahame-White and Gates, and the latter had some kind words to say concerning my progress in the factory. This seemed a good opportunity to ask them if there was any remote possibility of my working my way on to the flying school, seeing that I could not produce the £75 fee. I talked around the point for a while, and finally G-W, probably to get me off the subject, told me I would never make a pilot—I just wasn't the type—but if I had some money to waste they would put me on the school for £50. Gates, who well knew that I wasn't in any danger of delivering £50, or anything like it, chuckled sarcastically and agreed. This was obviously final.

So all I needed was a miracle that would produce £50. Relatives and friends told me that, if I wanted to break my neck, it would be at my own expense, not theirs. After numerous barren explorations, I was reduced to trying the least likely prospect of all: the family lawyer. From childhood I remembered his kindly face, which, I thought, even on a lawyer might mean something. I told the white-haired Alexander Crossman why I wanted to borrow the money, and waited for the kindness to vanish from his face. It didn't. He looked at the top of his desk for a few minutes, and then said something about wishing he were a young man again. I left his office with £50. Incidentally, he lived to see my name in headlines, and was gratified accordingly.

Thus had Fortune decreed that my aviation career should be staked by a banker and a lawyer—which I took to be Fortune's way of advising me never again to be surprised at anything.

When I handed Gates the money, and told him how I had got it, he said nothing. He looked grimly at me, shrugged his shoulders, and sighed deeply. Suddenly he started laughing, picked up the telephone, and called the school office. I was officially a flight student.

The planes used in the Grahame-White school were boxkite biplanes of about 1911 vintage, generally resembling the early Farmans. Tandem seats, with the control stick on the right side of the front seat, were mounted close together on a skimpy structure of struts overhanging the lower wing, wide open to the air, without side walls or windshield. If you didn't fasten the buckled strap you could fall overboard with no difficulty. There were no instruments whatever. Behind the wings, at the rear of the structure that carried the seats and the tanks, the uncowled Gnome rotary engine, of alleged fifty horsepower, spun with pusher propeller between the booms that carried the tail. About eight feet ahead of the pilot, carried on another set of booms, was an extra elevator, a relic of earlier "canard" designs, having no obvious purpose unless it was to give the pilot something reassuring to look at. The ailerons were not cross-connected; they hung down when at rest and were raised by airflow, so that when the pilot pulled them down on one side those on the other side floated up on their own.

Nobody ever knew just what the performance was, but a top speed of forty-five miles an hour would be a good guess, with a landing speed slightly lower, leaving a very meager margin for climb. A couple of the older machines, steadily gaining weight from the splices and fittings of countless repair jobs, soakage of oil thrown out by the engine, and contributions from the birds that roosted in the rafters of the hangars, could not be relied on to clear the local treetops with two people aboard, so they had to be reserved for solo flights or for short hops with instructor within the limits of the field.

The engine was operated without the luxuries of a carburetor or a throttle; its controls consisted of a plain tumbler switch for the ignition and a small ordinary tap for the fuel supply, located where the pilot (student) could reach down to them with his left hand. With the tap, the operator supplied more fuel or less to the engine until it seemed to be adjusted for maximum power, which was judged by the sound of the engine. It was often difficult to get the setting right, but no trouble whatever to get it wrong, in which case the engine spluttered or stopped. The engine was "throttled" by switching it on and off ("blipping"); but even that operation could be fouled up, because if the switch were left off for too long, the engine choked and refused to pick up again. Running an early Gnome was a sporting proposition.

For school purposes the student sat in the pilot's seat of the boxkite. The instructor sat in the slightly raised passenger seat immediately behind, from which position he could barely reach forward to the stick with his right arm in order to help the student with the elevators and ailerons; but he had no control at all over the rudder or over the operation of the temperamental engine, except for what effect he could get by shouting into the student's ear. With this limited management the instructor occasionally had a hectic time with a nervous student who was vague on the subject of left or right rudder or who switched the engine off or on at exactly the wrong moments.

It was nothing unusual to watch a boxkite, a few feet off the ground, yawing unsteadily to the right while the anguished shouts of the instructor could be heard above the buzz of the engine: "Left rudder . . . *left*, I said. . . . LEFT, you bloody idiot." The instructor was equally helpless when, for example, the student used far too much engine for taxiing, and knocked off chunks of airplane structure against a fence or a hangar. It is hardly surprising that "dual control" instruction was limited to straight flights close to the ground.

All school flying was done in dead-calm air; when the flag on top of the hangar showed signs of disturbance, the school adjourned. In long periods of bad weather a student, taking his turn, might be lucky to get in ten minutes' flying a month. So, by far the most part of our school-work was done in the early mornings or late evenings of the long English summer days.

Our whole flying course consisted of three stages: "dual straights," "solo straights," and "circuits." The dual straights were made with the instructor; you took off, flew along a few feet up, landed at the other end of the field, turned around on the ground, and flew back. Principally you were learning how to land, but you incidentally picked up a little experience of rudder control and maybe some slight acquaintance with the ailerons. When the instructor was satisfied with you, which might or might not be quite a long time, you continued to do the same thing solo until it was at last decided that you were ready for "circuits." This meant that you would go off alone and fly around the field.

Your first "circuit" was your great day, for you had never made a turn in the air with an instructor to show you how to do it, and you were never going to. Your first turn was a breath-taking venture of your own, and you took your choice from a variety of recommendations as to how it should be done. Some instructors supported the Wrights' original theory that you must bank; others recommended a very wide turn that needed no noticeable banking; and at least one students' booklet (still to be found in the London library of the Royal Aeronautical Society) warned you that "the ailerons are used to keep you on a level keel while turning."

Naturally, before starting on this great adventure, the student received parting instructions, which varied according to the instructor. Jack Lillywhite's were usually the most concise: "Shove off and break your blasted neck."

Students had an infinite genius for discovering new problems, so first-circuit performances were always well attended. Sometimes a student would wobble away out of sight, still trying to make up his mind to attempt a turn. In such cases he might finally get around and return to the field, or sometimes his boxkite would be reported from some distant meadow, where it had come to rest either in one piece or a large number of pieces. Now and then a student flew around in great shape, but balked at coming down; all his previous landings had been made from a few feet up, but now, with the earth several hundred feet below, things looked very different and he hated to shut off his engine. I have seen a student fly around until he ran out of fuel, landing with the loss of only one side of his landing gear.

When I started my flight training I was already well ahead of the game compared with most of the "customer" students. As part of my apprentice's ground job I had made a close friend of the Gnome engine and knew how it wanted to be run. In numerous joy rides with pilots who had let me "try the controls" I had become usefully familiar with control action. I could even make a slight bank with modest confidence,

and one day Pierre Verrier had allowed me to handle his Maurice
Farman all the way around the pylons.

I had no doubt, therefore, that I could "take my ticket" in short
order. My problem, strangely enough, was to avoid taking it. An older
apprentice had given me a valuable tip: once I took my ticket the
school was finished with me, and I would get no more flying unless I
paid extra for it; so the thing to do was to stall off the tests and get in as
much solo flying as possible before the school manager caught up with
me. The "customer" students couldn't get by with this sort of thing;
but the apprentice students, having all sorts of excuses for irregular at-
tendance, and having "influence" with the timekeeper in the matter of
records, could ensure that their progress never looked very favorable.
This I did for months, becoming a most experienced pilot with an impressive total of about three hours of solo time.

Then, on August 4, 1914, World War I broke out with startling sud-
denness and caught me in a trap of my own devising. All civilian flying
schools were promptly closed down and I had no pilot's certificate.
About two weeks later our school was reopened as a naval training
operation. Fortunately for me, Grahame-White was now in the Navy
as Flight Commander, and he was able to get special permission for me
to run through my FAI tests. My certificate was No. 874, dated August
20.

CHAPTER V

THE AIRPLANE GOES TO WAR

War came to aviation, and vice versa, almost overnight. In late July 1914, a military airplane was the same as any other airplane, except that it happened to belong to the Army or the Navy. In early August it was still the same machine except that now it was expected to submit its fragile structure to the violence of shot and shell in order to perform some martial service—nobody knew what.

Saturday, July 11, 1914, might have been centuries away from war; it was the day of the great London-Paris-London air race. Walter Brock, the Grahame-White pilot, calculated that his Morane would make better time by carrying a light fuel load and landing halfway to refuel on the firm sands of Hardelot, a bright little seaside resort in northern France. So Harry Gist and I were sent across the Channel, lugging fuel funnels, a magneto, spark plugs, a spare propeller in case of a nose-over on the sand, and miscellaneous emergency bits and pieces. Brock flew in right on time; Gist and I gave him a swift refueling job and sent him on his way to Paris. In the afternoon he landed again on his way back, and we repeated the service. Lord Carbery had tried to beat the odds by carrying a non-stop fuel load; we heard that he had fallen in the Channel. Then the news was flashed that Brock had won the race. Gist and I gave ourselves full credit for the victory and blew our remaining expense money on a memorable celebration—with no glimmering of an idea that, barely three weeks later, Brock's Morane would have become a "military monoplane" and that we would be entering history's first air war.

Of course, we had read that some Austrian duke or prince or something had just been shot up in some unpronounceable Balkan town, and that Austria, Serbia, and a few other countries were furiously swapping "ultimatums" in all directions; but this sort of thing was an old-established sport for emperors and kings who had a lot of armies that needed marching around and who usually simmered down at one growl from the British Lion. We had more serious things to think about; Grahame-White's new seaplane was completed and ready for test, and there was work to be done.

Then, suddenly, on Tuesday, August 4, Britain was at war.

The outbreak of war threw our flying fraternity into complete pandemonium, for few of us intended to be left out of the conflict. What scared us seriously was the thought the war might be over before we could get into it. It was well known that Germany couldn't hold out long against the combined mights of Britain, France, and Russia, and the whole show might be over by Christmas. It didn't occur to us to wonder where our airplanes were to come from, and we hadn't the slightest notion what we were going to do with them if and when we got them. Everyone scurried around madly trying to find a quick way to get into the Royal Flying Corps or the Royal Naval Air Service, in spite of the fact that their appalling lack of serviceable planes had recently caused an uproar in Parliament. We just had a blurred and glorious vision of air warfare as a natural and essential part of the vast adventure of flying. And even if we could have known how pitifully few of us would be left alive at the end of the show, I don't suppose it would have made the slightest difference.

Britain's ultimatum to Germany to get out of Belgium was to expire at 11 P.M. With a flight student named Upton (who was to die flying against the Turks) I took off for London on a late night bus. We lined up at the tail end of a long, crowded line of impatient volunteers outside the War Office. It was a couple of hours before we reached an exhausted recruiting sergeant who took down our particulars and told us "we would be notified." Then, just in case the War Office didn't get around to us before the war was over, we crossed the street to the Admiralty, stood in another long line, and signed up for the Navy.

Day was breaking by then, but the early buses were not yet running; so we walked the eight miles back to Hendon, elated with foggy dreams of knightly combat such as come to eager young men who don't know what they are taking on.

Back at the factory, things were at a standstill; nobody knew what planes, if any, we were going to build or who might be around to build them. The flying school was closed down. Everybody was waiting for something to happen.

Two or three days later I received a War Office telegram to report to Royal Flying Corps headquarters at Farnborough. On my way there in the train I gave myself up to dreams of the glittering feats I was about to perform in history's first war in the air. My visions were entirely shapeless, because airplanes had never done anything serious in war, and even an airman's flighty imagination could not easily picture them as anything aggressive or ferocious.

We knew that, to the great Military Minds, the airplane could be no more than a newfangled mobile observation post, or a sort of rickety overhead cavalry scout lacking the aristocratic elegance, dignity, and stamina of the horse. Those were days when it was bad manners to have new ideas in the field of warfare and when a lively imagination was indecent, if not downright immoral. Suggestions that the air might become a great battlefield could come only from very irresponsible people—such as airmen.

Our regular "military airplanes" were plain, ordinary airplanes of the day, with no provisions for equipment unless you included a pocket for the observer's pad and pencil. There did exist two or three experimental models picturesquely fitted with mounts for machine guns, but hardly anyone seriously supposed that they could really carry a heavy gun and hit anything with it. Working air speeds were around sixty-five miles an hour, a very few fast single-seaters doing seventy-five or a little better. Six or seven thousand feet was a very respectable altitude, and took a long time to reach. No serious plans existed for producing planes that were much better. Most engines produced from fifty to ninety horsepower and ran when they felt like it, which was not their regular habit. However, such planes were all we knew, and we were impatient to find out what we could do with them.

The new Commanding Officer at Farnborough, Major Hugh Trenchard, a rugged martinet whose thunderous voice had long before earned him the name of "Boom," was destined for fame as history's first great air strategist, founder of the Royal Air Force, and, incidentally, mentor of America's General Billy Mitchell. When I was marched into his formidable presence he took one look at my glasses.

"Do you have to wear those glasses?" he roared.

"Yes, sir," I said, "I'm a little shortsighted, but . . ." I was about to explain that my glasses had never bothered me in flying, but I didn't get that far.

"Don't try and tell me," he boomed, "that you can fly with those things on. Get out."

I got out. Total time of interview approximately twenty seconds. In a last-ditch effort I tried to bluff my way through the medical officer downstairs. I was out of luck; the regular R.F.C. medical man, who might have had some sympathy for me in the current need for experienced men, was absent, and in his place was a doctor from a Guards regiment. This unbending gentleman sincerely believed that anyone with less than 20/20 vision was stone blind. He shoved me out.

I returned, crushed and despondent, to Hendon, and showed up next morning at the Grahame-White factory wondering if I could get my job back. But there was plenty for me to do if anyone could be found to get some work organized. People you thought were showing up for work were just dropping in to say good-by and pick up a few belongings. Half or more of our key men, in all departments, were off in the general direction of war—some had commissions, some were sergeants, some weren't quite sure what they were, beyond the fact that they had been accepted for the R.F.C. or the R.N.A.S. Grahame-White had gone into the Navy, with the lofty, two-stripe rank of Flight Commander, leaving behind vague instructions to "carry on." Gates had just been killed. And so, for days, confusion was master.

Soon army and navy engineers started to arrive at the factory with a profusion and confusion of plans, drawings, and programs for producing airplanes. In normal times I would still have been considered a beginner of small experience, but now my one year's work as an apprentice, much of it in the design office, brought me a sudden raise in status. For sixteen hours a day I sat down with the engineers, flogging through stacks of largely unreadable official drawings, trying to find out how we could build airplanes in our little corner of an embryo industry that had never before dreamed of "production."

At last we were instructed to produce numerous copies of the B.E.2c, a two-seat biplane of pedantic government design, which later on was so easily shot down by the enemy that it earned the dreary nickname of "Fokker fodder."

I didn't know it then, of course, but I was taking my small part in a historic stage of aviation's progress: the first struggling efforts to put airplanes into mass production. Our chief engineer now had the monumental task of organizing quantity manufacture in a business in which everything had always been handmade and interchangeable parts practically unknown.

About this time I managed to run through the delayed flight tests for my FAI pilot's certificate. I couldn't imagine now what I would do with it, but I supposed it might possibly come in handy some time or other.

Our production work on the B.E.2c got slowly under way and, in addition, there were various odd jobs to be done on planes, previously built by our factory, that had been commandeered for whatever work the military people could find for them. One of my assortment of jobs was what would today be called service engineering: I had to go around to various military stations and squadrons to straighten out problems of repairs, replacements, and maintenance. Everywhere I went, conversation revolved around the struggles of the tiny Royal Flying Corps in France. Men I knew well had already died and the war had hardly started. The prospect of going through the war as a factory groundling was depressing, yet with my glasses I had no chance of finding a pilot's job through normal procedures. So, as usual, I would have to try to arrange matters the hard way.

One day I was sent to Farnborough to investigate a broken Morane fitting. I wasn't the hottest of service engineers, but occasionally I appeared quite brilliant alongside men who were still expected to be soldiers first and mechanics when they had time. When I had finished this particular job, Sergeant Burroughes took me into the mess for a cup of tea. He was overworked and weary.

"I wish," he said, "we could get a few more fellows like you to join up. Most of our trained men have gone overseas. These new recruits don't know a rudder from a propeller, and we can't make mechanics out of lads who are always being pulled out to drill or polish buttons. You'd be a sergeant in no time."

In self-defense I told him about Trenchard and my glasses.

"Today they'll take you as a mechanic even with glasses," he said. "Anyway, Trenchard has gone to France and 'Splash' Ashmore is commanding here now. I know he'll grab you."

A loud bell clanged in my head. It hadn't previously occurred to me, with my elegant pilot's certificate, to join as a humble military mechanic, but at least this would be a very small foot in a large door. Before I left Farnborough that evening I had seen the Squadron Sergeant Major, Major Ashmore, and the medical officer.

Next day, at Hendon, I told the chief engineer what I wanted to do. He was not surprised. "I guessed all along," he said, "that you were working up to something silly like that." Three days later I was in the Royal Flying Corps, as No. 2891, 2nd Class Air Mechanic Courtney.

On my first day in uniform they gave me a large broom and told me to sweep out the two hangars of No. 1 Reserve Squadron on Farnborough's Jersey Brow. As a battling hero of the air, it looked as if I was going to make a good janitor.*

* When I visited the big Farnborough Air Show in 1970, I came across these two wooden hangars; battered and derelict, and submerged in the encroaching jungle of new engineering buildings, they were due for early demolition.

CHAPTER VI

CHASING A RAINBOW

1. *Kaiser Wilhelm to the Rescue*

So now I was in the Army's Royal Flying Corps with the lowest possible rank and the highest possible hopes—brash hopes that, somewhere among squadron activities, I could pick up a key to a pilot's job. I was taking a very long shot, but it was the best I could do. I had a year's experience in the mechanics and engineering of aviation, plus that rare document, a pilot's certificate, and I was innocent enough to suppose that my shining merits could not long remain unnoticed. What I hadn't realized was that this was the Army and that, in its age-old fashion, it would go to work to impress on me that I was just a number.

I was Air Mechanic, 2nd Class, commonly known as a 2nd A.M., so I had to be soldier, and the Army couldn't care less what else I might be. On the barracks square, leather-lunged sergeants from the Guards tried desperately to make soldiers out of us by the soul-crushing processes of drilling, parading, marching, button-polishing, and rifle-juggling. Just to get away from the drill sergeants I had to think up some sneaky tactics.

I already had a couple of friends among the overworked sergeants of No. 1 Reserve Air Squadron, across the field from the barracks. They readily agreed to make repeated requests for my "emergency" services as a trained mechanic. So, as the world's worst soldier, I managed to acquire one distinction: even Sergeant Major Street found time to congratulate me bitterly on the amazing success with which I contrived to dodge parades in order to get down to the hangars. Finally, still less than half drilled, I found myself formally posted to the squadron.

Work on our airplanes involved long hours and dreary frustration, for almost every airplane in halfway decent condition had been sent overseas, and we were left with a bunch of sagging crocks that, somehow, we had to keep flying for the instruction of new pilots. In addition, those few of us who knew anything about airplanes had to find time for training the new flood of recruit "mechanics" for whom no schools yet existed. My rainbow dreams of flying glory had started to look silly as they slumped into nightmares of struts and wires, cylinders and crankshafts, oil and grease.

Our hated enemy, Kaiser Wilhelm II, was about the last person on earth whom I would have expected to boost me up into the air. Unwittingly he did it. His Imperial Majesty's birthday was on January 27, 1915. For some strange reason, the rumor had been spreading that the Germans intended to glorify the event with an air attack on England, particularly on the assortment of military installations at Farnborough and Aldershot. What the Germans were going to use for this dramatic assault nobody seemed to know, and we would have been surprised to discover that they had any airplane capable of carrying a hand grenade halfway to Farnborough. But, anyway, the War Office put No. 1 R.A.S. on a heavy alert. We worked around the clock in icy weather patching up anything that looked as if it could be made to fly, wondering what use could be found for it.

Then it was discovered that, what with a couple of crashes and a little pneumonia, the squadron couldn't raise the required number of stand-by pilots. The Squadron Commander, Captain (later Air Marshal Sir Philip) Joubert, sent for me. Was it correct that I had a pilot's certificate? Yes, sir, it was. How much solo time had I? Six hours, sir. (Three hours would have been a lot nearer—but what the hell!) Could I fly a Maurice Farman? Yes, sir. (After all, Pierre Verrier had often let me take the controls at Hendon.) Sergeant-Pilot Victor Strugnell was told to give me a test on one of our "Longhorns." Struggy reported very favorably. They let me put in an hour or so of solo practice, and I took a few chances with some fancy banking to make it look as if this was all old stuff to me. I even carried my first passenger: Lieutenant Ellis, an Australian. I was officially put on the list of stand-by pilots.

Heaven bless Kaiser Wilhelm, mustache and all! I was in—a very little way—and my problem now was to stay in.

The "birthday" scare passed, of course, without incident. Now I had to discover means of hanging onto a flying job. There was a desperate shortage of instructors, and I offered to take less-popular instruction hours, such as weekends and early mornings, and so I got myself informally accepted as a flight instructor. In those days there were no systems or procedures for instruction. Anybody who could fly was supposed to be able to instruct, and the instructor's main function was to do his best to prevent the student from wrecking the airplane, especially on landings. It was a job in which the instructor often learned more than he taught. After a few weeks of this, the officer-instructors became used to having me around, and at last Headquarters took notice of me. I was allowed to wear wings and given flying pay, the only 2nd A.M. pilot in the Royal Flying Corps. (This, incidentally, has been a matter of some inquiry among historians of the Corps; at another station there was one other mechanic pilot, the afterward well-known "Oujie" Noakes, but he was a 1st A.M.)

Mostly I was instructing very new young officers on Maurice Farman "Longhorn" and "Shorthorn" pusher biplanes, with a good deal of leeway for putting in some solo practice on my own. Now and then a visiting pilot would turn out to be an old Hendon friend whom I could persuade to let me try out his craft. Before long I had an impressive list—for the time—of different types I had flown. I was lent out for a while to the photography officer, Captain Court-Treatt (afterward well known as an explorer), who reported that I was a good cross-country pilot who could always take him right over his pinpoints. So, one way and another, I rapidly made up a lot of lost time in collecting experience. But I didn't seem to be impressing anybody except myself, and unless something unusual happened, I looked like remaining an instructor and odd-jobs pilot. Then my good friend Lady Luck came back to work for me.

One afternoon Captain A. G. S. ("Ginger") Mitchell, in an expansive mood, let me take out the little Martinsyde S.1 "scout" that the squadron maintained for officers' practice. This was a very small, supposedly fast, badly unstable, and generally nasty single-seat biplane with a four-wheeled landing gear. Few of the officers cared much for it, so I was allowed to fly it now and then. When I felt I had the hang of it, I asked the C.O.'s permission to loop it—at that time looping required official permission—and I was told to go up to three thousand feet for the purpose. I had never looped before, but I imagined that I knew all about it. I climbed as required, pushed the nose down to pick up speed, and happily hauled back on the stick to make my loop. I knew nothing about the gyroscopic effect of a rotary engine on a very small airplane, and I don't know who else did. But it had precisely the effect of hard right rudder when the stick was pulled back, and in later years it was to be a famed, and sometimes lethal, feature of the Sopwith Camel.

Anyway, instead of going around in the neat loop I was expecting, I found the nose shooting off somewhere sideways. In my struggle to get oriented, the horizon appeared, disappeared, and reappeared from all sorts of confusing directions. When I finally got straightened out I was down to about a thousand feet. Knowing that half the squadron was curiously watching, I had to try again. I climbed back to three thousand feet—same result. Now I remembered uncomfortably that I had never seen anyone loop the Martinsyde, and I wished I knew why. Desperately I tried again, gyrating all over the sky in mystified efforts to get some sort of co-operation out of this unruly beast. Whether I ever did complete an actual loop I never knew. I gave up and landed.

I taxied to the hangar wondering what excuse I could provide for my dismal performance. Mitchell and a group of officers were standing there. Mitchell was laughing. "You were told to loop," he said to me, "not to try and pull the wings off." I noticed then that the others were looking strangely at me, and suddenly it all dawned on me: they thought I had been purposely putting on a stunt show. With the usual process of rumor, the story quickly circulated that I had learned stunt flying at Hendon before the war, and that only my lowly rank had deterred me from giving an exhibition previously. I said nothing to disillusion anybody. I was now established as an aerobatic pilot, with the embarrassing prospect of having to maintain that reputation. That immediate problem was solved for me, at least temporarily, when an officer cracked up the "Tinsyde" on a landing. A week or so later I was told to report to Fort Grange, Gosport, for a special "monoplane course." Nobody told me why, but obviously I had been placed somewhere on record as having progressed beyond elementary flying.

2. A Monoplane Expert

This "monoplane course" was a ritual of curious origin. A year or so previously there had been an epidemic of military crashes in which monoplanes had happened to predominate, so naturally some political headline hunter set up a squeal for the abolition of the murderous monoplane. It made no sense; some of our biplanes were just as tricky as some of our monoplanes. But it was easier for our air chiefs to compromise than to try to teach aeronautics to politicians. So the monoplane was reprieved and a soothing but pointless course of special training was set up at Gosport for pilots likely to be assigned to monoplanes. It is worthy of historic note, however, that the British prejudice against monoplanes was maintained throughout the war; no new monoplanes were ordered except the magnificent Bristol M.1, of which only a few were delivered and even those were relegated to secondary theaters of war. Such monoplanes as we had, we had had to buy from the French.

My monoplane course came near to ending my flying career just as it was beginning to brighten. The only monoplanes at Gosport at that time were some single-seat and two-seat specimens of the tranquil Blériot. I was placed under the command of a certain Captain H., an acidly haughty scion of an aristocratic family who was appalled at the idea of having to allow a lowly mechanic to fly his planes. He felt that anyone less than an officer was inherently unfit to be trusted with any government equipment other than a pick, a shovel, or a rifle. He started by unintentionally doing me a good turn. He came by just as I was about to take off as passenger with Flight-Sergeant-Pilot William McCudden (elder brother of the later-famous "ace" Jim McCudden), whom Captain H. had previously grounded for several weeks on the pretext that there were not enough monoplanes for the officers. The sight of two non-officers in one plane was too much for Captain H., so I had to get out while a new young student officer named Norman Read, an American volunteer to the R.F.C. from Manchester, Massachusetts, took my place. For no evident reason, the Blériot stalled on a turn and dived into the ground; McCudden was killed and Read was very badly smashed up.

After that, Captain H. gave me the lowest possible flying priority, and I was a long time completing my assigned quota of monoplane hours. But my stay at Gosport ended in light comedy. On what was intended as my completion flight, the engine quit cold just as I took off over the end of the field. I turned sharply and barely scraped into a rough and unused corner of the field, where the Blériot leaped and bounded like a spring lamb before coming to rest—quite undamaged. This was Captain H.'s opportunity; he gave me a public and merciless dressing down for an incompetent landing. Then, still snorting with indignation, he climbed into another Blériot and took off. His engine quit also; he landed badly, bounced high, and wrecked his landing gear and propeller. The shouts of laughter from those who had heard him bawling me out must have reached him where he was. Head down, he walked back to the Officers' Mess by a circuitous route. I never saw him again—but he hadn't quite finished with me.

A clerk friend of mine in the Squadron Office had typed up the sealed progress report that I was to take back to Farnborough. He told me what was in it. It was signed by Captain H. and stated that I was a careless pilot and not likely to be any good. On the train I tore up the report and threw it out the window, trusting to find some way out of this menace before the inevitable copy followed up later. My luck held.

I reported next morning to Captain Wilson, the new Squadron Commander, who told me he had an immediate monoplane job for me. During my absence at Gosport the squadron had somehow acquired an ancient 50-h.p. single-seat Blériot, which had now been assigned to Netheravon, on Salisbury Plain. I was to take it there. I could see that it was a sadly battered specimen, but nobody told me its haunted history until afterward. It was probably the original home of the Gremlins. Nothing that the ablest mechanic could do would make it fly decently, and a new engine put into it would immediately develop troubles previously unknown to the Gnome engineers. I took off, and the Blériot promptly dropped the right wing and tried to dive me into Cove Pond. When I hauled it out of the dive it tried to stall; it became tail-heavy one moment and nose-heavy the next. If I ever got near to straight and level flight, the engine would splutter or cut out. And so on all the way to Netheravon. It took me two days and three forced landings to cover the sixty miles—it seemed much longer. But I made it.

And then Lady Luck really started to put in overtime for me.

At Netheravon they had a Grahame-White-built Morane, which was to be returned to the Hendon factory for overhaul. The Commanding Officer remembered me as a Morane "expert" from my earlier visits as a G-W serviceman; I had just flown in on a Blériot, so he apparently took it for granted that I also flew Moranes. Having no Morane pilot immediately available, he telephoned Farnborough to ask if I might fly this plane back to Hendon, and Wilson agreed.

I took special care to avoid telling the C.O. that I had never flown a Morane, for I didn't want to miss a chance like this. Only the best of pilots were supposed to fly this graceful, fast, but tricky monoplane, and I had long dreamed of the day when I could call myself a Morane pilot.

It has always seemed strange to me that the Blériot planes of those days are still well remembered, whereas the Moranes seem to be almost forgotten; this is all the more curious since the name of Blériot disappeared from airplane design some fifty years ago, whereas Morane-Saulnier designs continued into the age of jets.

The distinctive quality of the World War I Morane, apart from its speed, was its very high maneuverability, which was to have a major effect on my future. The Morane had no fixed stabilizer, so that its all-moving, balanced tailplane gave it an extremely light and sharp elevator control. The lateral control was by warping the wings, and the shape of the wing tips gave them maximum control effect but made them heavy to move. Sensitive handling was therefore needed to cope with this combination of light and heavy action in a powerful control; besides that, the clean lines of the plane gave it a flat glide, which called for more than usual skill in a landing approach. So it is not very surprising that, in those days, most pilots aspired to fly Moranes but not too many were competent to do so.

If I hadn't flown a Morane before this opportunity turned up, at least I knew enough about it to feel no lack of confidence. On my way to Hendon I gave the plane as complete an aerobatic workout as I knew how, and I arrived at my destination glowing with the feeling that I was now a complete pilot—if you could fly a Morane well, you could fly anything.

I returned to Farnborough ready to face anything nasty that might have arisen out of my "lost" Gosport report. But, if Wilson had ever seen it, he never mentioned it—I heard no more about it. A few days later my promotion to corporal appeared in orders.

3. Off to War

I had joined the Royal Flying Corps with the general notion of getting into whatever air combat was available; but I still hadn't arrived there. I had been posted to two squadrons, one after the other, that were formed at Farnborough for overseas duty, but in each case I had been taken out before it left for the Middle East, on the grounds that I was wanted at Farnborough. This was all very distressing, but in fact it was very fortunate for me, because both those squadrons eventually took a terrible beating from the desert sands, the climate, and the shortage of supplies, which caused them far more losses than the desultory combat they encountered.

I hesitated to apply to be sent to France. I knew several sergeant-pilots who were flying in action, but no corporal-pilots. Then, again, a medical officer had hinted that my glasses would be a bar to my acceptance for combat duties. It seemed that all I could do was to wait for my sergeant's stripes and then see what I could manage. My problem solved itself very suddenly.

One evening Captain Wilson told me I was to leave from Brooklands (midway between Farnborough and London) at daybreak next morning to take an Avro 504 biplane, with the first of the new long-stroke Gnome engines, to R.F.C. headquarters in France. I presumed that this was just some sort of ferry trip, but I thought I might as well ask Wilson if there was any chance of my remaining in France. "Of course," he said. "You're posted overseas." Then he told me that, owing to the short notice, I could take his car and driver to go to see my mother overnight in the south of London, and the driver would wait to take me to Brooklands early next morning. For a mere corporal, I was leaving for war in comfort and style.

My mother was now proudly content. She had been worried that Britain could not possibly win the war unless all three of her sons were in it. My brothers had been in the fighting for some time, Tom in the Australian artillery and Arthur in the Navy, and now that I would be fighting in the Royal Flying Corps the Empire was safe by land, sea, and air.

Duly I arrived at Brooklands, checked over the new Avro with Major Barrington-Kennett, and, in the daybreak of a bright spring morning, took off for Saint Omer and war.

CHAPTER VII

A New Kind of War

1. Introduction to War

It had not yet been six years since Louis Blériot first staggered across the English Channel with inches to spare, and an air crossing of that historic ditch still held a flavor of romance and adventure. The distance was barely over twenty miles, but it was an area of notoriously treacherous weather; the other coast could rarely be seen, and strong cross winds prevailed which could drift a slow airplane far off course, perhaps to come down in the sea or in enemy territory. Our unfaithful engines were not particular where they quit, and a wide stretch of rough water seemed as good a place as any. The long list of airmen "missing" in those few miles had already started to be compiled.

To the very raw pilots who were now being sent out to war, the Channel crossing was no inconsiderable hazard, for we had had no time to train them in the mysteries of air navigation. They learned to follow railways and highways with the aid of a compass; but that wavering instrument was so involved in errors and corrections that their faith in its honesty was practically zero. The mists, fogs, and winds of the Channel appeared, therefore, to guarantee that they would somehow get lost, and many of them set forth with confidence at a low level. There were stories of how two or three of them had flown northward, heedless of compass reading, across the broad and misty estuary of the Thames River under the impression that they were crossing the Channel, and of how they had at last landed near some eastern English village to inquire, in their best schoolroom French, what part of France they were in.

To try to obviate such mischances, the authorities devised what was probably history's first example of ground aids to air navigation. They cut two large white crosses, a couple of miles or so apart, into the chalky coastal fields near Folkestone, these crosses being lined up with Cape Gris-Nez in France. A new pilot, heading for war, was instructed to follow the railroad until he found one of the crosses. If he then couldn't see the other one, visibility was too bad for a crossing. If he could see both crosses, he was to fly a straight line between them, correcting for drift. At the same time, he was to note his compass indication; and then, no matter what that indication was, he was to stick to it until he reached the other side.

For my own first crossing I felt loftily superior to such expedients and, a little more than an hour out from Brooklands, I turned out over the water, flying at two thousand feet at sixty-five miles an hour until I picked up my landmarks on the French coast without difficulty.

The flying field at Saint Omer, which was my destination, was still under French military control, but it was also the main staging point for British air activities, and there was a profusion of units trying to get organized. After landing my Avro I taxied it around in this hotbed of bilingual confusion until at last I was able to hand it over to the Royal Flying Corps's Aircraft Park, where my new-type Gnome engine was awaited with great curiosity. Then I hurried off to Headquarters to discover what was next in store for me.

The Commanding Officer to whom I was to report was—of all people—Lieutenant Colonel Trenchard, whose last words to me several months before at Farnborough, had been "Get out." While waiting to enter the lion's den I briefly considered taking off my glasses, vaguely hoping that Trenchard wouldn't remember me. Fortunately I thought better of it; he remembered me all right, but I needn't have worried. My file was open on the table in front of him. "So," he said, "you managed to get here, glasses and all." This time, however, the fearsome Boom was smiling, and there was a note of congratulation in his rumbling voice. He went on to say that I was being posted to No. 3 Squadron to fly Moranes, and that my promotion to sergeant was already in the works. While waiting for the car that was to take me to the squadron, I got my sergeant's stripes, with the crossed-propeller badge, from the HQ storeroom.

No. 3 Squadron had just moved south from Choques to Auchel, a village a dozen miles behind the war front in the Lens coal-mining area, where the high conical slag heaps made a good landmark for the homing pilot. I reported to the Squadron Commander, Major Don Lewis, a pilot who had specialized in artillery direction and who was notoriously so contemptuous of anti-aircraft fire that he was eventually killed by a direct hit. He started to introduce me to my Flight Commander, Captain T. O'Brien Hubbard, but we were already well acquainted: "Mother" Hubbard had been a frequent military visitor to Hendon before the war and had once rewarded me, for services rendered, with a joy ride in his Henri Farman.

After preliminary briefings, Hubbard turned me over to Sergeant Jim McCudden, in charge of engine overhaul, to show me around. Hidden in the future was the fact that Jim would himself eventually learn to fly and become famous as one of the war's greatest fighting "aces."

Our Morane "Parasols" were among the various planes that we had had to acquire from the French while British production plans were still floundering in the morass of bureaucratic design programs. They were equipped with 80-hp Le Rhône rotary engines and were similar to the Morane Model G's, which I had helped to build at Grahame-White's before the war, except that their wings were raised above the fuselage to give the crew a better downward view, and the passenger space was much enlarged. This change cost something in performance, but the powerful and tricky control remained the same.

The planes—and, incidentally, the workshops—were housed in over-sized canvas tents that we had acquired from the French; they kept out most of the rain, wind, and dust but none of the cold of the local climate. Our flying field was a reasonably level stretch of ground on top of a low hill, so that it was well drained and gave us none of the familiar troubles with mud. But it was short by any standards, and particularly for Moranes, which landed faster than most other planes. Nobody bothered much about this; we just took that much more care to land very short. It was not until later, when Lieutenant Vachell overshot into the adjoining stubble field, turned over, and was burned to death, that some work was done to lengthen the landing run.

With McCudden I checked over my plane. It wasn't very new. It had been Hubbard's mount, but he had taken over a new plane that had just been brought up from Paris, and passed his along to me. The fabric was weathered and patched in spots, the cowling and other metalwork was dented and scraped here and there. But, as far as I was concerned, it was the world's most beautiful object, for it was the first airplane that I could call mine.

I gave the engine a couple of runs. Then, ballasting the rear seat with a mechanic eager for a joy ride, I put in an hour or so of flying and landing practice. Now I was all set for war.

2. *Learning the Hard Way*

Next morning, Hubbard gave me a map and told me to go out and cruise around to get familiar with our sector of the front, which extended roughly northward to La Bassée and southward to Arras. I was to keep well on our side of the lines, where presumably I couldn't get into any trouble, and collect a general idea of landmarks, trench systems, and other features of the scenery. It sounded simple enough. I took off alone; the Morane handled just as well with or without a passenger and climbed better without one. I decided that three thousand feet was a good-enough altitude for a sight-seeing excursion.

I was never sure afterward what I had expected the battlefield to look like. What I saw was a vast confusion of zigzag ditches running everywhere for miles in all directions, with shattered buildings and hamlets dotted haphazardly around, while the whole landscape was pitted with craters which made it look like a badly roughed-up section of the moon. I believe I expected to see unmistakable British and German front-line trenches, with something definite in the way of "no man's land" between them; in spite of all I had heard, I could not realize that sometimes the opposing lines were within a few yards of each other. For all I could tell, any of these trench assemblies could be the front lines.

In the air were four or five solitary planes, at a considerably higher altitude than mine, going about whatever business they had in hand, and some distance to the north I could see clumps of black dots in the sky, which I vaguely assumed to be anti-aircraft fire.

And then I had my first sharp lesson. Having no clear notion where the front lines were, I must have crossed them or come near to doing so. A large ball of black smoke appeared suddenly ahead of me, followed almost immediately by a roaring crash. The plane shuddered and shook, a triangle of fabric flapped loose on my right wing, and I could see daylight through the hole in it. Three or four smaller holes appeared close by. This was something that called for no deep thinking. Swinging the plane hard around as only a Morane could be turned, I put the nose down and streaked in the general direction of home, and I heard the next two bursts as dull thuds far behind. It was my first, but by no means my last, dispute with Archie.

"Archie" was the Royal Flying Corps's pet name for anti-aircraft fire. The name was derived—inevitably, for the British—from a currently popular music-hall song, "Archibald, Certainly Not," which had nothing to do with the war. The name Archie had an intimate ring that went well with a personal system of military discouragement in which the whole business was duck shooting on a grand scale. In the days when six thousand feet was a good altitude and sixty-five miles an hour a respectable airspeed, an airplane was not too poor a target if a pilot flew straight for long enough, and our wood-and-wire structures were full of vital spots where one hit with a chunk of steel was enough to wreck the whole plane. We learned to spot batteries whose gunners were particularly accurate, and some seemed to be expert in guessing the pilot's next move; so Archibald became, in fact, a personal and deadly enemy, to be faced when necessary and outwitted when possible.

Archie even wore a uniform, for the Germans used high explosive with a black shellburst, whereas the Allies used shrapnel shells with white smoke. In days before fighter planes ruled the skies at much higher speeds and altitudes, Archie was the war pilot's best enemy.

When I got back to the squadron, secretly proud of my Archie damage, I expected a reprimand from Hubbard for carelessly venturing out too far. But "Mother" was casually amused, and told me I would learn as I went along. Having found that my plane could be patched up in two or three hours, he suggested that, as I had already met Archie, I might as well take the afternoon long reconnaissance with Lieutenant Selby as observer. Since new pilots were usually assigned only the short missions, this put me slightly ahead of the game.

There are times when accounts of early efforts to fly in war seem rather improbable. Later generations grew to think of air warfare in terms of fighters, bombers, and other specialized classes of airplanes, with their complex backgrounds of training, tactics, and technology— even by 1917 such distinctions were well developed. So it is not easy to imagine the conditions, during that first year of the war, in which any airplane was anything you could make of it.

Our planes were not designed for any particular kind of operation, and no provision for any sort of warlike equipment went into their structures. Their performance was nothing like what it might have been when cleaned up for factory tests, for they were now cluttered with brackets, racks, fittings, and reinforcements to carry odd bits of speculative gear that would never have been tolerated in their original design. Their fabric and structures were patched with sundry repairs, and were weathered and sagging from life in the open. Their engines, which at best had been temporarily providing miserly horsepower, were now weary from long overtime hours and nervous from the ministrations of greenhorn mechanics.

The flying skill of the average pilot was still at the stage where a sharp, steep bank was considered stunt flying, and the simplest air navigation was an abstruse art. There were no established procedures for any particular mission. Beyond learning to fly, pilots were not trained for any specific class of work, and they were free to develop their own individual methods of carrying out any assignment. One result of this was that, when general business was slack, we were liable to invent our own assignments; if some new idea occurred to us that looked as if it might accomplish something, we simply asked the C.O's permission to go out and try it.

We knew too well that high military authorities did not think much of the airplane's possibilities, and in sober fact we ourselves had nothing more than our own optimism to support our faith in the airplane's military potential—no trace of previous experience was available. So we felt that it was up to us to try anything and everything to find out for ourselves what we could really do before we could hope to convince the ruling skeptics.

So if, today, it seems that we were then running a harebrained kind of an air war, the explanation is that we were still trying to discover how to run one at all.

3. Observation Tours

High Authority had conceded, from the start, that airplanes might just possibly be useful for observation work. But even on that point there were many doubts, because the vibration and rocking of the airplane inhibited the use of binoculars or a telescope. So originally the airplane's full observation equipment was the note pad and pencil for jotting down whatever the observer could see with the naked eye.

However, very early in the war, certain generals had cause to be grateful for information obtained from the air. On a number of well-recorded occasions, vital information was brought back by pilots who were out looking for something else. A result of this was that, while reconnaissance flights usually had some specific objective, pilots were allowed considerable latitude in making excursions or detours to pick up anything useful they could.

Usually we flew "high," around six thousand feet, where Archie was the main menace. But sometimes due to weather or for some especially close inspection, we flew as low as might be necessary, in which cases machine-gun fire from the ground could be nasty. For some strange reason it always seemed excruciatingly funny—to everyone except the victim—when somebody took a bullet in his bottom. I knew at least two men who suffered that painful indignity, and we tried to protect ourselves against such ignominy by placing a sheet-steel plate under each seat cushion. The unlikely story has often been told of the British pilot who, having run out of ammunition for his automatic pistol, continued his attack by trying to throw his steel plate into the enemy's propeller; but it is a true story—its hero was Lieutenant Arthur Payze, of our squadron.

Our routine reconnaissance assignments were rarely abandoned except for mechanical failure or impossible weather; if anything interfered with predetermined plans we tried something else. On one such occasion I started off with an observer and a routine program, but by the time we had reached working altitude and had set off over the enemy lines, we saw that there was a heavy haze below, through which little could be seen for observation purposes. Well, it was a fine day, with a clear sky overhead, so we decided to keep going anyway, in case we came across anything worth a report.

We had been cruising eastward for a little while when we became aware of a strange state of affairs: the customary Archie bursts were absent. The Hun was evidently not shooting at us, although, far to the north, we could see bunches of black dots where some other R.F.C. customer was being waited on. We guessed that the haze that dimmed our view was also hiding us from Archie. Emboldened by this happily peaceful situation, we set off on a wide sweep southward far out over enemy territory, climbing all the time in case we might later need the altitude to help us to get home. Eventually we came back to our side, flying unusually high, somewhere near Arras, where the French were holding the line and where the haze seemed to be clearing.

I started to let down for home; we had seen nothing interesting, but we had enjoyed a nice, calm, peaceful ride.

Peace was savagely shattered by a roar of Archie shells bursting nearby. Apparently a large battery had opened up on us—but the bursts were white, the mark of our own guns. I was still wondering what this was all about when a second salvo came up. This lot rocked us; several holes appeared in the wings, accompanied by all sorts of whistles and pings. A whiff of fumes and a cold trickle on my leg told me that my tank or a fuel line had been hit. And in days long before airplane parachutes, a pilot had no greater fear than the dread of fire. I promptly switched off the engine, swerved wildly into a tight diving spiral, and kept going until it was time to look for somewhere to land.

Forced landings were a feature of daily life, and we were experts at them, but the best-looking fields could contain hidden booby-traps, and you never knew what your luck was until the plane came to rest. In this case I had the added handicap, as I skimmed over a hedge into a long field of stubble, of wondering whether I was going to get some more "friendly" gunfire from any angle at any minute. By the time the

Morane had rolled gently to a stop, I felt as if I hadn't taken a breath for twenty minutes. My observer and I climbed out and polluted the air with sulphurous comments on the ways of idiot gunners.

Two cars came screaming up the country road and soldiers in blue jumped out. A French officer vaulted the gate, and, revolver in hand, started to sprint across the field toward us, bent on a dramatic capture. After a few yards he must have become aware of the plane's markings, for his run suddenly slumped to a slow and sheepish walk. My French developed spluttering eloquence. I wanted to know whose side he was on anyway, and why the French Army gave guns to artillerymen who couldn't even recognize a French-built airplane. By now the captain looked so distressed that I had to add something about their excellent shooting.

His story of mingled explanation and apology contained a streak of prophecy, although none of us then suspected it. He told us that the French anti-aircraft people had been warned that the Germans were believed to be building some sort of copy of the Morane. (And indeed the revolutionary Fokker fighter must already have been under construction; in silhouette from below it would be quite indistinguishable from our Morane.) Moreover, we had been approaching from far over the German lines, apparently immune from German Archie; we were flying very high, as the German reconnaissance planes always did; and the French had no Morane squadron in the Arras sector. It all sounded reasonable enough; maybe we had unwittingly asked for trouble. A reverse flow of apology and explanation got under way. A couple of French soldiers were left to guard the plane, and we were taken back to the French battery headquarters for dinner while our squadron was notified.

The incident led indirectly to occasional emergency co-operation between our squadron and the French artillery. I did a few "shoots" with French batteries and eventually found myself wearing the Croix de Guerre with Palm.

Artillery has always needed the services of well-located observers to let it know what, if anything, it was hitting. Artillery observation therefore became an early function of the airplane, and it developed into a specialty under conditions of trench warfare. Our C.O., Major

Lewis, had made this his own particular line of study, so No. 3 Squadron became leaders in that kind of work.

Artillery co-operation varied from directing actual bombardment to registering targets for later use. We had progressed from the earlier system of dropping weighted messages tied with fluttering ribbons, to the use of heavy and primitive radiotelegraph transmitter with a range of perhaps a dozen miles. With these we could tap out simple signals to batteries, or correct their gunfire by a code that used a clock number for direction (12 o'clock being north) and a letter for distance from target. The additional weight and bulk of a receiver was more than we could manage, so signals from battery to plane were made in code letters laid out in white cloth strips on the ground, which usually told us that the battery was ready to fire, or was delayed for some reason, or was changing its list of targets, or that we could go home.

The procedure was for the plane to fly over the battery to read its signal, then fly over the lines to the target area, radio the "fire" signal, watch for the shellburst, and radio back the correction—repeating the dose as necessary.

It was an unglamorous but hazardous occupation, and often a nerve-wracking one. We did this work in all weathers, which often meant flying very low over German target areas and back and forth over the trenches, giving the enemy ample time to figure what we were doing so that he could plaster us with Archie, machine guns, or any other hardware he had to offer. Losses among artillery-co-operation planes were often exceptionally heavy.

Perhaps the most trying—and too frequent—situation was having to work with a battery of green gunners fresh out from home. They would confuse both their signals and our own, firing when we were not ready to observe, or not firing when we were. Sometimes, zigzagging around the target to dodge ground fire, we would frantically repeat the "fire" signal and watch for the shellburst that never came. On one memorable occasion I gave up in disgust, went home, and telephoned the battery to ask what the hell. Answer: they had run out of shells and had been waiting for a fresh supply to come up. Such was the military supply situation in mid-1915.

Directing a heavy bombardment that preceded a major ground offensive was nearly always a hectic experience, particularly when poor weather compelled us to fly low. Initial plans usually fell into disarray as the attack developed, and nobody knew just who was firing at what. It was quite easy for planes to fly into barrages intended for the fellows on the ground, and there were frequent cases of direct hits on our planes as they scouted round trying to gather information for transmission to the gunners.

"Shell bumps" from passing ammunition were a ghostly sort of disturbance. My first taste of this was during one early-morning bombardment, when my Morane was wildly jolted by some unseen hand and I glanced up to see an enormous shell glinting for a moment in the sun, apparently loitering in mid-air looking for some place to go. When I reported this startling event to Hubbard, he told me casually that that was something else I would have to get used to: it was merely a high-trajectory heavy howitzer shell slowing up at the top of its path on its way to business.

The problem of co-ordinating an artillery barrage with an advancing body of infantry was, and probably still is, a headache for tactical planners. It brings up the story of Flight Sergeant* Burns; I did not know until quite recently that his heroic action is recorded in official histories of World War I. Burns was a giant of a man and, for an old-time soldier, of a singularly amiable and easygoing disposition. Inevitably he was known as "Tiny," and in our sergeant's mess it was regularly suggested that he was lucky to be in the Royal Flying Corps, because if he were in the infantry, the Germans could not possibly fail to hit his massive structure. Tiny occasionally wearied of this joke, which turned out not to be a joke.

In 1915, when everything was in a state of primitive experiment, the problem of keeping track of advancing infantry was acute. Portable radios were many years in the future. Field telephones were soon knocked out. The kite balloons were too far back to see enough detail. So of course the airplanes were called up to fly over the attack area and report to the guns, with their clumsy radios, what was going on. A few hectic sorties soon demonstrated painfully that, if we flew low enough to distinguish enough, we would not last long in the showers of hardware pouring out from both sides. Somebody suggested using

* "Flight sergeant" was a rank indicating the senior sergeant of a flight; occasionally he was also a pilot—Burns was not.

infantry officers from the attacking units as temporary flight observers, hoping that they could better distinguish their own units from above than our people could. So we tried taking up such men; they had never flown, and they frequently discovered that they never wanted to fly again. Results were, if anything, slightly worse.

I don't know whether it was Tiny's own idea or whether he eagerly picked it up from someone else. Anyway, Tiny was an expert at signaling with the Aldis lamp, whose bright, focused beam could, even in daylight, flash a message that could be read a long way off. He suggested that, as an experiment, somebody—himself, of course—who understood the working of airplanes, should go forward with the infantry and, with some simple code, flash information to planes flying overhead at a practical height. If the idea worked, it could be expanded into a general program.

Thus it happened that, on the first day of the battle of Loos, Tiny Burns went over the top with the infantry. In relays we watched the area where he was expected to be and we picked up many of his signals and tapped the information back to the guns. Late that night Tiny was brought back to the squadron smothered in mud. He told us grimly but cheerfully of a day spent mostly lying on his back in shell holes, sighting his lamp on the Moranes above. Notes were compared and improvements worked out. A little sleep, and he was off again to the trenches and shell holes. The second day of the experiment brought even better results and, at least where Tiny was, we knew a good deal of what was going on.

That night Tiny did not return to the squadron. He never did. The Flight Sergeant had died in a shell hole—like an infantryman.

4. Night Flight

It would be a long time before night flying, as a regular habit, became a practical proposition. Exhibition flights at night, within gliding distance of an airfield, had been a popular prewar novelty. And occasionally some reckless character, on a clear bright night, would get himself talked about by attempting a cross-country trip. But, under most conditions, navigation for any distance would be virtually im-

ossible, and, of course, in the event of a forced landing in the dark,
rospects of getting down without a crash would be negligible.

My first night flight, therefore, was the result of special circum-
tances, and it was nearly my last flight.

Late one afternoon I was out on the field when one of our observers,
lieutenant "Hoppy" Cleaver, came hurrying over with an urgent
nessage from the C.O. It seemed that, early the next morning, there
vas to be some sort of infantry offensive farther north. The artillery
hat was to open the attack had belatedly discovered a group of im-
ortant targets that still needed to be registered. Our Brigade wanted
he job done immediately.

"I told them on the phone," said Hoppy, "that we couldn't possibly
egister more than a few of those targets before dark, even if the gunners
vere shooting a damn sight better than usual. But the Brigade said
hey wanted the job done, and they didn't care if we had to stay out
ll night."

Needless to say, none of the comfortable characters at Brigade
Headquarters ever flew at night, if at all. I told Hoppy I had never
one any night flying and, as far as I knew, none of our other available
ilots had. Hoppy said he hadn't either, so this would be as good a
hance as any to find out what we could do with artillery in the
ark. The C.O. had said that it was up to us if we wanted to try it;
f not, he could tell the Brigade that their order had come too late.
We definitely wanted to try it.

The mechanics worked fast. The bulky transmitter set, with its heavy
torage battery, was hurriedly loaded aboard my Morane, the antenna
eel bolted to its bracket, and the whole works wired up. I told some-
ne to put a flashlight in the side pocket of my cockpit, for we had no
uch luxury as instrument lighting. Meanwhile Hoppy was on the tele-
hone getting his target pinpoints. At last he limped up with his maps
nd notes and, of course, his trusty cut-down Winchester, without
vhich he never flew and which he considered ample armament against
ny and all foes. We took off into a watery sunset and turned north
oward the target area. The sky was covered with a thin high overcast,
ut the air was calm and reasonably clear.

For a while it was routine: back and forth between battery and
argets; "Ready to fire," "Fire," observe shellburst, transmit correction,

dodge around to confuse Archie, "Next target, please." Sunset fade
into twilight; twilight darkened into night; landscape details fade
gradually, leaving only the more prominent objects in ghostly gloo
to indicate location or direction. The smoke of the shellbursts becam
flashes. I wondered vaguely how accurate Cleaver's observations migh
be, but that was his problem—I was now much too busy with the flyin
as I followed the directions he shouted in my ear.

Every so often Cleaver tapped my shoulder and shouted, "Lower.
From what little I could see below, I knew I had several hundred fee
to spare, but I thought I had better check my altimeter and reache
into the side pocket for the flashlight. It wasn't there—must hav
been dropped, or forgotten, or something. Too bad. Archie had give
up for the night, but varying volumes of machine-gun chatter could b
heard above the engine noise; I supposed the enemy below wa
giving us what attention he could, and I hoped he could see as littl
of us as we could of him. It occurred to me that probably I ought t
be scared, until I realized that I was enormously enjoying the heav
intoxication of trying something I had never done before and wonde
ing how it was all going to work out.

My sense of time vanished in my concentration on control and o
checking the few dim landmarks that guided my erratic course. At la
Cleaver shouted, "Finished—home." So now—how did we get home

I started tensely into an uneasy and wavering climb, for only i
cidental stars flickered through the overcast sky, and the blacked-ou
warscape below showed nothing but a few dim and distant ligh
on which to focus for steadying my flight. But, as I got higher, mo
lights became visible and I could relax into a more normal contro
My compass was somewhere in the darkness of the cockpit and wa
no help; but a faint remaining glow in the sky showed me where we
was, and I could head in a generally southward direction, feeling reaso
ably sure that our squadron landing flares would be visible from
long way off against the darkness of the earth. And, sure enough, ther
they were, unmistakable away ahead toward my right.

The flare system was totally simple: four two-gallon fuel cans wit
tops cut off and stuffed with rags soaked in kerosene. Three cans wer
set in line with the wind, and at the upwind end of the line the fourt
can was set at a right angle to form an L. The smoky flames fro

hese flares provided negligible light for landing, but they located the anding area and indicated the wind direction. Moreover, used properly, hey provided the necessary perspective for control during approach —but, like most of our pilots, I had no training, no experience, and no dea about how to use them properly.

I ought to have made a long, straight approach into the wind oward the short leg of the L., but I was tired, I guessed my fuel night be getting short, and I was in a hurry to get down. Anyway, I lidn't see why I shouldn't keep my southward course and then make a last-minute westward turn into the L. Now I banked for my turn, and something went wrong; my bank had destroyed all perspective, and the nice neat L had transformed itself into some other strange pattern. Then, suddenly, all the lights went out.

Now, I wondered, why on earth would they want to douse the flares just as I was about to land? Had some idiot mistaken me for an enemy plane, or what? The answer was easy, but I had no time to work it out before the crash: the flares had vanished simply because I had dropped below the top of the little hill on which the field was situated.

The Morane slammed into the slope of the hill and wrapped me up in a tangle of wires, struts, splinters, and fabric. Utter surprise took charge of all other emotions. It seemed to me that the earth had inexcusably jumped up and hit me, and that I had encountered a new phenomenon of nature which needed investigation.

I called out to Cleaver, but the wreckage was ominously silent. I heard the shouts of men running and stumbling down the hillside, and then hands were weaving me cautiously out from among the bits and pieces. A worried voice called out, "Where's Mr. Cleaver?" Suddenly I felt very cold—some weeks previously another Lieutenant Cleaver (no relation to Hoppy) had simply fallen out to his death from George Pretyman's Morane in very rough air. Now, it seemed, Hoppy was missing, and I was numbly trying to imagine when and where my weaving flight in the dark might have dislodged him.

I worked my limbs until I decided that I didn't need the stretcher and that the iodine and plaster could wait until we knew more about Hoppy. And then we found him. When we hit he had been catapulted ahead—still clutching his beloved Winchester—and had landed in a large clump of thorn bushes, where he had been briefly knocked out. He was now struggling with the thorns, and he was easily located by the appalling language emanating from the bushes. He had much to say about the thorns, the artillery, and the Brigade, and his voice was much too loud and firm to come from a seriously injured man. Together we staggered over to the waiting medical officer.

5. The Bombers

Last time I heard from No. 3 Squadron, which was fairly recently, they were flying "Canberra" jet bombers with NATO forces in Germany. But fifty years earlier, in 1915, nobody ever called us bombers; we were just trying to get the general idea.

It seems always to have been the instinct of the warrior to try to get somewhere over the top of his foe, so that he could drop something nasty on him. There must once have been a gleeful satisfaction in rolling rocks down a hill onto the enemy, or in pouring boiling pitch on him from high battlements. So it is probable that the idea of dropping bombs from flying machines was a good deal older than thoughts of spying from them. Long before war came along to open up real business opportunities for bombers, we used to hold bomb-dropping competitions, using bags of flour or chalk.

So when war came, we took to bombing with enthusiasm, although we may now wonder what good we thought we were doing. For one thing, we had little chance of hitting anything worth hitting, and, for another, anything we did hit was unlikely to suffer too seriously from the little twenty-pounders that were the best we could carry. Still, we tried, and if we weren't carrying other heavy gear, we would not miss a chance to take along two or four bombs and leave them off somewhere with the best of vicious intentions.

Bomb racks, homemade in the squadron workshop, were attached at some convenient location on the outside of the plane. The bombs were slung on the racks with improvised catches that were supposed to release a bomb when the pilot pulled a ring, usually a retired spark-plug gasket, attached to a wire running from the cockpit. Now and

hen the bomb would come loose at one end and hang up at the
ther, dangling precariously with good prospects of falling off over our
wn lines or threatening a catastrophe when the plane landed.

The idea of safety devices on the bombs took some time to sink
n; at one time, No. 3 Squadron used French-made melinite bombs
hat had no such device, until one day one of them blew up while
eing loaded aboard, killing Captain Cholmondeley and a dozen fel-
ows standing around. After that we used the twenty-pound Hale bomb,
vhich had a little wind-driven arming gadget.

Bomb-aiming was an acquired art, unrelated to science: the pilot
ooked over the side and pulled the ring when so inspired. This system
ractically ensured that the target was the safest spot in the area. My
irst "bomb raid" was combined with a reconnaissance trip during which
was supposed to drop two twenty-pounders on Don railroad junc-
ion, in Belgium. After I dropped the first bomb the railroad re-
nained exactly as before, but I saw a haystack fly apart about a quarter
f a mile away. I circled and dropped the second one, and my story
s that Archie spoiled my aim; anyway, I never did see what happened
o that bomb.

However, history would excuse us; there was to be a lot of "scientific"
ombing in World War II that fared no better.

Sometimes we took a few hand grenades, and to this day I can't
hink why, except that those were days when you tried anything. These
renades were of an ancient type that had no timing device; they went
ff on contact after the pin was pulled. One day Lieutenant Corbett-
Wilson took out a few grenades for some unremembered purpose; his
Morane was seen to disintegrate for no evident reason, and we sur-
nised that he had thrown a grenade and hit one of his own wires or
truts.

Then there were the famous "flechettes," famous because of the
orror stories invented about them. They were small, pencil-like steel
larts, released from a can a couple of dozen or so at a time. Devised
riginally for use against cavalry, they were supposed to terrify whole
egiments of Uhlans by dropping in ghostly silence clean through
nan and horse. It is a pity that there seems to be no honest evidence
hat anybody was ever hit by one.

I think the record shows that I was the last pilot to try to do something useful with the grenades and the flechettes. It was a disastrous effort—as I shall recount further along.

6. *The Mystery Passenger*

Captain G. L. Cruikshank, one of our flight-commanders, was eventually to be shot down and killed by the famous German "ace" Oswald Boelcke. But before that happened, he was to enter the pages of history as pioneer of a daring type of air operation that was to flourish extensively in World War II. It all started on the day when he brought a clumsy-looking civilian onto the flying field and set him to swinging a Morane propeller.

Swinging propellers for starting engines was always a hazard to new or careless mechanics; it was particularly so in earlier days, when ignition switches were often defective and an engine might fire when the switch was supposed to be off. In warning novices about being careful, we sometimes scared them so badly that some of them faced a propeller as though it were a firing squad. So it became a regular source of airfield entertainment to watch a timid beginner going through a sort of formal dance in which he gingerly grasped a blade, jerked it feebly, leaped wildly to safety, and then looked back dejectedly to see why the engine hadn't started.

But when Cruikshank brought out this quaint character to swing his propeller, there seemed nothing very funny in trying to make a fool of the poor devil.

He was a stockily built fellow with a walrus mustache and thick-lensed eyeglasses. His heavy corduroy pants were stuffed into high boots, and a belted lumber jacket and deerstalker cap completed the picture of something that never left the farm—although, in fact, he turned out to be the schoolmaster of a Belgian village. Cruikshank sat in the cockpit and exchanged shouts of "contact" and "coupé" with this rustic apparition while the latter kept jerking spasmodically at the propeller and finally got the engine started. Cruikshank promptly stopped the engine, and the performance began all over again. This went on for more than an hour. Evidently this was something more than a joke, and we all wanted to know what was going on. But Cruikshank was evasive.

For the next couple of days our peasant performer showed up for several repeats of this mystic training course, until at last he could put his powerful arms into a hefty swing guaranteed to start any startable engine. I was working on my plane at daybreak one morning when I saw the schoolmaster, in his usual attire plus a pair of goggles, climb into the observer's seat behind Cruikshank with a heavy bag, and off they went into the dawn. An hour or two later Cruikshank came back—alone. After a couple of days, Cruikshank went out alone, and came back with the schoolmaster, who hurriedly went off in a car with a staff captain.

When this strange act was repeated, it was easy for us to guess the reason for that propeller-swinging business. If Cruikshank were landing a man behind the enemy lines, he risked the stopping of an engine that could not be effectively idled, and his passenger would have to be able to restart it for him.

It was on the third or fourth occasion that Cruikshank went out alone and came back alone, with several bullet holes in his plane. Instead of a waiting rustic, there had been enemy soldiers, but Cruikshank had spotted them before he stopped his engine. Weeks later, the news seeped back: our schoolmaster had been trapped by the Germans and shot as a spy.

The French Resistance movement of World War II produced innumerable stories of that kind of operation, aided by radio, parachutes, night flying procedures, and other modern improvements. But Cruikshank's name is honored in the records as the pilot who introduced aviation to the cloak-and-dagger business.

CHAPTER VIII

IMMELMANN'S GERMAN MORANE

On October 21, 1915, I learned painfully that the opening phase of the air war was over, and that the days of blind and hopeful experiment were about to be brutally ended by a deadly new air weapon.

For me it was a long day. In the morning I was notified of forthcoming promotion. And by nightfall I was flat out on a stretcher, headed for a few months of hospital, an early and very disconcerted victim of the new era.

The muddled battle of Loos was petering out dismally in senseless infantry slaughter, and over our section of the front there hung an air of stagnation and stalemate. We had a natural hunger for action, but no worthwhile action seemed to be in sight.

Just before lunch Major Lewis sent for me and handed me the good news: he had recommended me for a commission "for service in the field," and headquarters approval had just come through. In a few days I would be exchanging my sergeant's stripes for the "pips" of a second lieutenant.

I hurried back up the hill to our messroom, a French villager's parlor that the sergeants and corporals shared with two million flies, and told them my news, which obviously called for a celebration. I sat down with Sergeants George Thornton, Jim McCudden, and Freddie Mayes to discuss a program. Thornton promptly claimed that this had to be a joint celebration: he had just had news from home of the birth of his first son.

Then we remembered that this was a very special date for celebration purposes: it was Trafalgar Day, in glorious memory of Admiral Lord Nelson. And somebody raised the question, long popular with facetious Britons in an emergency: "What would Nelson do?" Certainly, in our situation, Nelson would have gone out to raise some sort of hell with the enemy. That settled it: Thornton and I would try "the Nelson touch"—if we could think up something.

We discussed this and that possibility, in the course of which Mayes brought up the subject of kite balloons. As far as we knew, nobody had ever knocked one down from an airplane. If we could figure out a scheme for doing it, we would open up a promising new line of business. We tried to think of a suitable weapon; we knew nothing of incendiary bullets or rockets, such as would be used in later years for this particular form of sport. Then McCudden remembered a recent squadron order: our old hand grenades and flechettes had been declared obsolete, and the Equipment Officer was going to bury them when he got around to it. Why waste them?

A can of flechettes might promote a lot of leaky holes in a balloon: not much of a prospect, but possibly worth trying. Grenades looked a lot more promising; these, as I mentioned before, had no timing device but exploded on contact after the pin was pulled. One hit with a grenade on a gas-filled balloon would do the trick.* Now we settled down to work out a program.

I found Hubbard and talked to him about it; he said it was all right with him if the C.O. approved. I went down to the squadron office to get the Major's permission. Lewis looked dubious at first, and then the idea seemed to amuse him. He finally agreed that it might be a worthwhile experiment.

The afternoon was fine and clear as my Morane was pushed out. Thornton loaded himself into the observer's cockpit with a rifle, as many grenades as we could find room for, and three cans of flechettes. I took off, with a proud feeling that Nelson would have approved, and with no thought that I might not see No. 3 Squadron again.

We had already decided on our prey, a large sausage usually to be

* In his book, written after he became a famous ace, McCudden mentions that we also took a Very pistol for incendiary purposes. I don't remember that, but anyway we never got around to using it.

found floating high over Salomé, near La Bassée. Our plan was magnificently simple. I proposed to approach the balloon in a sneaky
fashion, as if I were heading somewhere else, then suddenly turn and
glide swiftly down on it—a steep dive would make it too difficult to
throw the grenades. I would zigzag around close to the top of the
balloon, signaling Thornton by hand when to throw the grenade. I
relied on surprise, the Morane's maneuverability, and the interference
of the balloon itself for protection against unpracticed gun crews with
their unwieldy infantry machine guns.

After we crossed the lines, Thornton used one can of flechettes for a
drop test; we had never used them before. They were so clumsy to
handle that he gave up and threw the other two cans overboard. We
approached our quarry in a wide circuit and got ready for action.

A few poorly placed Archies dropped behind as I shut off the engine,
swerved, and slid rapidly down on the sausage. The surprise seemed
complete; not a sound came from the ground guns. Over the top of
the balloon I circled and weaved, with brief straightaways for Thornton's grenade work. We had noticed no effect from our first three or
four grenades, and now I began to sense something ominously strange:
I was expecting to arrive within unmissable distance from the balloon,
but although we were gliding without power, we were not getting
any nearer to it. I must have known, if I had thought about it, that
the balloon could and would have been pulled down, but it had never
occurred to me that this might be a high-speed operation. My eyes
had been glued on the gasbag, and I had lost track of everything else.

Now I glanced around at the general scenery, but it was too late.
The balloon was almost down to the ground, we were somewhere
around a thousand feet up—and the machine guns came alive with
a dreadful chatter.

Quite obviously, our balloon strafing was over for the day. I had
run myself into a trap and I had to get out of it. I immediately put
the Morane into what, in later years, would have been called "evasive
action," and I was reasonably confident that the clumsy guns of the
balloon unit would have a hard time trying to hit me so long as I
could keep that up. But I had to get home, and I knew I had little
chance of getting back across the forward lines at that altitude. There

was no prospect of climbing in that area; if I continued to dodge around I would have no rate of climb at all; and if I didn't, I would be too good a target.

All I could think of was that if I flew well back into German territory, there would not be so many guns round and I could, with ordinary luck, regain enough altitude for getting home. I dived right down to the canal bank and started to follow it eastward, so low that I would be a hopelessly fast target for any chance gunner on the way. The canal ran into a river, and I followed that for a while. I don't know how far back I went, but at last I gathered enough nerve to start pulling up in a widely circling climb. Thornton jettisoned our remaining grenades.

All seemed well; I reached about six thousand feet without any sign of trouble, and then started on a beeline for home—which was probably just what some calculating Archie gunner was waiting for. A black cauliflower blossomed right overhead. There was a loud crump and a violent jolt. A few seconds later the next one hit us. I don't remember hearing a sound, but a hundred hammers hit me in the neck and shoulders, everything shook and rattled, fabric flapped, wires slacked, and I waited for the whole works to fall apart. I must have swerved with the shock, for the next bursts sounded vaguely distant. I could feel a sticky trickle down my neck and back, but I had no idea whether or not I had been badly hit, and I could not tell whether my dizzy headache meant something serious or nothing much. Pulling myself together, I cautiously tested the controls. Everything seemed to be working, and the engine buzzed smoothly. For the moment, at least, I was still flying.

I managed to look back at Thornton. His face and hands were streaked with blood. He was cursing vigorously and grinning broadly, and he called out something about being all right. A minute later he shouted in my ear that our rifle had been damaged. I didn't know how, but who cared? I wasn't going to fight anyone. I was no longer interested in what Nelson would have done—I just wanted to go home.

Now I could dimly make out the jagged lines in the distance where the front trench systems were. If I could avoid any more Archie, and if I didn't pass out, and if the plane held together, perhaps I could make it. Then came another shout from Thornton: "Something coming up fast behind—looks like that German Morane."

It was, as we knew later, Immelmann and his new Fokker, fresh from his first few easy victories. But, at that moment, I knew my pursuer only as the "German Morane" about which so many vague and disquieting rumors were going around. I wasn't sure now what he could do to me, but he wouldn't have to do much to finish us off. I was definitely unhappy. While waiting for final punishment I thought rapidly over what little I knew of this mystery plane, and what I remembered gave a faint shred of hope.

Some three weeks earlier I had been casually watching one of our B.E. observation biplanes a couple of miles away when I noticed that it was being overtaken by a smaller monoplane, which suddenly dived behind it and swooped up under its tail. The B.E. wallowed as if surprised or hit, while the smaller plane continued upward in a steep climbing turn, heading back the way it had come. If this was an attack, the attacker must have had the surprising capability of firing ahead. Vaguely I recalled the prewar Morane-Saulnier experiments for firing through the propeller, but that scheme had been rejected by the Allied military authorities. The Germans also had long ago toyed with some such project but had abandoned it. The whole idea was assumed to be a dead letter.

The B.E. had headed homeward, and the monoplane had hovered dimly in the distance, making no attempt to renew the attack. After a while it had headed in our general direction, and we had watched it. It had cruised round until it was some way above and behind us, and then started to dive. I had swung around to turn under it, which would spoil the pilot's aim if, indeed, he was shooting ahead. He immediately cut short his dive, pulled up in the same stunt turn, and passed over the top of us. It was then that I could see the familiar Morane outline and the German black-cross markings. He went off into the distance, came back, started another dive behind us, and evidently again thought better of it. He pulled up again and went off out of sight. Within the next week or two stories started to come through from various squadrons, and the stories were all the same: the dive from behind, the burst of fire from under the victim's tail, the spectacular climbing turn of the getaway, the long hesitation before a second attack, if any. A few days before this balloon expedition of mine, Lieutenant Johnson had come back to our squadron with his observer, Corporal Elmer Roberts, badly wounded. Roberts told me he had not been looking to the rear—observers rarely did so at that time—and had been taken completely by surprise. But he had seen what looked like a Morane with black crosses as his attacker climbed steeply away.

The picture of a new and deadly enemy started to take shape. But there was something puzzling about the whole business. If this very fast plane could shoot through its propeller—as now seemed certain—its pilot had us cold no matter what we did, and surely he ought to have known that. So why the wary formula of approach, the hesitant fishing for a surprise, the hit-and-run system of attack? The elaborate method of retreat—later known widely as the "Immelmann turn"—looked like the performance of a pilot who was concerned far more with getting out of a fight than into one.

So, sizing up my present microscopic chances of survival, I concluded that I was up against a fearsome weapon in the hands of a pilot with much skill and little enterprise. So long as he didn't discover that we were already crippled and entirely helpless, I thought I might just possibly dodge attacks as they came up and work my way home between attacks.

My idea was soon put to the test. Thornton called out that the other plane had started to dive behind us. I held my breath while I made a hopeful guess at the time it would take the attacker to pull up under my tail, and then banked suddenly and sharply to the right. At once there came an appalling noise from behind; it was my first experience with the savage explosive chatter produced by the business end of a machine gun at close quarters, mixed with the curious crackle of bullets passing close by. I could feel or see no signs of a hit, and as I straightened out for my next swerve I saw over my shoulder the black Maltese crosses on the Morane-shaped wings as they went up past me in a steep climbing turn.

Thornton watched the enemy as he retreated into the distance, and kept me posted. Some little time went by during which I made some good homeward mileage. But I knew the show was not yet over, for Archie had not resumed firing, as he would have done if the German plane had quit the job. So I was not surprised when Thornton shouted in my ear that our friend was heading toward us again after picking up some altitude. The second attack followed exactly the same pattern as the first, except that this time I swung hard to the left, and a lot of good German bullets were wasted in another stuttering burst.

By now, however, the German pilot must have noticed something that told him that he had nothing to worry about from us, because, after climbing away, he just made a wide circle and came straight back. From then on, I was a pigeon dodging a hawk.

From Thornton came repeated shouts of "Here he comes." But I could get only odd glimpses of him, and I couldn't tell where he was coming from. It was now a confused affair of nerve-wracking bursts of gunfire while I weaved, twisted, and dived in all directions, wondering whether my Morane's damaged structure could take what I was giving it, and rapidly losing my hard-earned altitude. My back was throbbing, my head was buzzing, and my thinking had reached the stage of "What's the use?"

At last he hit us. A burst of fire from somewhere behind sent bits and pieces rattling around the cockpit, and my seat shook as bullets glanced off the steel seat plate. A couple of bullets hit my left leg, took a chunk out of it, and knocked my foot off the rudder control. My right foot shot forward, sending us into a wild left-hand skid. And then the engine stopped; a steel bullet was later found embedded in the smashed "bloc-tube" fuel control. This was it!

Blindly I shoved the nose down, waiting with no remaining hope for the finishing burst. It never came. Later on, I found out why.

I leveled out and glided dazedly onward. I seemed to be somewhere over the front lines. Coming up from below was a jumbled vision of a shattered landscape of trenches, barbed wire, shell holes, mud, and the miscellaneous debris of war. I had no landing problem —there was no place to land. A crash of some sort was inevitable, but I had passed the stage where a little thing like that would worry me. I just kept going until we hit. I don't remember the landing; I was told later that I hit a wing on a post of some kind, swung around, and stayed more or less upright. Faintly, through the buzzing in my head, I heard Thornton's voice—he was mumbling something about "a hell of a celebration."

A group of Scottish troops dragged us out of the plane and into a sort of cellar or dugout. Men with bandages and bottles gathered around, someone stuck a hypodermic needle into me—and then it was nighttime and I was bumping along on a stretcher on my way to the field hospital in Béthune.

Thornton had been astonishingly lucky. He turned out to have a large collection of cuts and punctures and a messy lot of blood to go with them, but none of them was deep or serious, and the medicos were able to patch him up for return to the squadron.

The field hospital was swamped with human wreckage from the Loos battle, and the overworked doctors, nurses, and medical orderlies were asleep on their feet. I didn't see any beds; we lay in rows of stretchers on the floor. A Guards corporal was put down beside me and we started talking. Just before he had himself been hit by a sniper he had seen our "fight" from the ground, and he told me more about it than I knew myself. I learned that, when I made my last frantic dive toward our lines, the plane with the black crosses hadn't followed me; it had turned back and gone off. I didn't know it then, but that was to be the basic pattern of German air fighting: they preferred to remain over their own territory. It is possible, of course, that Immelmann thought he had finished us off, or he may have run out of ammunition, or his gun may have jammed; but later records inclined me to the less charitable view that he just wasn't going to venture over our side of the lines. Anyway, whatever his reason, I had no cause to complain about it.

The next day Captain Hubbard showed up at the hospital with his observer, Lieutenant Charles Portal, who had sometimes flown with me. I had been reported missing the previous evening, but now they had found out where I was. They had a few jovial comments to make on the subject of "celebrations." Then Portal (who was to achieve fame as Marshal of the Royal Air Force Viscount Portal of Hungerford, Chief of the British Air Staff in World War II) said I would doubtless like to know the identity of my not-quite executioner; he showed me a translation of the morning's official German communiqué, which indicated that I had been shot down by a "Lieut. Max Inglemann," a name that meant nothing to any of us at the time. We found out later that Immelmann was the pilot of the only Fokker flying in our sector at that period, and German propaganda had already started to work overtime to advertise him as the invincible terror of the air.

CHAPTER IX

HISTORICAL DIGRESSION
THE FIGHTER-PLANE STORY

1. *Dim Prospects for Fighters*

The gladiatorial glamour of the single-seat fighter plane has long bewitched public imagination, and the purveyors of romance and sensation have given it almost exclusive billing in air stories of World War I. The modern generation, therefore, can be excused for picturing the first war in the air as a continuous series of knightly jousts between fearless "aces," in which any pilot's war achievements were to be measured simply by the number of enemy planes he was supposed to have shot down.

All this makes for good, rousing drama, but it sometimes makes rather a hash of history. So at this point I propose to take time out from my main narrative to review the story of the fighter plane as I saw it emerge suddenly from practically nowhere to take its place in the forefront of military air history in the face of substantial doubts as to whether such a plane could ever have any practical existence.

It may be difficult, these days, to recall the fact that the fighter plane was actually a late-comer to military aviation. Among the earliest thoughts concerning possible uses of airplanes in war it was, of course, vaguely contemplated that some sort of aggressive gun-carrying plane would be needed to harass or destroy any intruding aircraft that might be rendering useful service to the enemy, and numerous primitive experiments were conducted with airborne machine guns. Those efforts

were invariably unpromising, because they led to the general conclusion that the carrying of a gun would defeat its own object. The gun
itself was a shockingly heavy item, and when you added the weight of
ammunition, gun mounts, structural reinforcements against recoil and
vibration, and working space for a gunner, you came up with a load
that sadly depleted the already scanty performance then available.
However, weight wasn't the only performance problem: it was obvious
that aggressive gunnery was possible only from pusher-type planes, since
they offered gunners a wide, unobstructed field of forward fire, which
was not possible in tractor types; but pushers were notoriously slow
because of the forest of booms, struts, and wires necessary for carrying
the tail clear of the propeller. Before the war, therefore, and during
its earlier stages, the logical picture of a prospective fighter plane
emerged as a large, heavy pusher, much slower in speed and climb
than the unencumbered working planes it was expected to attack.

It was all highly discouraging, but it was tried just the same—with
results that were mainly as had been predicted. The British and the
French turned out an assortment of clumsy gun-carrying pushers,
which, on rare occasions, scored a "victory" over some enemy who was
careless enough to wander within range. I was eventually to spend some
months of combat duty on one of our more unwieldy pusher models.
They called us "fighters," and we learned to put up a blistering defense
when the enemy chose to attack us; but, as fighters, we were too slow
to catch up with anything that didn't want to fight.

The Germans went into the war with, apparently, no serious ideas
at all concerning air fighting; they had no planes that could claim
even the feeble fighter capabilities of the British Vickers and F.E.'s
or the French Voisins and Farmans. In that respect, perhaps, they were
lucky, for at least they never became obsessed, as our officials did, with
the "pusher gun-bus" formula for fighter planes, and they were left
with relatively open minds to consider something better when it
eventually came along.

So, during the first year of the war, there didn't seem to be much
that could be done about air fighting. Every squadron, including ours,
had its stock of Lewis machine guns, and we assiduously learned to
assemble and fire them. But when we took them into the air, their
weight was a bad strain on our limited climb capacity, they were

clumsy to handle in a cramped cockpit never designed for gunnery, and they rattled violently and dangerously when fired from our home-made gun mounts, which consisted of sockets made from pieces of sawed-off tubing bolted to the side of the cockpit. So we hardly ever bothered to take them. On practically all missions, we relied, for offense and defense, on the observer's rifle and the pilot's automatic pistol, the latter being, in our case, a .45 Webley-Scott.

My first air fight was with an L.V.G. biplane, which looked enormous as it approached our much smaller Morane. We met casually on con-verging tracks over the German lines and then flew parallel courses, two or three hundred feet apart, while both observers banged away over the sides with single shots from their rifles. This sort of battle seems rather ludicrous today, but at the time there was nothing humorous about it. The idea of combat maneuver never entered our heads, because each pilot was trying to give his gunner a steady plat-form, and for my part I sat at the controls with the helpless feeling of being a naked and unmissable target at that range. What protection we had, of course, lay in the extreme difficulty of sighting a rifle, in a cramped cockpit, crosswise to a turbulent slipstream, but on occasion a plane was brought down by a chance hit in that haphazard process. This particular duel ended when the German shut off his engine and dived; I hoped we had hit him, but more likely he was on his way home after finishing whatever job he'd been doing. It was no use diving after him over his own territory; we couldn't fire forward at him anyway. So we continued on our way, while Archie resumed his familiar attentions.

Fights of this kind occurred sporadically and left us quite unprepared for what was to come. Pilots and observers had no reason for keeping regular watch to the rear, for only a pusher plane could attack us from behind and pushers were too slow to overtake us.

And so, until the late summer of 1915, prospects were dim for the development of anything startling in the line of fighter planes.

Then, with sudden violence, a deadly destroyer plane appeared on the scene. Its author was not British, French, or German, but a highly imaginative Dutchman named Anthony Fokker, who had picked up a discredited French weapon and persuaded his adopted German masters to use it against us, which they proceeded to do with catastrophic effect. The story of that dramatic episode in military air history has been told in many versions. However, apart from being an early victim of this disaster, I happened also to be more closely associated than most chroniclers with the circumstances and the personalities concerned. So I propose to give my version of that story.

2. The Birth of a Killer

It was not long after the "German Morane" had put me out of action that everyone knew it to be a Fokker monoplane. For a year or more, the new destroyer inflicted such appalling losses on allied airmen that this milestone episode in the air war is remembered as the "Fokker scourge." Moreover, it gave the Germans such a long lead in the development of fighter airplanes that, for still another year, we would continue to suffer sadly in our muddled efforts to catch up with them.

Anthony Fokker deserves lasting credit for his part in changing the whole course of air warfare, but it seems to me that most histories provide a questionable record of just what he did and how he came to do it.

The familiar and now generally accepted story is, briefly, that Fokker, "inspired" by a captured French Morane-Saulnier plane fitted with a crude and suicidal system of deflector blocks for shooting ahead through the propeller, was asked by the German generals to devise a more practical plane of the same nature; that he then "designed" his famous "Eindekker" fighter monoplane, for which he "invented" the novel device of a synchronizing gear for firing bullets forward between the propeller blades. There are traces of truth in that story, and Fokker, always the supersalesman, was glad to promote and encourage it. But it is a garbled story, and I was in a peculiar position for getting at the facts.

I first met Tony Fokker in England in 1921, and in subsequent years I think I became as friendly with him as it was possible to become with that brusque and often studiously surly character. I worked with him and for him on several projects in Holland and America, and I flew most of his postwar military and commercial models. In the course of that long association we often debated the origins of early fighter-plane developments; and since he was well aware of my earlier Morane associations, he was reasonably candid with me concerning his own wartime efforts.

My connections with Morane-Saulnier went back to the days of my apprenticeship, when the Grahame-White Company built M-S planes under license. Our factory was then, of course, in contact with Morane engineers, so that Morane projects and plans were regular subjects of discussion. During the war, I flew most types of Morane planes, and I have been in touch with the company on and off since then.

As I mentioned before, all early contemplations of air fighting quite logically assumed that the shooting would have to be done by a gunner wielding his gun through as wide a field of fire as he could get. But, late in 1913, the Morane-Saulnier firm went to work on a very different idea. The thought came rather easily to them, since they had long specialized in small, fast, and highly maneuverable monoplanes. But it defied all accepted concepts of aerial gunnery—it actually proposed that the pilot himself should be the gunner.

The Morane scheme was to take their well-known fast tractor monoplane, clamp a machine gun rigidly on top of the fuselage so that it could fire straight ahead through the propeller, eliminate the weight and drag of a gunner with his equipment and accommodations, and leave it to the pilot to attack the enemy by aiming the whole airplane at him. Thus the plane's high speed and climb could be preserved, and the pilot could overtake and outmaneuver any prospective victim, aiming his gun by the use of the sensitive and powerful Morane controls.

The problem of a gear for shooting between the propeller blades was not considered particularly difficult. Such gears had been devised in the past, but nobody had found them of any practical value with the clumsy controls of the heavy planes to which they were fitted. Raymond Saulnier, a notably inventive engineer, proceeded to design his own gear to suit the nimble Morane.

The French military authorities were not enthusiastic about such a radical proposition. They had certain doubts about trying to shoot bullets through a fast-spinning propeller. But, above all, they could not swallow the idea that even the best of pilots could take any accurate aim along gunsights that pitched and swayed in response to the notoriously unsteady action of airplane controls. To them it seemed quite obvious that guns were for gunners, not for pilots.

However, Robert Morane, head of the company and himself a first-class test pilot, was confident that he could prove his point. In April 1914—four months before the war started and eighteen months before the Fokkers came on the scene—the plane was ready for tests.

And then fate played one of its dirtiest tricks in air history. The gun-gear flunked its ground tests; it failed to prevent the propeller from being hit by occasional bullets. Saulnier was mystified—he couldn't find anything wrong with the gear. It was not discovered until very much later that the trouble was not in the gear; it had come from the worn belts and the uneven charges of old and defective ammunition that the French Army had supplied under the somewhat excusable impression that this sort of stuff was good enough for simple tests and might as well be used up. So, as a stopgap measure, in the hope of getting on with air gunnery tests while the trouble with the synchronizing gear was being investigated, Morane proposed to fit triangular steel blocks on the propeller to deflect impinging bullets. He himself made satisfactory flight tests with the blocks, prior to preparing for official gunnery tests.

But the French military experts announced that they had seen enough; they had never been able to find much sense in the project anyway, and they were not interested in further experiments that involved splashing bullets up against the propeller. They wanted no more of it, and Morane had to shelve the whole scheme.

Then came the war. Roland Garros, already internationally famous as an aerobatic Morane pilot, went off to the fighting front, where he quickly realized the damage he could do if only he had the sort of fighting plane that had been so casually rejected a few months previously. He returned to the Morane factory in Paris with permission to take the plane out to see what could be done with it against the enemy. He was not going to wait for further experiments with the gun-firing synchronizing gear; he would settle for the simple deflector blocks. *The gear remained inertly in the plane, installed but disconnected.*

Garros took his "destroyer" plane into combat action, and promptly proceeded to shoot down almost every enemy airplane he could find to attack. He brought utter consternation into the ranks of enemy airmen;

and when he couldn't find anything in the air to attack, he went after anything on the ground that seemed worth shooting up.

Unfortunately, his reign of terror was too brief to stir the sluggish official imagination into a realization of the vast possibilities of this new air weapon—Garros was a flying genius, and you couldn't expect the average pilot to emulate this notably reckless character! One day, less than a month after he started his hair-raising operations, Garros was shooting up a German train at close quarters when a lucky shot from one of the train guards hit a fuel line and forced him to land. Garros was taken prisoner, his plane was put on exhibition in Berlin, and German airmen were free to take a good look at the freakish craft that had been making life miserable for them.

And that is where Anthony Fokker came into the picture.

Tony always liked it to be believed that the German generals asked him to examine Garros' plane and to produce a similar deadly fighter for the German air service, but this story is unlikely on the face of it. Fokker was a foreigner with no particular engineering qualifications; there were several well-established German aircraft companies whose reputable engineers would certainly have been called upon to undertake such a job. Moreover, there is not much evidence that, apart from natural curiosity toward a startlingly novel type of airplane, the Germans themselves were much impressed with this Morane of Garros. They regarded the deflector blocks as a suicidal device—which it wasn't —and, like the French, they doubted that the average pilot could effectively aim a fixed gun by maneuvering the entire airplane. They also were inclined to attribute this Morane's success to the famous aerobatic skill of Roland Garros rather than to any specific merits of the plane.

The perceptive eye of Anthony Fokker, however, saw this plane in a very different light; in fact, he saw it just as Morane had seen it and had vainly hoped the French air staff would see it. Fokker himself was an enterprising pilot, and what he lacked in formal engineering training he more than made up for with an intense and practical imagination reinforced by a supersalesman's ability to promote his often unconventional schemes.

First of all, it was instantly obvious to him that the fixed-gun principle would be effective in the hands of any first-class pilot, provided that the plane was as maneuverable as a Morane. Then he noticed something that the others had missed: Saulnier's disconnected gun gear was lying there for him to examine. If he could make it work, he could dispense with the clumsy deflector blocks, which reduced performance by decreasing propeller efficiency. It took him a couple of days to make the changes necessary to adapt it to a German gun, and he then made the thorough tests and checks that the French could have made long before and had failed to do. It worked. This was such a startling development that Tony thought up a famous fable to account for the inspiration behind his suddenly brilliant "invention."

The fable goes that Fokker, remembering his boyhood pranks of throwing stones that would pass between the revolving sails of the Dutch windmills, suddenly got the bright idea of devising a gear that would allow bullets to be fired forward between the blades of a propeller; and how he then, within the miraculously brief period of forty-eight hours, conceived, devised, built, and perfected such a gear to replace Garros' awkward deflector blocks. This was one of Tony's tongue-in-cheek yarns, but it is still generally accepted.

To Fokker's own initiative must go the credit for what eventually happened. He enlisted the support of German air officers of aerobatic inclinations, such as Max Immelmann, who were only too anxious to get their hands on a plane more agile than the ponderous crates that formed Germany's air equipment. He scared the higher ranks with visions of what would happen if the French were to come over with a few dozen fixed-gun Moranes. And so he was given the chance to go ahead with his E.I fighter.

In later years Fokker objected indignantly to the frequent suggestion that his E.I was practically a Chinese copy of the Morane, and after a fashion he was nearly right. Earlier on, he had, as a first-class pilot, greatly admired the maneuverability of the prewar German Hanuschke monoplane, which was hardly distinguishable from Garros' Morane; so when he built his own M.5 he unblushingly adopted almost every line and dimension of the Hanuschke, although he did make some changes in the rudder shape, the landing gear, and the internal structure. It was no great task to fit the unarmed M.5 with a machine gun and Saulnier's synchronizing gear, thus creating the E.I fighter, which explains the legendary rapidity with which that historic plane was first "invented."

And thus the fighter plane was born.

As the Fokker E.II, with 100 hp in place of the original 80 hp, that fighter went into production. In the hands of Immelmann, Boelcke, and their successors it massacred Allied airmen, who then and for a long time afterward had no defense against it and nothing to compete with it.

3. Immelmann and His "Turn"

The depredations of the "Fokker scourge" against Allied airmen got under way very slowly. This was because, to start with, only Anthony Fokker and a few of the more enterprising German pilots had any firm faith in the possibilities of this new method of attack.

A couple of Fokker's new fighters were put into the hands of Max Immelmann and Oswald Boelcke on a sort of trial basis. As it turned out, Boelcke was the more capable and successful fighter, but Immelmann was the more spectacular pilot, and when the Fokkers started to spread havoc among their enemies, most of the glamour fell on Immelmann. The German authorities quickly realized that they had beaten the Allies to the use of a deadly new weapon, and their propaganda services went to work to proclaim their new form of superiority.

They proceeded to build up a mythology around Immelmann that, thanks to the romantic propensities of air-story writers, has survived practically intact to this day. He was presented to the world as a bold and fearless fighter, the "Eagle of Lille," the "first of the aces," the invincible terror of the skies. The superlatives were laid on so thick, that, when Immelmann was shot down and killed (as the result of carelessly straying across the path of a lumbering F.E. pusher much slower than his Fokker), the flabbergasted Germans refused to believe it—they claimed that his plane must have broken in the air.

So, for the sake of several points of history, I think the Immelmann legend is due for some sort of overhaul.

As a pioneer air fighter, Immelmann deserves great credit, and it is probable that no better man could have been found for the Fokker's trial operations. He was an unusually good pilot, a serious student of his equipment, and an imaginative innovator in the tactics of air combat. His approaches from blind spots, his attacks out of the sun, his use of aerobatics as a means of confusing such defense as the enemy might have, and other tactical inventions, were quite unthought of before Immelmann, and they were passed on to become the standards of air fighting practice.

But the record does not show Immelmann as a daring and tenacious fighter. In a sky full of sitting ducks with negligible defenses or none at all, he averaged during the ten months of his fighting career less than two victims a month—fifteen in all, which is a poor score even allowing for the fact that he had no experience to start with. His approach was cautious, cagey, and elaborate, and if he missed on his first attempt, his getaway (the famous "Immelmann turn") was spectacularly urgent. And if he came back for a second helping, he took plenty of time to look things over. I have read much about his deadly marksmanship, and I can only reflect that he missed me with a large quantity of bullets.

However, Immelmann left another distinctive mark on the air history of the period by his firm reluctance to venture out of the sanctuary of his own territory. He developed, though he probably did not invent, the principle that the function of fighter planes was to defend the airspace over their own areas and not to go out, as we did, looking for trouble elsewhere. I ought to be grateful for that shyness, because I owed my continued existence to it, but I could not admire it. It has been said that this restraint was officially imposed on Fokker pilots in order to protect the "secret" of the Fokker gun gear, but in fact there was no particular secret to protect.

To the Royal Flying Corps it always seemed normal and natural to carry the war to the enemy, even during the days when our planes were hopelessly outclassed by those of the Germans, and we never did understand their reluctance to carry it to us. Even the famous Boelcke was not ashamed to proclaim their uninspiring slogan: "Let the customer come to us." The result was, as not many histories point out, that almost all air fighting of World War I took place over the German side of the lines.

Immelmann bequeathed his name to the language of airmen with the expression "Immelmann turn." However, even this expression has somehow wandered into the realms of mythology. My dictionary and others I have looked up say that this is "a maneuver in which an airplane is first made to complete half a loop and is then rolled half of a complete turn." In fact, Immelmann never made such a turn, never could have made it, and never would have used it in combat even if he could. The warping wings of the Fokker E.II could not provide anywhere near enough lateral control to half-roll the plane as it slowed to near-stalling speed on top of a loop, and it would be a long time after Immelmann's death before a plane existed with enough speed and control for that maneuver. In any case Immelmann was too clever a fighter to use a stunt that would leave him suspended upside down, with almost inert controls, for enough seconds to make him a limp target for an enemy gunner.

The "turn" that Immelmann actually used for his getaway (and I saw him use it often enough) was simply a very steeply banked climbing turn, requiring much skill in those days when stalling was greatly feared. It was an impressive feature of stunt flying before the war; the French called it a "chandelle," and the Americans later adopted that expression. Immelmann, however, was certainly the first to make combat use of it.

So I am still curious to know where Mr. Webster and the other lexicographers dug up the definition they now give.

4. Germany's Long Lead

In the records of the two years of air fighting that followed the introduction of the first Fokkers in the summer of 1915, most histories seem to me to be curiously misleading. They usually leave the impression—some of them state as a fact—that the Royal Flying Corps soon suppressed the "Fokker scourge" and promptly proceeded to batter the enemy with efficient new fighters. That is what should have happened, but it didn't. Those histories abound with stirring accounts of how the R.F.C. fought back with its D.H.2's, Sopwith Pups and Sopwith two-seat fighters, F.E.2's, Nieuports, and Spads; what those records rarely or never make clear is that this equipment was dismally feeble for the job we did with it.

The fact is that, during those two years, the Germans maintained a vast superiority in fighter planes while British officialdom fumbled around in confused efforts to come up with something better. They were years in which the R.F.C. pursued its aggressive fighting policy only at heavy cost, culminating in "Bloody April" of 1917, when our losses rose to record heights. We would have to wait until the summer of 1917 before our Sopwith Camels and S.E.5's came along to even up the score. I went through most of a year, including Bloody April, of that underdog fighting, of which I shall later give some account, and I would like to straighten out a few kinks in the fighter-plane records of that period.

The startling success of the Fokkers, from late 1915 onward, easily convinced the Germans that this class of fighter—the single-seat, fixed-gun tractor—was the only class worth developing. Soon earlier Fokkers were replaced with improved Fokker models, and new types of similar fighters were added, such as the Albatros, Pfalz, and Halberstadt. Before long they had two fixed guns firing ahead instead of one. Engine horsepower was greatly increased. The training of German pilots in fighter tactics could be concentrated on this one class of fighter, a vital factor in those days of rapid expansion of the air war.

But the British Army procurement chiefs, powerfully influenced by the pedantic and academic attitudes of the government's Royal Aircraft Factory, were not at all convinced that this was the best kind of fighter. If they had been, they could easily and quickly have procured a fighter directly comparable to the Fokker, or even a bit better. Instead, they seemed determined to avoid anything that might appear to be following in the footsteps of the very non-academic Anthony Fokker. So they tried everything else.

Against the growing array of specialized German fighter power, they threw a heterogeneous collection of assorted types and models, all involving different principles of tactical operation and pilot training. Under the title of "fighters," the Royal Flying Corps was given two-seat tractors and single-seat pushers, two-seat pushers and single-seat tractors, all underpowered by German standards, most of them obsolescent and many long obsolete, reinforced at odd moments of emergency with whatever planes could be begged or borrowed from the Royal Naval Air Service, or from the French Army, which contributed the few Nieuports and Spads we had.

Fortunately for Britain, the R.N.A.S. was directed by more imaginative technical minds than those of the R.F.C., and it is of historic interest that for a long time the only experience R.F.C. pilots had of guns firing through the propeller was on Sopwith planes originally designed for the Navy. On the other hand, the Royal Aircraft Factory ("The Factory," as it was generally known) remained stubbornly obsessed with the ancient conviction that a real fighter had to be a pusher, and F.E. pushers designed by The Factory continued to be dumped onto the R.F.C. almost up to the end of the war.

One tragicomic episode occurred when, at one time, under pressure of bitter comments from the fighting fronts, The Factory reluctantly designed a fighter on the general principle of Fokker's planes: a single-seat tractor with a fixed gun firing through the propeller. I had to do some of the factory tests on it. It was called the B.E.12, and it proved to be unquestionably the worst "fighter plane" ever produced by anyone anywhere at any time. After several of them had wallowed catastrophically in action for a few weeks, General Trenchard, hard pressed as he was for fighters, flatly refused to accept any more.

Perhaps, however, the B.E.12 was not a total loss, because it was so bad that it shocked the Royal Aircraft Factory into a serious effort to produce an effective fighter for the R.F.C. The result was the S.E.5, one of the finest of World War I fighters and the only really admirable plane that The Factory ever designed. But the S.E.5 did not get into practical operation until the middle of 1917. Along with the Sopwith Camel, which came along at about the same time, it gave the R.F.C. a chance to meet the Germans on equal terms—for the first time since the Fokkers had started their devastating operations two years previously.

CHAPTER X

The War Becomes Serious

1. *Resurrecting a Commission*

When I attempted to return to circulation, following personal repairs made necessary by Archie and Immelmann, I found progress obstructed by the startling discovery that I had died a hero's death. It took me a little while to learn of that event.

I left the hospital late in January 1916. It was a volunteer hospital that gave only secondary attention to military paper work, and I was issued vague orders to report to some office at Farnborough, where I expected to find my commission waiting for me. At Farnborough nobody knew anything about the commission or about me, and they could find no instructions as to what to do with me. So, on general principles, I was sent to the huge military camp at Aldershot, where there was a severe shortage of drill instructors for the infantry recruits of "Kitchener's Army." I pleaded with everyone in sight that I knew nothing whatever about drilling. The answer was always the same: How could I be a sergeant and not know how to drill a squad?

Early next morning I was directed onto a vast parade ground, where I gazed glumly at my new clients, a mob of about fifty fresh recruits, most of whom looked to me as if they had never obeyed an order and probably never would. I coaxed them into some kind of line-up and tried to remember the commands for a simple marching routine. I got them started off toward a high brick wall, which they reached be-

fore I could think up the magic words with which to turn the formation, and they piled up in helpless laughter against the wall. I called on
a passing Australian sergeant for guidance, but he was laughing too
hard to be of any use. At that point some infantry sergeant major
came by and put me out of my misery by taking over the squad. They
sent me back to Farnborough that evening.

When pay parade turned up—with no pay for me—I induced the
Paymaster, Major Burch, to investigate. Next day he showed me a
report. "Here you are," he said sadly. "You're dead. It says here:
October 22nd, 1915, 2891 Sergeant F. T. Courtney, previously reported missing, now reported killed in action." It transpired that, on
the evening I was shot down, No. 3 Squadron had reported me missing, and after that my plane had been confused with another plane,
whose pilot had been killed. It was not a remarkable error in those
hectic days—but the serious point was that, with my unfortunate death,
my commission had died also. So I had to get a resurrection project
started.

For a while I puttered around on miscellaneous flying jobs with a
squadron that was forming to go overseas. One morning in March I
found that the squadron, with Sergeant Courtney, was posted to
Gosport, where I went in a squadron truck. When I got there I was
told that Second Lieutenant Courtney was posted to Dover, so I
went back to Farnborough—in the squadron commander's car—to
complete commissioning formalities and incidentally to pass a parting
evening in the Sergeants' Mess. The news had gone ahead, and that
evening a dozen or more sergeants were waiting for me. There was
Jim McCudden, not yet on his way to fame. There was "Spider" Webb,
whom I was to see shot down in sickening flames a year later. There
was Bill Lawford, who was to survive to make history's first scheduled
airline flight and later to end his days as a civil air traffic controller.
And there was an elderly character, whose name I forget, who after
the third drink always claimed to have flown a Blériot during the Boer
War—which ended in 1902.

It was rough. They called me "sir" once or twice in every sentence,
handed me drinks with one hand while saluting with the other, and
held mock requiems for my fall from princely sergeant to paltry
second loot.

Next morning they accompanied me in a body to Sergeant McCarthy's tailor's shop. There was no time for me to get an officer's uniform, so, with elaborate ceremony, they removed my stripes and insignia—leaving bare-looking light patches on the weathered cloth where they had been. They sewed a second lieutenant's "pip" on each shoulder, strapped a Sam Browne belt around me, and, saluting incessantly, paraded me down to the train for Dover.

And then, inevitably, back to Farnborough. For, after a few days at Dover, I was posted to the Royal Aircraft Factory as military test pilot.

2. Military Test Pilot

On my way from Dover to Farnborough I had to stop off for briefing at an administrative office in London, where a staff colonel gave me a rousing lecture concerning the importance of my new job. The Royal Aircraft Factory, he reminded me, was the official nerve center of military airplane research, design, and development, and I was about to join its staff at this most critical period for military aviation.

It was regrettable (continued the Colonel) that the enemy had obtained the jump on us with their new Fokkers, but this would be a strictly temporary situation. We now knew just what was required to defeat them (the Colonel honestly believed this), and the Royal Aircraft Factory, with the massed brains of its scientists and engineers, was designing mighty new warplanes, in all categories, that would swiftly establish our lasting air supremacy. I was about to be the only member of that experimental staff with practical combat-flying experience, so naturally my own contribution to that momentous program would be vital.

It all sounded very wonderful, and I hoped the Colonel was right. In any case, however, it was obvious that I was heading for something very new and special in the way of flying jobs.

The Royal Aircraft Factory was a remarkable pioneer institution with a very checkered record in the technical history of aviation. When I went there in 1916 it was already a venerable government activity, having been known as the Army Balloon Factory in days when airplanes were still only a dream. In modern times it functions as one of the world's great aeronautical research organizations under the title of Royal Aircraft Establishment—its name having been again changed in 1918 to avoid confusion of the initials R.A.F. with those of the newly formed Royal Air Force.

However, a less glorious phase of its history occurred during World War I, when The Factory overreached its functions as a research organization and set itself up as the virtual arbiter of military aircraft design. Its disastrous influence on the equipment of the Royal Flying Corps brought it into deep disrepute as a bungling engineering bureaucracy, about which calamity I had a few things to say in the previous chapter.

But when I arrived at The Factory as a budding test pilot, I was unaware of any such possible political distractions to my job. I thought of The Factory only as the Abode of Genius, where I would cease to be a mere ordinary pilot and become a flying partner of men of science in the urgent search for higher levels of aeronautical knowledge.

And as it turned out, The Factory was to provide me with training in the problems, processes, and perils of experimental flying such as I could never have obtained at any other time and place. Certainly our flight-test section can be regarded as the pioneer of what is today called engineering test flying; it operated as part of the Engineering Department, in close association with scientists and engineers whose names would in future years be famous in aviation technology. Hitherto, test flying had been a haphazard business, consisting mostly of brave efforts by skilled pilots to get the best they could out of some new plane or gadget; now we raised flight techniques and studies to the levels of engineering standards in a manner that had probably never been attempted anywhere else on an organized basis.

The fast-expanding air war was raising strings of new questions for which engineering had practically no answers, so there was no limit in sight to the scope of our work. The planes we flew in our innumerable experiments were of about a dozen different types and sizes, ranging from The Factory's little S.E.4a single-seat tractor to the big F.E.4 twin-engine pusher as well as assorted aircraft from private manufacturers. Usually these were in various states of modification by endless experiments with wings, tails, controls, stability, power plants, equipment, accessories, and anything else that seemed to need testing in that pioneer period of restless research for rapid progress.

As his share of the engineering work, the test pilot played a wider and more responsible part than he was ever likely to play again. Laboratory equipment, instruments, and procedures were still rudimentary, and the only conclusive tests on almost any subject were those conducted by the pilot in flight. Since flight instruments were few, never very sensitive, and often full of errors, the information they gave was usually subject to whatever interpretation the pilot decided to put upon them as the result of previous experience and of consultations with an organized body of experts.

The pilot's personal judgment was constantly under strain: on the one hand, his observations and reports had to be as accurate as possible; but on the other hand, the pressures of war's necessities often left little time for prolonged and cautious procedures, so that perilous short cuts to knowledge had frequently to be attempted. If a new experiment got us into trouble, we had first to examine what the trouble was and then find a way out of it, which was not always easy— there were no parachutes to provide escape from threatening disaster.

Looking back on those days, I have often thought that the absence of a parachute contributed substantially to our education; a pilot was sometimes forced to learn valuable lessons while trying to ride down a stricken plane he would hurriedly have abandoned if he had had any means of doing so.

It was while I was at The Factory that it embarked on a new program, which then looked very fanciful but was to have a lasting effect on piloting sciences, flight training, and aircraft engineering: for the first time in air history, we began to make systematic studies of stalling, spinning, inverted flying, and aerobatics in general. The fighting tactics of the new Fokkers were too easily effective against pilots who, like most of ours, had been trained to avoid firmly all forms of "abnormal" flying and leave aerobatics to the experts. The information we gathered was passed along to the training people with the result that, within a year, it was not uncommon for even elementary flight students to be performing stunts that exhibition pilots would have been proud of not long before. I like to think that I played a substantial part in initiating and developing that program.

It was going to be a very long time before flight and test instruments began to approach anything like the intricacy and efficiency that they have reached today. But, in one respect at least, our experiments with instruments were well ahead of their time. Dr. Keith Lucas was developing gyroscopic equipment such as bombsights and turn indicators, and I was lucky enough to be assigned to work with Lucas in that line of research. As a two-man operation, Lucas and I produced amazing results in blind flying and in experimental bomb runs; unfortunately, war conditions left no prospect of getting such intricate equipment into production for operational use.

Lucas firmly believed that flying would one day be almost entirely dependent on gyroscopes; he was never to know how very right he was, for he was killed in a crash in one of his experiments.

The fascination of those days of pioneer research flying would probably never be recaptured. For everything was new, previous experience hardly existed, and almost nothing was predicted or predictable. It was at The Factory that I learned the very fundamentals of the test pilot's art: a habit of careful, accurate, and unremitting observation, an open mind that took nothing for granted, a willingness to try anything at least once, and a readiness for quick decision in emergencies.

3. Back into Battle

After several months of this factory work I found I was beginning to get restless.

In trying to sift out my thinking, such as it was, I had to conclude that I was afflicted with an unreasonable itch to get back into combat. This I did not understand, for I was no belligerent hero, I was not at all anxious to shoot at anybody, and I certainly disliked being shot at. Probably I felt that, much as I enjoyed my job, I could regard it only as a non-combatant civilian job in disguise—and it was not for that that I had made strenuous efforts to get into the Royal Flying Corps. Then again, when I had first been sent to The Factory, I had vaguely assumed that I would eventually be returned to combat duty on one of those wonderful new warplanes that (as my staff-colonel friend had assured me) I was to help design and build. But now I had had enough experience of The Factory to realize that, while its research work was admirable, its capacity for designing new military planes was painfully poor.

So, getting back into combat wasn't anything I wanted to do, it was something I had to do.

At last I tackled Colonel Mervyn O'Gorman, the Factory Superintendent, on the subject; I gave him what I thought was a lucid explanation of why I wanted to transfer back to a combat squadron. O'Gorman was a charming gentleman, but he was strictly a civilian engineer carrying an honorary military rank as an ornament to his high official position. He had only dim notions on such matters as combat activities, and he obviously didn't understand what I was talking about. He told me that I had been specially assigned to this test-flying work, that I had shown myself well adapted to the job, and that I was expected to remain permanently at The Factory as part of its development team.

Shortly afterward I had to take a "new" airplane over to France— an obsolete R.E.7 The Factory hoped it had rejuvenated with some new engine installation. I was to demonstrate its questionable merits to General Trenchard at Royal Flying Corps Headquarters. "Boom" Trenchard had long remembered me favorably for the fact that, after he had rejected me for the R.F.C. at the beginning of the war, I had worked my way in anyhow, "glasses and all." He told me that he would be glad to have me back under his command, but that he had no jurisdiction in the matter of getting me away from The Factory. However, he said, if I could furnish him with a plausible excuse, he could apply for my transfer. I had an excuse all ready.

I pointed out that I had been running practically all the tests at Farnborough on the F.E.2d, which was the old F.E.2 fighter now powerfully reinforced with the new Rolls-Royce engine. No. 20 Squadron was now being equipped with F.E.2d's, and I suggested that it might be a new and valuable idea if my tests could be extended into combat conditions. It was a somewhat thin excuse, but at least it was a novel one, and Trenchard thought he could make it work. He did.

Not long afterward I was reporting to Major Mansfield, commanding No. 20 Fighter Squadron, at Clairmarais, France. It was September 1916.

CHAPTER XI

BACKGROUND FOR "BLOODY APRIL"

1. Combat on Pushers

At the time I was knocked out of the air, in October 1915, serious air fighting was a new and bewildering invention, which the Fokkers of Immelmann and Boelcke were just beginning to test out. Now, when I returned to the battle eleven months later, it had developed into a familiar and spectacular addition to the arts of killing.

The "Fokker scourge" had been carrying off our airmen like a spreading plague for several months until the Royal Flying Corps's first single-seat fighters, the D.H.2's, came on the scene. They did much to relieve the worst of the earlier Fokker pressures on the R.F.C., but with their obsolescent pusher design, they were never the superlative planes they are often reported to have been, and they were soon outclassed by new models of German fighters, while most of our planes continued to be pitifully incapable of any effective defense.

But we did have a number of planes, such as the F.E.'s to which I was now assigned, that could at least fight back when they were attacked, even though they were much too slow and unwieldy to take the offensive. With them we carried out our so-called fighter patrols by cruising around over hostile territory with chips on our shoulders, defying the enemy to attack us. When they did, they had all the advantages of the initiative, but they did not always escape lightly, and occasionally they fared very badly.

At this point I may as well mention that, in this chapter, I do not intend to offer the customary blow-by-blow accounts of the assorted air battles that filled the ten rugged months of my second tour of combat duty. Acres of print have gone into stories of air fighting: the weavings and circling of the combatants; the dives and zooms for position; the attacks and evasions; the bursts of gunfire with hits or misses; the jammed guns; the crumpling wings and flaming tanks; the homeward struggles with crippled controls or failing engines; the tragically empty seats in the mess at dinner—all these are familiar drama to readers of the innumerable records of air fighting. After enough experience, one dogfight was pretty much like another, and I propose therefore to offer a less familiar impression of the conditions under which we fought in days when we had to face a constantly superior enemy.

The F.E.2 was a remarkable airplane—which is not intended as a compliment, because the most remarkable facts about it were that it was ever called a "fighter" and that it was retained in service for so long and in such numbers. It was a ponderous, 2-seat, pusher biplane of nearly 50-foot span, as compared with the 28-foot monoplane span of the Fokker. Its great size and rocklike stability make it as maneuverable as a cathedral, and it was impossible to dive it: at anything much over a hundred miles an hour with nose down, the elevator control would overcome the pilot and the stick would push itself hard back into his lap while the plane leveled off. I had devised a trick method of diving it by first hauling it up into a stall and then holding it down when it fell off into a dive, but enemy fighters were not disposed to wait around while I performed this ceremony.

It had twenty-eight exposed struts and booms for its wing and tail structures (and eleven more for the landing gear), with endless fathoms of connecting wires. With these built-in head winds, no amount of power could give it any useful speed, so when our F.E.2d's acquired the 250-hp Rolls-Royce engine, as compared with the 120 hp of the original F.E.2b, the increase in speed was almost negligible. The extra power did, however, give us a generous improvement in climb— and we needed it.

Fighting on the F.E.2 was like no other kind of fighting. The gunner's field of fire was an entire, unobstructed hemisphere of airspace ahead, while the sometimes painful stability of the plane gave him a solidly steady platform to work from. On the other hand, anywhere behind and below the plane—and that was a lot of space— an enemy was completely safe from the F.E.'s gun, and the F.E. control was much too sluggish to evade attack from the rear. So a single F.E. could be sunk in short order by a fast and nimble enemy with the ability to get quickly behind it. This fact fooled the Fokkers for a long time into the belief that the F.E. was naturally easy meat.

But a formation of several F.E.'s was a very nasty unit to attack. Our procedure, when attacked, was to break formation and swerve off in all directions, milling around and trying merely to keep as close together as reasonably possible. The Fokkers didn't like this at all, because an F.E. was in danger only when lined up squarely with a Fokker's fixed gun, whereas a Fokker was in danger any time it got anywhere at all in front of an F.E. And, with several F.E.'s weaving closely around, there was almost no time when a Fokker might not find itself heading the wrong way under the gun of at least one F.E. The great Immelmann himself was knocked off by an F.E.2b in just such an unorganized brawl.

My first fight on an F.E. was fairly typical of those that followed in the next few months. Five of us were pounced upon by two formations, totaling nine Fokkers. Within a few minutes we had shot down two of them, and the others ended the argument by vanishing in all directions, knowing very well that we couldn't go after them. Our own damage was negligible. This sort of outcome, not unusual at that period, encouraged some of our officials to claim that the F.E. type was obviously a better fighter than the Fokker type; but a plane that could do no more than defend itself was no inspiration to a fighter pilot.

I had never expected much from the F.E. as a fighter, but it had served the purpose of getting me back into action. I kept my eye open for a chance to get into some fighting work that was more like flying and less like driving a tank.

I thought I had found it when, around Christmas of 1916, Harry Pagan Lowe flew over to see me on a Sopwith two-seat fighter from No. 45 Squadron. Lowe had been Chief Draftsman at Grahame-White's before the war; we had kept in touch, and he knew that I was bored with the F.E. He had come to ask if I would care to transfer to No. 45, which was badly in need of experienced pilots.

I had already flown this Sopwith type at Farnborough; it was very pleasant to handle, and its performance was excellent for the 110 hp of its Clerget rotary engine. But for me its chief attraction was that it was the first British plane to give the pilot a fixed gun firing forward through the propeller.

I put in my application for a transfer to No. 45 Squadron.

2. A Switch to Tractors

No. 45 Squadron had come out from England with its Sopwith fighters barely two months previously. But it had already taken such a beating that it was back at a "rest" area in Boisdinghem for refitting and for more crew training in the techniques of the new two-seater type of fighting that this plane was supposed to conduct. Nobody considered, at the time, that the squadron's troubles had been due to anything much worse than inexperience plus, perhaps, an overdose of bad luck.

Before long, however, we were going to find out, at heavy cost, that we were up against more drastic difficulties than mere inexperience, and we were due to compile such a record of losses that we would earn the title of "The Suicide Club."

Many circumstances combined to produce this situation, but behind it all was the collapse of the two-seat-fighter concept, a theory long and firmly held by certain British authorities who continued to distrust the Morane-Fokker single-seat formula for fighters, on the grounds that it offered too limited a scope for gunfire and observation. They contended that a plane with a forward-firing fixed gun for the pilot ought also to carry a rear gunner to protect the tail. They conceded that such a fighter, having to carry a crew of two, would necessarily sacrifice something in speed, climb, and agility; but they claimed that this would be more than offset by the fact that the crew could see all around and could fight with both ends of the plane. We were about to find out that this theory couldn't have been more wrong.

Our first fateful discovery was that, in air fighting, there is no substitute for performance. So long as our single-seat foes could outspeed, outclimb and outmaneuver us, they had all the combat initiative, they could attack or break contact as they chose, and nothing we could do with our guns could give us anything but a defensive capacity.

Our two guns, one forward and one aft, were intended to be a menacing combination, but they turned out to be not even a combination; for, while the pilot was weaving the plane around in order to use his fixed gun, the poor gunner in the rear had little chance of taking effective aim from an unpredictably swerving platform largely obstructed by a swinging and bobbing tail. So only one gun or the other could be effective at the same time, and what we had was two independent gunners, back to back, neither of whom knew what the other was trying to do, and each of whom wondered what was going on when he heard a burst of fire from the other end of the plane.

That situation might have been improved by some workable system of communication between pilot and gunner, whose cockpits were a yard or more apart with a tank in between. But, for the exchange of warnings, instructions, and comments, the only equipment we had was a primitive forerunner of the "Gosport tube." It consisted of two rubber tubes running from one cockpit to the other; at one end of each was a small speaking funnel, and at the other end a forked connection for carrying sound to two tin cups—often homemade from shoe-polish cans—buttoned under the ear flaps of the flying caps. With this refined device a message, spoken clearly during calm intervals, could be interpreted four times out of five; but in the stress of combat, a message was either unspoken, unheard, or totally incoherent.

Of course, the proponents of the two-seat fighter theory took it for granted that pilot and gunner would learn to work together, practicing prearranged maneuvers and tactics. An excellent idea, except for the fact that we never had enough planes or time to carry it out. As casualties mounted, it became practically impossible to keep the same two crew members together, and eventually a plane might go out on a fighter patrol with a pilot and gunner who hardly knew each other.

Although the operation of these Sopwiths was new to the Royal Flying Corps, it was by no means a new type of plane. It had originally been designed for the Royal Naval Air Service, which had made excellent use of it for their particular purposes. But it was admittedly obsolescent when the Navy handed over a large number of them to the R.F.C. in response to frantic calls for anything that could fight. They were still good planes, but not nearly good enough for the arduous tasks assigned to them in the face of a greatly superior enemy. Anyway, they were the best planes we could get at the time, and we did the best we could with them.

3. The Suicide Club

After a few weeks of refitting and what we hoped was suitable training, No. 45 Squadron left Boisdinghem to return to the fighting front. Our field was a large piece of farmland at Ste. Marie Capelle, a few miles north of Hazebrouck. We were in trouble from the start, and we got deeper into it as we went along. Lowe was one of the first to be killed.

The early Fokkers had now been replaced by a new crop of German fighters, twin-gunned and demonstrating performances with which they could literally run rings around us. For a short while, as long as we had enough practiced crews, we could hit back at these enemies with gratifying effect, and they showed their respect for us by their reluctance to attack unless they substantially outnumbered us. But, as our old hands were gradually picked off, to be replaced by newcomers with less and less training and experience, the going began to get progressively tougher.

Our really serious troubles started early in the game, when the Staff began to load upon us other duties, which those chair-borne gentlemen apparently supposed would be merely incidental to our fighting.

We soon had cause to envy the simple life of the single-seat fighter pilot. He had nothing to do except fight, and he was free to do the best he could for that single purpose. Once a fight started, he had nobody else to consult or consider in the handling of his plane, his guns, his tactics, or his maneuvers. Few other jobs could be wished on him, because his small plane had no space for the stowage of unrelated equipment. And if our two-seaters had been left to do nothing but fight, we could at least have planned and developed our tactics to make the best of what performance we had.

However, the Staff decided that, instead of using us as fighter protection for regular photographic planes, we should do both the fighting and the photography ourselves. After all, said the Staff, there was plenty of room in the gunner's cockpit for a camera installation, and he ought to have plenty of time between fights to take photos. Worse still— from our standpoint—our Sopwiths had come to us with the long-range capacity that the Navy had required of them for long overwater patrols, and we had about five hours' fuel instead of the usual 2½–3 hours' supply. This encouraged the Staff to send us out farther and keep us out longer, for photographic purposes.

Now, on almost every fighter patrol, two or three of the planes were required to carry cameras, and we were given charts of areas and points to be photographed. And since the camera planes were supposed to be part of the fighter formation, the whole patrol was tied down to sets of tracks over the localities specified on the charts. The enemy's higher performance gave us little freedom to attack in any case, but now what little of that freedom we had left disappeared in the need for attending to photographic requirements. All fighting initiative had to be left to the enemy, giving them all the time they needed to climb, mass, and maneuver for the most favorable attack conditions, while we plodded along the prescribed tracks waiting for what was coming to us when the enemy was ready.

Our fighting objective was no longer to destroy the enemy; it was to try to ensure that at least one of our camera planes got home. The Germans quickly learned to take advantage of the restraints we were working under, and their attacks steadily grew bolder and more effective.

We became used to losing two out of five planes or three out of eight, and there were occasions when we wondered how any of us got back at all. Often the planes we got back with were not usable any more. We began to run out of replacement planes, and at one time, in a desperate effort to keep the squadron up to strength, headquarters tried to fill our gaps by calling on the French for some superannuated Nieuport two-seaters—which at least gave us something to laugh at, because the Nieuports had only 2½ hours' fuel and couldn't even keep up with the Sopwiths.

It was, however, the extent of our crew losses that became crippling and eventually notorious. At best, the production of our training schools at home was hardly adequate for keeping up with the casualties that the R.F.C. had been suffering from the Fokker scourge and its developments; it was totally unable to supply us with competent pilots for the strenuous work that the Sopwith squadrons were expected to do. Most records tell the story—which is frequently dismissed as an improbable fable—that pilots were then being sent out to war with as little as a dozen hours of solo flying time. In fact, however, we sometimes wished that our new pilots had all that much experience; some of them had a good deal less, and one officer named Evans came to us as a "fighter pilot" with only four hours of solo, having never carried a passenger and never fired a machine gun.

In the matter of gunner replacements the situation became so chaotic that it was almost funny. As casualties whittled down our normal airman resources, we were reduced to calling for volunteers from line regiments. Soon even those were hard to come by, because rumors about the "Suicide Club" were filtering down to the infantry, who became sarcastically curious to know why we couldn't supply our own gunners. Almost none of those who did volunteer had ever been up in the air; no qualifications were required of them beyond the ability to load and fire a Lewis gun, and there was rarely time to give them any sort of air training before they went into action. Yet, with nothing but their courage to recommend them, some of those fellows performed magnificently.

Too often, however, those unsung heroes were airsick in the whirlings of a dogfight, or else they used the gun installation as something to hang onto instead of to shoot with. Then again, we occasionally got specimens such as my completely fearless Scottish infantry lieutenant: full of guts and ignorance, highly belligerent and trigger-happy; he itched to shoot at anything, everything, or nothing, regardless of range. In one dogfight in which our Sopwiths received unexpected reinforcements from some F.E.'s from No. 20 Squadron, he opened fire on one of the F.E.'s merely because it looked different, and I had to kick the rudder hard to throw his aim off. The only things I ever knew him to hit for certain were our own tail, rudder, and wing tips.

It was from a very small infantry lieutenant that I first heard the grim new title we had acquired. A Methodist clergyman in civil life, he reported to us one morning as a volunteer gunner. He told me that, when headquarters at Saint Omer had given him his posting to No. 45, somebody had advised him cheerfully not to bother to take much kit—he was not likely to last long in the Suicide Club. He wanted to know what kind of a joke that was supposed to be. It really wasn't much of a joke—he was among those "missing" the following afternoon.

In March I was promoted to captain and sent as flight commander to No. 70 Squadron, which also had Sopwiths. I arrived at Vert Galand to be told that three of the six planes of my new command had gone out that morning and had not returned. Except for flying over different territory, life in No. 70 was much the same as in No. 45; the two squadrons shared the title of Suicide Club, although there was some debate as to which of them offered the shorter life expectancy. I was not long in No. 70 before I found myself back in No. 45, in command of "B" Flight.

My first experience of the responsibilities of command brought me no joy. For it was now my dismal duty to pair off the pilots and gunners of my flight for the next day's sorties. We had perhaps three or four of the original gunners left in the squadron, and the eager courage of the newcomers was no substitute for skill and experience. For pilots we were in no better shape; I think I was one of three survivors of the eighteen pilots who had left Boisdinghem, and only a few other pilots had much experience. It would be murder to send out a green pilot with a green gunner. So then what? Should I send out an experienced gunner with a pilot who could hardly fly, or an experienced pilot with a quite useless gunner behind him? There was nothing to do but guess and trust to luck.

It was in such conditions that we went through Bloody April, the month of the Royal Flying Corps's highest losses, losses that had been steadily building up for two years while the R.F.C. pursued its proud policy of unrelenting aggression over enemy-held territory in the face of far superior German fighter power. Thereafter the situation would

change, for the first of our really effective fighters had begun to trickle
into France, and by the late summer of 1917 the Camels and the
S.E.5's would be out in full force to even up the score.

Meanwhile the losses of the Sopwiths were becoming the subject
of muffled but widespread comment. As far as we ourselves were
affected, it wasn't so much the losses themselves that distressed us; we
knew very well that the whole R.F.C. was going through a tough
time. What perturbed us was that the Staff appeared greatly to over
estimate the capabilities of our Sopwiths, and we were losing too
many men and planes on ill-considered assignments that we were too
feeble to carry out.

Sometimes we amused ourselves with the suspicion that there must
have been a special government department devoted to inventing
troubles that the Sopwiths had not yet met. At one time some Supply
genius decided that the specially refined castor oil ("Castrol") used
in our engines was too costly; so they shipped us large quantities of
ordinary pharmaceutical castor oil, which was much cheaper. Thereafter
the squadron was happily grounded for most of a week while we
dismantled our engines to remove the waxy deposits that had gummed
them up. Then we went back to Castrol, returning the other castor
oil to the Brigade with explicit suggestions as to what they might
do with it. Another time we rejoiced to hear that our 110-hp engines
were being replaced by new Clergets of 130 hp. Unfortunately, some
one forgot to order propellers with the steeper pitch necessary to absorb
the higher power; we had to fly with the old propellers, and throttle
off our extra power to avoid engine overspeeding.

To have survived those tough months in No. 45 I needed a heavy
overdraft on my brimming store of luck. On the various occasions when
they shot up my plane or gunner, the Germans seemed to have
developed the knack of missing my person completely and never doing
quite enough damage to the plane to prevent my reaching at least
our side of the lines. But this sort of luck could not go on forever
and, like most of us now, my early eagerness for battle had worn very
thin. Attempts had been made to boost our morale by feeding us
repeated rumors that we were "soon" to receive the new Sopwith
Camels. In the mess huts we regularly chanted that rousing Scottish
refrain, "The Campbells Are Coming," with suitable mispronuncia

tions. But somehow the Camels didn't come (until shortly after I left the squadron).

Meanwhile, in honor of the "stiff upper lip," we were expected to maintain the fiction that our punch-drunk Sopwiths were still mighty engines of war. And, in the same spirit, the Brigade continued to send us out on jobs that we were too feeble to complete. The casualties continued, and our new Squadron Commander, Major van Ryneveld, who was not supposed to make combat flights but couldn't hold himself back, was only briefly in command before he joined the list of severely wounded.

Stories of my departure from No. 45 went the rounds for a long time afterward, with gleefully lurid versions of what I was supposed to have done or said to our Brigadier General. There was a complicated background to the story, because others besides our squadron were becoming seriously concerned with the Sopwith losses. Anyway, I was now, in point of experience, considerably the senior pilot in the Sopwith squadrons, and I had already had several clashes with the Brigade, usually in efforts to make sense out of some of our missions.

One day the Brigadier—who had never himself flown in any serious action—visited the squadron and broadcast some ill-timed comments that implied we were not using our planes to best effect. I replied with some undiluted remarks concerning the Brigade's directives. A few days later I was sent home, and I have to admit that I was not inclined to dispute the sentence—if that's what it was.

And when I got home, they gave me the nicest job I could have asked for.

CHAPTER XII

The Great Training Era

1. Fighting Schoolmaster

Back in England I was given two weeks' leave, now several months overdue. Then I reported to R.F.C. Headquarters in London. Colonel Warner, the Personnel Officer, put on his heaviest professional scowl as he dug up the matter of my indiscretions toward the Brigadier General in France; but he was rather halfhearted about it, with hints that General Trenchard's comments on the affair reflected more sympathy than censure. The worst I could expect was that further promotion would be unlikely to come my way.

Then he waved the subject away, switched his expression to a genial grin, and announced the newly invented job to which I was being appointed. I was to be Fighting Instructor to the 18th Wing, a command that covered six or eight major training stations in the London area. There were no precedents for this kind of work, and I was to have an unusually free hand in devising, testing, and applying methods of introducing new pilots, who had completed elementary training, to the arts of air combat.

The mere creation of this job made it evident that military aviation was entering a new era. Today, when everyone gets a "training course" for everything from launching missiles to threading needles, it is not easy to realize that, for three struggling years, the combat pilot had had to learn his perilous trade in the hardest possible way. He was given skimpy instructions in the bare rudiments of handling an airplane, and what he learned afterward about air warfare was—as in my own case—mostly a matter of how long he survived to learn his own lessons. We all knew that an appalling proportion of losses were due to lack of training, but up to now there didn't seem to be much that could be done about it; there was no organized collection of knowledge concerning what to teach or how to teach it.

Now at last, in the field of primary training, the revolutionary ideas of Major Smith-Barry, who had long been a voice crying in the wilderness for systematic training procedures, were suddenly accorded enthusiastic official approval, and his historic Gosport School was about to be established. But "advanced training" was still a foggy concept, and this new fighting-instructor system was the first tentative step in that direction.

After the rough going of my latest ten months in France, this new job was the richest of gravy. I was directly responsible only to the Wing Commander, Colonel Robert Loraine, a renowned pilot of early prewar days and, incidentally, one of England's great dramatic actors. I set up my own schedules at the various stations, and several types of planes were always at my disposal, all fitted with the newly invented gun camera, which was an invaluable tool in the program. Probably, to start with anyway, my "courses" were somewhat primitive, but at least they lent a reasonable degree of skill and a vast amount of confidence to the lads we were now sending out to man the R.F.C.'s new crop of fighter planes. For me, at any rate, it was intensely rewarding work.

By the end of 1917 the rising tide of official concern with training programs had risen to a flood. Training was no longer to be left to the haphazard teaching of any transient pilot who happened to be appointed "instructor." A program was called for based on the new and startling theory that instructing was itself an art that had to be learned, and Smith-Barry became the central influence in this program. His Gosport organization became the "School of Special Flying," and the principles it established were to spread throughout the world as the basis for all flight-training systems. It started by training instructors, and eventually it was training special instructors to go forth and train still more instructors in the gospel according to Gosport.

I was sent to Gosport to absorb the philosophy of the great Smith-Barry and to acquire the distinctive title of Gosport Instructor.

2. Gosport Instructor

Major Robert Smith-Barry (known to all as "Smith-B") was an amazing character. A magnificent pilot, in spite of injuries from a 1914 crash that forced him to limp around with a cane, he was a caustic humorist and, although a professional soldier, totally contemptuous of musty military conventions. Even in the face of his ferocious demands for efficiency, he managed to make himself beloved and respected by all who knew him—with the probable exception of a few highly placed stuffed shirts who resented the astonishing success of his unorthodox methods.

He was obsessed with the belief that far higher standards of piloting could quickly be established if only old taboos were removed and a spirit of calculated enterprise were brought into the business. He thought that the accepted principles of sedate caution were merely wasting time as well as dulling the ardor of the student. He wanted a new type of instructor: not the old semiretired "flat-turn kings," nor brand-new pilots who themselves could barely fly, but the most expert pilots he could get hold of, specially trained in his own methods of dual-control instruction.

New students, under Smith-Barry, found themselves going out in all kinds of wind and weather and confidently performing, within their first few flights, maneuvers that in earlier days would only have been timidly approached after many weeks. The instructor stayed with the student all the way through aerobatics and emergency procedures, until the student was highly proficient or was rejected as unsuitable. Unlike some of the wooden methods of today's government-approved instruction, the Gosport system encouraged the student to develop his own flying techniques. There were no rigid right-and-wrong ways of flying: what mattered was what a student could do with a plane, not how he did it.

My first encounter with Smith-B gave me a good taste of his strong medicine. I flew into the field at Gosport to begin my qualification as

Gosport Instructor. I made my approach in a steep and elegant side-slip, turned my Avro neatly into the wind, made a perfect landing, and taxied up to the hangars. Anyone watching would know that here came an accomplished pilot!

Before I could get out of the cockpit, an officer limped up, frowning heavily. A major's crown insignia was on his shoulder and I knew who he was.

"Courtney, aren't you?" he asked. I admitted it.

"Well," he said, with biting sarcasm, "I always heard you could fly. Yet you come here, I suppose, to be a Gosport Instructor, and I see you landing *into wind*. What's the matter with you?"

I stammered something about "usual procedures."

"This is not the place," he said, "for usual procedures. Here we land and take off down wind, cross wind or any old direction, but not *into wind*. Any damn fool can land into wind. Besides, what was all that taxiing for? Can't you judge your distance from the hangars?"

I soon knew what he was driving at. A Gosport Instructor was not supposed to waste his time in the simplicities of ordinary flying; every takeoff and landing, and as much as possible of his regular flying, was supposed to simulate some difficulty or emergency: use of minimum space for landing and takeoff on good or poor surfaces, coping with sudden engine failure at low altitude, dodging obstacles on or near the ground, operating the plane with one or more controls damaged, discovering new maneuvers or new ways of doing old ones, making quick recoveries from unusual attitudes, and a hundred other points that could be more readily passed on to students if the instructor could make them appear to be casual procedures in routine flying.

I long ago gave up trying to describe the extreme degree of precision that we developed in doing everything with airplanes that could possibly then be done—hardly anyone believes me. Yet I will claim that flying, regarded as the fine art of handling airplanes, reached a peak of glorious efficiency in the Gosport of those days that has never been surpassed. In fact, it has never been allowed to—today, ten minutes of the old Gosport flying would cause any pilot to lose his license.

On a later occasion, Smith-B told me to take up his Morane "Bullet," a tiny French fighter monoplane that would probably have made its name in fighting history only for the fact that the designers had apparently arranged the cockpit for small pilots only. Smith-B kept it as a sort of personal airplane. I squirmed into it with difficulty and found that, with my long legs, my knees were jammed up against the tank and I could barely move the rudder. I told Smith-B so.

"Oh, never mind that," he said. "With my busted leg I can't do much with the rudder either. Shove off and see what you can do with it."

I shoved off—to learn a little more of the things you could do with an airplane when you had to.

Smith-Barry became colonel, and was then made brigadier general in charge of training, with an office in London. He promptly battered military traditions by throwing out old but sacred files to make room for the limited records he wanted. A shock wave passed through administrative circles, and when the expressions of horror reached him, General Smith-Barry immediately demoted himself to colonel and posted himself back to Gosport, where, it seemed, flying was more important than filing.

After the war, Smith-B flew with a civil private pilot's license. A little while before he died he wrote me—I was then living in America —bemoaning his troubles with the civil air authorities when he occasionally lapsed into some of his old Gosport habits; according to him, flying had now degenerated into a dull and quiet pastime for old ladies.

While the Gosport system was being activated throughout the training stations, I was engaged in assorted instruction work at Northolt, near London, where two or three training squadrons were functioning as best they could with whatever planes they could get: ancient Maurice Farmans, war-worn B.E.2c's, unwanted Martinsydes, mislaid Spads, and (probably by some administrative oversight) a few brand-new Bristol Fighters. It was a strange miscellany of activities. We even picked up a little combat work by using our Bristols to chase raiding Gotha bombers over London; we could never climb fast enough to reach their altitude, but we sometimes came fairly close, and on one occasion, one of our observers, Captain Keevil, was killed by a chance enemy volley.

Then the first of the "branch" Gosport schools was established under

Captain (later Air Vice-Marshal) Stanley Vincent, one of Smith-B's original team, assisted by Gilbert Martingell and myself. The unit was called the "Special Instructors' Flight," with the urgent task of mass-producing qualified instructors. It was rather a hectic job because of the short cuts we had to take to get rapid results.

It was while the S.I.F. was operating at London Colney, a large field about twenty miles north of London, that we encountered the war's latest and most encouraging phenomenon, the large-scale influx of the Americans.

3. The American Contingent

At London Colney our Special Instructors' Flight was stationed at one end of the field when the first large batch of American "cadets" came for training to a squadron at the other end. They were a new, refreshing, and sometimes disconcerting experience to British officers, who were settling down stolidly to a war that, it seemed, had always been going on and probably always would be.

Since the start of the war occasional American volunteers had appeared in the Royal Flying Corps, often calling themselves Canadians to avoid certain legal entanglements. But now that the Americans were arriving en masse, quite a few problems came with them. In the first place, they had a vast surplus of enthusiasm; they felt that they had to cram a backlog of three years of experience into as many weeks or days. It was a most admirable attitude, but not an easy one to handle, and it cost them more lives than we cared to see them lose. Elliott White Springs, afterward my friend for many years, was among this crowd, and his stories of their adventures became classics.

Our S.I.F. and the American training unit shared most of the same mess facilities, and it took a little time for the "Yanks" and the "Limeys" to get adjusted to each other's outlandish customs. Discipline was one factor. Among the British the almost religious attitude of the Old Army toward authority largely prevailed, and we were still trying to get used to the untamed Australians. Those of us who were not old soldiers developed a sneaking envy for this newly imported

irreverence toward rank and tradition, but we found it a little difficult
to absorb. The impatience of these newcomers was sometimes a
strain, but it was not new to us; it was the same irrepressible eagerness that we had had at the beginning of the war, but we, by now,
had had plenty of time to simmer down—they hadn't.

Colonel William Larned, a pioneer American sportsman pilot (and,
incidentally, a longtime amateur tennis champion), was in charge
of U.S. aviation technical headquarters in London, and I first met him
at London Colney, where he housed the D.H.4 that he used for his
general flying and touring purposes. In our subsequent associations, I
learned much about the monumental headaches of his technical job;
the United States had entered the war with nothing like an adequate
aircraft industry to support its military aviation, and Larned had to
find ways and means of helping to equip American squadrons with
such British and French (and, I believe, a few Italian) airplanes and
engines as could be obtained in the wild technical, industrial, and
political scramble of production and procurement.

Later, when I was transferred from training work back to military
experimental flying, I was officially assigned to give Larned's office
what assistance I could, my first job being to help with a difficult project
for installing a large batch of 150-hp Monosoupape Gnome engines
that the Americans had acquired from the French (who were glad to get
rid of them) into a line of Sopwith Camels acquired from the British
(who were reluctant to release them). There were other confusions,
such as the fiasco of the first consignment of Curtiss "Jennies" delivered to England, and some of the early troubles with the Liberty
engine, which led me to become almost an honorary member of
Larned's staff.

Bill Larned was philosophical about these setbacks, regarding them
as a good lesson to the United States not to neglect its aircraft industry in the future. He was convinced that, in spite of appearances at
the time, America must eventually lead the world in aviation; and
Colonel Billy Mitchell, who joined a couple of our discussions, could
talk fervently for hours to the same effect. Larned invited me to join
the aircraft company that he (a very wealthy man) intended to set
up in the United States after the war.

As it happened, after the war the United States resumed its indifference toward a powerful aircraft industry; Mitchell was punished for denouncing that lapse; Larned's company was never formed. It would be ten years yet before I moved to America.

4. The Wild Russians

Our Russian cadets were an uproarious experience. After Kerensky's revolution, before the Bolsheviks took over, a bunch of about two dozen young Russians were sent to England for flight training, and they arrived at Northolt under a Major Abakanovitch—it saved time to call him Abby. The project had been sketchily organized, and nobody seemed to have bothered about the language problem. None of us knew a solitary word of Russian, and only three or four of the cadets could make themselves understood in odd bits of English. But several of them spoke good French, so for a while I found myself with the job of interpreter/instructor. There were no pilots among them— Abby was a Cossack who was always looking for a horse—but a few had air combat experience as gunner-observers, and many had fought in the infantry. They wore some sort of Russian army cadet uniform, an elegant dark-blue affair that they always kept spotless.

We enjoyed every minute of these people, but we found them hard to fathom. They were a strange mixture of dead seriousness and hilarious abandon. As flight students they were quick to learn and mostly showed great promise as pilots. Their military discipline would have charmed a Guards sergeant, and they accepted commands or reprimands with a curious sort of courtesy.

Abby quickly puzzled the officers' mess. Apparently he found scotch whisky to be an acceptable if feeble substitute for his native vodka, and he was frankly disappointed that even the thirstiest British officers could not keep up with his fabulous rate of consumption. Nobody ever saw him drunk, and we used to debate whether it was the Russian army or the climate of The Steppes that had provided this priceless training.

The cadets were a superstitious crowd, openly revering assorted charms and sacred medals which presumably helped them on their way. They had a quite oriental and fatalistic attitude toward crashes, death, and injury that was sometimes helpful to us and sometimes not. We had an old B.E.2c that was in fair enough shape for training purposes but was a hand-me-down from a night-flying squadron and was painted a dull black all over. One of my brighter cadets was ready for his first solo, so I sent him off on this B.E. I noticed his lack of enthusiasm and that he crossed himself before climbing into the cockpit, but he made no comment. He took off, made a straight stall not far from the ground, and dived in. By great good luck he wasn't too badly hurt, and after he was taken off to the hospital, I asked one of the other cadets to go after him and find out what had happened. Apparently no explanation was needed: you send a man off for his first solo on a plane painted the shade of death, so what else would you expect?

One afternoon I was flying into Northolt when, ahead of me at about fifteen hundred feet, I saw a Bristol Fighter apparently in trouble. It was winding strangely into a closer and closer spiral until, in a series of turns that was not a spin, it dived into the ground. It looked as if the rudder had jammed, which may or may not have been the case. I landed alongside the wreck and saw what was left of something in a Russian uniform. It turned out to be Cadet Kopyloff. When I got back to the hangar I was staggered to find the rest of the cadets laughing uproariously. It seemed that Kopyloff had just won some sort of sweepstake among the cadets, and now the poor devil wouldn't be there to collect.

Another first solo, performed by a Russian less enterprising than most of them, provided a long-enduring Northolt legend. This time it was on a venerable Maurice Farman, and the cadet climbed in proudly wearing on his smart blue uniform, as he always did, the Cross of St. George gained in infantry fighting. The Maurice Farman had a rate of climb of nothing much and, when our cadet had reached a small altitude against the southwest wind, he suddenly developed a strong disinclination to attempt a turn. He kept going—straight and level—and passed from sight.

An hour or so later Major Chadwick sent for me.

"A call from the Guildford police has just been passed on to me," he said. "They think they've got a captured German pilot in the clink there. He seems to have stolen one of our planes and had a forced landing on the Hog's Back. Ten to one it's our Russian. Take a car and see if you can collect him."

After much negotiation with the Guildford police and the local Home Guard, I gathered up their prisoner and eventually got the story. Our cadet had kept on his way until the Hog's Back, a range of hills, loomed up in front of him. He saw a nice field and landed in it. He climbed down to confront a farmer armed with a formidable pitchfork. The farmer saw only an airman, speaking a strange tongue and wearing on a strange uniform what could only be an Iron Cross. The farmer formed his own conclusions, prodded the pilot into a barn, locked the door, and called the police. The police, who knew as much about Russians as the farmer did, locked the man up and called the nearest air station. What the other cadets had to say to him that evening would have been worth hearing.

Some of these cadets turned into first-rate pilots, and I often wonder what happened to them. Ivan Smirnoff, later a very famous pilot with the KLM Royal Dutch Airlines, told me he thought most of them were liquidated by the Bolsheviks on account of their imperialist contaminations, and the only one I ever heard of again was Batourin, who, a dozen years later, was reported to be a senior officer flying seaplanes in the Black Sea.

5. The Royal Air Force Takes Over

On April 1, 1918, the Royal Flying Corps ceased to exist, when it was unified with the Royal Naval Air Service into the new Royal Air Force. The name of the R.F.C. would live on in the most glorious records of military history, trailing an infinite nostalgia for the days of our early despised and puny efforts. But at least our mourning was tempered with a pride that our struggles were now to be rewarded by the recognition of a mighty new force: the force of Air Power.

If the birth of the Royal Air Force produced a vast commotion in political and administrative circles, it passed almost unnoticed among the flying men, whether on the field of battle or at home. The war still raged, and the change didn't make it look any different.

We had heard a lot about what our new sky-blue uniform was

going to look like, and, faithful to tradition, we found nothing about it to praise. We ridiculed the bananas on the cap badge, we sneered at the brass buttons that would liken us to doorkeepers, and we would miss our Sam Browne belts, that unmistakable trade-mark of the officer. But most of all, we shuddered to think that the proud letters "RFC" on our wings would now be replaced with "RAF," which thitherto had been the label for the dismal airplanes and engines of the Royal Aircraft Factory. The Factory would slide out from under that unloved designation by changing its name to Royal Aircraft Establishment.

The official uniform of the R.F.C. had been the double-breasted, high-collared "maternity jacket," infinitely smart and dashing, but really quite uncomfortable, and too warm in hot weather or indoors; mostly we wore the usual infantry jacket. Now we discovered a belated affection for our old, distinctive garment. Outside of staff offices, few bothered to hurry into the new uniform; perhaps it seemed to proclaim too loudly the end of the R.F.C.

It was at the naval air stations that the shock of the change was more immediately felt. The new Royal Air Force adopted army titles of rank; the present distinctive titles would not be invented for some time yet. Navy traditions being what they have always been, it was a dreadful thing for a Navy Captain to have to call himself a Colonel, or for a Lieutenant Commander to become a Major. The nautical lingo of a naval air station had to be revised to conform with land-lubber vocabularies, and the distressing effect on old-time Navy men was enough to bring tears of compassion to a visitor's eyes.

A new government department, the Air Ministry, came into being, and its reorganized Technical Department gave me a full-time appointment for carrying out officially the kind of testing and consulting work that previously I had been doing as incidental and occasional jobs. I became again a military test pilot, stationed at Norwich and working mostly with the firm of Boulton & Paul, which had an unusually large program of design, production, and development in various types of aircraft, from small fighters to large flying boats. As a side line to this job, I had to visit other contractors and fly many of the numerous new models that were then coming out for the expected continuance of the war.

I was now virtually a civilian in uniform, so when the war ended some months later, I was able to face with relative confidence the too-often painful transition from military to civil life. What lay ahead for aviation in the postwar years nobody could guess. But at least my good luck so far had placed me in a position for latching onto one or other of the various developments that seemed bound to take place.

CHAPTER XIII

AFTER THE STORM

The Great War, as we called it, was over. Those of us who considered aviation to be our regular business had to take a puzzled look around to see where that upheaval had left us. Aviation had gone into the war with nothing that could seriously be called a warplane, and it had come out of it with nothing but warplanes. So, since this had been "the war to end all wars," we were apparently out of business. Our visionary faith in aviation's glorious future was still in working order, but we had to start all over again to find out where the road to it lay.

There is not much support for the general assumption that World War I gave an immense boost to the primitive business of aviation and set it on its feet. At the end of the war it was far from being on its feet. Perhaps the best that could be said for the new situation was that the public had come to accept aviation as one of the facts of life. Having seen so much flying during the war, it now knew that the airplane was here to stay. It was even ready to agree that, one way or another, airplanes would eventually be put to common use, although it was not at all clear what that use might be. Airplanes had proved themselves mighty weapons in the hands of fearless warriors, but the average citizen was in no hurry to take himself or his business up into the air.

Aviation technology had made little obvious profit from the war. An enormous amount of effort had gone into engineering development, but most of it was of the slipshod and wasteful variety that naturally resulted from trying to meet immediate wartime needs in a hurry. As far as anyone could see, all the progress we had made in airplane design during four years of war was to take slightly refined versions of prewar airframes and fit them with more or bigger engines. Even in the matter of engines there was little to show for four years of scrambling effort and huge expense. The great majority of the numerous wartime engine models went into the discard, while a few other types were dumped onto a cluttered market at "surplus" prices for those who could find means of using them up. Only three or four designs, such as the Rolls-Royce and the Hispano, were found worth developing for postwar use.

There was, however, one solid gain that had not yet become evident, but soon would be: wartime expansion had attracted to the industry a large new infusion of technical talent, able and anxious to tackle the innumerable experimental developments that wartime experience had suggested but wartime priorities had sidetracked. Moreover, the arts of flying and handling planes had enormously improved, simply because there had been so much more flying than peace conditions would have called for; although air navigation was in the same primitive shape as it had always been in, with no better equipment or aids than had been available before the war.

So, in effect, aviation in 1919 was picking itself up out of the confused litter of war and starting again to hack its difficult way along the path of progress that it had been forced to abandon in 1914. Only, this time, it had wider resources at its disposal.

★   ★   ★

The next decade, therefore, was an immensely important period in the history of aviation development, because it was during those years that aviation emerged vigorously from the rather artless concepts of the past and embarked on the wide program of engineering and scientific experiment that was to lay the foundations of most of the advances of the future. Unfortunately, the history of progress during that decade is not easy to follow today, partly because much of it involved a long succession of detailed technical achievements of which only the more spectacular—and often less important—seem to have left much of a general impression. Another outstanding reason is that America on the one hand and Europe on the other took off along widely different paths in their respective approaches to postwar progress, and the student of factual history is liable to become seriously misled if, as often happens, he fails to make an objective comparison of events on opposite sides of the Atlantic.

In postwar Europe a powerful, new, and permanent influence appeared on the scene that for many years had no great impact in America: governments found themselves compelled to give firm support to effective peacetime aviation industries. The fighting was supposed to be over, and everyone was signing peace treaties with everyone else; but Europe's international rivalries still festered to show that, if the spirit of war was officially dead, it would not lie down. Military air establishments were everywhere sharply curtailed, but in England General Trenchard's creation, the new Royal Air Force, was already established as an independent partner of the older services, and its future efficiency could be assured only with the backing of a sound, versatile, and progressive aircraft industry. An Air Ministry, of Cabinet status, had been founded, of which a Directorate of Technical Development was a most important division.

In the absence of an immediate need for new military planes in large numbers, government support consisted largely in promoting, sometimes by direct contracts and sometimes by indirect encouragement of private ventures, the development by industry of wide ranges of experimental planes, engines, and equipment, most of which required corresponding research in all branches of aeronautical engineering and science. Comparatively few of these ever went into production —many remained generally unheard-of—but all served the purpose of building up the engineering background of an efficient aviation industry.

Other major European powers adopted similar plans, and even defeated Germany evaded peace-treaty restrictions by evolving advanced aircraft models in Switzerland, Denmark, Italy, and elsewhere.

Civil aviation in Europe looked, for a while, like a dubious weakling that would somehow have to fend for itself. But it was soon realized, especially in Britain, that civil flying organizations could constitute a substantial reserve for military aviation, besides contributing still further to the support of the aircraft industry. Government assistance, therefore, took the form of fostering private enterprise in civil and commercial flying developments. A small subsidy was provided to keep alive the pioneer passenger airlines that commercial interests were struggling to maintain; private flying (which would provide a national reserve of pilots) was officially promoted by government-sponsored competitions for light airplanes and the small engines required to power them, while a system of local flying clubs was encouraged for the training of new pilots and the maintenance of serviceable airports in widespread locations. By mid-1919 the Air Ministry was administering the airworthiness certification of civil aircraft and the licensing of aircrews.

American aviation, during that same period, followed an entirely different course. After the war the United States withdrew across the Atlantic, anxious to be clear and stay clear of Europe's turmoil. It saw no further need for substantial military air commitments and their costs, and when General Mitchell loudly demanded a vigorous air force he trod on enough toes to land himself in a court martial. Again, as before the war, government support for military aviation was too sparse to encourage the formation of a substantial aircraft industry. Civil aviation, for many years, had no official standing at all; in rejecting the League of Nations, the United States incidentally cut itself off from the international commercial flying agreements that were being organized through the League, and it provided no early substitute, so that it was not until 1927 that provisions came into effect for the certification of civil aircraft and aircrews.

Just the same, however, the United States Government evidently felt that America's place in the new era of aviation should somehow be asserted, and it concluded that this task should be performed through operations conducted by the government itself, thus, of course, effectively crowding out private enterprise. To begin with, air-mail services were set up by the Post Office and operated by the Army, the effect of which—as I shall explain at length in a later chapter— was to obstruct the development of public passenger airlines for about ten years. Then government efforts were dedicated to a succession of "national prestige" performances. A group of Navy seaplanes, sup-

ported by a fleet of warships, was sent out to make the first air crossing of the Atlantic. Similarly a group of Army planes, provisioned
en route by the Navy, made the first flight around the world. In national air races, military planes, flown by military pilots, competed
with predictable success against the less bountiful resources of civilian
sportsmen.

In 1923, the United States Government shattered international
sporting traditions by entering Navy seaplanes and crews in the
Schneider Trophy contest, which, since its inception ten years previously, had been regarded as a strictly civilian sporting event. Military airmen, flying government planes, regularly pursued trophies, records, and "firsts" that, in other countries, were generally regarded
as the business of private sportsmen or industry pilots.

Many writers of popular aviation histories appear to regard these
performances as evidence of America's outstanding progress during
those postwar years. More objective historians, however, have to conclude that such activities were little more than feats of military showmanship in which the few planes employed were mostly special models that brought negligible nourishment, technical or financial, to the
American aircraft industry. It is, therefore, the regrettable fact that the
industry remained during that period, as it had been before the war,
sadly backward compared with that of Europe. This general situation
prevailed until the time that Lindbergh's sensational New York–
Paris flight let loose a passionate public interest in flying and trig-
gered the explosive expansion that was soon to bring the nation to
the forefront of aviation—which is a story we shall come to.

Anyway, my personal record of progress in experimental, commercial, and sport flying during most of the immediate postwar decade
continues to be a story of developments in Europe, because that is
where almost all the important action was then taking place.

★　　★　　★

For my own part, the war had provided me with experience, knowledge, and skill far beyond anything that earlier, peacetime conditions
could have offered. Now I had to see what I could do with them.

I got out of uniform as soon as I could, which was in January

1919, without the foggiest idea where my career, if any, might be heading. The aircraft industry was almost motionless, with war orders being canceled in all directions. The government was already facing the problem of distributing the thin slices of the small cake of military orders that were now in prospect to those firms that stayed in the business. I had made no effort to line up any sort of job, simply because I had no idea what jobs would exist or who would have them to offer. I just tried to spread the news that I was available. However, with the experience and contacts I now had, I guessed I would be able to keep up my supply of bread, even if I had to wait a while for the butter.

I had hardly qualified as a civilian before the world-famous Geoffrey de Havilland offered me a job as company test pilot to his concern, the Aircraft Manufacturing Company. My immediate task was to test their prototype twin-engine bomber, the D.H.11, which had not been canceled and had not yet flown. But also, with a view to future commercial flying and new military types, D.H. had a good deal of research flying in the mill on an assortment of experimental planes. I was off to a good start.

The D.H.11, being of De Havilland design, inspired all a test pilot's confidence; its A.B.C. "Dragonfly" engines did not. The Dragonfly was a thoroughly bad product, which fast-talking salesmen had induced the Air Ministry to order in large quantities and which, fortunately, had not gone into service before the war ended. It was a metallic assembly of infirmities, some of which I had already met in other planes, so I was doubly horrified when Major General Brancker, a director of the company, insisted on coming up with me on the first flight. I hated, in any case, to take unnecessary passengers on experimental flights; even on large planes in those days, I never cared to risk the distraction of a copilot on the first trip. I tried to scare Brancker out of the idea with a lurid story of dangerous engines. Which was silly of me, because Brancker, one of the earliest Royal Flying Corps pilots, had never been scared of anything in his life, and if the engines had been twice as bad, he would have been twice as anxious to come.*

---

* Shortly afterward, Air Vice-Marshal Sir Sefton Brancker became Britain's first Director of Civil Aviation; he lost his life in the crash of the R-101 dirigible in 1930.

After a few days of the usual ground tests I took off, with Brancker in the copilot's seat, from the same field at Hendon and in the same direction as I had, seemingly centuries earlier, taken off on my box-kite for my pilot's certificate. I had reached about a couple of hundred feet over the railroad line bordering the field when, with no warning, the starboard engine shattered its intestines and stopped dead. There was nothing ahead but a hill, a church, and a lot of houses. At once I started a turn to the left, against the power of the port engine, hoping that my untested controls were equal to the job. The controls responded dutifully, and I had just about got headed, down-wind, back toward the field when the port engine developed bronchitis and coughed itself down to idling power. I held my breath as I approached the telegraph wires clustered along the railroad embankment; I wasn't sure I could pull up over them without stalling, but I was quite sure the plane was too big to go under them. I pulled up, missed the wires by an unknown number of inches, rammed the nose hard down, and kept going to make one of my best Gosport-style down-wind landings.

"Good show, old boy," grinned Brancker, who obviously hadn't been worried for a moment. "We'll put in the spare engines and take another crack at it."

Before long, two or three firms who hadn't enough work to employ their own full-time test pilot asked me to do sundry tests for them. My experimental flying for De Havilland usually left large gaps of time for changes or modifications, so I had no difficulty in getting his permission to do some of this other work as well.

In the summer of 1919 De Havilland's associated firm, Aircraft Transport and Travel, started the first commercial scheduled airline, between London and Paris. I was called on to function as reserve pilot on the line, to help with the numerous technical problems involved in this new operation, and to make studies for the planning of future passenger planes.

At last the Aircraft Manufacturing Company closed down; it was too big an outfit for the small size of its postwar orders. De Havilland took over such work as it had, and hopefully set up his own small company at Edgware, near Hendon; his early struggles to survive gave no hint that this would one day develop into one of aviation's largest businesses. Thirty years later it would put the first jet transports out over the airways.

Meanwhile I had received enough requests for experimental assistance to encourage me to take up the precarious business of freelance test pilot and consultant. Those were days of incredible expansion and variety, such as are never likely to be seen again. Freed from the limitations and restraints of war, new ideas and suppressed brain waves broke out in all directions. They were still days when technical data were mostly scarce, elementary, or questionable, and the only reliable principle of research was "build it and fly it." I had long been hopelessly addicted to trying out anything new that I could find to try, and now I was to spend many eventful years in numerous branches of that satisfying, if somewhat hazardous, occupation.

CHAPTER XIV

THE LIVES OF A TEST PILOT

. *The Evolution of a Profession*

A while ago someone sent me—from Hong Kong of all places—
a newspaper cutting of a syndicated story that, in the course of
some historical comments, referred to me as a "famous test pilot."
The old-timer naturally likes to know that he is remembered here
and there, and I am content to be remembered as a test pilot. For,
during a great part of aviation's history, the test pilot's work has
generally been regarded as calling for the most skilled, most exacting, and, incidentally, the most hazardous kind of flying, because
essentially it has involved coping with problems and emergencies
unknown to previous experience.

The history of test flying has passed through three fairly distinct
phases. In the long years of the earliest phase, when the answers to
most aeronautical problems had to be sought in actual flight, the
test pilot took his chances and whatever experience he had and took
off in search of the information. The result was that his observations,
discoveries, reports, and opinions were prime ingredients in the early
accumulation of aeronautical knowledge.

The inventors of the earliest flying machines usually wanted to,
or had to, fly their own contraptions. A notable exception was
Professor Langley, whose age prohibited such pastimes and whose
engineering assistant, Charles Manly, undertook to fly his device in

the undeclared race with the Wright brothers to effect the first pow
ered flight. And so it happened that Manly crashed his way int
test-flying history without even flying. Something buckled on th
Langley plane as the catapult tried to launch it from its houseboa
and it took Manly for a quick dive into the Potomac River. Man
was probably luckier than he knew, because Langley's plane had que
tionable controls and Manly had no flying experience—such as th
Wrights had acquired with their gliders—so he was an odds-on favorit
for a much worse crash if he had managed to reach any appreciabl
altitude.

Around 1910, as I mentioned previously, airplane flying cease
rather suddenly to be the private mania of a few eccentric "inver
tors," and a new breed of men, mostly of sporting inclinations, ha
started to take to the air. This fresh market brought out a rash e
all sorts of new flying devices from inventors and designers, whe
as often as not, found reasons why someone else should test them
There was usually little difficulty in finding somebody who, for cas
or for fun, was happy to try out some new plane or gadget. Man
of these, especially in France, were mechanics who had someho
picked up enough ideas about flying to be capable of making inte
ligent observations on whatever went wrong—as something usuall
did. Such people could probably be regarded as the original tes
pilots. However, many others were types who knew nothing an
cared less about the details of the planes; there was not much i
their minds beyond the sporting possibilities of getting up into th
air, defying gravity as long as they could, and maybe getting dow
without a crash.

I knew many of these "fly-anything" boys; they were usually ver
skillful pilots—they had to be to survive at all—and their cheerfu
disregard of all kinds of risks left a long-standing public impressio
that all test pilots were crazy men. This attitude became an emba
rassment when test flying began to develop into a serious busines

Gradually the more practical designers came to realize that the
needed something more than mere piloting skill for the testin
of their new devices. They started to choose pilots who would tak
risks when necessary but would avoid them when possible, and wh
could be relied on for information or suggestions that would hel

to correct defects or effect improvements. Designers of that sort treated a competent test pilot as an engineering collaborator, expected him to be candid in his criticisms and comments, and respected his findings—even if they didn't agree with them. Most of my work, fortunately, was in association with designers and engineers of that sort.

But there was another type of designer who resented any suggestion from the pilot that there could possibly be anything imperfect about his planes. If he found himself with a pilot who insisted on changes or modifications that might cost money or cause delay, the pilot was liable to be told: "All right; if you don't want to fly the plane as it is, we can always find someone who will." Which was true enough, because the "fly-anything" boys were always available, eager to demonstrate their fearless skill and unconcerned with such trivial matters as reasonable precautions or critical observations. When I eventually went into the business of professional test flying, I lost a number of jobs that way—and sometimes got them back when my replacement produced more wreckage than information.

I was exposed to the vicissitudes of test flying in my early apprenticeship days, before the First World War, when as was often the case, it was uncertain whether a new plane would get off the ground, let alone what it might do if it ever got well up into the air. In doubtful cases we apprentices might be appointed expert observers, lying flat on the ground alongside the expected takeoff path to see if any space appeared between the wheels and the surface. If it did, the plane was said to have flown, and much joy spread around. But even a reputable designer could occasionally produce a distressing failure.

Our Grahame-White design office had turned out some reasonably successful models, and great things were therefore expected of its revolutionary prewar "military biplane," so called because it was hopefully fitted with a built-in mount for carrying a machine gun. At last the plane was enthusiastically wheeled out for test. With its predicted rate of climb of five hundred feet per minute, we could count on at least a snappy takeoff. In those days we didn't use blocks under the wheels; during engine run-up a dozen or more men held the plane back, pushing in front and pulling behind, until the pilot signaled for release. Tense with the excitement of the occasion, we hung onto the plane, while the pilot, Louis Noel, ran up the 120-hp Austro-Daimler engine to his satisfaction. With throttle wide open, Noel waved his hand. We all let go, those in front throwing themselves on the ground so that the lower wing could pass over them. The plane didn't budge. Grimly we all now pushed on struts and outriggers to get the machine rolling. At last it lumbered along under its own power, slowly gathering speed as it approached the hedge at the far end of the field. Somehow Noel hauled it into the air in a soggy stall, barely clearing the hedge. It sat down heavily on the other side—and never flew again.

In an earlier chapter I referred to the pioneer training I had had in real test flying at the Royal Aircraft Factory in 1916. With that experience behind me I should have known better than to undertake to try to fly the Kennedy "Giant," at Northolt in 1917. This plane was a four-engined monstrosity of 142-foot span, by far the world's largest airplane at that time. It was the job that first brought me to general notice as a test pilot, for it was much publicized as a mystery plane—the chief mystery being whether anything so enormous could ever get off the ground.

Its Salmson engines—two tractors and two pushers—produced an impressive total of 1000 horsepower, but who knew whether that was enough? Nobody dared to assert positively that it wouldn't fly; there were several reputable engineers associated with the job, and there were rumors that its immense size and span were about to confer on it special lifting powers hitherto unknown. Moreover, the government was cautiously prepared for a possible success; it had promised Kennedy financial support once the plane had flown, and it had permitted me, as a Royal Flying Corps officer, to be assigned to the tests.

After months of preliminaries, we came to the great day of flight. Alone in the huge, totally enclosed cabin, I taxied laboriously to a point in front of the hangars at Northolt Air Station where the ground fell away in a gentle slope, up which a good, steady breeze was blowing. Wondering what I was in for, hoping for the best but sublimely confident that I could cope with the worst, I opened up

(1) A Grahame-White school box kite, 1913–14.

(2) FTC (left) with students and mechanics and damaged box kite. January 1914.

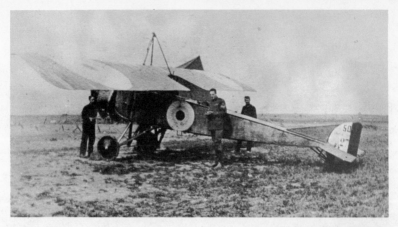

(3) No. 2891 Sergeant-Pilot F. T. Courtney with Morane-Saulnier "Parasol" monoplane. No. 3 Squadron, Royal Flying Corps, Auchel, France, June 1915.

(4) Bullet-deflector blocks on propeller. British experiment on B.E.12 fighter, tested by FTC in 1916.

(5) F.E.2d pusher fighter of No. 20 Squadron, Royal Flying Corps. 1916.

(6) ABOVE: FTC's well-worn
Sopwith 2-seat fighter, "Little
Erbert." No. 45 Squadron,
Royal Flying Corps,
France, 1917.

(7) RIGHT: FTC commanding
"B" Flight, No. 45 Squadron,
Royal Flying Corps. Ste. Marie
Capelle, France, March 1917.

(8) Kennedy "Giant" biplane (with C. J. Kennedy) tested by FTC at Northolt, England. 1917.

(9) Crash of Boulton & Paul P.8 "Atlantic." Norwich, England. 1919.

(10) First slotted wing. Handley Page experimental monoplane mounted on D.H.4 fuselage. (Note also slotted ailerons.) London, 1921.

(11) FTC with "Siskin" fighter for arctic engine tests. Kiruna, Swedish Lapland, January 1924.

(12) BELOW: Pre-starting rotor on early Autogiro by pulling on rope. Farnborough, 1925.

(13) Early Autogiro piloted by FTC for British Air Ministry tests. Farnborough, 1925.

(14) BELOW: Left: Juan de la Cierva, inventor of Autogiro. Center: Sir Samuel Hoare, British Air Minister. Right: FTC, pilot. Farnborough, 1925.

(15) Cartoon by German General Ernst Udet: his impression of pre-starting rotor of Autogiro during FTC's demonstration at Tempelhof airfield, Berlin, 1926.

(16) Gold cigarette case presented by Juan de la Cierva to FTC on successful conclusion of Autogiro trials for British Air Ministry, 1925.

(17) Crash of Autogiro C.6c, pilot FTC, after losing blade at 250-foot altitude. (A second blade, foreground, came off just before the crash.) Photo taken by Mrs. Courtney. Hamble, England, 1927.

(18) BOTTOM: D.H.34, of early British passenger airline services to Continent, 1922.

(19) Croydon commercial airport, London. 1922.

(20) FTC in Parnall "Pixie II" light airplane racer, with 1000-c.c. Blackburne motorcycle engine. Lympne, 1925.

(21) FTC with Martinsyde "Semiquaver" racer (300-h.p. Hispano-Suiza) before London Aerial Derby, July 1920.

(22) BELOW: FTC (hand to head) emerging from wreck of Martinsyde "Semiquaver" after winning London Aerial Derby, July 1920. (Back to camera, Fred Raynham).

(23) Presentation of King's Cup for air race around Britain, July 1923. L. to R.: FTC, winning pilot; Duke of Sutherland (representing King George V); Sir John Siddeley, owner of winning plane.

(24) Multiengine aerobatics: FTC looping "Bourges" bomber at reception for crew of American N.C.4 transAtlantic seaplane. Hendon, England, 1919.

(25) BELOW: Dinner in New York (1931) for pilots who had made or attempted trans-Atlantic flight. L. to R. (upper) L. Yancey, C. Lindbergh, FTC, A. Lotti, H. Connor, B. Balchen; (lower) C. Chamberlin, Amelia Earhart, Dr. Kimball (meteorologist), Ruth Elder, Peter Brady (New York City rep.), J. Fitzmaurice, Lowell Thomas (speaker).

(26) Mrs. "Ginger" Courtney, copilot of
FTC's Dornier "Wal" flying boat, on arrival at
Royal Air Force seaplane station,
Calshot, England, 1927.

(27) BELOW: FTC's Dornier flying boat
(two Napier engines) in Horta Harbor,
Azores, 1928.

(28) Burned-out rear engine of
Dornier. Photo taken while
drifting in Atlantic, August 1928.

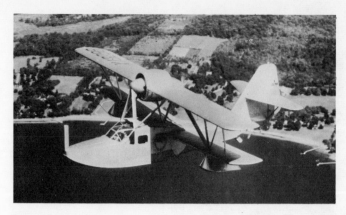

(29) FTC testing prototype Courtney Amphibian designed by him for Curtiss-Wright Corp. Over Long Island Sound, 1934.

(30) Saunders-Roe experimental military flying boat R.2/33, being towed to moorings after test flight, 1938. (FTC at pilot's station above, engineer Kerry at forward gun hatch below.)

(31) FTC with Navy PB4Y2 for trans-Pacific ferry flight, 1945.

the engines. I started to pick up speed reasonably fast, and now I began to struggle with the ponderous controls in an effort to coax the monster off the ground. The rumble of the wheels stopped. I was in the air—and I tensed myself for some heavy work ahead. A few seconds later I reached level ground at the end of the slight slope. Again I felt the rolling of the wheels. The plane ran into a soft patch of ground, slowed and stopped, still under full throttle. I couldn't even get it to move for taxiing back. I cut the engines and turned the problem over to the tow truck.

A committee of investigation studied the situation. From the track marks in the earth, it was decided that the wheels had lifted off for a hundred yards or so; there was considerable debate as to whether the tail skid had ever left the ground. Finally, it was officially declared that the plane had "flown." Nobody asked me to make another trial, which saved me the trouble of declining; I had already found out enough to know that, if I had ever reached full flight, the enormously heavy controls would have been far beyond my physical strength.

For years the huge Kennedy sat out in the open, crumbling away in wind and weather, a famous and ghostly landmark for thousands of pilots flying into Northolt, while assorted lawsuits revolved around the claim that I had flown; eventually someone carted away the remains. Meanwhile, when someone would occasionally ask me, "Did you *really* fly that damn thing?" I would mutter something vague and change the subject.

When, in 1920, I left De Havilland to venture into free-lance work, there was negligible aircraft production; but the world of aviation engineering was spending most of its available money and brains on a splurge of experimental projects that reached out into all sorts of unexplored fields for new aeronautical knowledge, and I was happy to discover that my reputation in the field of experimental flying was already substantial. Jobs on all kinds of airplanes began to trickle in, and some of them involved developments unusual enough to bring me considerable publicity. The newspapers took to calling me "The Man with the Magic Hands," because, according to them, I was supposed to be able to do anything that could be done with an airplane.

This gaudy title earned me hoots of laughter in the club bar, but it did me no harm in bringing more jobs along.

My constitutional curiosity where anything really new was concerned occasionally led me to fly some very questionable contraptions. But usually I tried to fly with great care and caution, seeing that my own neck was as easy to break as most of the surrounding structure. However, taking chances was all in the day's work when there was no other way to get results—and, incidentally, I was test flying for ten years before I ever wore a parachute. Yet, of the various crashes that came to me from time to time, only one put me in the hospital; usually I got by with nothing worse than a headache, a few cuts and bruises, or skinned shins.

There was a long period when the problems of the test pilot were by no means confined to the cockpit. In days before intricate instrumentation and elaborate recording devices were available for supporting test verdicts, the reports of qualified pilots were very nearly the only means of assessing the major characteristics of a new plane or device. It naturally followed that those reports became a weighty factor in deciding vital questions such as acceptance or rejection, sales and contracts, expensive changes or modifications, and similar terrestrial matters that were not supposed to be any of the pilot's direct business. Consequently he often found himself under conflicting pressures, technical, commercial, and even political, which strained his judgment, increased his risks, and occasionally killed him. Obviously this state of affairs was a major handicap to conscientious test flying, and it encouraged some designers to employ the "fly-anything" pilots, who were unlikely to come up with inconvenient or expensive criticisms.

Gradually, however, progress brought general recognition of the fact that the interests of engineering development were poorly served by the employment of test pilots who either hadn't enough experience to uncover defects or could be persuaded to ignore them. Military customers, in particular, became increasingly resentful of flight defects or deficiencies that should have been corrected in new types of planes before they were delivered. At last, therefore, test flying came to be accepted as a job for an experienced specialist, and his o-operation with design and engineering staffs became comparatively asy.

However, even where the test pilot was working smoothly with the ngineering staff, it was still possible for non-technical management o make substantial contributions to his headaches, because management's needs to produce specific plans and programs were too often n conflict with the wide uncertainties of experimental aviation— problem that, incidentally, does not seem to have disappeared even oday.

On one occasion I had arranged to make the tests of a new single-ngine prototype heavy bomber. After studying the situation I de-ided that the flying field alongside the factory at Yeovil was passable or routine flying but too small to leave a safety margin in case of xperimental troubles. I asked that the tests should be run at a large Royal Air Force field at Andover some fifty miles away. The chief ngineer supported me and the management reluctantly agreed. The plane was dismantled, shipped across country, and re-erected at the new ield. Over several weeks I completed the tests, with no emergency roubles at all.

I had no doubt that I would be engaged for the tests of a new xperimental plane that the firm had on the way. But then one of the directors told me: I had done a good job with their last plane, but ny sense of caution was too expensive; it had cost them a lot of noney to transship the plane, with all the test supplies and personnel, o a distant field, and it had turned out, after all, to be quite unnec-ssary. I could test their next plane on condition that I would be villing to fly it from their own small field. After much hesitation I de-lined, and another pilot was engaged. On the first takeoff run omething went wrong. There was no room to stop the plane within he limits of the field, and the pilot was forced to try to complete the akeoff; he didn't make it, and in the ensuing crash he lost both egs. The plane was not rebuilt and the design was abandoned.

The first flight of a prototype used to be a regular source of unsched-ıled troubles for the test pilot, for it has always been—and still is— ın occasion of much interest and excitement. Too often an enthu-siastic company executive would plan to organize the event as a thrilling spectacle for his friends and associates. On the day of the hoped-for flight, at any sign of delay or postponement, impatient spectators would start to get restive, plaintively pestering the pilot and the technicians with the monotonous question: "When is it going to fly?" Before long the test-flight staff could expect to feel executive pressure to hasten or by-pass final checks and inspections in order to get the plane into the air. The standard request was: "Couldn't you make just one short flight? Surely you can fix all those details afterward." I have known several crashes to follow that sort of intrusion, including at least one good one of my own, which I shall recount in due course. Anyway, as the result of experience I learned to conspire elaborately with the engineers and mechanics to try to keep management reliably misinformed as to prospects of a first flight, so that I might be left to conduct tests without mob distractions.

By 1928, when I moved to the United States, flight testing had begun to pass into the second phase of its history. The day had gone by when almost any experimental flight was a blind step into the unknown. By the late 1920s most of the basic problems of flight, of performance, control, and stability, and of adequate structures had, in the main, been overcome. Engines were more reliable and powerful. New and far more accurate instruments had been developed. Laboratory equipment had taken over much of the testing of structures and components that previously had depended on flight tests, while more sophisticated wind tunnels were widening the range of preflight aerodynamical information. A test pilot could take off with at least a reasonable foreknowledge of what the plane was about to do. Parachutes were standard equipment for giving airmen a chance to escape from insuperable difficulties.

On the other hand, as earlier problems receded or vanished, new problems took their places. Higher speeds and altitudes, larger and lighter structures made of new materials, complicated power-plant and fuel installations, totally new forms of operating equipment—these and numerous other advances brought with them new problems in design and construction, and the test pilot was working in fresh fields of exploration. The pilot's handling of his plane was becoming increasingly dependent on new instrumentation and gadgetry, which relieved him of many responsibilities and added others, for such equipment was itself largely experimental and subject to critical malfunctions.

Generally speaking, therefore, the second phase of test-flying history was a period during which experimental flying had begun to lose its reliance on the personal verdicts of professional test pilots and came increasingly under the influence of rapidly developing instrumentation. It lasted, roughly, into the early part of World War II.

My first job in America led me into a strange sideline in the way of test flying. In 1928 I was engaged as Aviation Adviser to the New York investment firm of Hayden, Stone & Co., which already had substantial interests in several aviation concerns and was expanding its activities into the new flood of projects generated by the "Lindbergh boom." An excited public, stirred into a vast new enthusiasm for aviation by Lindbergh's sensational flight, was anxious to pour a deluge of money—something American aviation had hitherto sadly lacked—into anything that looked like an aviation business, and innumberable new aircraft enterprises were mushrooming all over the country. Their eager schemes all called for extensive financing, and aviation shares added their own special glamour to the stock market uproar of 1929.

My job for Hayden, Stone was to investigate, for investment purposes, the technical organizations, programs, and products of a large assortment of companies. As part of these studies I had to fly a wide variety of airplane types which these new or expanding companies hoped to finance, promote, or sell. My reputation for test flying in Europe having accompanied me to the U.S.A., inevitably I found myself, usually informally, in the business of recommending and testing modifications and improvements that, hopefully, would increase sales prospects in a wildly competitive market. A national magazine, suitably impressed by these random activities, referred to me as the "Airplane Doctor."

When the Hayden, Stone group formed the Curtiss-Wright Corporation, I moved to that concern as Technical Assistant to the Vice-President, Engineering, the renowned Charles L. Lawrance. C-W started life as a very versatile collection of subsidiaries involved in the design and construction of practically every class of airplane, from little puddle jumpers to large passenger airliners, seaplanes and amphibians, as well as an assortment of air-cooled and liquid-cooled engines. Although these extensive activities were gradually curtailed by the onset of the Great Depression, they provided me with several years of experimental developments of all kinds.

Those years turned out to be very eventful ones in aviation's history, because it was during the 1930s that American aviation, which had for so long lagged behind that of Europe, now reversed the earlier situation; with the Boeing 247, the D.C.3, and similar sleek, fast monoplanes, America initiated the series of swift and original advances that brought it to the leadership of the business. In 1940 World War II had broken out in Europe, and the sudden demand for powerful warplanes in all categories rapidly pushed airplane design and operations to new levels of complexity.

And so the history of test flying was inevitably carried into its third, and presumably final, phase. Now the personal initiative, authority, and responsibility of the individual test pilot became merged into the collective procedures of engineering test teams of which the pilot might or might not be the supervisor. Each test flight became an organized sortie planned in detail for specific objectives by engineering groups, with an increasingly elaborate array of instruments to measure and record the data, while continuous radio communications provided instructions, advice, and information from the ground.

The days that I still like to think of as the Golden Age of test flying had vanished into the past.

My last venture into test-flying activities was, for me, a disconcerting demonstration of the march of progress. As copilot during tests of a four-engine jet transport, I had the intermittent duties of handling the plane manually, at speeds up to 600 knots, while the plane's captain supervised a small army of technicians as they checked, adjusted, and calibrated a fantastic array of electronic equipment; this impersonal gear then proceeded to fly and navigate the plane automatically with a degree of smoothness and precision that no human pilot could hope to equal. When the tests were finished I was willing to salute the wondrous achievements of science; but somewhere in the back of my mind there lurked a sort of unreasonable resentment that a pilot of modern high-speed planes was now no match for a collection of black boxes.

2. *Leaves from a Test Pilot's Notebook*

I think that, in the minds of most people, the chief problems of the test pilot's job are concerned with the trials of prototype aircraft; an atmosphere of danger and suspense inevitably surrounds the pilot who takes into the air a plane of new design that has never flown before and therefore is presumed to hold hidden threats of defect and disaster.

There has, however, always been a much wider if less glamorous field of test flying which concerns itself with aerodynamic or mechanical experiments, control and structural investigations, power-plant studies, changes and modifications to existing planes, and endless checks of new components and equipment. Tests of that sort could be tedious and dull, or they could be just as dangerous, exciting, and fascinating as the trials of the most obstreperous prototype. Some of my most hectic moments in the air have developed when some apparently trivial experiment has set up a chain of disturbances that defied me to get the plane back on the ground in one piece.

The history of test flying is, by the nature of the job, a long record of occasions when the pilot found himself in extreme peril in the air, but stories of test-flying adventure are often difficult to relate with reasonable brevity, because they call for lengthy technical explanations of whatever the trouble was. However, the following somewhat random notes concerning a few experiences of my own may serve, along with various incidents related in other chapters, to give a sketchy picture of test-flying activities in the pioneering years of that profession.

PROTOTYPES. It seems probable that, in the course of my career in experimental flying, I tested more prototypes than any other pilot has had a chance to do. This is chiefly because, during the long years when "build it and fly it" was the only reliable system for testing anything, and when new models were much less expensive to develop than they are today, constructors were less hesitant to speculate on a new design if it showed prospects of some military, commercial, or experimental success, and consequently prototypes were far more numerous.

Some prototypes would get into trouble in the first attempt at takeoff and were wrecked before they ever got into the air; seaplanes with porpoising tendencies were notable offenders in that respect. Others proved to be a menace from the moment they left the ground, so that the pilot was faced with an often desperate struggle to return them to earth as soon as possible. Sometimes a radical new design, on which the pilot braced himself for all sorts of treacherous trickeries, would run through its trials in gentlemanly fashion, while some apparently simple and innocent-looking plane might turn out to be a vicious hellion.

Traditionally, the first flight of a prototype has attracted an assortment of inquisitive spectators who could become a serious distraction to the pilot if he couldn't keep them out of his hair. I learned about this the hard way in 1919, in the course of one of my first jobs as a civilian test pilot. I was preparing to make the first flight at Norwich on a twin-engine biplane that was particularly high-powered for its day, and everything was ready except for certain final engine check runs. But a Very Important Person had been brought along by the Managing Director to see the first flight, and he had a train to catch. I was taken aside by the Managing Director, who heavily impressed on me that we had already completed many successful engine runs, that these final runs did not seem to be essential for one short flight, and that it was most important for the Company that the VIP should see the plane fly. Unwisely I gave in.

An observer and I climbed aboard, and I taxied out for the takeoff. Just after I left the ground, the port engine quit suddenly and completely as the result of a simple fuel-flow defect that (as we discovered afterward) the final runs would have revealed. The plane swung sharply to the left before my untested rudder control could check it, the left wing dug into the ground, and the plane cartwheeled over. The nose broke off in one piece with me strapped into it, and I was pulled out with a few cuts and bruises. The observer suffered from a bad bang on the head and lost a few teeth. The company lost a fine airplane. I don't remember whether the Great Man caught his train.

That expensive lesson taught me to try to keep test flights away from people who wanted to be entertained, and on a later occasion it was as well that I did so. I was getting ready to make the first flight of a Dutch military prototype, the Koolhoven F.K.31, a single-engine two-seat fighter, at Rotterdam's Waalhaven airport. That afternoon, as we were making final adjustments and inspections, a string of limousines rolled onto the field and disgorged the company's Managing Director, the Secretary of the Aero Club, the Mayor of Rotterdam, and most of the City Fathers, with a sprinkling of uniformed officers—all come to see the first flight as though it were some civic unveiling ceremony.

I had had no warning of this visitation, and there was a gusty wind blowing which I did not like for a first flight. After I had suffered the usual rituals of introductions and handshaking, someone announced that I would fly in about half an hour. I didn't argue with anybody —I just walked around the back of the hangar, jumped into my car, and vanished for the day. From my hotel I telephoned the Chief Mechanic, Tom Delaart, to have the plane out at daybreak next morning, when the air was likely to be calm and the Mayor would probably still be in bed.

Next morning, test conditions were perfect, and nobody was around except the mechanics. After a few preliminary ground runs I took off. I had reached a couple of thousand feet when I felt an increasing amount of play in the rudder control. I knew that the pilot's foot control was connected to the rest of the rudder mechanism through a shaft to which it was attached by two horizontal pins that were supposed to be secured by nuts. We found out later that, in the confusion and haste generated by the Mayor's visit, a distracted inspector had overlooked the fact that the nuts had not yet been fixed in place. Now the engine vibrations were steadily shaking out the pins. First I felt the control loosen as one pin fell out; then the second pin fell out, and the rudder was on its own.

Now I had only the ailerons for a ragged and uncertain system of steering, complicated by variations of engine torque and slipstream swirl with every change of throttle setting—and all this on a plane that had never flown before. A parachute would have come in handy about then, but I didn't have one. I weaved and wobbled around the sky for I don't know how long—probably half an hour or so—until I learned to keep a reasonably steady course; and I couldn't have done that except for the fact that the aileron control was of the differential type, which reduced the necessity for rudder action. At last I gathered the courage to attempt a landing approach. I slithered down uncertainly between the masts of two ships in the harbor, and all I can say about my landing is that it could have been worse. One thing, however, I could say for certain: if I had made that flight in the gusty air of the previous day, the Mayor and his party would have been entertained by a spectacular crash.

(Incidentally, as a footnote to history: I eventually flew this plane in the Dutch Military Trials, and my official government observer on those flights was Dr. von Baumhauer, who was destined to die in 1943 with the great American test pilot Eddie Allen in the crash of the prototype Boeing B-29.)

Probably the most complicated prototype to be tested before the days of modern gadgetry was the Boulton & Paul "Bodmin" of about 1924, a large non-military plane of complex steel construction which carried its engines in an "engine room." It was the first serious experiment in increasing long-range reliability by making the engines and their accessories accessible to the engineer in flight. Its two Napier engines were mounted inside the fuselage; the forward engine drove two tractor propellers out in the wings through clutches, gears, and shafts, while the rear engine similarly drove two pushers. Between the engines there was sufficient room for an engineer to work so that, if necessary, he could declutch and stop one engine and attend to its ailments while the plane flew along on the other.

For the first flight of such an unusual airplane, with no military secrecy involved, I could find no means of keeping the newspaper people away. Before takeoff they plied me with innumerable cheerful questions of the kind that only newsmen know how to ask, such as whether I thought the long shafts might break and the broken pieces flail around to chew up the wings or pull the fuselage apart, and what chance I thought the engineer might have between the two engines in the event of a crash. It seemed almost a shame to disappoint them.

But I had to—the first flight, and a couple more, passed off with no trouble at all. The plane flew very well, and Martin, the engineer, successfully operated all his gears and gadgets.

So the newsmen took me into Norwich for lunch—and got themselves a little story after all. As we left the restaurant, a hurrying messenger boy on a bicycle ran hard into me, knocking me into the gutter, breaking my glasses and cutting my face. So the story of the "hazardous" Bodmin tests wound up in a set of solemn speculations as to whether a test pilot wasn't safer in the air than on the ground.

A prototype that had a peculiar test background was the three-fuselage Siddeley "Sinaia." I flew it in 1921 and it missed, by a few minutes, a chance to end my existence. It was a twin-engine bomber of some 90-foot span, with a main fuselage to carry the tail and two other fuselages, extending well aft of the engine nacelles, to carry gunners. The Sinaia test was one of those jobs on which the pilot can run a lot of risks from causes that are only indirectly technical.

For one thing, the plane was fitted with two liquid-cooled, 500-hp Siddeley "Tiger" engines, which had undergone only sketchy bench tests and no flight tests at all; an experimental plane with experimental engines can always be counted on for a packet of troubles and delays. Worse than that, however, was the fact that nobody was any longer interested in plane or engines; the whole project had been started during the war and had never been canceled, although there was now no prospect for a further contract. All anybody cared about was to complete this contract—which included test flights—with the least possible effort and expense. Under those conditions, nobody consciously neglected anything, but on the other hand nobody could work up much enthusiasm for making the changes or corrections that the pilot thought necessary for the completion of the flight tests.

I flew this unloved plane at Farnborough a number of times; all flights were short, because the two engines could never be persuaded to run simultaneously for any length of time. Then, one evening, after I had noticed some increasing slackness in the elevator control during the landing approach, I suggested a special inspection of the elevator cables. We never arrived at that inspection—for, while the plane was being wheeled into the hangar, the main fuselage buckled wearily in the middle. Some fuselage bracing wires had pulled adrift, which they would obviously have done in the air if the flight had lasted a few minutes longer. Nobody was interested in making repairs, and the Sinaia and its Tiger engines vanished into almost-forgotten history.

CONTROLS AND SUCH. I sometimes suspect that a good many pilots regard their elevators, ailerons, and rudders as rather straightforward hinged appendages that could be designed without too much strain on engineering brains. It is probable, however, that as many test-flying hours have gone into the development of controls as into all other airframe features put together. Control effects are highly complicated, chiefly because the action of any one control affects, or is affected by, the action of the other controls, as well as by the stability, balance, and dynamics of the plane itself. Control design has therefore never lent itself to a mathematical engineering approach, and some of the best airplane designers have occasionally come up with surprisingly poor control systems.

Consequently, flight testing has always been the only reliable way to arrive at a satisfactory control system.

At this point it is worth remembering that the fame of the Wright brothers rests heavily on their appreciation of the control problem. They never claimed to have invented an airplane; what they claimed was a fully *controllable* airplane, and their control patents turned out to be their chief asset.

I think that, at one time and another, I have run into every kind of trouble that controls could produce, some of them very nasty troubles indeed. I have handled controls that were too feeble to function or too heavy to move; or, by contrast, controls so powerful and sensitive that vicious overcontrol was a menace to the structure. I have met controls that were excellent at low speeds and dangerous at high speeds—or vice versa; overbalanced controls that tried to overpower the pilot; controls that reversed their intended action by warping the fixed surfaces to which they were attached; controls that became jammed by mechanical defects or aerodynamic loads; controls that fluttered wildly enough to break themselves or other parts of the structure; controls that behaved sedately most of the time but could think up special treacheries under special conditions.

Most such troubles came to us, of course, in days when we were having to devise new systems to enable the power of one man to cope with the control loads on ever-faster and -larger planes; that problem had eventually to be solved, as it is today, by the use of hydraulic or electric servomechanisms.

Apart from his three basic controls, the modern pilot is familiar with a number of auxiliary controls, such as flaps, slots, tabs, spoilers, and air brakes. These are hardly ever to be seen in pictures of earlier planes, and so it seems to be generally supposed that they are comparatively modern inventions gradually introduced in the course of progressive improvements in design. It may therefore come as news to the modern flying generation that these devices are of ancient vintage, conceived—and in some cases well developed—before anyone could find adequate employment for them.

The idea of wing flaps for reducing landing speeds was a very early one. I made what were probably the first organized test of wing flaps on the single-seat S.E.4a biplane at Farnborough in 1916. They were, in fact, very elaborate tests, because the flaps were not only pulled down (by a hand crank on the control stick) for slow landing, but could also be raised above normal position for reducing drag at high speed. Within the next couple of years, I had tested a variety of different flap schemes. Some of them were hand operated, with clumsy and slow-acting mechanisms; others were automatic, and they usually provided the pilot with disconcerting surprises by snapping into action at exactly the wrong moments.

But flaps aroused no general enthusiasm, for a simple reason that applied also to most other promising inventions of earlier times. These devices all called for extra structure, reinforcements, fittings, and mechanisms, which added too much weight to the frail wings of the day and thus practically canceled out the extra lift they produced. What little advantage still remained was not worth the cost and complications. So the flap idea went to sleep until the days when heavily built wings, heavily loaded, came into use; it would be some fifteen years before I flew in America with split flaps on the DC-2 and with Zap flaps on a Berliner-Joyce. By the time it was my daily job to handle the elaborate Fowler flaps and their complex variants on modern bombers and transports, a quarter of a century would have passed since my early flap experiments on the S.E.4a.

The invention of wing slots was one of the three or four most important advances in the history of aerodynamics. But it arrived far too early for its own benefit, and it was not until it could be applied to the heavily loaded wings of modern design that its immense advantages could be put to use. When I made the first flight tests of wing slots for Handley Page in 1921, on an experimental monoplane specially built for the purpose, the flights caused a sensation in the industry. The United States Army was so impressed that it promptly gave Handley Page an order for several fighters fitted with wing slots. Unfortunately I eventually wrecked the plane in an overambitious demonstration of slow flying, and such was the financial condition of the industry at the time that even the famous Handley Page was unable to raise the funds necessary for carrying on experiments with a device that many designers thought too complicated for practical use.

If there is one control device that appears to be completely modern it is the "spoiler." It obtains its effect by "spoiling" the airflow over the wing and killing the lift, and only in quite recent years has it come into familiar use as an air brake and as part of the lateral control on large, high-speed jet planes. Yet, in fact, I made the first spoiler test in 1920, even before the first wing slots appeared. The test was a one-shot affair, and it was so nearly disastrous that we did not dare, at that time, to repeat it. The story may be worth relating in detail.

This spoiler scheme was a part of the general research program of Geoffrey de Havilland, for whom I was then flying, and the idea was to provide a means of rapid descent without having to dive or increase speed. At various times I had tried out several kinds of air brakes, but none of them had been very effective. So now we were going to try a spoiler to kill the lift on the top wing of a biplane, leaving only the lower wing to support the plane, and thus cause rapid loss of altitude.

Our installation was made on a D.H.16, the four-passenger airline version of the D.H.4. A narrow slat was inlaid spanwise across most of the upper surface of the top wing, somewhere near the front spar. The slat could be raised to a vertical position by means of a small hand wheel in the cockpit; there was no provision for rapid action or quick release, as we supposed that whatever happened would happen gradually. We had completed and checked out the mechanical installation at Hendon, without yet having set up any test program, when we had a call from an airline at Croydon (for which I flew in my spare time) asking if they could borrow a D.H.16 for the early London–Paris run the next morning. There was no rush for the spoiler tests, so De Havilland told me I could take the airline run and bring the plane back to Hendon later. The mechanics loaded ballast into the passenger cabin, and I took off for Croydon, the other side of London.

I crossed London at ten thousand feet. The weather was beautifully clear and, as I approached Croydon with plenty of time to spare, my curiosity told me that I might as well give the spoiler a little tentative test before landing. To give myself plenty of room, I climbed another couple of thousand feet. Then I started to turn the spoiler control wheel, a little at a time. Nothing happened. I turned it some more— and then some more. Still nothing happened as far as I could observe. I wondered if the control had come adrift somewhere, and carefully I kept on turning. Suddenly everything happened.

Apparently there was some critical point at which the spoiler started to take effect, and now I had reached it. I had never imagined that a plane could shake so violently without falling apart. It pitched, heaved, rolled, shuddered, and vibrated as the turbulent airflow set up by the spoiler swirled around the wings and tail, battering everything it could get at. Instinctively I cut the engine, and my flying earthquake seemed to fall flat out of the sky. For a few moments I clung to the control stick with both hands, vainly trying to steady things up; but then I had to release one hand for turning the spoiler wheel back. I turned it as fast as my shaking grip would allow.

But now the eddies and vortexes around the upper wing, once generated, were having too much fun to give up. The wild bucking showed no signs of diminishing as I jerked away at the wheel, and it occurred to me with no amusement that the control had probably broken and that the spoiler was not intending to close down at all. The ground was coming up at a frightful rate, and I was down to about three thousand feet when peace returned almost as suddenly as it had departed.

As soon as I landed at Croydon I put inspectors on the plane to look for damage and then telephoned De Havilland. He was not surprised that violent turbulence should have occurred if things had been allowed to go far enough; what he had not expected was the sudden onset of the turbulence and its reluctance to die down. Obviously there was nothing simple about spoilers, and they were going to require a considerable experimental program; and at that time we could not see enough use for them to justify that expense. So further tests were postponed indefinitely.

It would be forty-three years before I again handled spoilers, this time as a practical, power-operated control on a jet transport.

ENGINES. When an engine gets up into the air it is not the same article that probably delivered suitable power on the factory test stand. The air that goes in and out of it and tries to cool it is changed in quality and quantity by speeds, altitudes, temperatures, humidities, and other factors, while vibrations, cowling, plumbing, ignition, and accessories contribute their own special effects. Today, highly complex and expensive test-stand installations are employed to try to reproduce flight conditions on the ground; but they never quite manage it, so that flight testing remains an indispensable process in engine development.

For years, however, flight testing was practically the whole job. For one thing, we didn't know enough for setting up anything like adequate ground installations, and anyway we couldn't afford such luxuries. It was much easier, cheaper, and quicker to put an engine straight into the air once it had undergone its routine runs on the brake. Test instruments were few and elementary, and test records depended largely on the pilot's reports, aided by whatever could be discovered by subsequent examination of the engine's insides. The science of fuel rating was in its feeble infancy, and many an engine won or lost on test according to its luck with the fuel it was getting.

At the outbreak of World War I, the British were in a bad way for engines. It was just as well that the French were on our side, because nearly all our so-called military planes were equipped with French air-cooled engines—mostly Gnome and Le Rhône rotaries of 50 and 80 hp; the Renault V-8, of 70 hp; and a few odd Anzanis and Clergets. When I went as military test pilot to the Royal Aircraft Factory, in the spring of 1916, the war had been going on for well over a year. Yet, apart from Rolls-Royce, which immediately established the outstanding position in the aircraft engine field it holds to this day, the British engineering industry had still accomplished practically nothing in that vital field.

A major, and eventually almost catastrophic, cause of this stagnation was the fact that the industry had been confused and discouraged by the government's action in permitting its own Royal Aircraft Factory to compete in the business of designing and building aircraft engines, a business for which The Factory had neither the experience nor the inspiration. Why this should ever have been allowed to happen is a secret that lies buried with long-dead politicians. At any rate, the fumblings of the Royal Aircraft Factory with its dreary "RAF" engine designs were a leading factor in keeping British engine procurement fouled up practically throughout the whole war.

The Factory's products were a series of 8- and 12-cylinder air-cooled vee engines, from 90 to 120 hp, based on sickly efforts to copy and improve upon the earlier Renaults. Nobody ever called them good engines, but, being of official design, they were built in thousands for the Royal Flying Corps for lack of any better British engine in their class. When higher power was needed, the demand for Rolls-Royces far exceeded possible supply; The Factory's efforts to produce a new liquid-cooled engine were farcical, and again we had to call on the French, with an order for a batch of 150-hp Hispano-Suiza engines, the first of which was sent to Farnborough for our tests.

At The Factory I was assigned a good proportion of the engine flight work. I tested the Rolls-Royces in numerous installations, tractor and pusher. The smooth and trouble-free running of those engines was a new experience in aviation. Accessories were a different story, and most of our R-R problems arose from inadequate ignition systems and endless experiments in locating and installing the radiators and plumbing for the liquid cooling systems.

I nearly lost our Hispano first time out. We installed it for test in a B.E.2e, which normally had 90 hp, so with 150 hp it went up like a rocket. At about seven thousand feet I leveled off. I don't know what they had done to the oil system, but as soon as I started to fly level, oil streamed out straight at the cockpit. Within a few seconds I was smothered with the hot and messy stuff. I went back into a climb, and the bombardment stopped, and I took off my oil-blinded goggles to see if I could spot the trouble. I couldn't, so I throttled back to go down. As soon as the nose dropped, the cascade of oil became worse than ever, and the best I could think of was to stop the propeller to cut off whatever pumping action might be doing the trick. I switched off and flew at a stall until the propeller stopped. The oil storm abated; but now the cockpit was saturated, my hands and feet were slipping on the controls, oil was pouring down my face and neck and blowing into my eyes from cowling and structure. Fortunately, I knew just about every square yard of Farnborough Common, so my dead-stick, half-blind landing was not as bad as it might have been. Anyway, my Hispano was intact, so a study could be made of its oil-scattering propensities.

However, it was with the RAF engines that I got as much experience as I shall ever want of what engines should not do. The standard 8-cylinder, 90-hp version was running reasonably well in numerous production planes, but, with its crude cylinder design, its cooling was always marginal in spite of the big air scoops that cowled it. Now wartime urgencies were demanding more and more power, and our experiments were largely devoted to hasty attempts at squeezing a little extra power out of the same engines, with lower fuel consumption and less drag for cooling. Such efforts usually wiped out the engine's already slim margin of reliability, and if there was any part of those engines that didn't let me down at one time or another I can't remember what it was. The 120-hp, 12-cylinder version had a similar history, and its enormous air scoops fouled up the design of every plane it went into.

At one time some wildly optimistic official decided to try to extract 105 hp out of the 90-hp engine in one fell swoop, merely by fitting it with cylinders of bigger bore. I collected the test job. Three test engines were built; two were installed in two B.E.2c's, the third being held in reserve. I took off with the first one, with Walter Barling as observer. (Walter in later years designed the U. S. Army's first giant airplane, the "Barling Bomber.") I climbed steadily, and at three thousand feet, about five minutes after takeoff, unscheduled noises started to come from ahead. I got set for trouble. I put my hand on the switch (which, incidentally, was at that time on the outside of the cockpit so that propeller-swinging mechanics could see for themselves whether the switch was on or off). At thirty-five hundred feet there was a shattering clatter as an overheated piston jammed in the top of a cylinder and the connecting rod tore free from the piston, flailing around and chewing things up generally. I promptly cut the switch as bits of metal and puffs of oily smoke whizzed past the cockpit. The propeller jarred to a stop. I went down to make a routine spot landing right outside the factory gates, where the crash truck and fire extinguishers usually waited.

There were some brief engineering discussions in which it was decided that nothing could be judged from this one test. So Barling and I climbed aboard the second B.E. and took off. The second flight was almost an exact duplicate of the first, and I delivered another wrecked engine at the gates.

Over lunch there was a big discussion; nobody came up with any bright ideas, and the less optimistic engineers were in favor of putting the third engine into the air and getting the whole thing over with. I didn't mind, and by late afternoon the third engine had been installed in place of the first one. This time Barling had had enough for the day, and he sent Lynam, the propeller expert, with me. By now I was finding the procedure monotonous; again the noises started at three thousand feet, and at thirty-five hundred feet the engine duly started to come apart. But by this time I had concluded that if they wanted a test to destruction they might as well have it. So I left the switch on for about fifteen seconds while two or three more cylinders and a section of crackcase disintegrated riotously; then Lynam, who was nearer the engine than I was, started waving distress signals, and the possibility of fire suddenly occurred to me. After we landed they took the engine to join the others in a post mortem, but I don't remember hearing any more about the 105-hp scheme. We had disposed of a new project in one day and much less than an hour's flying time.

It was with the 90-hp engine that I had my first fire in flight, although this was not the fault of the engine. It was just another instance of our lack of experience in requirements that are routine today, such as providing drainage for leaking fuel. In one of the tests for a new carburetor on a B.E.2c, I was to try a quick pickup with a stone-cold engine. I climbed to about ten thousand feet, switched off the engine, and stopped the propeller, so that the engine could cool off completely during the glide. At about fifteen hundred feet I dived to get the propeller turning for restarting the engine, and I put the switch on. Fortunately the propeller was slow in starting, and I was down to about three hundred feet before the engine got going. Just as fortunately I happened to be heading for the factory gates, a mile or two away. As the cold engine picked up, it promptly backfired, and a couple of seconds later wisps of black smoke began to come back from somewhere in the cowling. The wisps rapidly became clouds in which flickers of flame appeared. I did not know then, of course, that during the glide a stuck needle had been allowing fuel to dribble into the new, lower cowling that had been fitted to accommodate the carburetor and had no provision for drainage. But for the moment I was not interested in causes. I pulled back the rod that turned off the fuel, and put the plane into a steep sideslip to carry the increasing smoke and flames clear of the cockpit. But I had to straighten out for landing; and then the choking smoke and ominous heat closed around me. The wheels had hardly touched before I had my belt unfastened and was on my way overboard. I landed on my feet but couldn't get clear of the tail, which promptly knocked me down. The plane went rolling toward the factory gates, almost into the arms of Jim Winter and his gang, who had observed the smoke from the emergency post and had their fire extinguishers all ready. The whole affair occurred so fast that damage was relatively small. If I had been two or three hundred feet higher up, or over ground where I couldn't land, another mysterious and fatal fire, such as the one that had killed Edward Busk on another B.E.2c, would have had to go on the records.

Between wars, much of my engine testing consisted in searching for low-drag means of cooling the increasingly popular radial air-cooled engines. The clean simplicity of the Townend ring and the modern NACA cowling were not arrived at before we had spent years trying out a weird assortment of slitted and perforated engine enclosures and cylinder helmets for that purpose.

Arctic flying, on the other hand, offered more of the cooling stuff than was needed. Earlier on, most such flying was carried out with liquid-cooled engines, which could have their cooling systems filled, immediately before starting, with boiling water to get things generally warmed up. In the winter of 1924 I was sent to Kiruna, in Swedish Lapland, with a ski-equipped fighter to find out how air-cooled radials would behave in a steady forty degrees below zero. I don't remember just what difficulties we had expected, but I know that we hadn't thought of engine starting as a serious problem. Yet sometimes I spent half a day just trying to get the engine started, falling back at last on the crude process of holding red-hot bars of iron in the air intakes while the propeller was being swung. Unless I took off again almost immediately after a flight, we had to go through the whole clumsy business again. Otherwise we were in difficulty with congealed oil, frozen fittings, stiff controls, and a collection of other troubles which today present no problems but which we had to fix then as we went along. Our antics were usually watched by groups of gaily costumed little Laplanders, who must have wondered why we didn't give up and stick to something reliable, such as reindeer.

As time went by and knowledge accumulated, the more adventurous aspects of engine flight testing began to disappear. There would always be surprises, and occasionally disasters, when new engines or new installations went on trial in the air, but in most cases the safeguards of elaborate test equipment and instrumentation are able to ward off the threats of the unknown and the unexpected.

PROPELLERS. Considering the enormous loads inflicted on a fast-spinning propeller—centrifugal, gyroscopic, bending, twisting, and other loads—it is remarkable that propellers have given comparatively infrequent trouble in experimental flight history. On the other hand, when propeller failure does occur, those loads are liable to produce impressive violence. Occasionally, if rarely, a modern built-up propeller sheds a blade, in which case the departing blade behaves like a savage projectile, smashing everything, human and otherwise, in its path, while the now unbalanced forces in the rest of the propeller can rip an engine clean out of the plane.

The one-piece wooden propeller, which today is used mostly on small private planes, was for a long time all we had. It was a relatively frail device that, however, stood up well under normal conditions, but was easily damaged by anything unusual. Breakage or splitting could lead to intolerable vibration, or even to fatal accidents when flying chunks took out some vital part of the airplane structure. Pusher-type planes, which were in extensive use for many years, were particularly vulnerable to propeller damage from objects falling overboard; early in World War I we learned the hard way not to let spent cartridges drop back into propellers.

It was a disconcerting experience when a combat pilot shot off his own propeller. This was not infrequent in the early days of synchronizer gears for firing between the blades, and it happened twice to me. Our early gears were simple mechanical jobs operating through a series of cranks and levers in which a loose pin or a slight misadjustment could throw off the timing and send bullets through the blades instead of between them. It was not quite as catastrophic as one might expect. What happened (in my cases, anyway) was that both blades were perforated alternately in the same pattern, and when one let go the other followed almost simultaneously, leaving a couple of stubs mounted on the engine. Nothing was out of balance, and the thrust on the blades, plus centrifugal force, would throw the amputated pieces well clear of the plane. So the pilot's principal worries were to cut an overspeeding engine, dodge any neighboring enemy, and find some place to land.

Sometimes an entire propeller decided to go off on its own, usually because of a faulty hub attachment or a sheared shaft. The pilot's luck generally depended on where the propeller went after leaving, and things happened so fast that there wasn't much he could do about it. There might be a jolt of some kind as the propeller took off, and the engine would start to overspeed. Meanwhile the propeller, relieved of the plane's drag, would shoot on ahead, barely visible as the usual blurred disc; but as it quickly lost spinning momentum it also lost headway, and it would become clearly visible to the overtaking pilot in the form of a wavering and menacing obstruction drifting back into the plane, I relate elsewhere how, in a race with a low-wing monoplane, my propeller came off and struck the fuselage as I overtook it, doing no special damage. On another occasion, in level flight,

I lost a heavy four-blader that carried enough spinning momentum to go well ahead; it immediately started to drop of its own weight, passing closely but harmlessly below my landing gear. Other people have been less lucky, in cases in which the propeller has wandered back into a biplane structure, smashing the bracing and wrecking the wings.

I once had the strange experience of losing a propeller without knowing it. I was flying peacefully along on a Maurice Farman pusher when the Renault engine suddenly roared into overspeed. I cut the switch and found a field to land in. Ducking under the tail booms, I went to the rear of the nacelle to hunt for the trouble, and it must have been most of a minute before I realized that there was no propeller there. What had happened was that the shaft had sheared, but the propeller, being a pusher, had held itself more or less in place until it had slowed up to drop down neatly between the booms. We later found the propeller, with its hub and stub of sheared shaft, a mile or two away.

When pioneer efforts were made to produce metal propellers, British officialdom was still prejudiced against the use of aluminum, so the Leitner-Watts steel propeller, produced around 1923, received considerable encouragement. I did a good deal of test work on it. It had blades built up of formed and laminated sheet sections welded together. Most of the time it worked well, but unpredictable welding defects could produce devastating results. On two test occasions I had the tip of one blade open up like a tulip when, evidently, a small bit of internal welding metal was shot out by centrifugal force. On the second occasion vibration was so violent that I landed with the engine ready to drop out of its mounting.

Also about 1923, America had produced the Curtiss-Reed aluminum-alloy propeller. It was a one-piece job and, in its pioneer form, it looked like a strip of bent tin with a hub in the middle. But it was very efficient and practical and in 1927, after a British firm had secured a license for it, the Air Ministry gave some orders for its use. It was, however, still a good deal heavier than a corresponding wooden propeller, and that got me into trouble.

I had been testing the prototype Parnall "Pike," a two-seat, multi-purpose Navy biplane. It was ready for delivery when orders came through that it had first to be fitted with a Curtiss-Reed propeller. With this extra weight forward, it looked as if we were in for a major modification for rebalancing the plane, until somebody's slide rule decided that we could do the job rapidly by rerigging the tail to a bigger negative angle. All went well during takeoff, climb, and cruising flight. But when I throttled back to land I found that the highly negative tail, deprived of the downthrust of the slipstream, could not bring the nose up. So I could not level off for a landing unless I used too much power to land with. After a vain attempt to figure out a solution, I made two or three passes at the field to explore possibilities of coming in fast with the stick hard back and leveling off by opening the throttle. It seemed barely feasible, but it didn't work. The touchdown itself wasn't bad, but the tail was high and I was going so fast on about half throttle that I would soon be through the wall at the end of the field. I had to close the throttle, whereupon the plane promptly nosed over, shoving the engine back practically in my lap. I couldn't get out until the mechanics had jacked up the engine sufficiently to free my legs. I suffered my regular damage—a couple of skinned shins.

3. Parachutes and the Test Pilot

The test pilot and the parachute are today intimate friends, but it is surprising how long it took for that friendship to develop.

The average citizen is now conditioned to regard parachutes as the normal and natural refuge for those in peril in the air: when in doubt, just step out. Most people connected with aviation know that the parachute is a venerable device, well over a hundred years old, used from balloons before the Wright brothers were born. So today I am asked, more often than ever before, why airmen didn't use parachutes in World War I or in the years of highly dangerous test flying that followed it. When I reply that we didn't use them because we didn't have any, it doesn't seem to be much of an answer. Why didn't we have any?

When you consider the desperate helplessness of the aviator whose wing has broken, whose controls have failed, whose plane is on fire,

or whose engine has quit over impossible terrain, you would reasonably suppose that, from the earliest days of flying, there would have
been a wild rush to develop an airplane-borne parachute. There wasn't.
And you would suppose that the test pilot, whose job it was to face
those risks in new experiments, would have been in the forefront
of the rush. He wasn't. Here and there an earnest parachute inventor
exhausted his substance designing and testing a hopeful specimen,
and then went out of business for lack of general interest.

After many years and the steady persistence of a few inventors, the
world of aviation began to notice somewhat vaguely that practical
parachutes were actually available. But they were received with no
notable enthusiasm, even by their principal beneficiaries, such as the
military and test pilots. The record reveals that official compulsion was
the original means of raising parachutes to their rightful place of honor.

There were all sorts of reasons why parachutes took so long to get
the warm welcome they were entitled to.

Until well after World War I, the only sort of parachute gear that
most people were familiar with was hopeless for ordinary airplane installation. For balloons, the chutes usually hung down below or over
the side, all ready to open when the man jumped. And even then
they often declined to open; I twice saw observers jump from kite
balloons that had been hit by enemy fire, trailing unopened chutes
until they crashed into the ground. Parachute jumps from planes had
long been a stunt feature of early air shows. I assisted at one in May
1914, in which a man named Newell sat on a tiny seat rigged on the
landing gear of the Grahame-White "Air-bus" with the chute piled up
on his lap. Newell "jumped" when Frank Goodden, sitting on the
lower wing, shoved him overboard with his foot. The main point of
interest in the show was that the chute opened—we were all wondering
if it would. (During the war, walking along a road in France, I ran into
infantryman Newell, who was spending all his spare time trying to
promote official interest in airplane parachutes. Apparently he was
regarded as a harmless nut.)

In 1916, at the Royal Aircraft Factory, where we were supposed to
look into everything, the subject of parachutes came up from time to
time. With the materials then available, the whole gear was evidently
going to be bulky and heavy, even if we found ways to stow it

compactly. And, if chutes often failed to open when loosely attached, they seemed even less likely to work if they were closely folded. At best we would require larger and heavier seats, with fatter and heavier fuselages to accommodate them, and this would have made a bad dent in such little performance as we had. No pilot could be found who was willing to accept this continuous sacrifice of performance in order to carry a parachute that he might or might not need, and that might or might not work if he needed it. At the tail end of the war it was reported that a few German airmen had been seen to bail out of disabled planes with parachutes. This provoked no special enthusiasm; it was generally concluded that, if these airmen had had the extra performance they had lost through carrying chutes, they probably would not have needed to bail out.

After the war the outlook for parachutes showed slight signs of improvement. With larger planes, higher power and better performance, and with improved materials for chutes, the stowage problems looked less serious. Several inventors, notably Irvin in America and Calthrop in England, came up with relatively light and compact chute packs and demonstrated widely their willingness to open. Still there was no rush to use them. It was a problem in psychology. Airmen tended to prefer the devil they knew to the devil they did not know and, except in the most hopeless emergencies, they would still rather try to ride their disabled planes to the ground instead of stepping out into thin air with a chute that *might* open. And, since airmen were a race of natural optimists, they mostly chose to forget emergency possibilities and leave the cumbersome parachute packs to the pessimists.

For test pilots in particular, the odds in favor of the chute did not seem attractive. So many of their problems arose during takeoff and landing—too close to the ground for the parachute to have a chance of doing its stuff. Ejection seats, with their intricate mechanisms, would have been a laughable idea until quite recent years.

Besides, it often seemed that parachutes, even when they worked, could merely take the pilot out of one set of perils into another. Even a kindhearted chute that opened promptly and lowered the pilot dutifully to earth was liable to leave him with broken limbs or a cracked skull, especially over rough terrain or in high winds. And there were cases when an opened chute became entangled with the tail

f a falling plane, dragging the pilot to his death. It is now easy to
ee that most such troubles were due to lack of training. A parachute
vas deemed to have done its job once it opened—what happened
fter that was another subject, and there was just not enough experi-
nce available for anybody to train anybody in it. Even today, with
 few million jumps to its history, the parachute can be a dangerous
ontraption in the hands of the untrained.

Perhaps the first, and for a time the only, operation in which pilots
ame to treat parachutes as an absolute necessity was when, in the
niddle twenties, the United States instituted air-mail services that
alled for night flying in practically all weathers with single-engine
planes. With negligible prospects of finding a landing place at night,
vith an engine failure or when lost in foul weather before the days of
adio navigation, the pilots had to be ready to jump at any time. They
lid so often enough to convince most of the world that the parachute
ad really arrived. But their case was considered exceptional.

As a test pilot I should have been one of the first to make at least a
how of support for the regular use of parachutes in experimental work.
But that wasn't easy either. I had had extraordinary luck in getting out
f tight corners. I had been on fire three times in flight and suffered
rom sundry failures of structures and controls and other difficulties
rom which I had somehow extricated myself without a parachute. If,
before parachutes were made compulsory, I had turned up at my various
obs lugging a pack and harness and asking the engineers to make
oom for them, I would only have created the impression that I had
started to lack confidence in myself and the plane I was to fly. My
continued existence seemed to prove that chutes were really a theoretical blessing but a practical nuisance. And I admit I had some such idea
myself. Besides, I had a sort of sentiment that possession of a chute
might encourage me to quit in an emergency that I ought to work
myself out of.

I think it was around 1926 that the British Air Ministry issued orders
that parachutes must be carried—if they could possibly be fitted into the
plane—on all experimental flights with government-owned aircraft. An
immediate beneficiary of this order was "Tiny" Scholefield, the large-
sized test pilot for the Vickers Company. He was about to make some
spin tests on the French-designed Wibault fighter when the new orders

arrived. In utter disgust he trussed himself up into the harness and squirmed into the seat, from which all cushions had been removed. He started his spin very high up. The plane refused to come out of the spin, no matter what he did. The earth was coming up painfully close when Tiny, who had completely forgotten his unaccustomed parachute, suddenly remembered it, and he was now forced to decide that it was the lesser of two evils. He jumped, and then realized that he had no idea what to do except that he had to pull something. His two hundred-plus pounds were hurtling toward the ground while he pulled wildly at anything he could reach: rings, buckles, clips, and straps. Suddenly, as he later described it to me, he was jolted as though cracked at the end of a whip, and the chute delivered his hefty frame into the top of a tree. The only casualty was a farmer who had run over to the Wibault's wreckage, couldn't find a body in it, and then passed out cold when he looked around and saw what he was sure was the ghost of the aviator walking toward him. Ironically, Tiny lost his life in a bomber that crashed on a minor test for which parachutes had not been considered necessary.

When the parachute requirement first reached me I was about to make a series of dive tests on a Gloster fighter to investigate the newly encountered phenomenon of wing flutter. We had to order a parachute and, while waiting for delivery, I went ahead with the tests anyway. By diving from higher and higher altitudes, I had set up increasingly violent flutter, happily assuming that I could always level off before a serious structural failure occurred. The Air Ministry, now worried about this flutter business, sent an R.A.F. pilot named Junor, a highly competent test pilot, to check and review my current findings while I went off on another job. I met Junor at the railroad station and gave him a full personal account of events to supplement my written report. He was hauling along a chute and harness, which he said he had orders to wear. The next day I heard what happened. Perhaps Junor, encouraged by the prospective protection of his chute, had decided to give the flutter as prolonged a study as possible. Anyway, he held his dive to a low altitude. As he leveled off, the wing broke. Junor jumped, but his chute was still trying to open when he struck the ground. This shook me badly, because it left me wondering whether, if I had had a chute, I wouldn't have done the same thing.

Outside of military circles, an offhand attitude toward parachutes continued to exist practically up to World War II. Military pilots were little bothered; they were compelled from the start to take parachutes along, and so became used to the discomfort of lugging them around and the nuisance of fitting them on and arranging the seat to suit them. Later, of course, with planes that needed mile-long runways for safe landings, it would not occur to a military pilot to fly without a chute. However, civilian test pilots, including myself, usually found excuses for leaving them behind unless the forthcoming test looked particularly risky or doubtful. Even during World War II, when I was testing bombers with a crew of five or six, we would conscientiously fit our individual chutes—if someone in authority happened to be around. But, as often as not, we just took the correct number of chutes and heaved them into a corner of the flight deck, intending vaguely to find time to fit and adjust them in case we should happen to need them.

Inevitably there were people who went to the opposite extreme, usually people who knew nothing about parachutes and imagined that you put them on like putting on a hat. During the late thirties, when airline crashes began to involve what then looked like a large number of passengers, there were sporadic public demands that all passengers should be fitted with chutes. Someone even made tests with an enormous chute that could carry a whole airplane, and then demanded that all airlines should be so fitted. Usually such people were very hard to argue with: they invariably quoted the case of the Titanic and declared that "the sanctity of human life should outweigh all other considerations," etc. One may still run into them occasionally.

The history of the parachute is about the same as that of most safety devices: nobody wants to be bothered with them until danger arises, and then it may be too late. Test pilots, as a race, are not naturally inclined to worry much about their personal safety, so it is not hard to understand why for so long they failed to become enthused about a safety device that offered considerable inconvenience and did not guarantee results.

CHAPTER XV

THE HERALD OF THE HELICOPTER

For more than a year, I was the world's only frequent and regular pilot of rotary-wing aircraft. This was the result of my long association with Juan de la Cierva, the brilliant and temperamental inventor of the Autogiro, which was the true precursor of the modern helicopter.

There are people in the helicopter business today who have forgotten, or never knew, that it was the invention of the Autogiro that swept away, with immense ingenuity, the fundamental problems that had beset the years-long attempt to devise a workable helicopter.

Most of the long line of helicopter experimenters had started with the idea that the main problem was to devise some means of producing vertical lift, but they soon discovered that this was just about the least of their difficulties. Before Cierva, nobody had made any practical progress in solving the far more serious control problems with rotating wings: the ferocious and unruly gyroscopic forces in the whirling rotors, the upsetting loads of advancing and retreating blades in forward flight, and the prospects of falling like a brick if the power gave out. The Autogiro overcame those formidable obstacles, and by putting rotary wings into easy and familiar flight, it opened wide the road to helicopter development.

I know that Cierva himself could have, and should have, devised a practical helicopter years before anyone else. Why didn't he? Why did he cling tenaciously to the Autogiro, which although it held the world's attention for a few years, gradually lost prestige and then sank into near oblivion? The answers lie in the complex character of a brilliant man whose genius was fettered with the pride of an over-sensitive nature. It is a strange and tragic story, with which, more than most people, I was closely involved.

In the summer of 1925 I was at Cuatro Vientos military airfield, near Madrid, where I had delivered a fighter plane from England. The Spanish officers, who well knew my reputation for trying out new and strange flying devices, told me that they had a real freak to show me. They opened the doors of a hangar, and I saw an Avro fuselage, with engine and propeller in front, tailplane and rudder behind. It had no wings, but on top was a mast supporting four large blades, hinged so that they could move up and down, apparently unconnected with the engine. They told me that it had actually made short flights; the blades apparently spun around on their own and lifted the thing into the air. It was, they said, the invention of an eccentric character named Juan de la Cierva. I gave it a quick look-over. I couldn't see how it would work; for one thing, it seemed obvious that the angle of the blades would make the rotor turn the wrong way for flight. The officers couldn't explain it. Perhaps there was some essential gadget I couldn't see or that someone had taken out. Well, anyway, lots of funny and useless things had been coaxed into the air at one time and another—this was probably just another one! An army car drove me to the station for my train to Paris.

In London a few weeks later I had a phone call that Señor de la Cierva would like to have a talk with me. At his hotel the next day, after the usual preliminary chit-chat, we settled down to a discussion. Cierva's English and my Spanish didn't meet at any useful point, but we got along fine in French. (He later learned to speak excellent English.)

I found Cierva (he disliked the omission of the "de la" from his name, but he had to get used to popular usage) to be a cultured, charming, and serious gentleman of about my own age. He came, I discovered, from a fine Spanish family whose considerable wealth had financed his numerous airplane experiments. Before getting onto the subject of design details, he told me that the British Air Ministry had shown an interest in his machine and had invited him to give a series of demonstrations, for which, if they proved his claims, he would be paid a substantial sum and receive an order for two aircraft. They had suggested my name to him and he wanted me to fly the machine in the tests.

It would, he said, be a simple and straightforward job; his Spanish pilots had already flown the machine without difficulty. After a while, however, he admitted that his pilots had made only elementary straight flights at low altitude; they had neither the confidence nor the experience for undertaking the risks of the elaborate maneuvers, fully stalled flight, vertical drops, and other abnormal flying called for by the official tests; nor were they qualified for making adequate studies and reports on flight behavior.

Having cleared the decks on that subject, we got down to technicalities. For two or three hours he explained to me the aerodynamic principles of his invention, how he had arrived at them, and the design methods by which he had carried them out. Very soon I knew that this was no crazy inventor, but an imaginative engineer who had braved repeated disappointment and employed persistent ingenuity in making the most important breakthrough in aerial locomotion since the days of the Wright brothers. I was fascinated.

The machine was assembled at Farnborough, and I went to work on it first with a few short hops and very soon with longer flights in which I could study the unique qualities and feel of this strange craft. Not the least of my problems was to become accustomed to moving through the air with no wings, supported only by the foggy disk of the blades rotating over my head.

The rotor was turned only by its passage through the air, which was the basic property of the craft that the scientists hadn't thought of before and that some of them took a long while to grasp. But before I could take off, the blades had to be given some sort of initial rotation; this we provided by wrapping a rope around four knobs, one on each blade, and then putting a gang of men to haul on the rope. With this comical procedure the rotor was turned up to less than half its normal flying revolutions; I obtained the remaining revolutions in a wobbling and staggering run over the ground before the machine could be airborne. But the primitive nature of the start was forgotten when, once in the air, the machine provided a tremendous impression of something totally new in aviation.

My first few landings, cautiously attempted, involved a short run after touchdown; the next few took only a length or two of the machine, and at last I was able to touch down with practically no run at all—and the landing gear had no brakes. By nightfall of the first day I felt I had the hang of the job, at least so that I could start to face the more exacting requirements of the official tests.

Within a day or two the sensational story had spread through the flying world of this new phenomenon of flying with rotary wings. The next time I flew, there was a crowd of spectators: generals, air marshals, including the great "Boom" Trenchard, admirals, scientists, engineers, pilots, politicians, newspapermen, and the plain curious, who swarmed around Cierva and me asking a million questions. Cierva's face beamed with delight in the midst of those who could find means of communicating with him; I had to handle the rest. One of the world's foremost aerodynamicists, Leonard Bairstow, took me by the shoulder. "I told you, Frank," he said, "that the thing couldn't fly. I still don't believe it. What have you got up your sleeve?"

Perhaps the most curious demand came from the Patent Office. Cierva's description of his claims, they said, were not sufficiently convincing; it seemed to them (as it had once seemed to me and lots of others) that the blades would evidently rotate the wrong way for flight, like a propeller going backward. They asked for a special demonstration flight. They got it. Cierva got his British patents.

Toward the end of October 1925 we were ready for the government tests. Observation instruments were set up on the ground, and the machine was equipped with such recording instruments as were then available. The tests were in four parts. The first three of these, consisting of all sorts of maneuvers and landings, I waltzed through in more or less routine fashion; nothing exciting happened, but already I was storing up a lot of information for future use. The fourth test was another proposition altogether: it called for a power-off descent, as nearly vertical as possible, from (if I remember correctly) about fifteen hundred feet.

Cierva was gaily confident about the whole thing. Nothing to it! All I had to do was to pull the machine up to a complete stall and hold it there while the rotating wings lowered me like a feather to the ground. I had other thoughts. With no forward speed my air controls would be almost or entirely useless. With my engine and propeller stopped and no way of restarting them, I would have no means whatever of recovering from any trouble; in fact, I would have less control than I would have with an ordinary parachute. How fast would I drop? And with no forward speed over a prolonged period, would the blades maintain enough speed of rotation? Preliminary tests at altitude would not help me much; there were then no means of reading vertical speed, and Cierva admitted that his own calculations were based on a lot of assumptions. I was entitled to suspect that they were optimistic.

We could, of course, try the whole thing out unofficially before making the official tests. But, if that were to wreck the machine, the tests would remain indefinitely uncompleted. On the other hand, if a crash occurred in the course of official tests and it were not too bad a crash, we might scrape by with sufficiently acceptable results. Those were days when a test pilot had to make up his mind how much risk the results might be worth; there were no means of protecting him with large expenditures in money, time, or research. I decided to take a chance, and to make my first long drop as an official test.

We put weights in the tail, to bring back the center of gravity and thus inhibit forward speed. I climbed up to my altitude, with something to spare for getting set. I shut off the fuel to the Le Rhône engine and watched the propeller slow and stop. With the little forward speed I had left, I used the elevator to pull up the nose. I held it there until the airspeed indicator flickered to zero and I could feel the craft sinking straight down. The only sound was the swishing of the rotor blades as they spun overhead. My eyes never for long left the rotor tachometer; the revolutions were staying comfortingly steady. I glanced over the side; the distant ground seemed to be coming up at a reasonable rate. So far, so good; I was beginning to enjoy myself.

I was a couple of hundred feet up when I suddenly observed that all was not well. Now, with a closer view of the ground, I realized that it was coming up at me with a speed that was already much too fast and seemed to be increasing. It was obvious that the machine was not going to be able to take it, and I wondered where that would leave me. But there was nothing I could do about it—and anyway I hadn't long to wait for the answers. My safety belt was already pulled up tight; from previous experience of crashes, I relaxed for the shock.

The machine hit squarely flat, with geometric precision. The landing gear crumpled like a set of matchsticks, the bottom longerons and struts caved in, assorted fittings and instruments dropped off; my seat collapsed and I was jarred as though the world's biggest elephant had given me a swift kick in the behind. But the extensive breakages had absorbed much of the shock, and the broken pieces held the body upright while the rotor continued to revolve lazily overhead. I stepped out stiffly over the edge of the cockpit. The gleeful crowd of watchers came rushing up and dusted me off.

The government observers were satisfied. They agreed that it had been an abnormal test to which no ordinary landing gear could have been expected to stand up. The whole series of tests was declared successful.

That night the elated Cierva threw a big dinner party at which he presented me with a costly gold cigarette case inscribed, ". . . recuerdo de unos experimentos que nos han hecho amigos para siempre."

For a while, Cierva lived in a blaze of glory. Scientific and engineering groups showered compliments and awards on him, and the aviation industry crowded around for design information. But there was much to be done. The present machine was admittedly crudely experimental; structural and performance data were scanty, and there had to be a period of planning and research. Money had to be raised for all this. Reasonable and sometimes critical questions had to be answered, and conflicting opinions had to be reconciled. Cierva had to step out of the glittering heaven of the brilliant inventor and settle down to hard, mundane facts.

He had asked me to join him in further development work, and he accepted my suggestion that facilities for progress would be much better in England than in Spain. I introduced him to Scottish friends of mine who were powerful in aviation engineering circles; they, in turn, brought in influential banking interests for the purpose of forming an Autogiro company.

But now, confronted by problems of conflict in design, engineering, and finance, a new Cierva gradually began to emerge. Always a gentleman of quiet charm, he yet started to reveal a highly sensitive hidalgo pride, of a kind that I had supposed existed only in romantic novels of Old Spain. It was a pride so intense that any sort of adverse comments or criticisms seemed to bring him physical pain, and it was to influence the whole Autogiro story.

Soon we faced innumerable engineering discussions with inquiring designers, and inevitably these produced difficult questions and critical comments—Cierva too often left an impression of evading problematic issues, for his attitude was that of a man who sincerely felt that he alone fully understood the new principles that he alone had discovered, and that therefore his word should be accepted without question on all points. To many, it was a discouraging attitude; as a French designer put it to me later: "I can discuss problems with an engineer, but I can't argue with a High Priest."

The financial situation brought me into the first serious contact with Cierva's extreme sensitivity. I had taken no part in his discussions with the banking people, but I knew that, in spite of the plaudits of the crowds, they were likely to take the unemotional view that we had a long way to go on the road to financial success. I met Cierva one evening after one of those discussions. He was glum and miserable, and I soon discovered that his pride was badly hurt by the financial terms he had been asked to accept. So I told him that, if he felt that way, he needn't bother with the banking people; I could show him how to make, quickly and easily, all the money he would need to put him far along his road.

I had already talked this plan over with my old friend Major Jack Savage, who had introduced skywriting into the United States. Jack had made a huge amount of money out of the advertising exploitation of his spectacular invention, and I believe it is true that he signed a million-dollar contract the same day he gave his first demonstration in America. I pointed out to Cierva the vast possibilities of a similar project in the United States with an aircraft as sensationally novel as the Autogiro. A couple of duplicates of his existing plane (never mind improvements for the moment) would be adequate for the job; they could be turned out in a few weeks, and they would cost little. Besides the revenue that would come from exhibitions and advertising, the shows would stir up the interest of the aviation industry at no extra operating cost. Savage was all ready to lend his experience and contacts to put the show on the road.

Juan looked at me as if I had slapped his face. He sat down, banged his hands between his knees, a habit he had when agitated, and tears came into his eyes. Could I conceivably be suggesting, he asked, that he, Don Juan de la Cierva y Codorniu should become a showman, trying to support the offpring of his brain and vision with the tawdry dollars of gaping American yokels? He was too genuinely shocked for me ever to raise the subject again.

So the bankers formed the Cierva Autogiro Company. I agreed to act as technical consultant and pilot for tests and demonstrations.

It seemed that the whole world wanted to make use of this fascinating and wonderful invention. From every country came requests or delegates asking for demonstrations, information, and design data. From America came Harry Guggenheim and Admiral Cohn. And the hard facts of the situation began to be more obvious: We really had little to tell them or give them. The initial demonstrations of the Autogiro had been too successful for its own immediate good. They had drawn universal attention to an exciting new principle of flight before enough data existed for its practical application to design. Cierva himself, dazzled by the bright lights that were focused on him, seemed unwilling to admit that there were any serious problems that he could not immediately cope with. The name and person of Cierva were as yet so much the essence of the business that he was trying to function as a one-man band. He delighted to have it that way but, in fact, there were too many instruments for one man to play.

Almost immediately Cierva commenced to center his interests in theoretical improvements. As an expert mathematician and aerodynamicist—and at that time no pilot—he could be very impressive in calculations of new rotor-blade sections and plan forms, blade-angle studies, problems of disk loadings and solidities, and new theories of controls. But my argument was that rotor refinements, important as they would eventually be, should wait until we had made the present machine more practical as a medium for tests and demonstrations. Everyone now knew that the Autogiro was wonderful, but the question was arising: Is it practical? The rope-hauled starting system was beginning to be a comedy, and the landing gear was so unsuitable that I was always on the verge of cracking up unless I nursed the machine with extreme care on the ground. Our first major foreign demonstration helped to prove that point.

At Villacoublay airport, outside Paris, a demonstration was arranged for officials of the French Air Ministry and members of the Cabinet, headed by Pierre Etienne Flandin, as well as the Spanish ambassador and the Belgian and Italian military attachés. The gusty and showery weather of January 27, 1926, was no excuse for delaying the show; Cierva had been telling everybody that the Autogiro was untroubled by gusts because they were absorbed by the hinging of the blades—which was quite true in flight, but not in ground maneuvering. I took off, hoping that, as usual, I would have enough luck to scrape out of the troubles that threatened. The top-hatted functionaries and the newsreel cameramen stood out in the drizzle on the concrete apron in front of the hangar and watched the flight with suitable amazement. But I could tell, from my drift on turns, that the wind was rapidly increasing, and when the trees on the distant side of the field started to wave violently, I knew a squall was coming up. I had to try to get down before it hit.

I landed precisely, with not an inch of run, on the prearranged spot just outside the apron, right in front of the guests and the cameras. Now I was helpless. As soon as the tail went down—and I had no means of preventing that—the rotor presented an angle to the increasing wind, which kept it whizzing round at almost full speed. In effect, the aircraft had landed but the rotor was still flying. For a few seconds the wheels dithered up and down, and then a gust picked up the whole machine, lifted it two or three feet, and turned it clear over to the left. I ducked deep into the cockpit, listening to the crackle and crunch of the splintering blades as they thrashed wildly into the muddy ground. When the noise subsided I unfastened my belt—and fell out of the half-inverted cockpit into a large puddle of mud.

That afternoon I saw the newsreel pictures, and they were worth the whole trip. Like a giant golfer gone mad, the whirling blades were shown smashing into the ground, distributing huge divots of wet earth and mud all over our VIPs. Naturally official conclusions were mixed; there were some who saw an impressive new principle of flight that needed improvement, but there were others who saw only a freak that could fly with regular prospects of crashing. If we had fitted a wider landing gear, with wheels out in front to allow the tail to remain high, we could have avoided such a crash. Cierva reluctantly came around to that idea, but he took his time about it.

On another occasion, this time in uniform as a reserve officer of the Royal Air Force, I had to give a demonstration before King George, Queen Mary, and an enormous crowd at the 1926 Hendon R.A.F. Pageant. The previous afternoon I made a test flight to see that things were all in order. The flight was normal and nothing seemed to be wrong when I landed. I didn't know that during the flight a fitting on top of the mast that held the check wires supporting the blades when at rest, had come adrift. I was halfway out of the cockpit, with the rotor idling overhead, when suddenly there was a series of loud crashing noises, the whole craft shook, splinters flew, and everything seemed to be coming apart. Something hit me on the back of the head and knocked me to the ground. By the time I got to my feet I could see what had happened: having now no ground support, the blades slowly sank as the rotor speed died down, until at last they were low enough to chew themselves up against the propeller in front and the tail behind. Things were pretty well wrecked; but we had a spare set of blades and enough other parts so that, by working all night, we were able to give Their Majesties and the vast throng their first view of a rotary-wing aircraft in full flight. The King, greatly impressed by this strange craft, personally congratulated me, but added what was probably the royal equivalent of "There must be an easier way to earn a living."

In our wide confusion of plans, a problem of first urgency was the initial spinning of the rotor. I discovered, with surprise, that Cierva was curiously reluctant to investigate the mechanical methods that seemed the obvious way to tackle the job. He wanted to discover some aerodynamic, non-mechanical solution such as deflecting the slipstream or whatever else we could think up in that line. I pointed out that our eventual goal, the helicopter, would need plenty of mechanical gear, and we might as well start on that sort of thing now. Then I found that a subtle change had come over Cierva's thinking which, I believe, altered the whole course of the project and eventually led it into a dead end.

From the very earliest discussions between Cierva and myself, we seemed to take it for granted that the ultimate aim of rotary wings was the helicopter. The Autogiro, we agreed, would hold the field while the special problems of helicopters were gradually surmounted. We even worked out a tentative mechanism (which, I think, has never yet been tried) for counteracting rotor torque. Cierva now commenced to reverse his attitude entirely: the helicopter, he claimed, would never be a practical aircraft because of the immense complications of its power drives and controls. Besides, the helicopter would never be necessary, because the Autogiro would always be able to do anything really useful that the helicopter could do, and much more simply, cheaply, and efficiently. This concept grew upon him, and in 1931 he expressed it clearly in his book, "Wings of Tomorrow," which tells his story of Autogiro development and is still to be found in many aeronautical libraries. He even reached the state of mind at which his personal pride was involved: the advocate of the helicopter now became the enemy of the Autogiro.

It took me some time to figure out Cierva's new attitude, but eventually I came to some conclusions: Cierva's flair was for the elegance of mathematics and the romance of aerodynamics. He cared little for mechanical engineering; as far as he was concerned, that was a rather crude relative of the plumbing business. The Autogiro was his, and his alone, and he could not bear to contemplate submerging its beautiful simplicity in a welter of shafts, clutches, and gears—which would not be his.

It was Cierva's reluctance to face mechanical problems that eventually led to the parting of our ways and to the nastiest crash I ever had—and, incidentally, to the only major and lasting change in basic rotor design on the Autogiro, one which has carried on into the modern helicopter.

It all started during preparations for the demonstration I gave at the Tempelhof airfield, in Berlin, in September 1926. After a check flight on the newly assembled machine, I happened to notice a misalignment between two opposite blades. Examination showed that the steel spars of all four blades were bent at the root. Cierva looked at them, and declared flatly that this could not possibly have been caused in flight by aerodynamic loads; it must have been done when the blades were crated in England. I ventured to disagree, and this revived an old sore point of some of our discussions: the horizontal hinges of the blades permitted them to flap up and down, but there was no vertical hinge to allow for fore-and-aft movement under drag loads. I had contended that the spars could conceivably suffer from such loads. This was definitely invading Cierva's special province, and he didn't like it. He stated that, first of all, such loads were too small to matter and that, anyway, they were taken care of by weighted cables that ran all around the rotor, from the middle of one blade to the next one, and were supposed to balance up drag loads all around.

Simple consideration, as others had pointed out, showed that this bootstrap arrangement could have no useful effect, and I had long ago suggested that a vertical additional hinge could relieve drag loads and, at worst, do no harm. Again Cierva's pride was at stake: surely he would have met such a problem if it existed!

Now all this argument was coming up again. There was a spare set of blades on the spot. We examined them, there was no bend in them, and I suggested that they now be installed for me to run another test flight. Cierva testily agreed. I flew for about ten minutes. Again the spars were found to be bent, but now I noticed something new: they were bent *forward*. This meant that the spars could be undergoing continual reversal of loads, forward under driving loads and backward under drag. Cierva was not a good actor and he was clearly flabbergasted. It was obviously something he had never thought of and, just as obviously, he was not going to admit it. He refused to discuss it and told me I could abandon the demonstration if I liked. I figured that the blades would last out long enough for this show, whatever might happen to them later. So I went on with the flights before ex-Crown Prince Wilhelm and a crowd estimated at two hundred thousand people; President Hindenburg had been expected to attend but was unwell. As usual, there was enormous public enthusiasm.

Back in England, my confidence in future tests was badly shaken. There were now clear-cut prospects of blade failure sooner or later. Possibilities of experimental trouble did not bother me; what I was worried about was Cierva's refusal to face these possibilities. I induced a couple of well-known design engineers, R. J. Parrott of Avro and Harold Bolas of Parnall, to take up with him the idea of a vertical hinge; as with me, he declined to discuss it. At that period there was no X-ray

equipment with which we might study the progressive effects of repeated reversals of bending on the spars. So I found excuses for stalling
off tests, and did as little flying as I could, hoping Cierva would see the
red light. At last the inevitable happened.

One day in February 1927, at Hamble, near Southampton, I took
the C.6c model up on test. By now I was tensely suspicious of the
slightest unusual noise or vibration in the rotor. At about a thousand feet I heard a curious groaning noise coming from overhead; I
decided to go down. I shut off the engine and started the usual descent. The noise immediately got worse and things started to shake.
I had to make a snap judgment, which was that, whatever the trouble,
it was increased by the greater angle of attack of the rotor. So I decided to decrease that angle by opening up the engine and "flying"
down in a partial dive. For a few moments I seemed to have guessed
right; the noise and shaking diminished. But I had no doubt now
that the rotor was going to break; it was just a question of whether I
could get back on the ground before it did. There was a long line of
trees ahead, and I followed it so that perhaps I might have something
relatively soft to fall into. I was still at about two hundred feet and
had passed beyond the trees when a blade let go with a loud bang.

For the next ten or fifteen seconds I lived through a long waking
nightmare. With my eyes wide open, I could see nothing but a white
blur, for the remaining three blades, whirling wildly out of balance,
shook my head around the cockpit as a terrier shakes a rat in its teeth
and my eyeballs were rattling in their sockets. For a fraction of a
second I glimpsed a railroad line below me, as one might see a single
frame in an otherwise blank motion-picture film. Then came a second
jolt, with another loud bang. For a moment I thought I had struck,
but it was only a second blade coming off, about ten feet from the
ground. If that had happened ten feet higher, I would certainly have
been killed. As it was, the surviving two blades, ninety degrees apart,
swung me over to dive the last few feet into the railroad line.

My safety belt snapped loose and I was flung out of the cockpit
into the ruins, striking my head on the rotor support as I went. At the
hospital they found that I had escaped rather cheaply, with shock,
concussion, and two or three broken ribs.

Later, when Cierva visited me in the hospital, he was obviously as badly shaken spiritually as I was physically. He assured me earnestly that there would be constructive reforms in his technical procedures and, to start with, vertical hinges would be added to the designs of the blade roots. Thereafter the vertical hinge was established as an integral feature of the flapping-blade installations. It still is.

However, like so many emotional reform movements, this one didn't last. When the shock of this alarming crash had worn off, Cierva let it be known that he still didn't think that the vertical hinge was really necessary; he implied that its main purpose was to pacify me. In subsequent discussions on various aspects of developments, I had to conclude that matters were going to proceed exactly as before. So Juan and I ended our association. I couldn't take any more.

Cierva, regrettably, did not accept my withdrawal very graciously, and he apparently decided that my picture should be turned to the wall. My work with him was a matter of official and international record, yet my name occurs only once in his book: a passing mention of "the British pilot, F. Courtney," who demonstrated the machine in Berlin. His account of the spectacular crash at Hamble, witnessed by a dozen or more people and dramatically illustrated in the press, was a rather wide detour of the facts. The book states: "In one of the earlier experimental models too much structural strength was built into the rotor blades. And this was the only Autogiro that ever broke a rotor blade in flight. Incidentally, the pilot was able to land the ship without serious injury to himself."

Yet, basically, his was a simple and sincere nature; he was just overwhelmed with a pride that could not admit an error or tolerate a criticism and which, as I think, lost him the high place in history that he might have reached.

For many years, Autogiro developments fumbled along. Mechanical drives for starting the rotor were adopted, and these eventually evolved into a device that enabled the machine to "jump" directly off the ground. A number of countries, notably the U.S.A. took up licenses and produced various models, and several attempts were made to employ Autogiros in military and commercial activities; but they never established themselves for any extensive or sustained operations. Finally, with the coming of Igor Sikorsky's helicopter, which admittedly owed a great debt to Cierva, the Autogiro faded into relative insignificance.

My last meeting with Cierva was a strange trick of fate. In 1936 I was on a visit to England from America, where I was then living, and on the evening of December 8, I ran into Juan in the "Hungaria" restaurant in London. I hadn't seen him for some nine years. He seemed dispirited and sad. We had a long talk over a couple of drinks, rehashing without rancor the days of the past. We parted friends again. And, after all, it was to be "para siempre"—for the next morning he was killed in the crash of a Dutch airliner at Croydon. He had devoted his life to the creation of an aircraft that could not stall, and he lost it in a plane that stalled on the takeoff.

CHAPTER XVI

THE AIRLINE STORY

1. The First Ten Years

Military aviation always had been a business prospect, however modest; once airplanes had flown it was pretty certain that, if they couldn't do much else, they could at least be employed in some fashion for observation, message carrying, signaling, or some other such auxiliary service to the soldiery. The Wright brothers knew this very well; they aimed all their sales efforts at the military, and they made their first sale to the U. S. Army five years after their first flight.

There was no such encouraging outlook for commercial aviation. To hope for commercial success, airplanes would have to sell services for cash to the general public, and for nearly twenty years after the Wrights first flew, it seemed that aviation had nothing much to sell to a public that had long been conditioned to regard airplanes only as dangerous and unreliable vehicles for carrying very small loads. When the Kaiser's war ended in 1918, the whole world knew airplanes as weapons, but there were no military air transports in that war, and it left the public with no evidence that airplanes could usefully carry anything except expendable military hardware.

The airline story, therefore, is that of the incredibly rapid rise of commercial flying from rags to riches in spite of formidable relays of obstacles—technical, political, and economic—that seemed specially devised to prevent any progress at all. Moreover, the story has strange twists, because the United States, which was always better adapted to airline development than any other country on earth, actually stayed out of the picture for most of ten years, a factor that the modern generation has not had much reason to remember. I shall get back to that subject further along, but meanwhile I shall sketch the birth of scheduled airlines and the first ten years of their growth, which were events that occurred in Europe.

As Europe tried to pull itself together after World War I, it seemed to a few of aviation's old-timers that the time was now ripe for air travel to be presented to a world that, they fondly believed, must be impatiently awaiting it. In earlier days a few trivial and short-lived operations had occasionally been conducted in most countries for carrying bits of fancy mail or a couple of adventurous passengers, with much uncertainty, for short distances; such ventures, unblessed by the licensing of aircraft or crews, were rather exhibition flights than serious commercial undertakings.

Now, however, committees of the League of Nations were convened to draw up agreements for international air travel, including provisions for supervising and certificating planes and pilots. Then, in a wave of optimism that refused to be damped by the towering obstacles in sight, British and French companies initiated scheduled passenger air services between London and Paris as soon as agreements were concluded. They were strictly commercial services, unconnected with any military or government operations.

And so the history of scheduled airline flying commenced on August 25, 1919, when pilot Bill Lawford, flying a two-passenger D.H.4A of "Aircraft Transport & Travel," took off from Hounslow, outside London, to make the round trip between London and Paris. The French started their corresponding service a couple of days later. Apart from a few disruptions caused by various reorganizations and changes of names, those services have been running continuously ever since.

I got into the act myself two or three weeks later, when, having completed the tests on De Havilland's new four-passenger D.H.16, I took it into passenger service over the line. For several years I continued to act as reserve and experimental pilot on the original routes, and on other routes as they opened up.

It didn't take long to discover that our bubbling optimism was sadly premature. We aviation people had the majestic impression that we were offering the world irresistibly attractive services; the general public didn't think so at all. We had been telling ourselves that flying was now a nice, safe business, but a skeptical public persisted in regarding it as a dangerous and uncertain method of getting around, to be indulged in only by those with a taste for adventure. We took our schedules very seriously and, considering the absence of aids to navigation, we maintained them surprisingly well. But the public was not ready to be impressed; our efforts were rewarded with much admiration and applause—but with little commercial revenue.

Operating costs turned out to be far in excess of our earlier crystal-ball readings, and the fares we had to charge—about four times the cost of surface travel—did not encourage a rush of tickets. Within a few months, prospects of survival looked pretty grim, especially for the British.

Other countries had quickly found it necessary to provide government financial help of some sort for their airlines, but the British lines were desperately trying to live up to Winston Churchill's dictum that "civil aviation must fly by itself." That wasn't one of Winnie's best guesses; it just couldn't be done. At last, in 1921, the government had to dole out a bit of a subsidy to help us to stay alive. It was a pitifully small amount but a stimulating one, because, in the public view, it amounted to official recognition of the need for airlines; so much so that it even attracted new operators. The Instone Steamship Company had already, in October 1919, started up the Instone Air Line, bringing Seven Seas experience into the Eighth Sea and, perhaps naturally, becoming the first airline to put its crew into uniform. Daimler Hire, renowned automobile operators, now took over most of D.H.'s A.T.&T. equipment and staff, and opened Daimler Airways, introducing refreshing concepts of commercial maintenance and scheduling. By 1922, we were offering regular passenger services between London and Paris, Brussels, Amsterdam, Cologne, Berlin, and intermediate cities, as well as charter services for tourists and others.

Air-mail services were a high-sounding concept that was—as I shall explain later—a major factor in obstructing airline development in America; but in Europe it was early realized that the mails would, for a long time, constitute only trivial, government-sponsored loads. European concepts of operation, therefore, were based on direct services to the traveling public; mail carrying was incidental. So our air-mail program was not taken too seriously; mail rates were high, and the public had to deposit letters in specially marked boxes that nobody could ever find. In my innumerable airline flights I can barely remember the occasional loading of a few small sacks of mail into the baggage compartment—it seemed such a minor part of the airline job.

The brilliant mail-flying stories of the French pilot Saint-Exupéry drew wide attention to the French Government's early air-mail services over distant colonial routes and relatively undeveloped areas. But there the situation was very different; those were primitive services which had the main purpose of surveying, establishing, and holding route franchises for later, more elaborate development—nobody cared very much what they carried, and the elementary planes they used were barely good enough for carrying mail sacks or maybe an occasional undemanding passenger.

But as we developed our passenger services, a picture began to take shape that was to provide the pattern for the rest of airline history.

To attract an always hesitant public, we had to have larger, more comfortable, and more efficient planes. We needed new and better instruments, particularly for blind flying, without which our bad-weather flights were excessively dangerous and night operations quite unpractical. Then, strange as it must sound today, we had only just begun to realize the need for extensive equipment on the ground to aid navigation in the air and to promote safety, reliability, and regularity; in the past such affairs had been taken care of almost entirely by the experience and skill of the pilot, and pilots had not yet been brought up to expect much help from outside the cockpit. Now experience was telling us that the pilot couldn't do everything.

Science and engineering were presented with an ever-lengthening list of previously unsuspected problems. And it was all wildly more expensive than we had ever imagined.

With such advances as we could afford to make, the flow of cash customers steadily increased, but never fast enough to catch up with the ever-expanding costs of equipment, development, and operations. However, no nation could now afford to abandon its air transportation, because the pioneers, in the first three or four years of effort, had at least proved that the highways of the air were practical routes of human travel. Airlines were here to stay. If, therefore, the costs of progress could not be met out of commercial revenue, governments would have to make up the difference. And, in one form or another, they are still doing it.

In 1924 Britain's assortment of four or five competing airlines was merged into one national government-supported company, Imperial Airways. Other countries had already taken, or were ready to take, similar steps, and today's pattern of national airlines was thus established. However, there was still five years to go before the United States seriously entered the airline business, and meanwhile progress in Europe was severely hampered by a set of obstacles that the U.S.A. would not have to face and that, in fact, made it virtually inevitable that America should eventually overtake and pass the pioneers. It was not so much a matter of the ancient frontier barriers of languages, passports, customs, and currencies; these were comparatively easy to deal with. Nor was it a matter of aircraft engineering—Europe already had a long start over the United States. The main trouble was that national geographic divisions were a multiple barrier to the development of ground facilities, which, as I said before, was a new sort of problem to people whose difficulties had supposedly always been in the air.

Take the case of night flying. Public services, and therefore revenue, must obviously remain severely limited without night schedules. Mail sacks didn't mind much if the pilot deserted them by parachute in nighttime emergencies; but for passengers we needed lighted airways with airports, intermediate as well as terminal, properly manned and equipped for regular night flying. Our current communications, weather services, and other such aids as we had, were good enough for skilled pilots in daylight, but for night work they were so precarious as to be impossible.

There were innumerable other problems, of which airport construction was far more serious than we then realized. Fast airplanes were never going to be developed so long as planes had to have large wing areas for taking off and landing on grassy, uneven, and often muddy fields. But paved runways—even if anyone had dared to contemplate their costs—would be useless to one country unless similar runways were available in other countries. Radio navigation could never be effective except under internationally organized installations and procedures.

Europe had no way to solve these problems except through the long, ponderous, and uncertain processes of international agreements and efforts. Different countries had different views as to what, if anything, should be done about such matters; and politicians in general were in no hurry to spend more money on civil aviation than they were already doing.

When once the United States took to airlines, it did not have to ask the consent or assistance of anybody else's country to cover thousands of airline miles with whatever installations were available and necessary to help passenger planes on their way, day and night. So, adding this advantage to the experience already gained in Europe, the United States had little difficulty in making up rapidly for the ten years' leeway it had lost, forcing the countries of Europe into the co-operation necessary for keeping up with American advances. Thus, in retrospect, the strange fact emerges that, no matter what progress European airlines made at the start, they would probably always have had to go slow until the U.S.A. took the lead in operating procedures.

However, those pioneer years were a colorful period of cheerful struggle against total inexperience and unexpected odds, and they saw the laying of the foundations of the great era of air travel that was to come. I shall try to describe the operating picture as we saw it in those early days.

2. *The English Channel*

The Channel—meaning to most travelers the Straits of Dover, which forms its narrow, eastern neck—holds a special place in the history of air travel. For, if it hadn't existed, it is very debatable whether the pioneer airlines would have rushed into the business so early and so hopefully, or could have learned so many sharp lessons in airline operations.

That usually turbulent ditch, little more than twenty miles across, had for centuries been a frustrating obstacle to the passage of armies, from Caesar to Napoleon—Hitler's turn hadn't yet come up. But equally it presented a notorious obstruction to peaceful surface travel over one of the world's busiest routes: the route connecting the metropolis of London with Paris and the other great European centers. The complications of transferring from train to slow boat and back to train were a tedious nuisance, practically doubling the time that would otherwise have been required for a London–Paris journey. Moreover, a large percentage of travelers intensely disliked—some even feared—the often rough water passage, and the seasick cross-Channel passenger had long been a standard subject for the cartoonists. Thus, as a traditional impediment to surface movements, the Channel became a standing invitation to air travel.

But if the Channel was a main incentive toward setting our airlines in motion, it was also a mean opponent to our inexperienced operations. The worst of England's often unlovely weather seemed to be funneled up the Channel eastward from the Atlantic, to be piled up in the bottleneck of the Dover Straits, where planes would have to cross. The rapidly changing nature of the Channel's weather played havoc with local forecasts and reports and, even when overland flying conditions were tolerable, visibility over the water had a habit of shifting by the minute in all directions.

It wasn't just a matter of getting across—during the war, thousands of planes had made the trip. We, however, were faced by the entirely new problem of trying to keep a schedule. This called for tackling whatever weather we found when we reached the coast; only under quite impossible conditions would we return to some coastal field to wait for a hole in the misty curtain. Blind-flying instruments and aids to navigation were then non-existent, and all flying had to be done by "visual" methods, which compelled us to fly under or around whatever murk we came up against. Flying under a very low cloud ceiling became a water-skimming job, and there were other causes besides low cloud ceilings that forced us to fly close to the water; poor visibility due to fog, haze, or heavy rain compelled us to keep low so that we could use the ruffled contours of the waves as visual references for piloting.

The topography of the Channel crossing was apparently specially designed to make life difficult for pilots. In bad weather we naturally preferred the shortest route across, and in fact, the insurance people required us to take this if possible. But at each end of that route were towering cliffs, the famous White Cliffs of Dover at one end and Cape Gris-Nez at the other. And there were occasions when these cliffs were a good deal higher than we were flying. So it was sometimes disconcerting, while you were straining your eyesight through the thick mists, to see the smooth, white haze ahead suddenly transform itself into the rough, white, vertical slabs of craggy chalk where the cliffs were, leaving you just about enough time to swerve for the safety of lower ground farther along. Nobody worried much about crossing the coast line at an altitude that cut things pretty fine; and there was the well-remembered occasion when Favreau, the happy-go-lucky French pilot, landed at Croydon with a few dozen yards of telegraph wire trailing from the landing gear of his Farman Goliath—he admitted he had had to cross the coast "rather low" over Folkestone.

The chances of being forced down on the water were a standard hazard of the route, because we used mostly single-engine planes, or else twin-engine planes that could not maintain altitude on one engine alone. If a plane dropped in, prospects of rescue were not very bright; the emergency systems, which were the best we could work out at the time, were too cumbersome and slow to be of much use. I remember that a French passenger Spad was lost in the sea in June 1922, and I believe two or three others dropped in at various times. The British airlines were lucky; we lost no planes that way, although close shaves were common enough.

In the middle of one crossing I had an oil-pressure failure, which brought the engine and propeller to a dead stop; but I was flying high on a fine day, and I had enough altitude to reach a grassy field on top of the Dover cliffs. My most creepy experience of this sort occurred in 1921, when I was taking a Westland "Limousine," with three passengers, from Brussels to London in unusually foul conditions of gale and heavy rain. Skimming low over the fields behind Cape Gris-Nez, I was checking my compass bearing before launching off over the raging Channel when the Rolls-Royce engine spluttered and stopped. I discovered later that a leaky fuel drain cock had been helping the engine to empty my tank. I landed in some muddy stubble less than a mile from the edge of the cliff, realizing grimly that, if my fuel had lasted for another two or three minutes, we would have been well out over the water and would never have been heard of again.

Another time, on a D.H.34 with eight passengers from Paris for London, I was flying low over the whitecaps in a thick and murky drizzle when, about mid-Channel, the smooth purr of the Napier engine suddenly changed to a hideous clatter; a tooth had broken in the propeller reduction gear, but at the moment I didn't know what had happened and it seemed that the whole engine was about to fly apart at any second. I switched course to westward, hoping to reach the low-lying polders of Dungeness if the engine would last out that far. It continued its ghastly racket all the way, but it kept going, and I sat down hurriedly and gratefully in the first good-looking pasture I came to, with only one fatality: a sheep. (Incidentally, I have often wondered how sheep know just where an approaching airplane wants to land, so that they can have all the fun of stampeding right across its path.)

Many of those trips were pretty rough on the pilot, but the passengers were, on the whole, an unworried lot. Hardly any of them knew anything about flying, so they assumed that whatever occurred was part of the routine of aviation. Most of them enjoyed it, some didn't like it at all, and a few were terrified. But many a passenger has told me that, however rough the air passage, he preferred it to the Channel crossing on one of those damned little boats.

3. *Pioneer Operations*

From their start in August 1919, the pioneer airlines offered their passengers comfortable and protected cabin space. The D.H.4A, which opened the London–Paris services, was a modification of the D.H.4 single-engine bomber, and it was put into temporary operation while special passenger designs were being rushed through. Even at that, however, it was provided with a totally enclosed cabin in which two quite comfortable seats were installed, facing each other with a small table in between. There were also small incidental furnishings, including inflatable life jackets in case of difficulties with the Channel crossing.

But the 375 horsepower of the Rolls-Royce engine was an expensive lot of horses for just two passengers. So while the D.H.4A was opening up the service, I was making the tests of the D.H.16, a very similar plane except that it carried four passengers. I took this new plane out over the London–Paris route in September 1919. Both these planes cruised at around 125 miles per hour; and it is worth observing that this was faster than airlines would move for many years afterward, for we had begun to discover that we just couldn't afford that kind of speed. The cash position told us that our available engines would have to haul larger, and therefore slower, planes to accommodate more customers.

In March 1920, only seven months after the service started, De Havilland came out with the D.H.18, which as far as I know, was the first plane ever to be produced specifically for airline passenger purposes. With its 450-hp Napier engine it cruised, with eight passengers in a roomy cabin with well-upholstered seats, at a little over 100 mph. The pilot was located in an open cockpit (nobody thought of enclosing the pilot in those days) in the back of the fuselage, behind and above the cabin. It was an extremely pleasant plane for pilot and passengers alike.

Then came the D.H.34, of 1922, which was very much like the D.H.18, but it carried a little more, flew a little slower, and incorporated a number of improvements based on the experience of the previous couple of years. A few other types of single-engine passenger planes were tried out from time to time, but the D.H.18's and -34's carried the bulk of British airline traffic for four or five years.

We did have a number of twin-engine planes, notably the British Handley Pages and Vickers, and the slow but economical Farman "Goliaths." So perhaps, today, it might be of interest to explain why we preferred to use mostly single-engine types when the safety of twin-engine equipment was apparently available. Almost the only reason why, at that time, more than one engine was used in any plane at all was because, with the engine power available, it was the only way to get enough power into a large plane. A safety reserve of power was no part of the idea—we couldn't afford the extra weight and drag of enough spare power—and none of these planes carried enough power to remain aloft if one engine failed. The best it could do was to take a little longer to come down, often under poor control. And of course, two engines offered two chances that one or the other could fail. Besides, soundproofing was ten years or more in the future, and a cabin was much noisier with two engines banging away at the sides than with one engine isolated up ahead. So, for our pioneer purposes, the single-engine plane won on points: it was faster, cheaper, quieter, easier to maintain, and hardly less safe.

Flight instrumentation was, and would be for a long time, of just about war's-end quantity and quality—except for the newly invented aperiodic compass, which was a revolutionary aid to our bad-weather navigation. We expected no precision from our elementary altimeters and airspeed indicators. There was usually a bubble bank indicator, and sometimes a bubble pitch indicator; nobody ever took any notice of them. Rate-of-climb indicators were not even thought of.

By modern standards the most notable absence from the instrument panel was that of any sort of gyro turn indicator, without which systematic blind flying was impossible. The very crude RAE indicator,* with which I had done a lot of experimental blind flying back in 1916, was too clumsy for airline installation, and I believe it was not until about 1926 that a usable production turn indicator was available.

But just the same, we did a considerable amount of impromptu blind flying, aided only by airspeed indicator, compass, altimeter, and a cultivated sense of the "feel" of the controls. I have been repeatedly told by medical and other experts, until I am tired of arguing about it, that this is a physical impossibility. But during the war, many of us had learned the fine art of disappearing into clouds to take refuge from excessive enemy opposition, and we applied the same methods to airline flying when an emergency forced us into zero visibility. Sometimes we climbed or let down through several thousand feet of

---

* This RAE—Royal Aircraft Establishment—indicator was an early effort to connect a gyroscope projecting outside the cockpit to a turn-pointer inside; every modern pilot has to understand the modern indicator, usually referred to as "turn-and-bank," of which the turn component is operated by gyroscope. An indicator of the late 1920s, the Reid-Sigrist, used by me on my Atlantic attempt, used flashing lights instead of pointer.

cloud. Such blind flying required great concentration and was very tiring; so we rarely did it from choice and never for fun—but we did it.

The one really big advance in our cockpit equipment was the radiotelephone, an invention in which great strides had recently been made. It could be operated only in flight, and it had its share of pioneering troubles; but when it was good it was very good. Its effective range was about a hundred miles, considerably more or less according to the weather and the altitude of the plane, and its value to us was immense and novel. It had also surprisingly high propaganda value to the ticket-sales departments: nervous passengers derived some obscure reassurance from the amazing fact—when they believed it—that the pilot could actually talk from the plane to the ground.

Then there was the language problem: the Anglo-French and the Franco-English of pilots and ground operators could produce astonishing and often hilarious confusion, especially in an emergency when someone got excited; on such occasions it was easy to appreciate what happened in the Tower of Babel.

Our methods of bad-weather flying over land would certainly not be tolerated today. In the absence of ground aids to navigation, we developed landmark flying to a fine art. Often skimming treetops in negligible visibility, we would follow highways and railroads when we could, or else cut across country until some familiar object, small or large, would tell us—we hoped—just where we were. We made a point, if possible, of notifying a ground station by radio when we were starting or finishing a Channel crossing. If we couldn't make contact we would—also if possible—circle low over one of the coastal airfields by way of signal. And if we couldn't do that, we went on anyway.

Of all the major airports on our early routes, the London terminal at Croydon was the most difficult in bad weather. When you left the airport, which was located on top of a hill overlooking the town of Purley, you had a couple of ranges of often cloud-covered hills to negotiate before picking up the railroad, which after coming out of the Sevenoaks Tunnel, proceeded in a virtually straight line to the coast. This railroad was a godsend to our navigation, and it became known as the "backbone of civil aviation." Coming back into Croydon in foul weather was not so easy; the "backbone" took you about as far as the Sevenoaks Tunnel and then left you to deal with the hills as best you could.

One day Andy Carruthers was bringing home his converted Handley Page o/400, which in spite of its hundred-foot span, retained the folding-wing feature designed for wartime storage purposes. The weather in the hills defeated him, and he crashed without hurting anyone. Reporting on the accident, he said he had been closely following the railroad when it suddenly vanished into the tunnel. There was only one thing to do, declared Andy with a straight face: fold the wings back quickly and fly through the tunnel. "And," he continued, "I'd have been all right only there was a damn train coming through."

One of my more disconcerting arrivals at Croydon occurred one evening when I was bringing the Instone Air Line's twin-engine Vickers Vimy back from Paris with a full cargo of a dozen passengers. Weaving my way through the hills in rapidly worsening weather, I was heading up the Purley Valley toward the airport when I noticed that the ceiling was dropping so fast that it now covered all the high ground, including the field itself. It was too late to turn back; below were the close-packed houses of Purley town, and ahead was only the thick murk of the city of London. But on my left through the edge of the clouds, which were just settling on the airport, I could distinguish a long, thin, white line. I knew at once that this was the perfect guide for a hurried landing, for I recognized it as the bank of chalky earth recently thrown up during the construction of a new road right alongside the boundary of the field, now some fifty feet above me. I gave the engines full throttle, picked up all the speed I had time for, pulled the Vimy up into a left-hand climbing turn, headed for the chalk line, and cut the engines just as I crossed a few feet above it. The few yards of visibility were enough to let me make a decent landing, although I had trouble finding the hangars until a car with fog lights came to guide me in. The passengers hadn't noticed anything unusual, and gave me their usual smiling thanks for a pleasant trip. I was glad somebody had enjoyed it.

The thought of air collisions occurred to us occasionally; but the general feeling was that, after all, there was a lot of air and not many airplanes in it. Then one day one of our D.H.18's, piloted by Neville

Duke, met head on north of Paris with a French Goliath, which was following the same highway in the opposite direction. All aboard the two planes were killed. Thereafter the more frequently used of our bad-weather routes were officially mapped out and we were supposed to keep well to the right. This was, I think, the first time that airline navigation procedures received any official attention.

This airline flying was not my regular job, but something I engaged in during intervals between experimental flight tests. My pilot's license covered all relevant British commercial types, so I would let the lines know when I was available "on call." A call, therefore, might easily be an affair of very short notice, and that could lead to complications.

One morning in 1923 I was having a leisurely breakfast at Croydon Airport, looking forward to a lazy day, when the Daimler Airways manager rushed in and asked me to take out the Berlin plane im-mediately. Everything, including passengers, was all ready to go, but nobody could locate the pilot. I had never flown the Berlin route, but that didn't bother anybody; so, borrowing a flying cap and a pair of goggles, I climbed into the D.H.34 and took off. During refueling at Amsterdam I collected a map for the rest of the route. I was well known there, and nobody asked me for papers and passport. At Ham-burg nobody knew me, and when I airily disclaimed any special in-terest in such trivialities as passports and licenses, I was promptly ar-rested.

Two of the longest German soldiers I had ever seen, with fixed bayonets, marched me to a distant office, where a fierce little man in a bowler hat told me I was invited to the local jail for a day or two, pending investigations. I made matters slightly worse by telling him that I often flew to Cologne, where I never had this sort of trouble; which gave him the chance to reply bitterly that the British Army was running Cologne, whereas the Germans were running Hamburg. Meanwhile my worried passengers had followed along, and one of them, a German of obviously some influence, talked earnestly to Bowler Hat. That official performed some elaborate scowling, and then in-formed me that I could proceed with temporary papers on payment of an immediate fine. The fine would be two million marks. I figured vaguely that, with luck, I might earn such a sum in the next twenty years, and resigned myself to the clink. Then a grinning passenger told me about the great German inflation, which was just then going into high gear. A few English pounds would pay my fine. I paid it out of Daimler's expense money, and that night I slept comfortably in a Berlin hotel.

A couple of weeks later, on another trip, the Germans gave me a more friendly demonstration of their Teutonic efficiency. Leaving Berlin for London, I was told that one of my passengers, a very high official, had to be dropped off at the former military airfield at Bremen. It had been raining for days, and that field, now poorly maintained by a caretaker squad, was practically a bog. I landed carefully enough so that I just failed to nose over, but then the wheels sank up to the axles—there was no earthly chance of taking off. A smart young German officer came up and offered to fix all that. In no time, a detail of troops pushed, pulled and lifted—always on the right parts of the plane, for they were ex-air-force troops—until they got the D.H.34 onto the tarmac. Having wiped it clean of mud, they produced some fuel and refilled the tanks. Then they pushed the plane up the ramp to a road leading onto the highway. Meanwhile another detachment had split up to halt traffic over a long, straight stretch of the main road. My remaining passengers climbed aboard, and with no trouble whatever I took off the highway en route to Amsterdam.

By the time I left England for America, in 1928, the European airlines had graduated to large, multiengine planes carrying twenty passengers or more, and services had expanded to much more of the Continent. New instruments now permitted blind flying in bad weather and at night, and a radio system had been developed for giving planes directional bearings from the ground. But there is great historic importance in the fact that there was no marked improvement in speeds, which remained around a hundred miles per hour.

Within a few years America was going to lead aviation into one of its revolutionary forward leaps; it was going to show that, for the first time in the history of any form of travel, it would be cheaper to go faster. But this was not yet imagined. It had been axiomatic in all forms of surface transportation that small increases in speed involved large increases in operating costs; shipping lines, for example, hesitated at increases of even two or three knots. As far as anyone could see, the same principles were bound to apply to airplanes.

So when we thought of airplane improvements, our visions of higher speeds were strictly limited; we thought rather in terms of larger planes, of more passenger space with finer furnishings and all sorts of in-flight services, of greater safety and reliability. Future long-range airplanes were pictured as something like hugh flying yachts, with cabins, bunks, lounges, and restaurant sections. Nobody could dream that planes might some day fly so fast that passengers would submit to being packed in like sardines for the few brief hours that a very long-distance flight would last.

There were reasons why we gave little thought to the prospects of much higher speeds. For one thing, these 100-mph planes were doing quite well as they were. There was then little loss of time on the ground; there was no heavy road traffic to impede access to airports, and airport procedures had few of today's time-consuming complications. However, engineers knew that the first requirement for really high speeds would be smaller wings, much more heavily loaded; but with such high wing loadings, airplanes would need a long, fast run over the ground, and they would never be able to get into the air from the grassy fields, which were all we ever thought of for airports and emergency landings. Nobody at that time could seriously contemplate the extravagant costs of long, smooth, hard runways as a standard feature of airport construction.

In 1928 America was just about to come into the airline business. Circumstances would be such that American developments would rapidly and radically change the whole picture.

4. The Cash Customers

Air passengers today are just anybody—everybody. The romance of the air and the thrills of flight have faded into the past, and people travel by air simply because that is the ordinary and normal way to travel. It even happens that, if someone takes a long trip by ship or train, he feels called upon to excuse his strange conduct.

But in the early airline days, a passenger was something very special.

For one thing, the great majority of our customers had never before been up in the air. For them this was not merely a journey, nor even a flight; it was a great event in their lives. So we treated them with a care and reverence that we hoped, would encourage more of them. In the first months of operations, schedules had to wait for the customers, and we would not think of taking off before they had all arrived. Some regulars got to know this, and they turned up when they felt like it. It was not too unusual for our limousine to call for a passenger at his hotel only to find that he was not yet out of bed, in which case the car driver would telephone the airport to announce the delay. Meanwhile we would try our best to entertain those who had already arrived, in surroundings where waiting facilities were very primitive or non-existent. This, of course, couldn't go on for long; gradually, with some timidity, we began to tighten up on the delay we would permit. At last, when Daimler Airways went into action, their manager, George Woods-Humphery, established the revolutionary principle that planes should take off exactly on schedule. This sort of thing lost us a few passengers, but gained us many more, for airport procedures became precise and swift, and little time was wasted on the ground. We were learning.

Passengers came in all shapes and sizes, and for a wide variety of reasons. A few of them were people who took naturally to airlines as a new, fast, and up-to-date form of travel, accepting the expected risks as part of the deal. Particularly on the German routes (Cologne, Hamburg, and Berlin), where distances were greater and time-saving more evident, we carried a considerable number of businessmen and officials concerned with the postwar revival of Germany or with the armies of occupation. There were others who were hesitant and doubtful, but willing to be convinced that airlines were practical. There were even quite a number who didn't like flying at all but preferred it to being tossed about on a cross-Channel steamer.

But the public in general considered flying as a highly dangerous method of locomotion and saw no point in paying three or four times the price of surface travel for the privilege of risking their necks. So, for the first few years, most of our passengers were people who were looking for some sort of thrill and didn't mind paying for it. Naturally, therefore, these new airlines were a great tourist attraction. American tourists, in particular, were one of our most substantial sources of revenue; for many of them a flight between London and Paris became a "must" for a European tour, and they were not to be deterred by any fears of the dangers of flight.

Where tourists prevailed, airport departure scenes usually produced emotional demonstrations that were of great entertainment value to the operating staffs. There would be the normal excitement and chatter of people about to embark on a new and perilous voyage. There would be the nervous twitchings and questionings of those who felt that they were probably about to die but were grimly determined to go through with the whole thing. There were the supercilious glances and comments of hardened air travelers for those who were making such a fuss about a simple trip. Theatrical celebrities about to make their first air trip were naturally accompanied by their publicity retinues, who made a great production of the departure.

The pilot was a Great Man, and there were requests for a personal introduction and probably an autograph. He was usually bombarded with impossible questions, for which he had to invent plausible answers.

Most trips proceeded without incident. However, under tough conditions, our first consideration was to complete the flight as nearly on schedule as possible, more or less regardless of whether the passengers took a shaking up in the process. Then, if we couldn't get through, we tried either to return to our starting point or at least to reach some airfield where cars for the passengers might be found to take them to a railway station. The French authorities gave us valuable help in our emergency programs by decreeing that an airline pilot had the right to have any express train stopped at any wayside station to take on stranded passengers. Now and then, however, because of weather or mechanical failure, the pilot had to land as best he could miles from anywhere, and I have spent many a miserable hour trudging across muddy ploughland in pouring rain trying to find that great French scarcity, a farmhouse with a telephone, while the passengers huddled in the cabin hoping for rescue in due course.

There were always a few customers who complained loudly, bitterly, and widely at such treatment; the famous writer H. G. Wells damned airlines in all directions after a couple of misfortunes with forced landings. But in most cases passengers took such troubles in surprisingly good part, and many of them even enjoyed the experience as a memorable adventure.

American tourists then (as now) were a mystifying species to their less exuberant European observers. Their bubbling enthusiasm, insatiable curiosity, and impatience to get going in all directions at the same time were inspiring, if somewhat exhausting, to us who liked to see our services appreciated. And they rarely did anything to dispel the popular impression that all Americans were Very Rich. Questions of safety did not usually seem to concern them much, and they might even show disappointment if they reached the other end without some exciting event.

Late one afternoon, flying to Paris on a D.H.18 with a load that included a boisterous American, I developed ignition trouble some distance north of Beauvais and landed in a field alongside the highway. I went into action to put my passengers on a Paris train before calling London for the service I needed. The American would have none of it; he was going to complete the trip by air if he had to wait a month. He promptly reserved all the available rooms in the main hotel of the small nearby town, and invited all the passengers to remain as his guests until the plane was fixed. Three of them accepted. By evening he seemed to have reserved everything else in the neighborhood that promised entertainment. He discovered a farmer's wedding party at an inn on the outskirts and descended on it with several cases of champagne, to the great local benefit of Franco-American friendship. The fact that he spoke no French whatever did nothing to slow him down. He occupied the next day in ensuring that there were no dull or thirsty spots within range. It took two days to fix the plane; if it had taken one more they would have had to send out another pilot.

We never ceased to be amazed at the American tourist's passion for high-pressure sight-seeing, which was now to be aided by the speed of flight. One summer's day in 1923, two D.H.18's were chartered for a party of fourteen American high school girls, with two teachers, for a trip to Holland. Perry flew one of them and I flew the other. Leaving Croydon early, we landed at Rotterdam in time for a quick breakfast. After which the party clambered onto a chartered bus and set forth. Early in the afternoon they came back, having "done" Leiden, The Hague, and Delft. Then on we flew to Amsterdam, where another bus took our explorers for a lightning study of that city and a quick look at the Zuider Zee. We landed them back at Croydon at dusk, exhausted but happy. They had made their first flight and "done" Holland—all in one day.

Since those exploratory years, when we thought we were doing well if we had more than a dozen passengers a day, the trickle of air travelers has swollen to a deluge, to be carried at far higher speeds for much lower fares. Yet those of us who have always been close to the business have watched, with dismay if not much surprise, while airlines' attention to passengers has steadily become more lopsided, to the point where flight speeds are now immensely frustrated by sluggishness of a multitude of ground services.

This has been not merely a matter of increased volume of traffic; it has been simply that airlines have historically concentrated their interest on the passenger in the air, and they have devoted heroic expenditure, creativity, and foresight toward vast improvements in flight equipment and operations. But airline vision has always had a blind spot for the passenger on the ground, who apparently was an incidental character not really in their line of business and who ought therefore to be handled unhurriedly or by some other, unconnected services or agencies.

This situation has now become a national and international problem of monumental proportions, far too complex for further discussion here, and it is going to get a lot worse before it gets better. However, it leaves one to wonder whether the fabulous costs of Supersonic Transports, which hope to provide higher airspeeds, which nobody really needs, wouldn't better be applied to higher speeds on the ground, which the cash customer will need for yet a long time on his way into the air.

5. Air Freight

In 1920 the concept of air freight was an infinitely remote one. Now and then we carried two or three small packages, which probably had to be extremely urgent to justify the high costs and general uncertainty of sending them by air. Occasionally something very special was put aboard, usually assigned to the "personal care" of the pilot—who had other things to bother about besides nursing someone's pet parcel.

There was a period when the jewelry business became a particular nuisance. Some serious jewel robberies had taken place in transit between London and Paris, and it was deduced that the complications of transfer from train to boat to train on the surface journey offered unusual opportunities to organized thieves. So some insurance genius came up with the idea that it would be safer if such valuables were handed casually without advance notice to an airline pilot just before departure.

One Saturday I was about to take out the Daimler Airways morning schedule when an official handed me a very small white package, with instructions to deliver it urgently and personally to a Mr. Lowenstein at his office on the Boulevard Haussmann, in Paris. By the time I reached that office it was closed for the weekend, and it took me until evening to locate Mr. Lowenstein. He took me around to the office, but refused to open the package until his partner came along, and he insisted I remain to witness the opening of the package. I was willing to do so simply because I was curious to know what this mystery was. I waited with increasing impatience for another hour or so until the partner showed up. Then they unwrapped the package, which contained a little box, and from it they tipped out, onto a velvet cloth, half a dozen huge diamonds. At least, I took their word that that was what those objects were—personally I wouldn't know a diamond from a piece of broken bottle. It seemed that I had been wandering around Paris all afternoon with several thousand pounds' worth of diamonds in my pocket. My interest evaporated when they asked me to sign some bit of paper about witnessing the contents of the box. I left them to it, and firmly declined any more such errands.

The first instance that I remember of a bulk air-freight shipment occurred during the big Dutch dock strike of 1921. An enterprising and publicity-minded department store in Utrecht hit upon the novel and daring idea of beating the strike by getting its current supply of women's underwear from London by air. The D.H.18, with the seats taken out, had something like three hundred cubic feet of enclosed space, and this we piled to the roof with cartons of feminine flimsies.

When I landed at Soesterberg, the Dutch military field outside Utrecht, I found that the store's publicity people had let themselves go. A brass band was blowing off stirring music, and I was greeted as a conquering hero by a welcoming committee that included the colonel commanding the field, the Mayor of the city and his satellites, and assorted store executives. Cameras clicked all around. The cartons were ceremoniously unloaded and piled high on a gaily decorated truck, and we set off along the narrow road to the town, an impressive procession of half a dozen limousines led by the truck. I was in the first limousine, with the Mayor. After that, everything was anticlimax.

The truck had been loaded with more enthusiasm than care. A little way along the uneven road, a couple of cartons slid overboard. Our limousine stopped to pick them up, holding up the following cars while the truck jolted innocently on its way. More cartons fell off— and more. When our car was covered with all the cartons it could carry, we hurried ahead, weaving around fallen cartons to try to catch up with the truck and leaving the other cars to continue with the salvage job. And so it went all the way into town. Outside the store a large crowd, attracted by the publicity, gazed in puzzlement at the arrival of this strange cortege: a half-empty truck followed at intervals by carloads of embarrassed dignitaries clutching armfuls of cartons.

During the first dozen years or so of airline operations, it was easy to predict that air freight was never going to amount to much. Past experience with all forms of transportation had proved conclusively that operating costs climbed steeply with higher speeds, so it could be safely assumed that the airplane, as the fastest and therefore the most expensive of carriers, was destined merely for a limited range of services in the express delivery of lightweight luxury items. This could hardly be described as "freight."

Then, as the 1930s came along, new signs had begun to appear that there might yet be some sort of future for the airplane as a freighter. There were outlying parts of the earth where new enterprises and projects, particularly in mining and exploring operations, were faced with the extreme difficulty, and often the impossibility, of moving supplies and equipment through wild and trackless terrain. The airplane alone could provide these outposts with any close contact with civilization, not because of its speed but because it could use the highways of the air where no other highways existed. A venturesome tribe of airmen sprang up to keep them supplied with scarce items of food and merchandise or occasional bits of equipment for which very high prices were willingly paid in camps cut off from all other ready sources of supply. These "bush pilots," as they came to be called, were the true pioneers of air freight; they took enormous risks with small planes loaded—or, more often, wildly overloaded—with whatever could be crammed into them or hung onto them. Flying over desolate territories and taking the weather as it came, they delivered cargoes that were commonplace merchandise at the starting point but had become luxuries at their destination.

From these operations it was not a big step to much more ambitious programs for moving loads by air that could not be moved by land or water, and soon the largest available planes were being roughly adapted for handling apparently outrageous loads such as structural materials or heavy mining machinery dismantled for piecemeal shipment and eventual reassembly at some otherwise unreachable spot in the wilderness.

Developments of this sort were of course impressive, but for many years they were generally regarded as too specialized, sporadic, and costly to encourage serious thoughts of air freight as a normal feature of air commerce. It required the vast military transport activities of World War II to convince all concerned that there were few classes of freight that could not practically be carried by air. In my numerous wartime ocean crossings with large bombers and flying boats, I sometimes shuddered at the sight of heavy metal parts, rugged crates, bins, drums, and sacks, which I was evidently expected to take casually up into the air, especially as I had long known the days when airplane loads were meticulously measured pound by pound and cautiously installed with religious respect for the frailty of the fuselage or hull.

However, the wartime military freight services, convincing as they were, had been carried on regardless of costs; the established airlines had at least some prewar experience in the economics, procedures, and technical equipment of passenger traffic, but practically none with regard to freight, which to them was a new business, to be examined carefully and approached cautiously. At that time, various newcomers, hoping for a foothold in air transportation, found themselves officially excluded from regular passenger operations, and some of them thought they saw profitable prospects in the development of exclusively cargo services. Their success soon brought the major airlines heartily into the freight business, and the subsequent enormous expansion of air-freight operations is now a familiar story of progress in modern commercial aviation.

It is now easy to predict the reverse of what we predicted when commercial airlines started fifty years ago and to forecast a still more astonishing future for commercial air freight, especially in view of the enormous capacity of forthcoming aircraft. For by now the passenger airlines have already taken away from the surface carriers a great percentage of long-distance travelers, and some limit to that expansion is in sight, whereas there is almost no practical limit to the quantity of freight that remains to be, and will be, diverted from the surface to the air.

6. America Takes to Airlines

When I left England for the U.S.A., in 1928, it had long been possible for a traveler to buy a ticket at a regular travel office for a scheduled flight in a multiengine passenger plane on any of several airlines operating between principal cities of Western Europe, and some of these services were even extending into Africa and the Middle East. I arrived to find that in America there was nothing that could seriously be called an airline system. There were numerous air routes over which an assortment of independent contractors carried sacks of Post Office mail in small and often outdated airplanes; here and there, efforts had been made to offer occasional passenger seats, but such traffic was entirely incidental to government air-mail operations and it was too scattered, unco-ordinated, and insignificant to be classed as airline service.

It was a puzzling situation. Of all countries in the world, America was endowed with the strongest incentives and the brightest possibilities for an intensive development of commercial airlines. It was the birthplace of aviation, possessing everything that aviation needed for its growth and progress: population, wealth, commerce, engineering, enterprise, inventiveness, and the wide distances that called loudly for air services and travel. And all these were within its own borders; it was quite free from the obstacles that international frontiers had placed in the way of European developments. So why, ten years after World War I, had America fallen so far behind Europe in a field in which, logically, it should have been a long way ahead?

This was a question of considerable historical consequence, and for an answer to it I have to refer back to my review, in Chapter XIII, of America's approach toward aviation progress in the decade immediately following World War I. What that amounts to, in brief, is the fact that the U. S. Government foresaw no military need to build and sustain an integrated aircraft industry after the war, any more than it had imagined such a need before the war, but it did foresee the probable value of air services and communications. And since no effective aviation industry existed which might initiate such services, the government decided that it should do that job itself with such planes as it had. However, the government was obviously not qualified to go into the business of public passenger transportation, whereas it could justify a project for speeding the federal mails. So, in May 1918, with Congressional applause and presidential fanfare, the U. S. Air Mail Service was launched, operated by the Army and carrying Post Office loads. Perhaps it looked like a good idea at the time, but it turned out to be a monumental obstruction to the development of airlines in America. It has become customary in some circles to hail this air mail as the foundation of U.S. commercial aviation, but this ritual claim is simply not supported by the record.

To start with, it immediately put the government into the air transportation business before private enterprise had a chance even to look at it. The whole operation was run on public funds, voted by Congressional politicians and disbursed through a political organization, the Post Office. The service, operated first by the Army and later by civilians employed by the Post Office, was managed with traditional bureaucratic inefficiency—in various phases of air-mail history there were public uproars concerning the high rate of casualties among the pilots, which sometimes approached wartime proportions.

After a few years of purely governmental operation, the services were contracted out to private operators, in bits and pieces all over the country, apparently with the general notion that under private management these services could now be called "commercial aviation." The country was officially mapped out into numerous air-mail routes, and contracts to carry the mail over each of these routes were issued on the "lowest bidder" principle—under conditions that virtually insured that the least possible money would be spent on services that needed large expenditures for serious development.

As a base for the growth of commercial aviation, everything was inherently wrong with this air-mail scheme. For one thing, there was nothing about it that was "commercial." The only loads provided for were government loads in the form of mail sacks, and the public was offered no effective access to the services either as passengers or as forwarders of freight. But it was worse than that; for if this scheme in itself provided no commercial service, it also effectively blocked all possibility of commercial development and ensured the further starvation of the aircraft manufacturing industry. It is true, of course, that there was nothing to prevent these new "commercial" operators from offering passenger services, but it is not hard to see why they were unlikely to.

Any airplane that could fly halfway decently and had a large enough cavity for stowing mail sacks was good enough for mail service. So the lowest bidder was likely to be the operator who used the least expensive of planes and engines, preferably from war-surplus stocks, and ran them with the simplest equipment. Who, therefore, was likely to give orders to the aircraft industry for newer, better, and therefore more expensive planes?

And as to passengers: air travelers required all sorts of space, comfort, attention, and services, at infinitely more cost than was called for by mail sacks. The Post Office was offering good money for carrying mail; there was no government department interested in passenger traffic. So, with a sure income from mail payments, what operator would speculate with passengers? And who, therefore, was going to give orders to manufacturers for the expensive business of designing and building commodious passenger planes?

And finally, what mail carrier was going to invest serious money to improve his service when he might lose his contract to a lower bidder next year?

In brief, the air-mail program was a patchwork of petty services that made it impossible for America to develop long-range passenger airlines. This was the dreary situation when, in 1927, Lindbergh's sensational New York–Paris flight stirred the nation into a sudden realization of America's immense potentialities for aviation and set off a near stampede in the direction of every sort of aviation project.

Early in 1929 two powerful new factors teamed up with the "Lindbergh boom" to clear the way for America to take its rightful place in the world of airlines. The first was that the incoming Hoover administration handed to its new Postmaster General, Mr. Walter Brown, the unenviable job of straightening out the air-mail muddle so as to make possible long-distance passenger airlines such as had long existed in Europe. The second was the fabulous stock-market boom through which the now air-happy public was ready to pour all the finances necessary for such airline developments: operations, airplanes, engines, equipment, and airports.

I had then obtained my first American job, as Aviation Adviser to the New York investment firm of Hayden, Stone & Co., a job that pushed me into the middle of these new airline activities. Through my old friend Dr. Edward Warner, who was now Assistant Secretary of the Navy for Aviation and whom I had known long before in England, I met Mr. Brown. From time to time I had discussions with him, particularly with regard to European developments, and took him for flights over some of the routes; so I got at first hand some idea of the problems he was up against.

The essence of Mr. Brown's program was, first, to map out the country into a network of long-distance routes. Then, air-mail contracts would be taken away from the jumble of small regional operators and given to large airline organizations capable of flying multiengine passenger planes over those long routes—incidentally carrying the mails. The small operators would then have to merge with the big fellows, or sell out to them, or go out of business. The whole program made elementary sense; airlines in America could not possibly function as a series of disjointed small operations. But putting that program into effect turned out to be an infinitely sticky business.

In various discussions, it was suggested that this new airline setup was now hardly a Post Office affair, and that it should probably be handled by some sort of aviation agency such as we have today. But European experience had already shown that airlines could not survive without a subsidy of some sort, and "subsidy" was a fighting word in American politics; it was much simpler to disguise a subsidy as "mail pay" and let the Post Office continue to handle it. In later years, as conditions changed, government support to U.S. airlines would have to change its shape, and a major political problem would arise as to what was subsidy and what was mail pay.

I had to be present at some of the political/financial battles in which the outgoing small operators and the new major operators had to try to come to terms; they were usually acrimonious affairs, in which I was glad my part was merely a technical one. There were cases in which Walter Brown had to force settlements on the contestants, and he had to be pretty ruthless in trying to bring order into this contrived chaos. He succeeded, and the airlines were set up as, in general, they exist today. But, long after he left the job, the political mud was being thrown at him in carload lots.

However, once the new operators went into action, progress was extremely swift. Before long the country was covered with federal facilities for night flying, radio navigation, meteorological services, and other forms of ground assistance such as nationally divided Europe was still struggling to organize. Elaborate airports were built, with long, paved runways that would soon permit the development of much faster planes. Civic and local enterprise rushed into the picture, and many cities, large and small, proudly built airports and other facilities to bring this exciting new traffic to their doors. Nothing like this could previously have occurred in Europe.

For the first few years the new airlines used types of passenger planes roughly comparable to those in Europe, with cruising speeds not much over one hundred miles per hour. But by 1933 America had started to lead the world in the high-speed types that we know today. And those types had upset the traditional theories of haulage: on airlines it was going to be cheaper to go faster.

In one capacity or another I had to fly most airline types at various times, but airline flying was rapidly becoming a specialty reserved for the lines' own pilots. However, now and then some special occasion arose that gave me the chance to play the airline captain. When Eastern Air Transport (later Eastern Airlines) made its opening flight, in October 1930, with the Curtiss Condor, I was more familiar with the plane than the line's pilots were. So I was appointed Captain for the round trip between Washington, D.C., and Fort Worth via Atlanta and other cities. One of my collection of distinguished passengers was Postmaster General Brown; another was the later-famous newsman of World War II, Ernie Pyle, who wrote an account of the trip for the newspapers.

It was indicative of the times that most of the airports on the route had never seen such a "huge" airplane as the twenty-passenger Condor. Before I left Richmond I had a message from Atlanta that they didn't think I could get my big plane into their little airport. This scared some of my passengers, who decided to take the night train on to Atlanta. When Brown elected to join them, the rest had to go out of politeness. With only my flight engineer, Ambrose Chabot (later Maintenance Manager for Eastern), I went on, landing at Atlanta with no difficulty, although with not too much room to spare. Next morning my flock of passengers arrived by train and, somewhat sheepishly, reboarded the Condor. With a few more ceremonial stops, we reached Fort Worth. Airlines had come to Texas. Which was sufficient excuse for Amon Carter, the well-known publisher, to try to knock us all out with a monumental Texas-style celebration that took no notice whatever of Prohibition, which was then raging. In fact, two or three of my passengers were in no shape to reach the Condor early next morning for the return trip. (And with my natural reverence for Cabinet rank, I will refrain from mentioning that Mr. Brown was one of them.)

Then there was the time Amelia Earhart and I jointly opened the Thompson Airline between Cleveland and Detroit, using six-passenger Loening amphibians. At that time there was every reason to believe that seaplane services between certain large cities would be particularly useful because, using the water, the planes could operate from close to a city's center and so save the journey to an outlying airport. Amelia was to fly one plane from Cleveland, while I flew another from Detroit. I had a small bet on with Amelia that I would get into Cleveland before she got into Detroit.

On the morning of the opening flights, there was a thick fog in the Detroit River, while Cleveland was clear. I knew it was not possible for Amelia to come down in such a fog, whereas I had it all figured out how I would take off, having done that sort of thing before. Using compass and careful timing, and allowing for river current, I would taxi to the middle of the river and take off by compass in the fog. I knew I would be well clear of the Windsor bridge, farther down. With a mechanic who was supposed to be a good seaplane man, and Cy Caldwell of *Aero Digest*, who was to write up the event, I taxied from the dock out into the fog and turned onto my takeoff course. Suddenly, from close by, I heard the booming of a ship's foghorn. I had rashly assumed that the fog would have kept shipping out of the middle of the river, but now I saw that I couldn't take off without the risk of slamming into a wandering vessel. I had no means of finding my way back to the dock, so I would have to moor and wait for things to clear. I cut the engine, told the mechanic to put out the anchor, and sat down in the cabin looking out the window while I chatted with Cy.

A little later, to my horror, I saw through the window the dim outlines of trees moving slowly along not far from the wing tip. I guessed at once what was wrong: the anchor was dragging and we were drifting closer inshore with the current. I leaped wildly into the cockpit, started the engine, and gave it full throttle in the general direction of open water. Then, leaving the engine ticking over, I hauled in the anchor to examine it. There was nothing wrong with it but it was a folding anchor, and the mechanic, whom I now discovered to be not as nautical as I had been led to expect, had unfolded the flukes but had forgotten to fix the stock. This time I fixed the anchor myself and checked that it was holding (which I should have done in the first place). A couple of hours later the fog dispersed enough for me to take off. But Amelia beat me badly. Having had a report that the fog was about to clear, she took off from Cleveland and cruised around over Detroit until she could see enough of the river to come down— only ten minutes after I had taken off with still a hundred miles to go.

In the airline days of the Ford Trimotor, the Curtiss Condor, and the DC-2, I managed occasionally to find experimental or other pretexts for acting as substitute captain over some of the route stages. But eventually new operating regulations, more stringently enforced, put an end to those opportunities.

In 1933 the Boeing 247 brought to aviation the new era of fast, clean, metal multiengine passenger monoplanes. By 1936 the Douglas DC-3 had started its classic airline career. With other types of American planes, it would be adopted by numerous airlines all over the world. With those planes would go American equipment and instruments, and American methods of using them. Few, if any, signs remained that, not so long before, America had had no airlines at all.

And with the coming of World War II, newer and larger passenger planes, designed for the airlines of America, would revolutionize war operations with a military transport service such as, in World War I, we could not even have imagined.

CHAPTER XVII

THE SPORTSMAN PILOT

1. Aviation's Debt to Sport

The earliest airplane "inventors"—I knew and worked with many of them in both America and Europe—were nearly always strangely solemn characters, so earnestly preoccupied with the problems of their own particular flying machines that they ignored, or even resented, public attention. The public, in turn, was not interested in their mysterious mechanical tinkerings, with the result that for several years aviation remained the obscure hobby of a few obscure people.

Then, around 1910, groups of sportsmen made the discovery that airplanes now seemed to be good enough to use for a dazzling variety of fun and games; and when the daring feats of the "intrepid birdmen" attracted the attention of a sports-loving public, aviation quickly began to make spectacular headway, long before it showed any signs of practical utility.

Sportsmen have always been addicted to racing anything that would move, so air racing was instituted as soon as it seemed barely feasible. Some of those early races took several days to cover a few dozen miles, while an enchanted public excitedly followed the daily succession of crashes and breakdowns that left results always in doubt. Freedom to frolic in three dimensions was a unique quality of the airplane, and this gave birth to the fascinating art of aerobatics, which started with mildly daring departures from cautious flying and evolved over the years into impressive demonstrations of masterly airplane control, besides making notable contributions to aerodynamic knowledge. Records for speed, altitude and distance became official statistics that served as milestones along the road of aviation's engineering advances.

Much of aviation's most spectacular history was made in the years when pilots competed for prizes and trophies offered for sporting performances that, in their time, seemed hopelessly difficult, dangerous, or foolhardy, and many of aviation's best-remembered names are those of men who earned public acclaim for their victories in such contests.

One of these was Glenn Curtiss, who did more than any other individual for the early progress of American aviation. He came vividly to public attention when, on May 29th, 1910, he won a prize offered for the first flight from Albany, the capital of New York State, to New York City. I became somewhat belatedly and distantly associated with that performance when, in a ceremonial celebration of that flight's twentieth anniversary, I flew Curtiss over that route. The trip treated Curtiss to some unexpected thrills—which was just as well, because it turned out to be his last flight.

The Curtiss Condor biplane, with two Curtiss Conqueror engines and seats for twenty-two passengers, was the ideal plane for taking Curtiss and the group of celebrants over the historic route. I had been doing some substantial redesign on the plane for the Curtiss-Wright Company and was appointed to fly it for this occasion.

The outgoing flight from New York to Albany, with all seats filled, was uneventful. At Albany Lieutenant Governor Lehmann put on a big luncheon affair, and after that, we started back, southward along the Hudson River. This was the route of the memorable flight we were celebrating, so Glenn Curtiss was invited to take the copilot's seat.

When we settled down to cruising, the air was reasonably calm and smooth, so I suggested to Glenn that he might like to take over the controls for a while. He was delighted with the idea. He hadn't touched an airplane's controls for many years, but he reared up like an old war horse scenting battle, seized the wheel, braced his feet on the rudder pedals, and went to work to relive old days. In his time he had hardly ever known a plane that didn't have to be manhandled all the time, so he kept up a series of small control motions just on principle. The big Condor wallowed and pitched a bit, but for a while we went along fairly normally. Then, with a west wind blowing from over the Catskill Mountains, we began to run into increasing turbulence.

Curtiss, as in days of yore, worked purposefully to correct every gust and bump. Above all, he kept in mind the pioneer pilot's ingrained principle of precaution against the risk of stalling: "When in doubt, push the nose down." At every good bump he pushed, just as he would have done on that other flight, twenty years earlier. Now, as the air got rougher, successive pushes kept putting the Condor into partial dives from which Glenn happily hauled it up when he thought it was safe to do so. Before long the Condor was performing like a roller coaster, and I glanced inquiringly at Glenn with a view to taking over from him. But he obviously had no remote desire to relinquish the controls; he was having the time of his life. So I felt that this was his day, and short of impending disaster, I was going to let him enjoy it.

Then the door from the passenger cabin flew open, and Frank Russell staggered to the flight deck. "For God's sake, Courtney, take over," he shouted hoarsely. "The passengers are all sick." With Glenn having such a good time, I had forgotten all about the people in the back. Reluctantly I took over, and Glenn sat back with the air of a man who has proved his point. He never flew again; a few weeks later he died from a long-standing malady.

Sports flying was, of course, an end in itself; but, in its heyday, it contributed immensely to progress in the design and development of airplanes and engines. In the tougher contests a pilot was expected, in the interests of sporting victory, to strain his equipment to its extreme limits, and such brutal in-flight testing often produced discoveries that might otherwise have been missed or long delayed in the more sober and serious processes of normal flight testing.

Racing and competition flying flourished widely in the 1920s and reached the height of its popularity around the early 1930s. In that era it was encouraged by many factors that no longer exist. During the Great Boom that preceded the Great Depression, airplane design was still very much in the formative and inquisitive stage, and everyone was trying something new. Dozens of manufacturers were producing innumerable different types of planes and engines, and competition flying was the accepted method of sales promotion. To the general public, airplanes were still something new and curious, and they were ready to flock in their thousands to see what all these planes could do when pitted against each other in assorted contests.

And so there were frequent air shows, from big national affairs attracting huge crowds to smaller, local ones. These shows featured races of all kinds, from tight dashes around a few pylons to long, cross-country events. Between races there were aerobatic demonstrations, mock air fights, dummy bomb drops, and anything else that anyone could dream up to give pilots a chance to throw airplanes around for the pure sporting fun of flying. Official "safety" supervision was rarely or never invoked to take the fun out of it. Military or naval planes usually showed up to give demonstrations of what the taxpayer was getting for his money, but the mainstay of the events was the flying of civilian airplanes by civilian pilots. These air shows contributed more than might be remembered to the growth of aviation; they were living showcases for the products and techniques of non-military progress, and they were persuasive recruiting grounds for future pilots and other air enthusiasts.

By the middle 1930s the persistence of the Great Depression had put a crimp in such activities. Few people could now afford to buy private planes, and the long list of manufacturers dwindled to the few that could manage to hold on in the hope of better times. The wide variety of planes and products, which had brought so much sparkle to competitive flying, no longer existed, and enthusiasm died from financial starvation.

After World War II little trace remained of the atmosphere of excitement and thrill that had once surrounded airplanes. To a once-awed public, they were now familiar objects of daily life. The new generation of sportsmen pilots had become conditioned, by a lengthening list of official flying restrictions, to fly prudently and sedately, and few of them had any excuse or inclination to become proficient in the trickeries of competition flying. Hardly any private owner would be eager to overload the insides of his expensive engine with the strains of full-throttle racing.

Today air forces and navies put on occasional shows in which the public may observe, free of charge, impressive demonstrations of military air activities. But such demonstrations have little resemblance to the contests that once drew thousands of paying customers to witness hot competition between sportsmen pilots. In a small way, such contests are sometimes revived here and there, but the days of their great glory have passed. Still, in their time, they rendered great services to aviation, and they deserve to be remembered.

2. The "Light Plane" Arrives

From the standpoint of the sportsman pilot, the state of aviation differed immeasurably after each of the two world wars. At the end of Hitler's war, comparatively few of the great number of wartime pilots showed any passionate desire to stay in aviation. In the experience of many of them, flying had become a heavily regimented business, governed by instruments, regulations, ground controls, and flight plans that severely damped the purely sporting joys of flying.

It had not been like that after the Kaiser's war. That struggle had seen aviation come of age; it was new and unrestrained, headed obviously for a future of unlimited adventure and discovery. The lure of the air was powerful, and of the thousands who had become pilots during those years, a large percentage sought around for means to keep on flying. But air forces had been cut to negligible numbers. Civilian flying jobs were scarce, and available usually only to the most experienced men. There were almost no planes that the ex-service pilot could afford to fly; war-surplus planes were cheap to buy, but much too expensive to operate. There was nothing else.

A few European plane makers toyed cautiously with the idea of producing planes for the private owner of moderate means. But market prospects were hopelessly nebulous, and there was little money floating around the industry for such speculative ventures. An even weightier problem was the fact that no small engines existed that might be suitable for such planes; and engine development would be another expensive speculation.

After a while the British Government, having now a separate Air Ministry, which was disposed to consider such matters, concluded that something ought to be done about this situation. The Ministry was not motivated by charitable thoughts of establishing an aeronautical welfare program; its plan was based on the hardheaded consideration that there was a national need to maintain, as economically as possible, a reserve of civilian pilots in case of future military emergencies. So it adopted the idea of offering prizes and other incentives for competitions that would encourage manufacturers to design and produce planes and engines small and cheap enough for the purse of the average private pilot.

The whole business really started in 1921, when the London *Daily Mail* offered substantial prizes for a glider competition, spurred on by disturbing rumors of how suppressed German aviation was maintaining its supply of pilots by the intensive development of gliders. Maurice Wright, Bill Sayers, and I pooled our efforts and finances into the design and construction of what we hoped was going to be the winning glider; but before we could work the bugs out of it, our homemade canvas "hangar" blew down one windy night and wrecked the glider inside it. This glider competition, held at Itford, in Sussex, aroused wide international interest.* It led the Air Ministry to conclude that the ideal low-cost private plane should be something on the lines of a glider fitted with a very small engine.

The Ministry, therefore, issued specifications in that category for the planes that would be eligible to compete for its prizes. Those specifications turned out to be hopelessly unpractical—for which the officials could hardly be blamed, for there was little but guesswork to go on. The winning planes were flimsy little affairs, with putt-putt engines often adapted from motorcycles, and I believe that not one plane built to winning designs was ever sold commercially. Just the same, the effort was very far from being wasted. The week-long competitions, held at Lympne, near Folkestone, and the races connected with them, were tremendous fun and attracted large crowds. The intensity of public interest in this class of flying was so obvious that it encouraged several manufacturers to venture into the "light plane" field with what they believed were more practical models, and still further competitions followed.

During the competitions, I flew several of the intriguing little types

* It was won by a Frenchman, Maneyrol, flying a French Peyret glider.

that were entered, but my special mount was the Parnall "Pixie II," a midget single-seat, low-wing monoplane of ingenious design, with sharply tapered wings of 18-foot span, powered with a motorcycle engine geared down to a matchstick of a propeller. Flying it was rather like flitting through the air on a noisy postcard. The pilot's goggles were its only windshield. Wide open, it could do somewhere around 70 mph, but the engine did not care too much for the full-throttle loads most of the contests called for, and it was very liable to cease operations at inconvenient moments. In races on rainy days, the wispy little propeller was occasionally chewed down, by a heavy shower, to a useless club, so that, one way and another, the Pixie gave me plenty of forced-landing practice.

In one of those unplanned landings I happened upon a remarkable piece of good luck mingled with a little comedy. At the end of one race I was heading the Pixie for the finish line a mile or so away, flying about fifty feet up over closely spaced hedges, ditches, and outhouses, when I smelled burning wood. This puzzled me, because there was no wood in the steel-tube fuselage structure. The explanation came fast. Suddenly the engine screamed into overspeed and, as I snapped back the throttle, I saw a blurred mass shoot on ahead and then come straight back at me as I overtook it. By the time I had ducked and heard something bang on the fuselage behind by head, I knew what it was. The friction of torque reaction on a possibly loose propeller boss had burned through the wood around the boltholes until the propeller was loose enough to take off on its own.

I had neither the time nor the altitude to look for somewhere to land in that cluttered area, but I didn't have to; there, straight in front of me, was the one possible place where I could have landed without crashing, a long, narrow strip planted in vegetables. All I had to do was to keep going and land. As I climbed out of the undamaged plane I heard a shout from behind and turned around to see a small farm boy running up with my little propeller in his hand. He said he had seen something fall off my plane, and was this it? I said thank you, yes it was.

As I said before, the popular success of these competitions attracted several manufacturers into the light-plane field, and the now historic De Havilland "Moth" led this general movement. According to official specifications, the Moth was too powerful (about 60 hp at first) to qualify as a "light plane," and it was not eligible for the early competitions; but it later sold in large numbers all over the world and I eventually helped to build it under license in the U.S.A. Other constructors joined the parade, the customers had an increasingly large number of models to choose from, and thus the foundations were laid for what is now generally known as "private flying."

Still, however, the ownership of a private plane was a relatively expensive business. And there was another big problem. The private flyer had almost no place to go, for few of the many wartime flying fields now remained in active operation, and the touring pilot could easily spend half a day in some far-out meadow, trying to get his little tank filled or to promote a ride into the nearest town. So then the Air Ministry followed up with another ingenious move which served its purpose admirably and, at the same time, induced the public to enjoy paying a large part of the costs.

It encouraged the formation of "Light Airplane Clubs," giving small subsidies for buying light planes that could be rented to members, and bonuses were awarded for training new pilots. These clubs were established close to numerous cities all over Britain; they were real clubs, with clubhouses, restaurants, bars, and lounges, and they derived a good deal of their support from non-flying members who just liked to watch the flying in comfort and mix with the flying fraternity. Club activities and interclub competitions and races—which soon became international—maintained a sporting and social interest in popular flying, which otherwise would have had a hard time surviving in the face of increasing costs, regulations, and restrictions. Many a Royal Air Force pilot who fought the Battle of Britain had started his flying career in one of these clubs.

In America during those postwar years, the would-be private pilot had none of the advantages that fell to his British counterpart. The government had no separate department for dealing with aviation and it apparently felt that private flying was not a subject for official interest, so neither the industry nor its potential customers received any sort of encouragement. Even when a few scattered constructors ventured to produce an occasional new type of plane that might serve the private pilot, there were no means of obtaining the airworthiness certification that could have helped to inspire confidence and promote sales.

On the other hand, the Curtiss "Jennie" wartime trainer, with its heavy but serviceable 90-hp "OX" engine, was available from surplus stocks in large numbers and at trivial cost, so that the story of American non-military flying for many years was very largely a story of the old reliable, but not very inspiring, Jenny and the venerable OX engine. In 1927 the way was cleared for more lively action when the U. S. Department of Commerce began to function as the regulating authority for civil aviation, and conditions were established under which private flying could develop on an orderly basis. By the end of the 1920s the Lindbergh boom had stirred up so much flying enthusiasm that numerous constructors all over America had gone into the business of producing a wider variety of planes for sportsmen pilots than Europe was ever likely to see.

3. The Palmy Days of Racing

Races of any kind are usually supposed to be contests of speed, and the unobstructed paths of the air promised limitless possibilities of speed to the pioneer sportsman pilot. But speed had nothing much to do with the results of early air races. Engines, which regularly broke down or broke up under normal loads, did so even more readily under racing strains, and a resulting forced landing was apt to do away with parts of the plane or all of it, and occasionally the pilot as well. Pilots lost their way through unskilled navigation or bad weather, and gusty winds were sometimes more than primitive controls could cope with. The winner was more likely than not to be the pilot whose luck— aided, perhaps, by a little skill—held out longest. All these uncertainties made for great excitement among the racers and the public that followed their fortunes.

With the general progress of aviation, such hazards gradually disappeared or receded until speed at last became the main deciding factor; but by then speeds had become so high, so expensive, and so predictable that the sporting element evaporated, and air racing lost most of its public appeal. Before that happened, however, there were two or three decades during which hard-fought races were a splendid feature of the aviation scene.

Races varied all the way from major events, usually with the most powerful planes available over long, cross-country courses in pursuit of valuable prizes or coveted trophies, to more intimate (and often more exciting) contests in which small craft chased each other around closed circuits in full view of the spectators. Some races were for speed only; others, especially with light planes, were handicap events, while sometimes separate speed and handicap prizes were awarded in the same race. In any case, races were not considered worthy of the name unless they called for full-throttle operation, which dragged every available ounce of power out of the engine.

I won the first race I ever entered. It was a major event, the London Air Derby of 1920. I won it with an improbable start, some sort of a speed record, and a spectacular finish.

This Derby was begun as an annual event in 1912, a race around London over a course varying from one hundred to two hundred miles. The start and finish were at Hendon Aerodrome, where it was a great social event, attracting numerous celebrities as well as large crowds of the public. As an aircraft apprentice I naturally had had vague dreams of one day flying victoriously in that race, but after the 1914 contest the event was shelved because of the war. When it was resumed in 1919 I had hopes of winning it as De Havilland's pilot with the powerful D.H.9R, but we couldn't get the plane ready in time.

For the 1920 race I hunted around for a promising mount. No luck; all the best planes already had their pilots. I resigned myself to being a spectator. Then, late in the evening before the race, Freddie Raynham telephoned me. He had hoped to fly the Martinsyde "Semiquaver" the next day, but he had had a minor crash while testing another plane and his wrenched knee was still too troublesome to allow him to fly. He asked me a superfluous question: Would I like to take the Semiquaver? He thought that, if I cared to take a chance with a plane I had never yet flown, I might have time in the morning to give it a quick tryout before the race.

The Semiquaver was by far the hottest prospect. It was a tiny, beautiful biplane with a 300-hp Hispano engine, built for nothing but speed. But there were snags. It was a brand-new design, and

Freddie had been able to give it only a couple of short preliminary tests before it was set up on a stand at the Aero Exhibition in London. Now, practically untested, it was to put its tremendous speed into a race of two laps, each of a hundred miles with six turning points, around London.

Early next morning I went out to Hendon. The plane had been dismantled from the Olympia Exhibition Hall, and the mechanics were now assembling it on the field. If they worked fast, I might have an hour or two to make a short flight and at least find out what the plane felt like. I discussed it with the engineers, who told me all the things about it that still had to be tested. I knew test flying; I knew that if I flew it now I was bound to find something that needed some essential change or adjustment—which might take hours or days. And that could well leave me out of the race. I decided to "go for broke" and take off into the race with no previous flight.

The dispatcher's flag dropped, I took off, swung low around the central pylon, and headed for Brooklands, the first turn point, about twenty miles to the south. I was combining a test flight with a high-speed race, and I soon began to make discoveries. First, the propeller pitch was too high, overloading the engine, cutting down revolutions, and raising water temperature. Then the radiator was too small, with an overflow pipe so located that the propeller swirl threw any steam or boiling water right at the open cockpit. I was to find out later that the landing-gear shock absorber had been pulled up tight to allow the plane to sit firmly on its exhibition stand, and nobody had had time to slack it off; in other words, on this fast-landing plane I had no effective shock absorber.

I was certainly the busiest man in the air that afternoon. To begin with, I had to watch every detail of an entirely unfamiliar plane as I skimmed the trees and housetops of suburban and rural scenery at not much under two hundred miles an hour. Then I had the three-handed job of juggling control stick, throttle, and map, for I had had no previous chance to make a preliminary trip over the course, and I could too easily lose the race by missing a landmark or one of the turning points. But mostly I was occupied with the throttle, trying to hold all the power I could get while keeping the needle of the water temperature gauge at two or three degrees below boiling. Now and then when I took a few seconds out to examine the map or the landscape, a gush of steam would warn me to jerk back the throttle to let things cool off a bit.

Still going strong, I reached Hendon at the end of the first lap, where I was required to circle the pylons before going off again. At the speed I was doing I had to pull the Semiquaver around so hard that I had my first experience of "blackout," in which centrifugal force drags the blood from the brain. This now-familiar phenomenon was quite unknown at the time, and I didn't tell anyone about it for a long time afterward—I was afraid the licensing medical people might find that it indicated something wrong with me.

The second lap was easier; I had mentally registered the landmarks, and at least I knew my way. I swung hard around the Hertford railway station onto the last leg.

As the finish point came in sight a few miles away, I decided to hell with the temperature. I shoved the throttle full open and let her rip. As I shot across the line, an easy winner, I had to duck low in the cockpit as clouds of steam and boiling water spewed around. I had figured that, once I closed the throttle for landing, the steam would let up. It did somewhat, but it still came out in gusts that made vision uncertain. I didn't dare to risk overshooting, for I was sure I had lost too much water to go around again, so I tried to land as short as I could —and I happened to pick a rough patch at the near end of the field.

I had never landed the Semiquaver before. And when I hit a little ridge the unadjusted shock absorbers absorbed no shock. The plane bounded high, turned over, and skidded along on its back. In that position the cockpit coaming was about half a dozen inches off the ground. My head smacked on something hard, and for a little while I watched a brilliant fireworks display. Then somehow I squirmed out of the small gap between the cockpit and the ground, just as the stretcher-bearers of the St. John's Ambulance Corps arrived breathlessly alongside to pick up the pieces. It turned out that all I needed was aspirin.

In 1922 King George V presented a silver cup for an air race around Britain. Thereafter it became an annual event, and the King's Cup Race replaced the London Air Derby as the great race of the year. I flew the race in several years but, except for one year, I was never able to complete the course. A split propeller, a blown-out spark plug, a hidden ditch in an intermediate landing field were among the items that, in one race or another, put me out of the running. But, on the one occasion when I did finish, I managed to win His Majesty's large and lovely cup.

That was in 1923, when I flew an Armstrong-Whitworth "Siskin" fighter, which, cleaned up for racing, was good for about 175 mph at full power. Its Siddeley "Jaguar" was a 14-cylinder, double-row, radial air-cooled engine, which could produce 350 hp when it felt like doing so. But it was, at that time, a rather new type of design and it still harbored a number of experimental bugs which the company had been slow in eliminating.

The circuitous course of eight hundred miles from London to Glasgow and back gave my uncertain carburetor system plenty of time to produce periodic spasms of coughing, barking, and sneezing from an engine that seemed liable to give up at any minute but finally dragged me home to victory. It was a little later that I discovered how narrow the victory had been—my landing gear, which had survived several intermediate landings, collapsed as the plane was being wheeled into the hangar.

My failure in 1924 was another kind of carburetor story, for it turned out to be something of a technical milestone in aircraft-engine history, teaching us something that now has long been common knowledge but was new to us at that time.

The 1924 race started from Martlesham, near Ipswich. I was flying the same Siskin fighter with which I had won the previous year, and the engine had undergone a number of modifications we hoped were improvements. Among those changes were carburetor revisions, which included a large-diameter air-intake pipe leading vertically down through the bottom of the cowling, in place of the two smaller horizontal pipes that had previously taken air from the sides. On tests, everything seemed fine. I was odds-on favorite to win the race.

I took off on signal, leveled off at about one thousand feet, and headed with wide-open throttle for Newcastle, the next stop. It was a cloudless August morning, with a moderate summer haze that left plenty of visibility. After fifteen minutes or so, something that looked like a small sheet of metal flew back past my head, coming from some unseen spot in front. Nothing seemed to develop from that, so I just kept it in mind and went ahead. After a while I got the impression that the engine was slowing up, and soon my tachometer showed that it really was. I couldn't think why; it was running smoothly enough. I checked everything I could, but now the loss of power was getting serious; with no other indication of trouble, the engine was acting exactly as though I were slowly closing the throttle. At last I couldn't even maintain altitude, and I saw that I would have to land. I tried to reach the Blackburn Company's airfield at Brough, near Hull, about 130 miles from the start, but I couldn't quite make it and had to land in a field a mile or so away. I was chagrined and mystified.

I switched off the engine, climbed out, and walked round to the front to look things over. The first thing I noticed was a hole, about eight inches square, in the propeller spinner, which explained the piece of metal that had come adrift. But this obviously had nothing to do with my engine trouble; I could have left it just as it was or else removed the whole spinner with no measurable effect on performance. I was still puzzling when I heard something "plop" on the ground. I glanced down to see what looked suspiciously like a large lump of ice which must have fallen out of the vertical air intake. I picked it up. It was ice, all right. Ice—on a sunny August morning? Absurd! Ridiculous! Impossible!

After some time, a group of Blackburn mechanics came strolling over. I told them about the ice. They looked at each other, evidently not sure whether I thought I was being funny. The ice, unfortunately, was no longer available as evidence. They went over the engine with me, but couldn't find any particular trouble. One of them swung the propeller and I ran up the engine. Perfect. It was now much too late for me to go back into the race, so I flew over to Blackburn field, went into an office, and telephoned the Armstrong-Siddeley factory at Coventry. I was put through to the tough Mr. J. D. Siddeley in person. When I told him about the ice he blew up. He said he would discuss with me later my real reasons for quitting the race, whatever they were, but why did I have to tell *him* that silly story about ice? So a report was issued to the press that I had retired from the race because of a broken spinner—and, for all I know, that story still stands. Nobody who knew my record believed either the spinner story or the ice story.

So it was generally assumed that I had hastily invented a feeble cover-up for some serious failure of the Jaguar engine.

However, the company's design engineers were not so skeptical. They made carburetor studies and concluded that, at continuous full throttle, it was quite possible, even on a fine day and in the heart of a hot engine installation, for a humid atmosphere to build up ice in the carburetor and choke it. Today, of course, carburetor heaters are standard installations.

High-speed air racing with powerful engines eventually fell into the discard largely of its own weight. The really fast planes became much too fast for closed-circuit events, and all that was left for them was the long, cross-country contests. The sporting excitement faded out of these because modern aids to navigation, all-weather flight equipment, and the extreme reliability of modern engines removed almost every element of chance, so that results could be predicted with little risk of error. There was nothing left to justify the high expense involved. The last of such races was the MacRobertson race from England to Australia, in 1934; under modern conditions, no such race is likely to be seen again. In America, for some years, such events as the Bendix and Thompson Trophy races continued to be run, but civilian sportsmen were eventually elbowed out of the picture by the participation of military planes and pilots, against whom sportsmen had little hope of competing. At last the races aroused so little general interest that I don't even know whether they are still being run.

Races with light planes were really an entirely different kind of sport. For one thing, of course, they were far less elaborate and expensive and consequently were much more frequent and popular— besides being a lot more fun for both pilots and spectators. Moreover, light-plane contests developed a different class of flying skills from those required for the high-powered, long-distance events. Nearly all light-plane races were flown over several laps of a closed-circuit course around local landmarks, and often even more closely around a few pylons within range of a flying field. Handicapping the racers gave everyone a chance to win and still left room for ingenuity in outsmarting the handicappers, for flying skill in outmaneuvering opponents on the straightaways, and for gaining ground by close cornering on the many turns.

Since early flying days, pylon racing around a large airfield had always been a gloriously exciting sport. In the low-speed era before World War I, it was a matter of fairly ordinary skill to round a pylon closely and dodge other planes at the same time; besides, practically all those early planes gave the pilot a wide-open view so that he could see where he was going on a turn. Gradually planes became faster, with higher stalling speeds, and so were less manageable on close-hauled turns, while many of them had wing arrangements that blanked off the pilot's turning view on a steep bank. Again, when the light-plane club movement spread around Europe, in the 1920s, handi-cappers in the interclub events, functioning in meet after meet, became so well familiar with most of the competing planes and pilots that they could pre-estimate performances with an accuracy that could bring the planes into a bunch for a tight finish. This meant that the last couple of turning points provoked a struggle for position and flying room, which added enormously to the excitement but also called for special skill and care on the part of the pilots; and even then collisions were always a hazard.

In 1927 I was flying a D.H. Moth in a handicap race at the Bournemouth Air Meeting. In the approach to the second-last pylon I took the lead from Longton, who was flying a Blackburn Bluebird; looking over my shoulder, I saw that Openshaw was rapidly over-hauling us both in his Westland Widgeon. At the actual pylon turn, the other two were a bare few yards behind me. As I rushed on to the last pylon I thought I might just get around it before Openshaw could overtake me in his outside position; and if I beat him on the turn I might win. Openshaw didn't appear; I turned the last pylon alone and won the race. As I circled to land I saw a cloud of black smoke arising alongside the second-last pylon. And when I had landed they told me that Longton and Openshaw had collided right behind my tail and both had been killed. Longton was one of the best-known pilots in the R.A.F., and he had recently been giving me night-bombing training as a reserve officer. Openshaw had worked with me on several test jobs. The game was beginning to get rough.

In 1929, at the National Air Races in Cleveland, Ohio, I entered for several events. The last two of these were hectic affairs over a fifteen-lap, five-mile course around five pylons. By now pylon racing had become something of a madhouse business. On top of earlier hazards, there were now cabin planes with window structures, and often hazed panels, which further impeded turning view. Moreover, a lot of new pilots had entered the game, full of aggressive enthusiasm but not much skill or judgment to go with it. They had no idea how to turn pylons cleanly; they climbed, dived, or zigzagged around them, giving more peaceful contestants the choice of getting out of their way or getting killed. On the last turn of the last race, cutting the pylon as closely as I dared, I found that someone with a small cabin plane was apparently trying to put his left wing tip into the open cockpit of my Moth—although the chances are that he never even saw me. To get clear, I had to haul in even closer over the top of the pylon, and I "won" the race only to find that I was disqualified for cutting the turn. There were lots of complaints and some very close shaves; my teammate for the American Moth Company, Russell Brown, had a couple of feet taken out of a wing tip, but he got down all right. Fun is fun—but there can be too much of a good thing.

Not long afterward, American newspapers gave wide publication to some gruesome photographs of a cabin plane (I think this was in Trenton, New Jersey), its tail cut off in a pylon-turning collision, swooping helplessly through the air before plunging fatally into the ground. This was about the end of popular pylon racing; thereafter this great sport was either prohibited or banished into obscurity, as far as widespread public interest was concerned, by stifling restrictions.

4. Aerobatics—and the Sopwith Camel

The fine old art and science of aerobatics has apparently fallen largely into disuse, if not actually into disrepute. It seems now to be popularly regarded as a frivolous form of showmanship, akin to the act of "the daring young man on the flying trapeze." In the official view it is evidently classed as "dangerous flying," and its practice is burdened by so many restraints and restrictions that the sportsman pilot is heartily discouraged from making a regular habit of it. Which is a great pity, for the ability to maneuver an airplane in all attitudes in three dimensions is a unique art in which humans, who were not designed to fly, can beat the birds at their own game.

Apart from its sporting aspects, the practice of aerobatics has made large contributions to our technical knowledge of controls, stability, aerodynamics, and structures.

However, the claim that it is a "dangerous" practice is wholly false. There is no safer pilot than the man who has learned, from aerobatic experience, to handle a plane by a sensitive "feel" of all its motions and controls, so that he can cope with tight emergencies that outrun the help of his instruments. Instruments, at best, tell the pilot what a plane is doing; aerobatic experience teaches him to recognize what it is going to do. I have known few pilots who have been killed in aerobatic activities, and then it has usually been the result of carelessness or recklessness; but I have known many pilots—including myself —who have often saved their lives by the skills acquired in aerobatics.

Unfortunately, however, the art of flying by "feel" has of recent years been much disparaged instead of being encouraged; it has become customary to refer to it contemptuously as "flying by the seat of the pants." The words imply that this sort of flying is some sort of crude and primitive technique, vaguely associated with frayed old-time pilots who have failed to graduate to the modern "refinements" of accepting instrument dictation. The fact is, however, that flying by feel is simply the essential art of piloting, which old-timers were never taught to despise.

Yet it is curious how this seat-of-the-pants delusion seems to persist. A few years ago some doctor with a sense of publicity that surpassed any other sense he may have had, proceeded to demonstrate this idiotic notion by anesthetizing his rump and going through some process of stunt flying. He widely reported his "scientific" findings, which were that, during the stunts, his benumbed bottom prevented him from feeling what was going on. This, he announced impressively, proved that the ability to sense the actions of an airplane was indeed located within the seat of the pants.

The earliest approaches to the tempting possibilities of aerobatics were severely restrained by the fear of stalling, which was considered practically certain to lead the pilot to a sticky end by producing complete loss of control. A pilot's skill and nerve were judged by the degree to which he dared to bank; the really hot stunt-flying artists might even pull the nose up and bank at the same time, but they took care to gather plenty of speed first.

Sooner or later, of course, someone was going to try to fly upside down, and in about September 1913 the French pilot Adolphe Pégoud made himself famous by doing so. When, a little later, he demonstrated "looping the loop," he started a new flying craze. Before long the world's pilots were popularly divided into two main categories: those who had looped and those who hadn't. At the time of the outbreak of World War I, loops and steep climbing turns were about the limits of the aerobatic pilot's repertoire; such ventures as spins, rolls, and other elaborate maneuvers were still a couple of years away.

My own entry into the aerobatic field began with unstudied and casual efforts to satisfy my native curiosity as to what would happen when I tried something "different." As mechanic pilot in the Royal Flying Corps I would try "crossing" controls, skidding into turns, sliding out of banks, falling out of climbing turns, and anything else in which I could quickly avoid stalling by pushing the nose down. Gradually I lost reverence for routine attitudes of flight. After increasing experimentation I was left with the comfortable feeling that henceforth I was unlikely to get into any control troubles that I couldn't get out of, and I considered myself entitled to try anything with a plane that I felt like trying.

During the later years of World War I, stunt flying was considered as a normal and stimulating way of passing a flying hour. After the war the same general attitude prevailed in the flying clubs and among private pilots with aerobatic inclinations; nobody considered it specially dangerous, and it produced no unusual record of accidents. Low-altitude aerobatics by competent pilots was not frowned upon, and nobody bothered with parachutes.

Personally I enjoyed aerobatic flying to the point where I made a specialty of it, and for many years I was called upon to give demonstrations in various countries. Particularly, however, I found aerobatics to be a valuable tool in test flying; surprising things might be discovered in unusual maneuvers with a new plane that might never show up in normal flight. I extended my curiosity in that respect to large, twin-engine planes; I discovered that, by using the engines differentially to assist the controls, I could persuade a well-behaved bomber to loop, roll, and spin almost as well as a fighter. My first public demonstration of this took place at the welcome given in England, in 1919, to the American Navy crew of the N.C.4 seaplane, which made the first trans-Atlantic flight, and I still see it referred to occasionally.

No discussion of aerobatics can usefully proceed without reference to the Sopwith "Camel," the most maneuverable airplane of all time. The Camel earned its undying fame by defeating more enemies in combat than any other type of plane in anybody's service. It achieved its success, with no outstanding capacities of speed or climb, simply by being able to baffle the enemy with its extreme agility. As one of the best-remembered planes in history, it seems to deserve some special attention in these notes.

The Camel was the greatest paradox of the air; a very bad airplane that did superlatively good work. Its vicious habits killed a distressingly large number of student pilots before they could learn to defeat its treacherous intentions. But, once mastered, its very defects could be put to use, and almost anything could be done with a Camel short of passing it through the eye of a needle.

I knew the Camel as well as anyone did. Apart from training work with its standard model, I did a great deal of experimental flying on Camels fitted with different engines and installations, including an especially difficult one for the U. S. Army. There has never been an airplane out of which I extracted more of the sheer joy of flying.

Strangely enough, the savage Camel evolved largely from the calmest and most docile of planes, the Sopwith Pup. But, as it evolved in size, power, and weight, it picked up defects all along the way. With its tank at the back, it was tail-heavy at the beginning of a flight and nose-heavy at the end, all of which was complicated by the fact that it balanced quite differently with engine on and off. If any stability had ever been intended in its design, it never showed up. It would be possible to make an impressive list of defects that would have caused the Camel to be rejected under any conditions other than the wartime pressures of its day.

Probably its most disconcerting abnormality was the exceptionally powerful effect of the engine's gyroscopic action (almost always misdescribed by historians as "torque"—engine torque had nothing much to do with it). With engine off, the plane was a fairly well-behaved, if unstable, little craft; with engine on, it was something else again. For example, when the stick was pulled sharply back, as it usually is in quick turns, the whirling mass of the rotary engine had the same effect as hard right rudder, with reverse effect when the nose was pushed down. Similarly, of course, sharp use of the rudder took over some of the elevator control. So, on a close right turn, rudder and engine acted powerfully together; on a left turn they opposed each other. If you turned on engine power to hasten recovery from a spin, the least overuse could switch you into an inverted spin—in which case everything worked the other way around.

To the bemused student, already trained to expect conventional obedience from his elevators, ailerons, and rudder; the Camel's conduct was mechanical mutiny. His problem was to survive long enough to discover how much he was flying the Camel and how much it was flying him. Too often, he didn't.

The student was up against another insidious peril. The pilot who had learned to take advantage of the trickeries of the Camel could make it flick around like an exuberant swallow, often so close to the ground that it all looked deceptively easy. It was very difficult to convince an enthusiastic beginner that he had much to learn before he could do the same things—and the Camel did not forgive mistakes.

Much as I respected the Camel, it had no particular respect for me. It made various attempts, from time to time, to catch me out, and on one occasion it came disturbingly close to succeeding. One afternoon I went to Yarmouth Naval Air Station to try a new seaplane. It wasn't ready, so to pass the time I borrowed Commander Egbert Cadbury's Camel for a little aerobatic exercise. (There was a landing field behind the seaplane hangars.) At one point in a series of casual gyrations, I decided to make a snap roll to the right as I pulled out of a dive. I shouldn't have done it, because it threw a doubly heavy load on the right wing, first because of the pull-out from the dive and second because of the additionally high angle that a roll imposed on the "inside" wing. The Camel knew this and resented it.

With a loud crack, the bottom right wing broke. The front spar parted completely, the fabric split right across the wing, and I could see the splinters where the rear spar had cracked but was still holding. The struts were loose in their sockets, bracing wires were slack and flapping, and the whole structure shook and dithered. A few seconds more, and the whole works was bound to fall apart—and I had a thousand-foot drop to look forward to. Hard left rudder could not quite overcome the swing to the right caused by the drag of the broken wing. Instinctively I put the nose down slightly to get a little more speed for increasing rudder control; but the extra speed only caused the broken structure to shake even harder. I slowed up, and the plane swung again to the right.

Still the bits held together, and a couple of centuries went by while I vaguely compromised between too much speed and too little rudder control. The Camel wavered toward the ground in a wide right turn, which through no skill of mine, brought it into the middle of the flying field. I had no thoughts beyond a trembling hope that the wing would hold together until I could make some sort of landing— any sort of landing. The right wheel touched the ground, the Camel bounced around and then apparently decided that I had had enough. It came to a stop—right way up.

For several dazed minutes I couldn't move to get out of the cockpit. Captain Chambers, the C.O., walked over with some mechanics, looked at the broken wing for a while, and then said, "You know, Courtney, if I were you I wouldn't do that again." And I knew the Camel was snickering quietly and muttering, "I'll bet you don't, you ham-fisted oaf."

There never was, and there never will be, another airplane anything like the Sopwith Camel.

CHAPTER XVIII

Days of the Great Flights

1. Exploring the Eighth Sea

By the late 1920s and early '30s, advances in engine economy and reliability had encouraged the notion that aircraft were ready to explore and exploit the world's longest and toughest air routes. Perhaps they were—but only just barely, and often not quite. Anyway, the outlook was cheerful enough to stir up a mounting wave of enthusiasm for attempting very long, and preferably very dangerous, flying performances. There were oceans, deserts, jungles, ice fields, and mountain ranges to be crossed by untried paths in the skies; there were parts of the earth to be reached in flight that were almost or entirely inaccessible by surface travel. There were wide distances to be covered at speeds that only the airplane could offer.

And so began the days of the great flights, when dozens of airmen rushed in recklessly to pioneer new tracks through the Eighth Sea that would some day, perhaps, be popular airways. Success was elusive; its rewards were fame, achievement, and on rare occasions, fortune. Failure was a more common story, for obstacles were formidable, experience was trivial, navigation was doubtful, resources were scanty, and equipment was strained to the limits of what it could take—and too often it didn't take it.

For many venturers, the penalty of failure was death, a penalty that did nothing to deter others. A long record of disasters began to be compiled. Some pilots died before they ever got started, crashing in desperate efforts to get their overloaded planes off the ground. Numerous others, with their crews, vanished in lonely oceans, crashed into snowy mountaintops, perished in burning deserts, or froze in icy wastes in those days of irrepressible search for flying adventure. Among their ranks were several of my old friends and flying companions.

These were years during which sensational stories of daring flights over perilous courses became the staple news diet of a fascinated public, who lionized the victors, saluted the lost, and absorbed fiction with fact so that, even today, it is often hard to distinguish history from legend.

I suppose most people are more or less familiar with details of the great pioneer flights that thrilled the world in that era, even if some of those stories have begun to fade into the mists of the past. But I doubt if many people ever realized fully the obstacles and problems that pilots faced in preparing the flights that brought them to fame or failure. The actual flights, which were all the public usually heard about, were more often than not the least of the pilots' difficulties.

Such projects cost money, sometimes lots of it. Occasionally a pilot was lucky enough to be employed by some aviation concern which, for prestige or other reasons, paid the expenses. A few pilots could finance their projects out of their own funds or those of wealthy friends. But usually the aspiring airman had to scurry around trying to arouse financial enthusiasm with any excuse he could think up. Sometimes he could invoke patriotic fervor, civic pride, or some such noble incentive. Then there was the good old stand-by of dangling the bait of publicity for some commercial product in return for financial support. Even that form of persuasion was difficult, for while advertisers would spend freely if assured of success, they usually fought shy of being associated with a possibly disastrous or fatal project. Whatever sources he tried to tap, a pilot needed an unfamiliar form of courage and endurance to face the drudgery of promoting and wheedling, from skeptical and discouraging humans, the funds and concessions necessary before he could even put his plans into shape.

Many newspapers have made noble contributions to aviation's progress with their offers of prizes and trophies for historic performances.

But when a newspaper, with the best of intentions, provided direct financial support to a conspicuous flying project, it inevitably became a sharp pain in the pilot's neck. In return for its expenditure, the publication naturally expected to be given exclusive rights to a story, which it then felt obliged to maintain at a high pitch of public interest. The pilot was badgered and high-pressured, while toiling with his preparations, to endorse regular announcements of improbable plans and schedules, noisy predictions of victory, or any flimsy puff that might be built into a paragraph or a column.

If the project gained any great public attention, rival newsmen clamored for material, which the pilot was obliged to refuse, and this could lead to unpleasant situations. On one of my occasions, a rival reporter, repeatedly jumping in my way while pestering me with questions, tripped over a rope on a seaplane dock and fell into the water. He later claimed that I had pushed him in. This, if true, would have been such a praiseworthy deed that I never bothered to deny it, and from then on he made a fairly good job of deriding my efforts.

Of the various long-distance flights that were attempted during that competitive era, it was the ocean crossings that generated most of the atmosphere of suspense. An excited public watched eagerly for news that an airman had reached the other coast; tension increased as time passed and it seemed that he might be overdue. And if at last he was posted as "missing," hopes rose and fell as search and rescue vessels went about their usually hopeless task.

The immense reaches of the Pacific presented an endless variety of paths for aviators to challenge. But the vast distances, with their frequent need for pinpoint landfalls at tiny islands or atolls, demanded unfailing equipment combined with perfect navigation; any default in either one of those essentials could bring certain disaster. The tragic outcome of the Dole Air Race to Hawaii in 1927 made that painfully clear; nobody would ever know whether the missing planes had suffered engine failure or whether they had run out of fuel looking for the islands. The brilliant careers of Amelia Earhart and Charles Kingsford-Smith ended when, in spite of great experience and the best equipment available, they disappeared in those limitless waters. Altogether, the Pacific was too desolate an arena to attract challengers in any large numbers. Moreover, from the standpoint of public interest,

Pacific-flying enterprises were difficult to follow; few people carry a mental map of those vast areas.

The Atlantic, on the other hand, was far more familiar territory. Its routes, heavily traveled on the surface, were a standing challenge to the pioneers of the air. Twenty years were to pass between the first successful air crossing and the final conquest of the Atlantic by commercial aircraft, dramatic years that were to bring fame and glory to some and death to many more.

2. Three Atlantic Flights

There is probably a good deal of excuse for the now popular belief that Charles Lindbergh was the first man to fly across the Atlantic. The sensational impact of Lindbergh's crossing made it easy to forget two other trans-Atlantic flights, which had taken place eight years earlier.

I was well acquainted with the principal performers in those three events. And I was long associated, one way and another, with an assortment of projects for flying the Atlantic, until eventually I got caught up in that business myself. So perhaps I may usefully review and compare the circumstances under which the first three trans-Atlantic flights were made.

The first plane to fly across the Atlantic was the U. S. Navy's NC-4 flying boat, which crossed from Newfoundland to Lisbon, Portugal, with stops in the Azores Islands, in May 1919.

Three weeks later John Alcock and Arthur Whitten-Brown made the first non-stop direct crossing, from Newfoundland to Ireland, in a Vickers landplane.

In May 1927 Charles Lindbergh flew non-stop from New York to Paris, which made him the first person to fly directly from the mainland of America to the mainland of Europe. His open-ocean crossing was about the same as that of Alcock and Brown.

From the day in 1909 when Blériot first struggled across the twenty-two miles of the English Channel, the prospects of a flight across the two thousand miles of the open Atlantic inspired visions of high drama in some probably far distant future. Someone, of course, would do it eventually, but the problems were prodigious and failure meant almost certain death. Those visions materialized into a challenge when the London *Daily Mail*, in late 1913, offered a prize of £10,000 ($50,000) for the first non-stop flight.

There were two 1914 aspirants that I know of. One of them, Lieutenant John Porte, a retired British naval officer who was working with Glenn Curtiss in America, was to fly the Curtiss "America" flying boat with the financial support of John Wanamaker. He was to be accompanied by George Hallett, whom I still see occasionally. The other was Gustav Hamel, an English sportsman pilot for whom I used to do odd jobs as an apprentice. It was probably just as well that the war's outbreak canceled those early plans, for I think their chances of success were dim. Incidentally, by a cynical trick of fate, Hamel was to be lost in a flight across the English Channel in 1914.

However, in 1919, as soon as the war was over, the contest was revived with enthusiasm. Wartime advances, especially in engines, had made it reasonably possible to cover the distance non-stop, at least with the assistance of the westerly winds that prevailed over the shortest direct route: from Newfoundland to Ireland.

The hazards of the prospective flight were all the worse for being quite unpredictable. Engines seemed reliable enough, but their accessories were treacherous; they would be strained to the limit, with plenty of time to fail in so long a flight. Day and night piloting in tricky ocean visibility would be a formidable problem with the elementary instruments of the day. Nobody quite knew what the navigation problems were going to be, especially at a time when ocean weather reports and forecasts were mostly guesswork. Unforeseen mishaps, in any of a dozen forms, could force a pilot down in a desert of waters where only a miracle could bring rescue.

So when, early in 1919, a number of airmen prepared plans and planes for this perilous contest, the world kept excited watch on what promised to be the most thrilling sporting event that aviation had so far seen.

An east-to-west crossing against inevitable headwinds was a practical impossibility, so the British contestants were faced with the laborious necessity of crating their planes and shipping them over to be assembled in Newfoundland. In addition, fields had to be found in the hilly terrain and prepared in makeshift fashion for the long takeoff runs of planes heavily overloaded with fuel. All this had to be accomplished with the funds available from private sources, for there was no thought of official help in the event.

While all this was going on, the U. S. Navy was preparing a gigantic production in order to make what could be called the first trans-Atlantic flight. Some of the sportsmen in Newfoundland were almost ready to start when, on May 16, a group of three NC (Navy Curtiss) flying boats, each with four engines and a crew of four or five, set out from a Newfoundland harbor headed for the Azores. Their route was marked by a dotted line provided by a fleet of naval vessels stationed at frequent intervals. Flying mostly by day, they were to make stops in the Azores and then continue to Lisbon. One of them, the NC-4, commanded by Lieutenant Commander A. Read, with Walter Hinton as chief pilot, completed the trip, taking eleven days to do so.

This rather ponderous demonstration by a government department was the first trans-Atlantic flight. But so little impression did it make on the public and on history that when in recent years I have sometimes asked groups of pilots, including modern U. S. Navy pilots, "Who was the pilot of the first plane to fly across the Atlantic?" nobody has been able to answer me.

This Navy performance had pulled the rug from under the aspirations of the civilian pilots to be first across the Atlantic. However, it was still open to them to make the first direct crossing, and incidentally to win the *Daily Mail*'s handsome prize. Harry Hawker, in a desperate effort to beat the NC seaplanes, started off while there was still much to be done on his Sopwith plane. His plane never reached the other side; and while the public was mourning the loss of one of Britain's most brilliant pilots, Harry reappeared in dramatic fashion. It turned out that he had had trouble with his radiator shutters, which had caused his engine cooling water to boil away—and he had had the miraculous luck to ditch alongside a lonely little freighter, which, having no radio, could not announce his safety until it arrived in port many days later. Then Freddie Raynham's Martinsyde ran out of field length on his overloaded takeoff run, and crashed.

Three weeks after the NC-4 arrived in Lisbon, Jack Alcock took off from a rough Newfoundland pasture in his twin-engine Rolls-Royce

Vickers "Vimy" wartime bomber, headed for Ireland. With him was Arthur Whitten-Brown as navigator. I had flown with Jack a couple of times before the war, when I occasionally gave him a hand with the Sunbeam engine, which he was testing in a Maurice Farman. He was a rugged pilot with the stolid endurance that was needed for manhandling a "Vimy" for long hours on end.

The modern pilot can hardly appreciate Alcock's achievement unless he has tried to fly a heavy plane through storm clouds with no blind-flying instruments of any kind. Alcock did this at night over a feature-less ocean, and he repeatedly evaded disaster by the narrowest of margins, often losing control and regaining it within a few feet of the water. At last, after more than sixteen hours, he managed to scrape across the Irish coastline with a failing engine, landing with minor damage in the first available open space.

Sir John Alcock was the first pilot to receive knighthood for a feat of airmanship, and this honor brought welcome prestige to the new profession of civil flying. His flight, however, led to no particular developments, technical or otherwise. The Atlantic had been flown, the big prize had been won—and that was that. There was no further incentive for anyone to emulate so obviously hazardous a feat. And so things remained for eight years, until 1927, the year of Lindbergh's fabulous success.

When the rush started to compete for the Orteig prize for the first non-stop flight between New York and Paris, it aroused a new wave of interest. This time the contest was not confined to an Atlantic flight; it called for an intercontinental trip, of which the open Atlantic crossing was about half the distance. But inevitably public interest concentrated on the Atlantic aspect of the challenge.

Since 1919 there had been big technical advances in aviation. Air-planes, engines, accessories, fuels had been improved to permit the carrying of greater loads with much higher reliability. And the loads could be in the form of more fuel for greater distances. In particular, new and more refined instruments had been developed which disposed of the worst problems of flying blind—at night and in bad weather—at least for experienced pilots. Only in cruising speeds had there been no noticeable improvement; for reasons I explained in an earlier chapter, these remained at little better than a hundred miles per hour.

In principle this was to be an international contest, with competitors free to start from either continent. But in practice it was essentially an American contest, because that same old business of the prevailing winds gave an overwhelming advantage to a pilot starting from New York. At the outset the race showed no special signs of developing into anything more than a passing wave of general excitement. But two factors were to combine to make it the most fruitful contest in air history.

For one thing, the timing was highly propitious. America had long lagged behind Europe in aviation developments, and it was just about ready to break out of this curious form of isolationism. A financial boom was in the making, and it needed only some impressive incentive to awaken the public to the vast possibilities of financial investment in aviation—which was just what American aviation had long been needing more than anything else. In that receptive atmosphere Lindbergh won the contest under a romantic combination of circumstances that turned an unknown airman into a national hero, stirred up a hectic public interest in America's place in aviation, and set the stage for America's later pre-eminence in the air.

It was the aftereffects of Lindbergh's flight, more than the flight itself, that made his performance a unique affair in flying history. It is not, therefore, surprising that Lindbergh and his trans-Atlantic flight should be well remembered by a generation that has long forgotten the others.

3. *The Success of a Failure*

My own trans-Atlantic efforts, in 1927 and 1928, had nothing to do with any prizes or contests, or even with any attempt to create a record. But it happened that, during those two years, other events occurred that caused ocean-flying ventures to take on the aspects of an epidemic. The world's newspapers whipped up almost daily stories of exciting flight projects, sensational records, and dramatic disasters. My particular activities got caught up in this splurge of headlines, but in fact they arose out of a program that originally did not contemplate an Atlantic flight.

I propose to tell the story at some little length, partly because I have never given my own account of an adventure that has received frequent attention elsewhere, and partly because it provides a fairly typical picture of the problems and risks that beset the pioneer in those hectic days of long-distance-flying enterprises.

It all started in 1926 with an ambitious scheme I had for interesting shipping lines in adding flying boats to their fleets to serve as high-speed auxiliary transports for mail and express. The essential idea was that the seaplanes could use steamship bases, operating organizations, communications, and services, becoming airborne simply for purposes of speed.

The scheme met with warm encouragement from a number of progressive maritime executives led by Sir Alan Anderson of the Orient Line; on the other hand, their more conservative and skeptical colleagues took the view that ships belonged on the water, where they had sailed for thousands of years, and had no business up in the air. My original plan, which called for demonstration and survey flights along the main steamship lanes between Europe and the Orient, was studied and debated for many months, but it ran into heavy problems of politics and finance. At last, after a long and complicated series of program variations, I found myself committed, early in 1927, to a demonstration which involved a round-trip flight; with a fully equipped flying boat, between England and Canada, via the Azores, Newfoundland, and New York. This, it was thought, would adequately impress the shipping people and lead to further developments.

As I had it worked out, it seemed a perfectly feasible proposition. And in fact it would have been, except for one major speculative factor: in the case of an established service, there would be an en-route organization for spares, repairs, and maintenance; I had no such organization, and I had to go ahead with a pioneer's optimistic hopes of escaping serious difficulties.

My own confidence was matched by that of several firms whose aid I needed in the matter of equipment. The flying boat I had chosen was the German Dornier twin-engine "Wal," which was by a long way the fastest and most seaworthy seaplane of its class; the Dornier

Company hadn't a new plane available, but they arranged to supply the plane that Amundsen had used in the Arctic, fully overhauled and repaired. The Napier Company offered to lend me two of their 450-hp "Lion" engines. The Marconi people came up with a complete long-range radio installation to work on maritime frequencies; it included the still-experimental radio direction finder—if it could be made to work. The instrument companies provided their latest models, and the Shell Oil Company arranged to lay down fuel supplies en route. Perhaps my most flattering endorsement came from a group of Lloyd's underwriters, who agreed to insure all this borrowed equipment.

My optimism tripped over its first major snag when I rashly assumed that, since all the principal equipment costs were being taken care of, I could meet incidental expenses out of my own funds, reinforced by contributions from friends. But I had badly underestimated those expenses in the first place. Worse still, I had failed to allow for the odd items of delay that habitually afflict aviation preparations. Dornier needed more time for repairs; the radio installations required special studies and checks—and so on and on. Funds were running low.

At this critical point a London newspaper, in collaboration with an American news syndicate, offered me a substantial contribution and other help in exchange for my exclusive story, and I was only too glad to accept. I didn't know what I was letting myself in for. Because, just about that time, news developments on the Atlantic front generated a flood of limelight that practically blinded my project. The Raymond Orteig prize offer had set off a sort of trans-Atlantic stampede, and several famous pilots were rushing preparations to be first across. A general assumption grew up that I was somehow involved in this rush, although the Orteig prize involved a non-stop flight, which could be no part of my program. My newspaper friends, perhaps excusably, wanted to tie in my story with all these other flights.

My plane was still being overhauled at Friedrichshafen, Germany, when Nungesser and Coli were lost at sea and Lindbergh made his famous crossing. But the newspaper thought it would still have a good story if I got started while trans-Atlantic flying news was still hot. I tried to cope with the pressure of daily publicity which urged me to get going. I flew my plane from Germany to England with my wife as copilot (she had learned to fly the previous year), while the Dornier people were still unsatisfied with the repair work. The Marconi people were discouraged by being rushed to complete their installations with insufficient tests and checks. I won't go into the innumerable other details of the confused situation which propelled me into action with equipment that was still half-baked or worse.

At any rate, I took off at last early one morning from Plymouth, headed for the Azores. My communications radio was working uncertainly, my direction finder not at all. The takeoff was a fearsome job, because the hasty repairs to the heavily loaded hull started to give way, and it was a question whether I could get into the air before the incoming load of water prevented my taking off at all. I covered one thousand miles while I checked performance and reviewed possibilities. In a short while I would reach the Azores, but the state of my equipment would almost certainly leave me stranded there, infinitely far from adequate help. I made my painful decision; I turned back and, late that afternoon, I reached the harbor of La Coruña, in the north of Spain. Later I flew the plane back to Germany.

Thus my 1927 effort ended in an unholy flop, made all the more dismal by the flood of publicity that had attended it.

My 1928 venture was quite a different affair. It had the bad luck to end in disaster, but the good luck to scrape through that disaster, by a narrow margin, without adding to the list of trans-Atlantic tragedies. And, in the process, it provided my crew and myself with a series of adventures that none of us would have wanted to miss.

A wealthy Canadian named Elwood Hosmer had tried to come to my financial aid in my former effort, but he had not been in time to alter the main course of events. Now he offered, as a strictly sporting proposition, to buy me a brand-new Dornier seaplane and take care of financial problems. His only condition was that he should be taken along for the ride. The Napier and Marconi people, and others who had previously lent me their equipment, cheerfully offered to support me again.

The plane was ordered from the Dornier production factory, which had been established at Pisa, Italy, to avoid Allied Peace Treaty restrictions on German aircraft production. The engines, radio, and other gear were shipped to Pisa for installation. My program was essentially the same as before, except that, this time, we obtained

Canadian registration (with call sign G-CAJI) and planned to start directly from Pisa to the Azores via Lisbon.

My crew, apart from Hosmer, who was appointed steward, was to consist of a flight engineer and an expert marine radio operator; the latter, a Marconi man who had volunteered for the job, was to join me at Lisbon. I needed no copilot or navigator; for its size the Dornier was very light on the controls, and for navigation I relied on a combination of my own dead reckoning and the radio direction finder.

After a few months the plane was ready, preliminary test flights were made, and we started on the air tests of our equipment. And then we had a bad shock. We couldn't get the all-important radio direction finder to work; its signals were completely drowned out by engine ignition noises—and there was at that time no practical method of providing ignition shielding. A flock of experts, English and Italian, were let loose on the installation; wiring changes cut the noise by about half, but it was still too bad.

We were losing a lot of time and sleep on the problem, which somehow had to be solved, when I woke up one night with a brain wave that produced an absurd but workable solution. When a bearing was required, I would climb an extra couple of thousand feet and then cut the engines. While I glided down, the operator would take his bearing, and then I would open up again. In the first tests the ignition was switched off altogether—not a very attractive procedure for open ocean work; but we soon found that, with a little practice, an operator could take his bearings through the small amount of noise that came from fully throttled engines. It was hardly the sort of routine that would appeal to a modern airline crew, but it turned out to suit our urgent purposes very well.

In early June, just as we were ready to start off, we were halted by a drama that was being enacted far away, at the North Pole. The dirigible *Italia*, on a polar expedition under General Nobile, was announced to be missing, and an air search was being hastily organized by the Italian authorities. Hosmer promptly offered our services, especially because of our long-range capability and because we knew, from Amundsen's earlier experiences, that the Dornier could operate effectively from flat stretches of ice as well as from water. I hurried from Pisa to Rome and discussed plans with General Balbo, Mussolini's air chief. Balbo was reluctant to interfere with our Atlantic plans, but said he would be grateful if we would stand by in case of need. Nobile was at last found by a Swedish airman and was brought back with the survivors of the dirigible's crash. We were released to go on our way—not suspecting that our little gesture would, later on, be usefully rewarded.

It was mid-June when we left Pisa, reaching Lisbon in a thirteen-hour flight. There we awaited our unknown radioman. A few days later there arrived Hugh Gilmour, an impassive character who promptly startled me by announcing that he had never before been up in the air. He went on to say casually that, as long as his ship had good radio equipment, it was all the same to him whether the ship stayed on the water or took off from it. He was totally unimpressed with the prospective dangers of Atlantic flying; he considered that sort of thing nothing to worry about after going through storms on some of the miserable little freighters he had served on. As it turned out, I couldn't have found a better man.

Some time was spent giving Gilmour enough air practice to check out his gear, and especially to get the hang of the eccentric direction-finding system we had devised.

I had given no thought to a mail-carrying project. But, at the last moment, the Portuguese Post Office asked me to take a small mail bag for what was to be the first air mail from Lisbon to North America. A cancellation stamp was hastily prepared, some mail was collected from those who had time to hear about it, and the mail bag was taken aboard. In spite of my subsequent misfortunes, the mail was picked up and delivered through the New York Post Office, and the few covers are now collector's items.

We left Lisbon Harbor for the Azores early on June 28. Cruising smoothly at ten thousand feet, we seemed to have left all our problems behind. Gilmour was busily in contact with an assortment of ships, from liners to frieghters, some of whom found it difficult to grasp the fact that they were swapping signals with a ship that was up in the air. I sent off to my wife the first ship-to-shore telegram ever sent from the air, and it was duly delivered to my home in London by the regular telegraph service.

Navigation was no problem; with our RDF we took regular bearings on the radio station on São Miguel Island, and passed over the top of it with an easy 150 miles to go to Fayal Island. After thirteen hours in the air I settled down to a smooth landing in Horta Harbor, and tied up to one of the mooring buoys. I had hoped to refuel quickly and take off before nightfall for Newfoundland—but our troubles had started. Just before I landed, two of the long wires that formed the Bellini-Tosi loops of our DF system had come adrift. Worst of all, the constant-speed drive, on which we relied for maintaining frequency on our air-driven transmitting generator, had broken.

A regular route organization would have had the spares and equipment to fix these little troubles in short order. As it was, it would take us months to get spares by ship, and we would have to try to rebuild and balance a tricky piece of mechanism with the simple machine-shop facilities of the local cable relay station. We did it, but it took us three weeks, including a couple of depressing failures on test flights.

While this was going on, some high-powered competition arrived on the scene. A supply ship of the French Navy showed up in the harbor announcing that it was there to service a CAMS flying boat the Navy had sent out to follow the same route as ours and that was due in a couple of days. The CAMS, commanded by Lieutenant de Vaisseau Paris, duly arrived—but apparently it only just made it. It was in trouble with engines and everything else, and was in no shape to go any farther; the supply ship was going to hoist it aboard and take it back home. The charming Lieutenant Paris was so deeply distressed that we made him a sporting offer to come along with us when we were ready. He was elated at the idea. But this was too much for the dignity of the French Navy, and when he cabled for permission he was bluntly refused.

At last we were ready to resume our journey. I had been receiving regular weather reports and forecasts from Washington and London, but these were often in such wide disagreement that obviously the time was far off when Atlantic weather information would be anywhere near adequate. At last I decided I would have to take my chances on scouting the weather for myself; if things looked good I could keep going, if not I could turn back.

On our first daybreak departure from Horta, headed for Newfoundland, we had a chance to test this program. There was only a moderate headwind as far as the little islands of Flores and Corvo, but beyond them the wind began to stiffen and the seas to pile up. Soon we were in heavy rain, with clouds so low that we were almost down to sea level. The storm-whipped water was a limitless sheet of foam. A big white object loomed ahead in the blur of rain and spray. It turned out to be the breaking of heavy seas as they smothered a smallish freighter plodding its weary way. We didn't envy the crew and I doubt that they envied us; they must have wondered, as we skimmed their masts, what sort of idiots would be out in an airplane over mid-Atlantic in that kind of weather.

It could, of course, be a local condition, so I held course while Gilmour checked with shipping. After a while he raised a Cunarder, which, from the position it gave, was about four hundred miles ahead. They reported a 35-knot westerly gale, with barometer still falling. That did it. With the best of luck we would run out of daylight at the other end and it would be no fun searching for a landing spot in Newfoundland in the dark. We streaked back to Horta, with the gale now behind us, in about half the time it had taken to go out. We had been about twelve hours in the air.

After that experience I decided, for the next attempt, to make an evening takeoff and fly through the night, so that I would have daylight to deal with any terminal problems. On August 1, at five in the evening local time, I took off on what was to be the Dornier's last flight.

At 6:30, neatly on schedule and under a clear sky, I passed Corvo and Flores. The sun was setting behind towering black clouds on the western horizon, and I guessed, without much worry, that we might be in for a rough night. Daylight was almost gone when I saw, stretched low across my track, the ominous roll cloud of the typical line squall. I knew now that the clouds ahead were thunderstorms and that I was going to have some work to do to keep the Dornier under control. I had had some thunderstorm flying experience, but I had never flown the Dornier blind or at night. I told Hosmer and Pierce, the engineer, to check everything possible and then take their seats, tighten their belts, and hang on. I pulled up into the cloud and leveled off at fifteen hundred feet—low enough, I hoped, to keep out of the worst of the violent updrafts and not too close to the water in case of control trouble.

Suddenly everything hit us; torrential rain with snatches of hail, lightning flashes that lit up the enveloping cloud to almost continuous incandescence, and a wild turbulence that tossed the plane around in all directions. For a while, regardless of heading or altitude, I concentrated on the flashing lights of my Reid turn indicator, with the main idea of staying as nearly right way up as possible. Perhaps somewhat to my surprise, it took me very little time to be certain that the highly co-operative Dornier was not going to get away from me, however much it was thrown around. My altimeter was showing gains and losses of several hundred feet as the fierce vertical currents played games with me; but this wasn't bothering me too much, and soon I was able to attend to my compass and maintain a reasonably good heading. My Lion engines were roaring smoothly. Now I was perfectly happy, and I didn't care if this sort of thing went on all night.

It went on for two hours, with brief intervals of relative quiet between one storm and the next. We emerged from the cloud below an overcast, and a prolonged period of peace convinced me that the worst was behind us. I told Gilmour to let out the antenna, which he had previously wound in as a lightning precaution, and start checking his Newfoundland stations, because I would soon be ready to climb so that he could take bearings on the way down.

With no warning, disaster struck. And then things happened with frantic rapidity. Suddenly came the bangs of a backfiring engine. A strange orange glow flickered on my windshield and, almost at the same moment, Pierce shouted in my ear, "The rear engine's on fire." I looked back just as the lower cowling released a flood of flaming fuel, which—as we knew later—had been fed into it by a broken fuel line. An inflight fuel fire is blood-curdling enough in the daytime, when all you can see is the torching flame with its trailing plume of black smoke. But at night it is a far more fearsome sight, for the flames appear longer and brighter and, instead of the smoke, there is a train of brilliant sparks that pour out far behind, swathing the tail and turning the plane into a winged comet.

Any number of things must have come to my mind during those few hectic seconds; but the only thing that seemed to matter was to get down on the water, somewhere in the blackness fifteen hundred feet below, before something blew up, or the tail burned off, or some equally final disaster took place. I cut the engine switches and shoved the nose down as steeply as I dared—if I dived too steeply I could plunge into the waves before I could see them soon enough to level off. At the same moment Fred Pierce performed a feat of quick thinking and courage that probably gave us the margin that saved us. He remembered that, for reasons connected with the fuel-system design, the only fuel cutoff from the gravity tanks to the engines was up in the nacelle, and with the propellers still spinning, the pumps were continuing to feed fuel into the flames. With the agility of desperation he clambered out onto the hull and up through the small access hole into the nacelle. Fumbling in the small space between the two engines, he started to turn off the cock under the rear gravity tank. He was still up there when we hit the water.

Gilmour behaved as though this sort of thing happened to him every day. He shouted something about "Looks nasty," rapidly wound in the trailing antenna as I had instructed him always to do when we were approaching the water, and then sat back to await developments. Hosmer's little cockpit was right under the blazing engine; for a while he stayed there to avoid getting in the way of any crew activities, but the heat soon forced him to squeeze his way forward through the little bulkhead door.

I had often claimed that I could set a Dornier down safely in any kind of sea, and now I was about to discover whether I had merely been bragging—although I will submit that this was rather an unfair test. I guessed that the waves would be high in the wake of our storm, but I had no idea of the direction of the wind or the run of the swells. It must have been at about two hundred feet that I could first make out dimly the whites of the wave crests, and a few seconds later I was skimming the breakers, which now gleamed a sort of yellow in the light of our flames. I really don't know exactly what happened then. I suppose I followed well-learned routines of rough-water seaplane work, and I remember that, for some instinctive reason, I held hard left rudder for several seconds before touching down. Then, as I went through landing motions, vaguely expecting some shattering blow, the hull slid onto the water with hardly a jolt and no bounce at all.

Almost at once I ran head on into a great wave, which broke over us and shocked us violently to a standstill.

It was just about midnight local time; we had been eight hours in the air and had covered something over half our distance to Newfoundland. We could spare a few seconds to congratulate ourselves on a safe arrival on the surface, but at the moment we were a long way from being out of danger.

For when we came to rest on the water the flames that had trailed aft now burned straight up, feeding on the fuel that had been flowing into the nacelle structure and, for all I knew, was still flowing. And their blaze was now surrounding the twenty-gallon gravity tank at the back of the engine. As the flames repeatedly flared up and died down, it looked as if the tank connections were giving way in the heat, dripping more fuel into the uncontrolled fire below. And if the fittings finally did give way, a mass of blazing fuel would be dumped down into the hull, where ten main tanks would promptly blow up. We could never have provided effectively against all risks of fire, and the only protection we carried was a little two-pound extinguisher to deal with small engine-starting fires. Pierce squirted this into the flames with no visible effect.

Unmindful of the heavy rolling and yawing of the boat as it drifted backward in the breaking seas, we stood or sat on the hull, drenched in spray, hanging onto anything we could grasp, and waiting numbly for the explosion. It was by far the most terrifying part of the whole affair, for we felt utterly helpless. I will never know how long this lasted; it might have been five or ten minutes, but it seemed like an hour before we were sure the fire had burned itself out. Pierce's stout effort in turning off the gravity tank had been successful, and what we had been watching was the burning out of the pools of fuel that had previously gathered in the nacelle.

Now I wakened to the drunken oscillations that were burying the wing tips in the waves and threatening the structure. I sat at the controls, "sailing" the craft with rudder and ailerons against the wind to keep it headed into the oncoming seas—a familiar art to the old-time seaplane man—while Pierce and Gilmour dragged out our sea anchor, attached its lines, and lowered it over the bow.

There is a ghostly fascination in riding out rough water in a low-lying seaplane at night. There is no real horizon, and each foaming comber appears to rush to the attack on top of a jagged hill of water, with the threat that it must inevitably break over the hull and swamp it through the open cockpits. But as the bow lifts to the oncoming swell and the air is thrust under the wings, the plane backs off like a boxer retreating from a blow, while the foam swirls past on each side and only the spray comes harmlessly over. Many a seaplane has capsized in a rough sea through the loss of a wing-tip float that failed to stand up to the incessant pounding, but the sea wings of the Dornier left us no such fears. With the sea anchor holding the boat head to wind, we felt we could now stay afloat indefinitely.

After a couple of hours the clouds broke up and the moon shone through. We considered our situation, and there seemed to be one slight remaining chance of continuing the journey. The seas were calming down, and perhaps by daybreak they might be smooth enough for me to try a takeoff with the forward engine alone. Dawn broke with a long rolling swell that would not be too bad for a takeoff if we could make it. We took in the sea anchor. Pierce made a general check and then cranked up the forward engine. After warm-up, I opened the throttle for a test run along the swell—if things looked favorable we could jettison some fuel and try a real takeoff. We had hardly gathered any speed before Pierce shouted a loud alarm; the rear engine was rocking so badly in its burned and buckled mount that it threatened to crash down through the hull at the first good jolt.

We gave up. The excitement was over; we sat around with the gloom of failure settling over us and faced the depressing task of finding help.

Our first SOS was picked up at once by the Cunard liner *Cedric*, which undertook to organize communications with other shipping. Very shortly we were in contact with four other liners and the Shell tanker *Achatina*. Taking DF bearings on their signals, we could chart a more accurate position than my earlier, dead-reckoning estimate, and Gilmour transmitted this to the ships. It seemed that there was now nothing more for us to do except to wait. And that easy thought led us into a serious mistake.

Our only electric power came from one small emergency battery; it ought really to have been enough, but now we used it rather prodigally in the exchange of more signals, especially with the *Achatina*, which thought it could reach us first. We forgot the fact that ships would take a long time to come up, and meanwhile we were drifting rapidly eastward in the Gulf Stream and the stiff breeze that had sprung up anew; and I don't think we realized that our proud big Dornier was no more than a small speck on the wide ocean. Around four o'clock in the afternoon the German liner *Columbus* broadcast that they had reached our position and could see no sign of us; they called for us to transmit a signal on which they could take a bearing.

We tried; but now our transmission signal was too weak, and our power was good enough only for reception. All we could do was listen in to the exchanges of messages between the frustrated ships as they discussed plans for further search, which, because of our failure to conserve our power, would now be pretty much a guessing game.

In due course the sun began to set over a calm ocean, and we were speculating what the coming night and following days might hold for us when a column of smoke appeared on the western horizon, followed by a tall funnel and then a large black hull. For a while it was heading straight for us and then, to our dismay, it started to turn south. Again it turned toward us, and kept coming. It was the 22,000-ton liner *Minnewaska*, under Captain Frank Claret, who, knowing a little about seaplanes, had made an extra-large allowance for our windage and had held an eastward course longer than had been planned. At that, he might have missed us except that, just as he was changing course, a keen-eyed sailor up in the crow's nest spotted the distant and intermittent flashing of the setting sun on our wing as we rolled in the swell.

By the time we were aboard the liner it was dark. Our mail bag was handed over to the purser. The liner had no adequate means of picking up our Dornier, and we unhappily left it where it was, thinking we had seen the last of it.

Four days later we steamed into New York Harbor. I was leaning idly over the rail watching a large tugboat, gay with bunting, that had drawn alongside. Someone grabbed my shoulder and, before I knew quite what was going on, my companions and I were being bundled into the tugboat. For a moment I thought we were being arrested for something. And then Grover Whalen, complete with formal attire and gardenia, mystified us further by greeting us in the name of the City.

We were landed at the Battery, from which a motorcycle police escort, with sirens screaming, rushed us to City Hall. Mayor Jimmy Walker, in all his legendary elegance, surrounded by a group of uniformed officers and city dignitaries, made a graceful broadcast speech of welcome, from which we learned that we were hero pioneers. For several days, as bewildered guests of the City, we were housed at the Ritz-Carlton Hotel, wined and dined, and fully equipped with new clothes and personal gear.

Well, it was very refreshing indeed to know that someone thought we were heroes at a time when we ourselves were wincing under a sense of dismal failure. Perhaps, however, our failure was not quite as complete as it seemed. A tragic succession of ocean-flying aspirants had paid for failure by vanishing to their deaths, and there were still to be many more. We, on the other hand, had set out to demonstrate that it was possible to operate airplanes across the ocean with reasonable prospects of surviving even the worst of misadventures. To that extent we had succeeded. But, by a twisted process of logic, in order to succeed in that demonstration we had to fail in the flight. It was left to us to squeeze what consolation we could out of that thought.

We even got our Dornier back. A week or two after our arrival I had a message that the Italian freighter *Valprato* had found it afloat in mid-ocean and brought it into Montreal. So it got there after all, if not exactly as planned. The Italian Consul in Montreal informed me that, on the personal orders of Mussolini, it was to be handed over to me without salvage claim, in recognition of our earlier offer to assist in the search for General Nobile.

The plane's structure had been smashed beyond repair while being hauled aboard the little steamer. But the Napier Company got their engines back. Their examination established the cause of our fire: a copper fuel line (there were then none of the modern fuel-line materials) had crystallized through vibration; it had first cracked so as to dribble pools of fuel into the nacelle and had then broken to allow the full fuel flow to flood the compartment; a backfire from the expiring engine had set everything alight. Marconi and the instrument people got back their expensive equipment virtually undamaged. The Lloyd's underwriters had only a few small claims to pay.

Elwood Hosmer, who had bought the plane and borne all the expenses, declared that he never thought anyone could get so much fun for the money.

Things could have been worse.

CHAPTER XIX

THE SEAPLANE STORY

1. *The Seaplane's Golden Years*

There was once a day when the great flying boat was the majestic Queen of the Air, and there was every reason to suppose that this must always be so. The huge intercontinental flying liners carried their passengers, in the spacious comfort of cabins and lounges, over thousands of ocean miles. Far from land, the big Navy craft patrolled the air for long hours over endless expanses of the seas. To the explorer and the prospector, the seaplane offered indispensable access to territories that no other vehicle could reach, for it could convert distant lakes, rivers, and bays into air bases that demanded no previous preparation. Many a primitive settlement in newly exploited lands had to rely widely on the seaplane for the transport of its supplies.

For the pilot, the seaplane united the ancient arts of sailing the waters with the modern fascinations of mounting to the skies, and I have yet to meet the pilot who, having once tasted the joys of seaplane flying, would not rather fly seaplanes than anything else.

Yet today the seaplane is a scarce object in the skies, and quite unseen over the great air routes of the globe. Here and there a few of them remain in use for special and infrequent purposes, but that is all. To the old seaplane hand this is a distressing state of affairs, and later on I shall speculate on how this came about. But first I shall talk of seaplanes as I knew them in days when one could not imagine aviation without them.

I have to digress for a moment in the matter of terminology. Many years ago it was officially decreed that the term "seaplanes" should be applied to planes mounted on separate floats, to distinguish them from the "flying boat" types, which carried their loads within the hull. It was a poor and misleading definition, because float structures are rarely adapted to endure for long the pounding of heavy waves, and such planes are more likely to be using inland waters than open seas. For purposes of distinction, the old term "floatplane" serves the purpose better. Today the term "seaplane" is most generally employed to designate any plane that flies off and onto the water, and that is how I use it here.

As an apprentice before World War I, I was introduced to what was then known about seaplane design. The *Daily Mail* had offered a prize for the first non-stop trans-Atlantic flight, and it seemed obvious at the time that, with all that water involved, a seaplane would have to be used. The Grahame-White Company had been asked to design a set of floats for the plane of one of the prospective contestants. The job of preparing a layout for this float system was passed along to me, and I was too flattered to realize that the chief engineer was merely giving me a test to see what a greenhorn would make of the problem. Knowing practically nothing about the business, I had the bright idea of inducing a French friend named Gondre, a mechanic at Hendon for the Morane-Saulnier firm, to borrow for me some drawings of the float system of a Morane-Borel monoplane, and these I scaled up to suit the prospective weight of the trans-Atlantic plane. When I proudly submitted my effort to the chief engineer, he laughed long and loudly. I never did know what was wrong with my "design," but at any rate this setback irritated me into the habit of studying whatever seaplane design material I could come across.

In my early days in the Royal Flying Corps I had no contact with seaplanes, which were supposed to be strictly naval craft. But shortly after I was commissioned, in 1916, an old Hendon friend, then in the Royal Naval Air Service at Lee-on-Solent, near Portsmouth, gave me a chance to put in an unofficial hour or so on his little FBA (Franco-British Aviation) two-seat pusher flying boat. As an airplane, it was not an inspiring job; its 100-hp Gnome engine was perched so high on its unstable airframe that the plane promptly stalled if you forgot to push the nose down before cutting power. But, as I played around with various experiments in takeoffs, landings, and water maneuvers, I found that in only one afternoon I had become completely "hooked" on seaplanes.

But the Royal Flying Corps had no seaplanes; it was going to be two or three years before a stroke of luck and a little conspiracy put me squarely into the seaplane business. By the summer of 1918 the R.F.C. had been merged with the R.N.A.S. into the new Royal Air Force, so that seaplanes were no longer officially beyond my reach. Meanwhile the war record of the Navy's seaplanes had been so impressive that the new Air Ministry had decided to establish a National Seaplane Factory for the purpose of expanding seaplane activities. I was then military test pilot in the east of England, where numerous wide and shallow lakes (widely known to tourist and sailing enthusiasts as the Norfolk Broads) offered excellent protected waters for seaplane testing; the Ministry gave me the job of prospecting this area for a suitable site for the seaplane factory.

The officials who assigned me this job evidently assumed that my very varied experience naturally included adequate acquaintance with seaplanes—and I wasn't going to tell them otherwise. I merely said that it was a considerable time since I had done any seaplane flying and that I needed a refresher course—which, heaven knows, was true enough. The Commanding Officer at Yarmouth Naval Air Station, Colonel (formerly Navy Captain) Chambers was instructed to give me the necessary facilities.

I hurried to Yarmouth and told Chambers the straight facts of my almost total inexperience of seaplanes. He, like a good sportsman, undertook to make an honest seaplane pilot out of me. He turned me over to those two famous masters of the seaplane game Majors (formerly Lieutenant Commanders) Cadbury and Leckie for a high-pressure course. It had to be high-pressure, for Yarmouth was strictly an operational base, with no facilities for training, and practically all flying was done from the usually blustering waters of the North Sea. I was first put through all the floatplanes they had, from the big lumbering Shorts, sixty-five-foot span with a single Sunbeam engine, to the snappy little Sopwith "Schneiders," twenty-foot span with a Gnome engine. They all carried the old float system, two boxlike, flat-bottomed main floats with a small auxiliary float to support the tail, so that on the water they sat at a high angle and were not easy to handle in a stiff wind.

Apparently I took naturally to the work, for soon Leckie was taking me out in the great operational F.2A flying boats, about a hundred-foot span with two 350-hp Rolls-Royce engines. As a final compliment he sent me off on my first "solo" (with two seamen-mechanics to handle the marine gear and fuel system) in an F.2A in as heavy a sea as most pilots would be expected to tackle.

More rough-sea practice on the big F-boats completed my training course. Rough-water seaplaning was once a regular feature of the trade, and it brought out the most emphatic differences between land-plane and seaplane flying. The judgment and execution of rough-sea takeoffs and landings are governed by the infinitely varying conditions and combinations of waves and swells; wind direction is a secondary consideration and often an added complication. Nobody would take on rough-sea flying just for the fun of it; a takeoff run is something like driving a fast truck over a field full of boulders while being drenched by a battery of fire hoses. But there were long years when seaplanes worked regularly with warships in open seas, when engine failures far from land were frequent, and when navigational aids or fuel ranges could not be relied on to bring a pilot back to sheltered waters. It was then that the ability to cope with rough seas was the pride of the old-timer who liked to call himself a seaplane pilot.

By the time Yarmouth had finished with me, I was ready to take on any seaplane job that came my way. With war's end, the seaplane-factory project was dropped; but before long I had made a promising start as a civilian free-lance test pilot, and the seaplane jobs started to come in. Soon I was testing floatplanes and flying boats in elaborate variety. For example there was the tiny Parnall "Peto," a floatplane designed to fold up into a watertight hangar on the deck of a sub-marine, from which it could be lowered into the water to fly around as a scout; and at the other end of the scale was the huge Saunders "Valkyrie," a three-engine patrol bomber about twice the bulk of the wartime F-boats. As time went on I became involved in the tests of every kind of airplane that could be made to get off the water—and many that couldn't.

Seaplane testing has always been a much more complicated and specialized business than landplane testing, because the performance of a new seaplane on the water has first to be tested and, if possible, perfected before flight tests can have much meaning. The design of seaplane hulls and floats, like the design of racing yachts, is an art and not a science. It is sensitive to even small variations of lines and dimensions, and the plane's designer never knew quite what his luck was going to be before water tests were undertaken.

Unlucky combinations of water forces and air forces could produce an astonishing variety of major and minor defects such as landplanes never meet. In the worst cases, the plane might turn out to be unmanageable in water maneuvers, or it might develop any of numerous forms of erratic behavior for fouling up takeoffs or landings. In fact, not infrequently an apparently promising seaplane never even reached flight tests, simply because it proved a complete failure on the water.

The test pilot's problems were compounded by the ever-present possibilities of sinking, something that could result either from the full violence of a crash or from some trivial defect that might lead to swamping or capsizing. On a couple of occasions I have been forced to run a plane hurriedly aground to avoid imminent threats of foundering, and one afternoon I was taken completely by surprise when an expensive Schneider Cup racer sank under me with no warning symptoms; it took several weeks of research to discover the cause of the trouble and only a minor change to correct it.

But, of all the innumerable troubles that can beset a new seaplane design, the worst and wickedest is "porpoising," a well-named and still poorly understood phenomenon in which the plane rears and plunges sharply quite out of the pilot's control, sometimes wrecking itself in two or three wild leaps from the water before it can be stopped. Experimental troubles with this menace began to get serious in the late 1930s, when higher speeds on the water resulted from increasingly high wing loadings, and expensive new techniques were devised in tests with models to try to cope with the problem.

Usually, from accumulated experience, I was able to detect the first signs of porpoising and to stop the plane before things got out of hand. But in the prototype tests of a large, four-engine British experimental flying boat, the Saunders-Roe R.2/33, my luck ran out after several flights in which I nearly lost takeoff control. The hydrodynamic experts had asked me to allow the porpoising to develop "a little" for study purposes. Unfortunately, true to its unpredictable nature, it developed much more suddenly and viciously than anyone thought possible. At the high-speed end of an attempted takeoff run, with a warning so slight that I had no time to do anything about it, the plane left the water in a prodigious porpoising leap from which it crashed down, completely stalled and out of control. Nobody was much hurt, but the plane was wrecked beyond repair.

Eventually, when I got into seaplane testing on an international basis, I could not help noting the extraordinary conservatism with which the British and American seaplane designers (who had co-operated closely ever since the start of World War I) had clung to design formulas originated by Glenn Curtiss in 1914. I became familiar with such widely diverse formulas as the broad, flat hulls of Dornier in Germany, the sharp, narrow boats of Rohrbach in Denmark, and the concave twin hulls of Savoia-Marchetti in Italy; these often had important advantages to offer in competition or combination with the Curtiss formula, but it was never possible to persuade British or American naval design authorities to consider any departure from traditions they had so firmly established. To my mind, this had a good deal to do with the eventual demise of the seaplane.

The modern flying generation, which hardly ever meets a seaplane, probably finds it difficult to appreciate the high importance and popularity that seaplanes attained in the late 1920s and most of the 1930s. Commercially they were in extensive use for the large-scale transport of goods and supplies to remote areas where new developments of various kinds were being carried out, where nobody had yet thought it necessary to build landplane airports, and where the seaplane was often the only means of ready access. The long transoceanic air services relied entirely on large flying boats because there were no landplanes in prospect with adequate range and capacity, and if there had been, few airports or runways anywhere could have accommodated aircraft so large and heavy.

For the private pilot, numerous models of floatplanes and small flying boats were available, and were widely used wherever lakes, rivers, and bays invited a visit; in those areas where yachting activities were general and where waterfront homes and hotels lined the shores, visiting by private seaplane became a fashionable institution. Those expanding uses of seaplanes were, unfortunately, ended by the stock-market crash of October 1929, and never managed to recover.

A remarkable performance of that period was the operation of a seaplane base on New York's East River at the foot of Wall Street, which enabled financiers and executives to commute from their out-lying homes almost to the doors of their downtown offices. A barge, sunk at one end, formed a ramp for amphibians to taxi up or for seaplanes to tie up to. A pier jutted out close by to provide a small patch of shelter from the tidal race of the "river." The remarkable feature of the operation was that it functioned surprisingly well, in spite of the fact that it was a very primitive installation and looked horribly dangerous. I used this base occasionally to take my bosses, and their friends and customers, to downtown New York or to take them home.

Getting in was not too bad; after picking a landing in the water it was not very difficult to taxi from the current into the slack water be-hind the pier. But departure could be a hair-raising business. The only way to be sure of enough control when making the sudden transition from the slack patch to the often swift current was to leave the ramp at practically full throttle, emerging into the open water where the pier or other structures obscured the approach of the haphazard traffic of tugboats and barges. On two or three occasions I avoided river craft by inches, and sometimes an incoming seaplane would appear suddenly around the corner of the pier, all set for a collision with an outgoing plane. Besides which, the water was always cluttered with chunks of floating debris that could easily stave in the thin plating of a fast-moving float or hull. Yet, as far as I remember, none of the many pilots who used this base ever had a serious mishap. This enter-prising operation also was terminated by the market crash.

It helped, however, to support our firm conviction that, in due course, most of the world's major cities would be served by large flying boats operating from well-organized air bases right in the heart of town.

The high point of seaplane development was reached in the latter half of the 1930s, when the giant passenger flying boat appeared to be on its way to establishing forever its supremacy in long-range air commerce. The reasons for those expectations seemed incontrovertible at the time. For very long ranges, and for the comfortable accommodation of large numbers of passengers on long trips, huge airplanes would be required, and engineers could see no practical technical limits to the sizes that flying boats could attain. Perhaps very large landplanes could also be developed, but their great weight would make them unusable except from long, level, and extremely solid paved runways. Such runways would be so expensive to build and maintain that even the wealthier countries could hardly be expected to provide them except at their own major air terminals; it would be out of the question to expect less prosperous communities in other countries to set up such costly installations at their ends of the lines. The giant landplane would have few places to go; but for the giant seaplane, generally speaking, water runways could always be found, or even artificially provided, for air terminals as well as for temporary and emergency refuges.

So the wide stretches of the Atlantic, the Pacific, and other long international routes were opened to air traffic by great seaplanes. There seemed no reason to doubt that the future of long-range air transportation lay mainly with ever larger and faster flying boats.

World War II was to change that whole picture—and, almost suddenly, the seaplane came to be relegated to a few minor functions in the parade of aviation's progress.

2. The Eclipse of the Seaplane

If World War II had been avoided or long postponed, or if military setbacks in that war had prevented the advance of our Pacific landplane bases, we might have witnessed an intensive program for the development of much better and faster seaplanes. But that didn't happen. Landplanes, apart from their advantages in ease of surface handling, had for a long time been attaining much higher speeds, while the unshapely seaplanes remained clumsy and slow, with every indication (for reasons I shall mention) that they were going to continue that way. So, as the war developed, the establishment of land-plane bases became a major military objective, and some of the war's bloodiest battles were fought to capture sites for that purpose. The once formidable and costly problems of building adequate landplane runways disappeared in the face of military priorities; special equipment, materials, and techniques were intensively developed to reduce run-way construction to routine procedure. Soon nobody was interested in bases for the dawdling seaplanes. As someone once put the situation succinctly, "When the bulldozer came in, the seaplane went out."

When the war was over, landplane runways had become available over most of the world, and, where they were not, nobody any longer hesitated to build them for the use of landplanes, which now far outstripped the best speeds that seaplanes could pretend to offer. As far as major airlines and similar fixed-base operations were concerned, the seaplane had finally gone out of business.

Still, it seems rather shortsighted to dismiss lightly the possibility of future military needs—perhaps serious needs—for a class of transport aircraft capable of widespread operations independent of fixed bases. Landplane bases, for the distant delivery or pickup of troops and sup-plies, need suitable terrain that can be continuously defended, as well as the equipment, materials, and labor for grading, preparing, and repair-ing runways. Even where these are available, the construction-time ele-ment might be vital in an urgent operation. On the other hand, a base for seaplanes of any size can be quickly established—and as quickly abandoned—wherever there is a sufficient expanse of reasonably smooth water for takeoffs and landings. These considerations carry even more weight today, when modern technology can readily provide airborne mooring equipment and ship-to-shore service craft.

But military planners are hardly likely to consider such possibilities so long as they remain unable to think of seaplanes except in terms of the slow and clumsy flying boats, which is all they have ever known. Yet the fact is that there never was any valid reason why water-based aircraft should not be as fast, and perform as well, as any landplanes in their respective classes. For many years the world's fastest planes were the Schneider Cup racing seaplanes, and to understand how the present situation came about it is necessary to remember the whole past history of flying boats.

The ancestor of the large flying boats was the 1914 twin-engine "America" of Glenn Curtiss. That type was progressively developed, through informal co-operation between the American and British navies, into larger boats, which performed excellent naval services during World War I and afterward. As a result, it came to be accepted that seaplanes were essentially naval craft, and, later on, this convention was, for no good reason, accorded official political approval. Thus naval technical offices became the sole repositories of design concepts, data, information, and approval, so that, when commercial operators took to seaplanes, the design of their planes necessarily followed naval practices.

But, in such navy designs, speed was never a matter of primary importance; the principal requirements were long range and long duration for wide ocean patrols, and seaworthiness for open-sea operations. The big seaplane grew up through the years as a seagoing naval vessel adapted for flight, never as a normal airplane adapted for use from water runways. This concept of the flying boat as a naval vessel was carried so far that quite a long time ago, with complete absurdity, seaplane design was officially designated as a branch of naval architecture, and its technical literature was fancied up with shipbuilding formulas totally unconnected with aircraft.

And so, while landplanes shaped themselves for higher speeds with streamlined fuselages, tucked-in landing gears, and other drag-reducing features, seaplanes wallowed through the air with their traditional "clunker" hulls, squared off with keels, chines, dead rises, steps, and other jagged nautical excrescences that had hardly changed since the days of Curtiss. Worst of all, basic design for high speed was virtually prohibited by navy specifications—I worked on many of them in recent years—which invariably demand that the plane be capable of takeoff and landing in waves several feet in height. It takes no great technical perception to realize that planes so handicapped have no hope of competing in speed with planes designed for operation from smooth runways.

There is every reason to believe that large, high-speed seaplanes can be developed for extensive operations from the moderately smooth waters of bays, harbors, rivers, and lakes. But any such development would require a totally new line of technical approach, uncluttered by naval traditions. Seaplanes in general, however, have so lost face that today there is little chance that such a program would receive any serious consideration.

3. Amphibians

There were always peculiar advantages in the use of an airplane that could operate equally effectively from either land or water. Amphibian planes, therefore, existed at least as far back as 1913. However, the hulls or floats for use on water were heavy, and so was wheel gear for use on land, especially when that gear had to include a mechanism for hauling it up clear of the water. So, in days when airplanes could do very little weight-lifting, the plane that carried both land and water equipment couldn't carry much else, and there was no real practical use for it. After World War I, with more powerful engines on hand, a few useful types were produced, and my first experience of them was with the Vickers "Viking" amphibian boat. This plane had a reasonably good performance, but it had some nasty flying tricks, and two famous British airmen, Sir John Alcock and Sir Ross Smith, were killed on the type.

The topography of Europe did not, in general, encourage much demand for this essentially more expensive class of plane. It was in America, North and South, where far-inland waterways, lake systems, and deeply indented coastlines alternated with large stretches of dry land, that amphibians quickly became popular. For many years, the most widely used type in America was probably the Loening, which was produced in both military and civil models. The modern Grumman amphibians, the best known types in modern use, are the Loening's lineal descendants.

The U. S. Army at one time made impressive use of Loening amphibians in international tours, and this encouraged some of us to hope that the Army Air Forces, having tasted the flexibility offered by water air bases, would develop a line of seaplanes for its own particular uses, which were totally different from the seagoing needs of the Navy. Unfortunately, that never happened, for the myth persisted that seaplanes were the exclusive concern of the Navy.

Amphibians employed retracting landing gears some twenty years before landplanes made a regular habit of it. They had to, because they could not possibly take off with wheels trailing in the water. Retraction had, of course, different purposes in the two cases: the landplane wanted to tuck its wheels away to diminish air drag, whereas the amphibian didn't care, in principle, where its rising wheels went so long as they cleared the water. Consequently, amphibians flew for years with their raised gears still sticking out into the breeze.

This difference of purpose gave the amphibian pilot one more thing to think about that instruments couldn't tell him. The landplane pilot *always* had to lower his gear before landing, and after a good deal of damage had been inflicted by forgetful pilots, all sorts of routines and warning systems were developed to remind him. But, with an amphibian, the pilot might or might not have to lower his gear according to whether he intended to come down on land or water. So the little matter of "forgetting the wheels" has always been a regular feature of amphibian flying, often hilarious and occasionally tragic. A descent on land with wheels up was usually harmless, but a descent on water with wheels down could be catastrophic.

At one time a mythical association was formed known as the "Dumbbell Club," the members being pilots who had put amphibians down on land with wheels up or on water with wheels down. I joined the club at Detroit in 1931, when, after giving a sales demonstration on a Savoia-Marchetti in the Detroit River, I landed smartly back on the airport with wheels up. (For this sort of performance a pilot must always quickly produce an excuse to cover his shame—mine was that my customer became excited by approaching airport traffic and confused me with his warning shouts.) The plane skidded to a stop in a few yards and canted over slightly on one wing float. A hoist was run out and the nose was hauled up, and the only damage found was the scraping of paint off the keel. I cranked down the wheels, took off again, and went back to the river.

I once came near to much worse trouble on a Sikorsky S-39. The stilted landing gear was actuated by a hand-pumped mechanism that could deal with each wheel separately. Flying in from Long Island Sound, I started to lower the wheels for a landing at Mineola. The left wheel went down obediently, but the right wheel refused to move. I decided to raise the left wheel, go back to the water, and deal with the trouble—but the left wheel declined to come up. Now I was really in a mess, due for a crash on either land or water. My passenger, Bo Sweeney, knew a good deal about this gear, and he practically dismantled it in the air while I cruised around trying to stretch out what fuel I had left. He got the right wheel down just as the fuel ran out, and I made a dead-stick landing and left the plane in the middle of the airport while the two of us went to the hotel bar to regain our composure.

One day I was at Teterboro Airport when a famous pilot of the trans-Atlantic flying era wanted to take a friend for a joy ride over New York; he borrowed a Loening amphibian from an operator whom (to save his blushes if he is still around) I will call Smith. The pilot was away a lot longer than expected, and Smith, who now wanted the plane for purposes of his own, was getting steadily more impatient. The famous man came in, forgot his wheels, and landed on the keel. Smith, now furious, had a number of purple remarks to make on the subject of careless pilots who didn't know enough to handle their wheels properly. The plane was jacked up and inspected for damage; there wasn't any. Still fuming, Smith got the wheels down, put his passenger aboard, and took off—and forgot to pull his wheels up before landing in the Hackensack River. The plane was wrecked.

But it wasn't always the pilot who forgot whether he was on land or on water. There was the classic story of the British air marshal who boarded an amphibian at a London airport to be taken on an official visit to the Royal Air Force seaplane station at Calshot. Arriving at Calshot, the pilot taxied up to one of the flying-boat moorings. While the mechanic was tying up to the buoy, the air marshal turned to give graceful thanks to the pilot for the flight—and stepped out backward into twenty feet of water.

Amphibian gear is useful for other purposes besides landing. For one thing, when lowered in the water it acts as a powerful drag anchor, allowing the pilot to apply plenty of power for maneuvering without gathering too much forward way. Particularly in later years, it came to be especially appreciated as a beaching gear. In days when seaplanes were made of wood, nobody minded leaving them at mooring for days or weeks; but when metal hulls and floats came into use, the salt-water corrosion problem led to the custom of bringing them ashore whenever possible and washing them off with fresh water. However, in the whole history of flying boats, nobody ever managed to design a beaching gear that could be easily and simply attached. Some of them were almost miraculously clumsy, requiring the floundering efforts of a wading or swimming crew to clamp the gear into place before the plane could be hauled ashore.

The beaching problem remained a major bugaboo in seaplane operations, and it was an important factor in the later decline of interest in seaplanes. With amphibians you simply lowered the gear and taxied ashore. It was an expensive way to meet the problem, because the weight of a full landing gear had to be carried all the time and detracted seriously from range and payload. But it saved a lot of headaches.

A few amphibians are in use today, but only in those limited spheres of operation where seaplanes are still employed.

CHAPTER XX

WORLD WAR II—AND AFTER

1. *Aviation in 1939*

If historians ever find themselves trying to specify a date for marking the practical conquest of the air, I would personally propose the year 1939. Since then, of course, aviation has made enormous advances, but these have served mainly to confirm and exploit the conquest. The year 1939 saw the Eighth Sea at last entirely open to navigation. There was no point on the globe that could not be reached by air with reasonable certainty, safety, and regularity, and there were many points that could hardly be reached in any other way. Commercial airlines, with landplanes and seaplanes, now spanned all the world's great ocean and land routes wherever there was any important demand for passenger and mail services, the last and most difficult route having been opened when trans-Atlantic services were initiated, just before the war.

The airspeeds of 1939 so far surpassed the speeds of surface travel that the airplane would have remained the normal means of fast transportation even if the vastly higher speeds of modern jets had never been attained. Unquestionably, by 1939 the conquest of the air could be considered complete; it now remained only for the world to make full use of that conquest. And, as it happened, the world was on the verge of using it to the widest conceivable extent. For, in that same year, World War II erupted, and every airplane of every class that the world's constructors could possibly design and build was pressed into the innumerable and expanding military services of the warring powers.

When World War II broke out in Europe, in September 1939, I was in England testing some new experimental flying boats. I was told to hurry back across the Atlantic and put my years of American experience into helping with the pressing job of procuring American warplanes for Britain. Then there was the Japanese attack on Pearl Harbor; America was in the war and I was invited by the Consolidated Aircraft Co. in San Diego to join their Flight Department. This offered me a chance to catch up in a branch of flying in which my experience had been lagging. Test flying of one kind or another had been my principal occupation for many years during which long-distance flying had entered a new era.

Non-stop flights over thousands of miles of land and ocean, which not long before had been the sport of the record breakers, were becoming routine. For several years I had not had much chance to keep up with this kind of flying, with all its navigating and operating problems, and I was anxious to get as much experience of it as I could. Consolidated (soon better known as Consair and then Convair) had undertaken a big wartime program of ferrying their various models of production landplanes and seaplanes to faraway points in all directions over land and over ocean, and as ferry pilot I could get all the long-range flying experience I could use.

In addition to ferry flying, the Flight Department carried out production flight tests of the innumerable planes coming off their assembly lines, most of which we would eventually ferry somewhere or other. Usually such "shakedown" flights were uneventful affairs, but they provided close contact with production processes and problems, and there was always the chance that some malfunction would stir up a bit of excitement or even something more serious. There was one incident that gave me an uncanny reminder of the part that luck had played in my flying career.

On the morning before Thanksgiving Day 1944, the Dispatch Office called me in early to make a routine shakedown test on a production B-24. When I arrived at the office I saw on the notice board that there were two B-24's for shakedown; Marvin Weller's name was against the first one and mine against the second. However, my plane was not yet quite ready; Weller's was ready, but he had called in to say that he would be delayed for a couple of hours. So the dispatcher switched the names against the planes, and I took off on the first one. I completed the flight, landed, and made out my report. As I left the office I met Weller, who was just coming in; I told him about the switch in planes, which was routine procedure anyway, and started off for home. I had hardly entered my door when the telephone rang, and the dispatcher had a grim story to tell me. Weller had taken off in the plane that was to have been mine. By one of those oversights that on rare occasions creep into some of the best production lines, that plane had been assembled, and somehow passed inspection, with insufficient attachment bolts in one wing. Shortly after takeoff the wing broke off completely, and Weller and his crew were killed.

2. Ferry Pilot

The ferry pilots of World War II engaged themselves in a brand of flying activity such as had never been indulged in before and probably never would be again. It was neither military nor civil flying. There were hundreds, perhaps thousands, of civilians whose job it was to deliver all sorts of military airplanes over all sorts of territory to keep the fighting fronts supplied in almost every part of the globe. Ferry pilots were a very heterogeneous crowd. Some were professionals of varied experience, some were transferred airline pilots who could bring to the job their special familiarity with organized airway procedures, others were amateurs with sketchy or limited experience that was now hopefully reinforced by hasty courses and check-outs in the planes they were to fly.

There were few, if any, group flights; most operations were in single-plane units, the basic purpose being to get a plane to its appointed destination and get the pilot back as soon as possible to take out another one. So long as enough pilots delivered enough planes to where they were wanted, it was a matter of secondary importance how they got them there.

Consequently the routine processes and precautions that in peace-time had been slowly developed for safety, regularity, and reliability were now submerged to suit wartime urgencies. Long chances were taken with weather; communications were often erratic and confused, and sometimes suppressed by radio silence in combat areas; planes were habitually overloaded, either with extra fuel for long stages or with urgently needed supplies—probably both; bases of departure and arrival, and intermediate stops, were often only marginally suited to operations; flight-crew fatigue was disregarded; flight plans were regularly prepared, but as regularly discarded to suit unexpected conditions. Under such circumstances, the civilian ferry pilots took risks that normal civil flying would never tolerate, and a long list could be compiled of wartime ferry pilots and their crews who died on the job, in various parts of the world, without benefit of military glory.

The delivery flight itself was only part of the job, often the most pleasant part. Before he could start off, the pilot had to concern himself with numerous preparatory tasks, such as a preliminary flight check followed by minor adjustments and the loading of the plane; then there would be crew consultations, navigation planning, and a volume of paper work connected with inventories, load sheets, receipts, clearances, and other documentary nuisances. Often I have taken off on a long trip at the end of an already tiring day of complicated preparations. Or perhaps, on the other hand, we would be quite unprepared. On one occasion I had to take a Navy-type B-24, at less than an hour's notice, from California to the Marshall Islands, a matter of more than six thousand miles, substituting for a pilot who had suddenly been taken sick; the Dispatch Office told me I would have time in Honolulu to buy a razor and a clean shirt.

At the end of the flight the now weary pilot had to go through the processes of getting somebody to accept the plane and its contents; usually this was quick and easy, but occasionally some finicky official would assert his rights to make a big production of it.

The roughest part of the whole job was the long trek back to the starting point. A pilot might have the rare luck to pick up a direct and comfortable ride home, but mostly he had to be a sort of hitchhiker on anything that was going his way, resting as and when he could at stopovers where accommodation was invariably overcrowded.

I believe ours was the only ferry group that handled both landplanes and seaplanes in large numbers over a wide variety of routes, and there was never a chance that the job could become monotonous. But I think I was able to extract much more than average interest out of flying these planes across stretches of thousands of miles of land and sea, by day and night and in all weathers; it gave me a sense of a personal share in aviation's progress from days when such flying could be no more than a dim and distant dream. Over mid-ocean, in command of a thirty-ton, four-engine miracle of flying metal, I could think back with a deep satisfaction and a kind of wonder to the time when, three decades earlier, I had ventured out across the twenty-two miles of the English Channel in a stick-and-string device of eighty horsepower, with only moderate assurance of reaching the other side.

Among the assortment of airplane types that were ferried in all directions, the PBY flying boat was in a class by itself. It seemed to be able to get into the air with anything that could be loaded into it, and, especially when fitted with long-range tanks slung under the wings, it gave the impression of being willing to stay up forever. On the other hand, its cruising speed was low, rarely much above 130 knots, and a good deal lower when the engines were eased back for maximum range or duration.

For the long over-water stretch between San Diego and Honolulu, the normal flight time for the PBY was about eighteen hours, but with headwinds and crosswinds I have taken over twenty-one hours for the trip, and others have taken even longer. It didn't seem to matter; there was always enough fuel left over to go a great deal farther. Besides, the roomy hull gave plenty of space to move around in, and it was equipped with bunks, an electric cooking stove, and other basic comforts provided by the Navy for the plane's regular job of long hours of patrol. The off-duty crew member, lounging in the huge gun "blisters," could enjoy a magnificent view of gorgeous sunsets and sunrises, star-drenched skies, and mountainous clouds. So, on a long ferry flight, conditions on board had the general aspects of an adventurous weekend on a small yacht.

We invariably carried a large supply of food, in case we had to come down at sea and wait for rescue. On our usual schedule we flew through the night, and daybreak occurred a few hundred miles out from Honolulu. Then we would breakfast on fried eggs and bacon, cooked on our stove and served on paper plates. Occasionally, however, when the automatic pilot went on strike or I had some other reason for remaining at the controls, I would prefer the simplicity of two or three hard-boiled eggs, cooked during the night and cooled off in the bottom of the hull; these I would eat while flying along, first cracking the shells on the control wheel. One morning someone handed me an egg. It was the wrong egg—and if anyone likes flying a seaplane with the contents of a raw egg splattered all over his lap, his hands, the control wheel, and the instrument panel, he is welcome to it.

A long overland journey on a PBY was quite a different proposition, and we made such trips regularly. In respectable weather it presented no special problems; there were always plenty of lakes and waterways available in case of emergency. In instrument-flying weather, however, we were up against the fact that the radio ranges marked courses between land airports that were no help to flying boats, and we had to be always ready to improvise special navigational methods. Once, when I was taking a PBY from the Pacific to the Atlantic coasts, the controller at Tucson, Arizona, instructed me to come in and land there; there was, he said, an unusually wide and severe storm ahead with icy rain, and all planes were being grounded until the storm had passed. The Tucson controller had no reason to be thinking about seaplanes, and I had difficulty in explaining to him that I could land there all right but would have trouble trying to take off again. The flight plan fell apart, and I had to detour about three hundred miles around the storm, intruding with questionable legality over Mexican territory, before eventually reaching the lake at Fort Worth, Texas.

This problem of emergency navigation under instrument conditions was particularly tough over mountainous territory, where the PBY had no hope of maintaining sufficient altitude on one engine—five thousand feet would be about the best it could do—and the radio ranges could not guide it to a water landing. It was a very threatening problem in our frequent winter ferry runs from Seattle to San Diego. For various reasons, these deliveries were nearly always urgent, and we often took off from Lake Washington, in Seattle, under conditions that normally we would not have cared to tackle. In the worst weathers it would have been easy to go out over the sea and skirt the coast all the way. But we were forbidden to do this for fear of agitating the coastal-defense radar network with alerts concerning "unidentified planes"; and once, when Charlie Lorber was forced to do this, there was such a hectic row that for a while we thought that Charlie had lost us the war.

So we had to follow a route that took us along the mountain chains of the Cascades and the Sierra Nevadas, and there was no reasonable way to detour around them. Flying blind in winter storms, with violent mountain-made turbulence and unpredictable icing levels, it was hard for the slow PBY to compete with the powerful upper winds which inflicted absurdly high angles of drift. Groping crabwise along the legs of the radio ranges, the pilot knew well that if he went far astray from them he was liable to end up against the craggy side of one of the numerous peaks that towered up into the murk; some of them reached as high as fourteen thousand feet or more, and they had already claimed the lives of too many airmen who had failed to keep out of their way. It was a route that I always followed with a steady prayer that both engines would stay on the job until more kindly conditions were reached at the southern end of the trip.

The PBY was never a glamorous plane, but it was a highly dependable workhorse of the air, providing amazingly versatile service for Americans and the other Allies alike. Those whose job it was to fly it will always remember it with a special kind of nostalgic affection.

The PB2Y ("Coronado") was a large, four-engine flying boat that nobody seemed to like very much or have much use for. It was clumsy and sometimes treacherous on takeoff and landing, and it had no obvious advantages over the smaller PBY except that it cruised about twenty-five knots faster. However, from the ferry pilot's standpoint, its very ample flight deck and cavernous interior, fitted with the usual Navy comforts, made it an amiable sort of barge for long hours of flight. I took a number of them out to Pacific bases, and others overland to Navy stations on the East Coast for distribution elsewhere. It was one of the latter that provided one of the more disconcerting incidents of my ferry-flying activities.

After these planes had been sitting around for some time at East Coast bases waiting to see who wanted them, they began to develop sundry ailments, including trouble with leaky fuel tanks in the wings.

It was decided to ferry them back to San Diego for reconditioning. On one of them, at Lake Worth, Texas, we repaired a couple of minor tank leaks that had developed during the flight from Elizabeth City, North Carolina, and the job looked safe enough to get us over the land crossing of twelve hundred miles westward to San Diego. As we went along, the flight engineer kept a suspicious eye open for tank trouble; except for some small seepages, nothing much happened until we were over the mountains about forty miles east of San Diego Bay.

Then a couple of leaks began to look unhealthy and were obviously getting worse. Fuel was dribbling from the trailing edges, first the left, then the right. Fumes were wafting into the cockpit, and I opened the windows to blow them out, but farther back in the hull the smell indicated that a nice explosive mixture was building up. I hastily radioed our San Diego base and gave them a short, sharp description of what was going on, while, at the same time, the engineer lowered the electrically operated wing-tip floats. Immediately they were down, we switched off the radio and all electric equipment to avoid a spark, which would have been likely to blow us apart. But I had to keep the engines running because I had little hope of making a successful power-off landing in one of the small, local reservoirs. Even a minor crash would probably produce a flaming disaster. I had to try for the bay. I remembered that two good friends of mine, Ed Musick of Pan American and test pilot Eddie Allen, had lost their lives in somewhat similar situations, and I just hoped for better luck.

As soon as I judged that I was definitely within gliding distance of the bay, I switched off all engines. I was not much too soon; a mile or two from touchdown something else evidently gave way in the tank structure, and a small cataract of fuel poured from the left wing and flowed down the side of the hull. With flaps still up I skimmed onto the water, and when I came to rest a pool of fuel quickly spread all around the plane. The company motorboat was approaching fast, and I tried to wave it off for fear its engine might touch off the floating fuel. But the smart boatman had thought of that already; he had had our radio message and could see the fuel dripping from the wings. He cut his motor, having nicely judged his course and distance so that he could coast past our bow while he threw us a line.

With the line secured, we drew the motorboat close and climbed hastily aboard. We rowed well clear before starting up the boat's motor and towing the big seaplane to moorings.

Just another ferry flight!

On ferry flights with the B-24 and its assorted cousins, I always felt that I was working harder. This, I think, was because the flight decks and other accommodations of the landplanes seemed so much more cramped than the spacious interiors of the flying boats. However, since the landplanes were faster, one had less time to endure discomfort—a philosophy that, incidentally, explains why passengers can tolerate the packed-in seating of the modern high-speed airliner.

It was during my first landplane flights over the Pacific that I realized, somewhat suddenly, that the war was altering all our earlier concepts concerning the future of long-distance aviation. Landplane runways were appearing where only seaplane moorings would once have been expected. This fact was impressed on me most vividly when I first went into tiny Johnston Island, out in the Pacific; I landed on a runway built out into the lagoon with dredged-up coral, that was about twice as long as the original island itself. It seemed clear enough, although I fought off the painful idea, that the days of the seaplane were coming to an end.

The business of taking off a landplane from a smooth, concrete runway is normally an uninspiring bit of routine, lacking the elegant nautical flavor of a seaplane departure. But our takeoffs on the four-engine B-24 for long Pacific crossings were anything but normal, and they contributed welcome excitement to the job of landplane ferrying. This was because of the huge overloads we started with, usually at night. Naturally we had a large load of extra fuel for long range; it was carried in the bomb bays in special tanks that could be dropped in an emergency, after a little delay for the opening of the bomb-bay doors. In addition, we were regularly expected to carry a heavy cargo of miscellaneous supplies, which were supposed to be listed on load sheets. On top of all that, however, everyone seemed to have some last-minute bit of gear that was alleged to be urgently needed at the other end.

The Flight Captain could always find in the cluttered fuselage all sorts of objects, large and small, that never appeared on his already weighty load sheets. I remember the occasion when, busily checking numerous papers shortly before takeoff time, I was asked by an officer if it would be all right to put a "few books" aboard; I said it would, and when I got over to the plane I discovered a couple of men trying to find space for two large and heavy crates of engine maintenance manuals.

So we never knew what our gross weight really was, and balance was something we had to take care of when we got into the air. All we were sure of was that we were unlikely to have any takeoff reserve, either of power or runway length. We therefore used to take off from North Island Naval Air Station, in San Diego, from a runway that led straight out over the sea, so that we would not have to try to clear higher ground ahead.

The takeoff itself was a tense procedure, with the whole crew at emergency stations for coping with any sign of power failure. Opening up the engines at the extreme beginning of the runway, holding the plane with the brakes until full power was reached, the pilot would release the brakes and then hold the plane on the ground as far as the last runway light before easing it cautiously and hopefully into the air. The copilot held the throttles wide open and pulled up the landing gear at the earliest possible moment; the engineer stood behind the console ready to push the superchargers to emergency boost; the navigator kept his hand on the control that would open the bomb-bay doors; the radioman held the lever that would drop the overload tanks; and all of us silently beseeched the twin gods Pratt and Whitney not to let us down, at least before we had the little altitude that would, if necessary, give us a chance to go around and land again. And so we stayed until the altimeter pointed to a thousand feet and told us we could relax.

The flight plan for the Pacific crossing usually called for initial cruise at seven thousand feet. But often, when I throttled back to normal cruising power at that altitude, the overburdened plane would sink wearily down to two or three thousand feet, where I usually let it stay until it had burned up enough fuel weight to be taken back to its appointed level.

The most tedious aspect of a wartime ferry pilot's job was the business of getting home after his one-way assignment. There were many groups of pilots who, like the military air transport services and their airline auxiliaries, stayed with their planes as they went back and forth with their various loads. But the ferry pilot had to hand over his plane at its destination and then find his way back to his base as best he could. And a good deal of the time it was not a very happy best.

Usually, in remembering the joys of ferry flying, I like to try to forget the long, dreary hours of transocean homeward rides in the stripped, cold, and noisy interior of a cargo plane, sitting in the phenomenal discomfort of a bucket seat or trying to sleep on a cold metal floor with anything that seemed usable as a pillow or a blanket, warming up from time to time on paper cups of alleged coffee. On transcontinental trips there were the endless hours of waiting, at airport after airport, for the odd seat that might be picked up on the overcrowded and dislocated airline schedules. Now and then we would fill in with a bus or a train. I have known times when it took me more than fifty hours, with five changes of plane, to get back from Norfolk, Virginia, via Chicago and Fort Worth, to my base in San Diego. Time on the ground, day and night, was spent moping sleepily in airport lounges, fearing to miss a seat on the next DC-3 to come through, whenever that might be.

The authorities did their best for us. The ferry pilot's job was considered urgent enough to earn us very high priority for transport accommodation, and often high-ranking people were "bumped" off the planes to make room for us. But demand for flight space was so high that even that did not always help us much.

However, the priority that gave us first call on seats also obliged us to take the first space available. On a return from far Pacific Islands, this didn't matter—we got bucket seats on cargo planes anyway. But from Honolulu to the mainland we tried to do better, and I learned from experience to juggle my priority papers so that they appeared just at the right time to secure for my crew and myself a seat on one of the very comfortable Pan American Boeing "Clippers" or the Navy's huge Martin "Mars" flying boat.

For a couple of years we carried out our work in civilian clothes, and this brought us increasing difficulties and embarrassment. Too often a senior officer, in all his uniformed dignity, objected fiercely to being bumped off a plane in favor of a weary and disheveled civilian who was merely a ferry pilot plodding his way home. On one occasion, at Fort Worth, I was the center of a near riot when a naval lady with two and a half stripes was officially bumped, apparently for my benefit, and her furious indignation was supported by two beribboned captains who were with her.

On naval and military bases, wandering around trying to find some office or other, we were sometimes intercepted as suspicious characters, and at Pearl Harbor I was twice hauled in by Marine guards to explain my unmilitary presence. So at last we were given a uniform, a slate-blue affair of a general airline type, complete with golden wings and badges. I spruced mine up with my few World War I medal ribbons, and it was a wonderful passport. It solved our priority problems, and on military bases the three stripes on my cuffs now brought smart salutes from soldiers, sailors, and sentries, who were apparently not sure whose navy I was in.

Getting a plane accepted at destination was not often complicated; usually the duty officer would sign the receipts and then see about providing the tired crew with a ride to wherever they could get some rest. But there was a period when small but important items, such as the navigating chronometer or the morphine in the first-aid kit, took to disappearing from the plane's inventory; special arrangements were then made for custody and receipts for such items, and this sometimes led to tiresome delays in the hand-over.

Once, when I took a four-engine flying boat into Norfolk, Virginia, a new and dedicated quartermaster told me he would not allow the plane to be brought ashore or anyone else to go aboard until he had checked with me every single item of the plane and its inventory list; he suggested I allow two days for this little business. I had to get the Commanding Officer to explain to him the facts of life in wartime aviation.

A crazy example of the antics of officialdom occurred when we were delivering some B-24s that were equipped with the oh-so-secret Norden bombsight, and someone discovered that security regulations required that this mechanical miracle be always protected by an armed guard. So the pilot was appointed guard; he was issued a revolver, which he put in one pocket, and some ammunition, which he put in another. Apparently nothing in the regulations required that the revolvers should be kept loaded or that the pilot should know how and when to use them. Personally, I hadn't fired a revolver since World War I, and all I remembered about guns was to be careful where I pointed the spout. On arrival at destination, the pilot was supposed to keep the plane far out on the field, solemnly guarding the mystic device until an army officer could come out to take responsibility for it. And in a hot summer I have stood for an hour, trying to take shelter under the wing from a broiling desert sun, proudly protecting our secret of victory against unknown and invisible forces.

3. The Last Lap

Aviation put an abrupt end to World War II with bombs that could now destroy whole cities at a single blow, and I left Convair's Flight Department when it closed down all but the remnants of its wartime activities. For the second time in my life I was surveying the scramble of aviation's transition from the destructive purposes of global war to the constructive processes of peace. But this time the picture had changed incredibly; it seemed to me that the past history of aviation was now a closed chapter, and an entirely new record was to be opened. As far as my own place in aviation was concerned, I felt that instead of being an old-timer in a field of steady progress, I had become a newcomer to a totally different kind of aviation.

I had seen aviation come out of the Kaiser's war full of the glamour of battle and not much else, leaving a shrunken and rudderless industry to wonder whether it had anything to sell in a world that had never known any serious peacetime uses for aircraft. This time a mammoth industry had a few million customers waiting for almost anything it could think of producing. The new peace was heavily diluted by a Cold War that ensured vigorous speeding of military air developments. But it was the fantastic expansion of commercial aviation that most deeply impressed the mind of the old-timer who had long taken part in its slow and often disappointing progress in the years between the wars. Now vast numbers of people, who might otherwise never have taken to flying, had become seasoned air travelers for numerous wartime purposes, and the immediate postwar years saw them lined up in their thousands for seats in the larger and faster transport planes that had revolutionized wartime communications and that the airlines were ordering as fast as the industry could produce them. The ports of the Eighth Sea were already congested with a flood of travelers such as those of the Seven Seas had never witnessed in all the centuries of their existence.

Dozens of new, subsidiary industries had sprung up to feed the airplane builders and operators with equipment and materials that before the war had been non-existent or merely in the process of tentative development.

Probably it was only the old-timer who would notice that the population of the aviation world had also completely changed. Between wars hardly anyone would have attempted to make a career in aviation unless he suffered from an uncommon mental condition known as "air-mindedness"; almost everyone in the business had once regarded it as something special and unusual and was intensely interested in every aspect of it. Now aviation, handling a hundred new technologies, had overflowed into such a wide variety of activities that its prewar professionals were somewhat lost in the crowd of newcomers.

In the design offices, in the factories, and in the flight-test sections, the old, adventurous days of blind experiment, of individual intuition, of guesswork and inspiration, of trial and error had passed away, and progress was now governed by intensive research in vastly improved laboratories, aided by libraries bulging with technical data and records in umpteen languages. The complex developments born in wartime had overwhelmed the general practitioners of aviation and had ushered in the inevitable era of specialists, a large proportion of whom were preoccupied with their own peculiar technologies and were only distantly interested in the airplane as a whole or what was done with it. One of the world's most successful designers lamented to me that he had had to give up trying to design airplanes; once upon a time he had had a fatherly control over every last detail of the planes he designed, but progress had turned him into an administrator of design committees, which concocted new airplanes from elaborate assemblies of intricate specialties.

These new complexities of design, construction, and equipment had added immensely to the costs of developing new aircraft, and new government requirements for certification had increased those costs far beyond previous experience; the full effects of this came as something of a shock to the industry, and some manufacturers lost a good deal of money in the underpricing of their new commercial planes before it was discovered how much they were actually costing. Experimental projects that might once have been lightly undertaken for a relatively small investment were no longer possible; it would cost many thousands or millions to try out a new idea or design.

Gone with the winds of progress was the pilot's cherished freedom to make what use he liked of the three wide dimensions of airspace. In days when airplanes had been infrequent dots in limitless expanses of sky, the prospects of collision seemed no more than vague and remote; now those prospects had changed to a constant and widening menace as increasing hundreds of much faster planes competed for airspace, often carrying heavy cargoes of human freight in flying conditions where they could neither see nor be seen. Radio communications that had originated as welcome aids to free navigation had to be elaborated into intricate systems of air traffic control, and there remained few piloting activities that were not closely governed by official rules, regulations, and restrictions.

Such was the new aviation to which I had to try to adapt myself. In little more than three decades I had been carried along on a flood of progress far beyond anything that could have seemed possible in the dizziest dreams of my early optimism; yet, for still another couple of decades, I was to stay with aviation as it swept on into the era of jets and supersonics, creating new forms of aircraft that would have seemed more astonishing except for the fact that we had lost the capacity for further astonishment. Finally, absurd as it would once have seemed, I would "progress" to rocketing missiles that would leave the air altogether.

Aviation was now a stolidly practical business which had left behind the enchantment of individual adventure that had once been its magic trade-mark. Being no specialist, I followed as long as I could the wider interests of the general practitioner in a variety of engineering and operating assignments, with as much work in the air as I could find excuses for. In my earlier years as a pilot, I did not imagine that there could ever come a time when I would not rather fly than eat, but now I had to admit to myself that the growing restraints of flight regulations had dulled my once insatiable appetite for flying any plane I could get my hands on. However, for working purposes, a commercial pilot's license came in handy on occasion, and mine was still valid as I passed the fiftieth anniversary of my original flying certificate of 1914. On that occasion, I could remember with amusement that in 1914 it was the prevailing view that a pilot's useful flying life would be about four years; the idea was that his "nerve" was unlikely to last out much longer than that.

At last there had to come a day when I turned onto the final leg of my aviation course. A younger generation had taken over most airborne occupations, and when I had to settle finally for desks and paper work, I hoped for a chance to satisfy my long-standing tastes for covering as much as possible of the expanding aviation field. The chance came when an opportunity arose for me to rejoin Convair in their Engineering Department, and I was assigned to writing specifications for new types of airplanes, of which, at that time, Convair had an unusually large number under contract or in design. There were four-engine flying boats, landplane and seaplane supersonic jet fighters, vertical takeoff planes and military transports, as well as airline planes ranging from twin-engine propeller craft to four-engine jets.

The writer of specifications takes no part in the constructive advance of aircraft design, but he gets a grandstand seat in the review of all that is being done. I could well remember the days when the specifications of a new airplane barely covered one sheet of paper; it consisted of a simple description of a stick-and-wire airframe, an elementary power plant, and some sketchy accommodation for whatever crew there was. Equipment, if any, was hardly worth mentioning, and if any predictions of performance were included, nobody took them very seriously. Now every specification was a thick volume compiled in consultation with every branch of engineering, operations, and sales, elaborately detailing the design, construction, equipment, furnishings, and performance of an enormously complex flying organism. To my mind, specifications were a great deal more than necessary technical documents; they were miniature histories of the evolution of aviation since the days when any airplane was good if it would fly.

For several years I carried on this work, interspersed with a few minor flying activities, until the calendar informed me that somehow I was about to reach the age of sixty-five, that deadline age at which industry now commonly assumes that the human machine must have rusted up, and I was expecting to be discarded accordingly. At that point, however, it was discovered that I possessed talents that were usable in the growing Convair missile business, and I was therefore put to work on engineering planning for their Atlas intercontinental missiles and associated military and space projects.

This transfer enabled me to enjoy the happy illusion that I had stayed with aviation until the end, for aviation itself was now absorbed into something they called "aero-space." My couple of years in that new, compound industry were interesting enough, because the nature of my job took me into most details of the missiles and their installations. But it was not aviation; there is no natural association between "aero" and "space," for the great ocean of air that carries the wings of the airplane on its world-wide missions is no more than a major nuisance and obstruction to the wingless, space-bound rocket. It seemed to me that I was now working merely on glorified artillery, which does nothing to arouse the enthusiasm of an old-time aviator.

So when, eventually, they retired me, it was no great blow. As a youthful optimist in the primitive days of flight, I had dreamed vaguely of some great Air Age of the future, hoping dimly that I might perhaps some day see a little of that dream come true. Now, between boxkites and missiles, I had survived to share the great adventure of aviation until the most fanciful of those early dreams had long been surpassed. I had nothing to complain about.

INDEX